Betrayal

Also by Naomi Chase

Exposed

Deception

Published by Dafina Books

Betrayal

NAOMI CHASE

Kensington Publishing Corp.
www.kensingtonbooks.com

DAFINA BOOKS are published by

Kensington Publishing Corp.
119 West 40th Street
New York, NY 10018

All Kensington titles, imprints, and distributed lines are available at special quantity discounts for bulk purchases for sales promotion, premiums, fund-raising, and educational or institutional use.

Special book excerpts or customized printings can also be created to fit specific needs. For details, write or phone the office of the Kensington Special Sales Manager: Kensington Publishing Corp., 119 West 40th Street, New York, NY 10018. Attn. Special Sales Department. Phone: 1-800-221-2647.

Dafina and the D logo Reg. U.S. Pat. & TM Off.

ISBN-13: 978-0-7582-8437-2
ISBN-10: 0-7582-8437-3
First Trade Paperback Printing: April 2014

eISBN-13: 978-0-7582-8439-6
eISBN-10: 0-7582-8439-X
First Electronic Edition: April 2014

10 9 8 7 6 5 4 3 2 1

Printed in the United States of America

For all my loyal Chasers

ACKNOWLEDGMENTS

My utmost gratitude to my editor, Mercedes Fernandez, for your patience and commitment to this series. Thank you for providing such great feedback and for seeing this dramatic saga through to the end.

A heartfelt thanks to my readers and fans who have been patiently waiting for *Betrayal*. I hope you'll think it was worth the wait.

ACKNOWLEDGMENTS

Prologue

Moaning with pleasure, Tamia tightened her thighs around the sweaty, muscular back of her lover.

He groaned her name, his hips pumping up and down as he drove into her. Deeper, harder, the slap of their naked bodies echoing around the shadowy room.

Tamia clung tightly to his shoulders, her nails breaking his skin as his thick, hard shaft pounded her core. He felt so good inside her, hitting all her sweet spots. It was as if they'd never been apart.

Gazing into her eyes, he lowered his mouth until his warm breath fanned her lips. "You thought I'd let you walk out of my life?" he whispered, the husky rasp of his voice sending shivers through her. "Is that what you thought? Huh?"

Lost in sensation, Tamia could barely breathe, let alone speak.

He thrust faster, his dark eyes boring into hers. "I'm never letting you go, Tamia. Never . . ."

Prologue

Chapter 1

Tamia

Time ground to a halt as Tamia stared up at Dominic Archer, stunned speechless.

She couldn't believe he was standing at her table, looking like he had every right to be there with his hands casually tucked into his pockets, a smile playing at the corners of his full lips. She couldn't believe he had the audacity to approach her after the way he'd nearly ruined her life, blackmailing her for sex by threatening to expose her past as a porn star.

As fury quickly replaced her shock, Tamia spat, "What the fuck are you doing here?"

His eyes glinted with amusement. "Hello to you too, Tamia."

"Don't 'hello' me, motherf—" Glancing around the elegant restaurant, she lowered her voice to an angry hiss. "I don't know what the hell you think you're doing, but we have *nothing* to say to each other."

"I disagree," Dominic said calmly. "I think we have plenty to talk about."

"I don't give a shit what you think." Tamia turned her head, darting an anxious glance toward the front entrance. The last thing she wanted was for her ex-boyfriend Brandon to show up and see Dominic standing at her table. There was no telling what Brandon would think—or do.

"You need to leave, Dominic. I'm serious."

"Why?" His eyes gleamed. "You expecting someone?"

Tamia scowled. "Not that it's any of your damn business, but yeah, I *am* expecting someone. He should be here any moment."

Or so she hoped.

For the past twenty minutes, she'd been anxiously waiting for Brandon to join her at Da Marco, the Italian restaurant he'd taken her to on their first date. She'd told him to meet her there at four o'clock. It was now ten minutes past the hour.

He's coming, she assured herself. *He's just running late.*

She didn't want to consider the alternative. That Brandon was at the justice of the peace this very moment exchanging vows with his fiancée, Cynthia Yarbrough. She couldn't bear the thought of it.

"Let me buy you dinner," Dominic drawled.

Tamia gaped at him, incredulous. "What part of 'I'm expecting someone' did you not understand?"

He looked amused. "Come on, Tamia. You don't really think he's coming, do you?"

Her eyes narrowed with suspicion. "How the hell do you even know who I'm waiting for?"

Dominic chuckled softly. "I think I can safely assume that you're waiting for Brandon. Which is unfortunate, since I heard through the grapevine that he's getting married today." He raised a thick brow at Tamia. "Did I hear wrong?"

She glared at him. "How did you know I'd be here?" she demanded, ignoring his question. "Have you been following me?"

"Of course not," he said with lazy amusement. "I had a business meeting this afternoon, but my client had to cancel. I was just about to leave when I saw you."

Tamia didn't believe him, not for one damn second. This was the same conniving motherfucker who'd had an affair with her while he was married. She couldn't believe a word that came out of his lying mouth.

Before she could light into his ass, the waiter appeared. After topping off Tamia's water, he divided a friendly smile between her and Dominic. "Will you two be dining together this evening?"

"No," Tamia said so sharply that the man looked startled.

Dominic smiled at the waiter. "Give us another minute."

"We don't need another minute," Tamia interjected through

clenched teeth. "He's not joining me for dinner. I'm waiting for someone else. In the meantime, I'd like to order the grilled scampi with orange honey salad."

"Excellent, *signorina.*" The waiter shot a sympathetic glance at Dominic before moving off.

Tamia picked up her crocodile Dolce & Gabbana handbag, one of many expensive gifts Brandon had lavished upon her during their recent trip to Italy.

"I'm going to the ladies' room," she coldly informed Dominic as she rose from the table. "I expect you to be gone when I get back."

With that, she turned and stalked off, feeling Dominic's gaze on her ass until she rounded the corner and disappeared from view.

Once inside the empty restroom, she slipped into the nearest stall and retrieved her smartphone from her handbag. After taking several deep breaths, she pulled up Brandon's number and pressed SEND.

Her heart sank when her call went straight to his voice mail.

"This is Brandon. Keep it short and sweet."

Tamia inhaled a shaky breath, debating whether or not to leave a message. If he'd gone through with marrying Cynthia, there was nothing she could say or do at this point. But if he was somewhere having second thoughts, she had to at least *try* to get through to him.

The beep sounded, prompting her to speak or hang up.

Gripping the phone, she nervously moistened her lips. "Hey . . . it's me. I'm at Da Marco waiting for you. I hope . . ." She trailed off, not wanting to sound too desperate. "I hope to see you soon."

She disconnected, closed her eyes and held the phone to her thudding heart.

Please don't let it be too late, she silently prayed. *Please let Brandon be on his way to the restaurant, not the courthouse.*

Drawing another deep breath, she stepped out of the stall and crossed to the row of sinks to inspect her reflection in the mirror. Her sleek bob was freshly straightened, her red lipstick was perfectly intact, and she wore a Dolce & Gabbana tapestry-print dress that molded her voluptuous curves. She'd been delighted when the Italian saleswoman had told her that the dress wouldn't hit the U.S. market for another four months. She enjoyed being ahead of the curve.

With a parting glance at her reflection, Tamia left the restroom and headed back to her table.

When she saw Dominic sitting there, a wave of incredulous outrage swept through her.

This motherfucker!

As she marched over to the table, he stood and smoothly pulled out her chair for her. Ignoring the chivalrous gesture, she thrust her hands onto her hips and spat, "What the fuck do you think you're doing?"

His lips twitched. "You might want to keep your voice down," he advised. "People are staring at you."

"I don't give a shit." But even as the angry words left her mouth, Tamia couldn't help glancing around. Meeting the curious stares of several other diners, she scowled.

Not wanting to cause a scene, she reluctantly sat down and allowed Dominic to push her chair back in. But as soon as he reclaimed the seat across from her, she began looking around for the waiter so that she could request her food to go.

"I ordered a bottle of Chianti," Dominic said, gesturing to the wineglass in front of her. "It's good. Have some."

"I don't think so." Tamia glared at him. "I thought I told you to leave."

"You did," Dominic said mildly.

"So why the hell are you still here?"

"I thought you could use some company." He raised his glass to his lips, his eyes dancing with humor. "Were you able to reach Brandon?"

Tamia's face heated. "None of your damn business."

Dominic laughed, leisurely sipping his wine.

Tamia hated him with every fiber of her being. But not even she could deny how fine he was with his hooded dark eyes, juicy lips framed by a trim goatee, broad shoulders, and muscular six-four frame dipped in Armani. His lazy West Indian accent only added to his immense sex appeal.

But it didn't matter how gorgeous he was, or that he was by far one of the best lovers she'd ever had. From the moment Tamia had met him, he'd wreaked pure havoc on her life, ultimately causing her to lose everything. Now that she was trying to pick up the broken pieces and move forward, she wanted absolutely nothing to do with him. The sooner he got that through his thick head, the better.

Tamia took a sip of her water and glanced impatiently around the restaurant. "Where the hell is that damn waiter?"

"Probably taking care of our order," Dominic drawled.

Tamia's eyes snapped to his. "*Our* order?"

"Yeah." He drank more wine. "I canceled your salad and ordered dinner for both of us."

"Excuse you?" *The nerve of this motherfucker!* "Who the hell told you to do that?"

He smiled lazily. "We're both here. We might as well eat together. Besides, this will give us a chance to discuss my proposal."

Tamia's eyes narrowed. "What proposal?"

"Glad you asked. I'd like to—"

"You know what?" Tamia cut him off, holding up a hand. "I don't even wanna hear it."

He frowned. "Why not?"

"*Why not? Why not?* Hmm, let me see. Maybe because the last time you approached me with one of your so-called proposals, I lost my boyfriend and my job, and I went to prison for murder."

Dominic grimaced, leaning back in his chair. "All of that was unfortunate—"

"*Unfortunate?*" Tamia echoed in angry disbelief. "Getting a speeding ticket is unfortunate. Falling on your ass in public is unfortunate. What happened to me was absolutely devastating, Dominic, and none of it would have happened if you'd stayed the hell out of my life. So, no, I have absolutely no interest in hearing your proposal, so you can just go fuck yourself."

Dominic hung his head, looking contrite for the first time since she'd met him. "I know I did you wrong, Tamia. That's why I'd like to make amends."

"How? You nearly destroyed my life, Dominic. There's nothing you can say or do to make amends for that."

"Maybe not," he conceded, "but I'd at least like to try."

"Why? To ease your damn conscience?"

"Nah," he murmured, watching as she agitatedly sipped more water. "This isn't about making myself feel better. It's about rectifying a mistake, righting a wrong—"

Tamia snorted derisively, shaking her head at him. "You are so full of shit, Dominic. And you're out of your damn mind if you think I'd be stupid enough to ever trust you again."

He looked at her with solemn eyes. "Everyone deserves a second chance, Tamia."

"Not everyone." She set her empty glass down on the table, then grabbed her purse and stood so abruptly she got lightheaded.

As she swayed for a moment, Dominic frowned in concern. "Are you okay?"

"I'm fine," she snapped.

"Maybe you should stay and eat something."

Tamia sneered. "Nice try, but I'd rather go back to prison than stay here and have dinner with you." She jabbed a finger at him. "You wanna make amends? Stay the fuck away from me."

With that, she turned and strode from the table without a backward glance.

Chapter 2

Brandon

Brandon felt like a contestant on one of those old game shows.

Except in this case he only had to choose between two doors, not three. And unlike a contestant on a real game show, he knew exactly what awaited him behind each closed door.

Or did he?

Over the past year he'd learned not to take anything for granted, because nothing was ever as it seemed.

Nothing.

And no one.

Behind Door Number One was Tamia, the woman who could have been his soul mate if things hadn't gone so horribly wrong between them.

Behind Door Number Two was Cynthia, the woman who'd gone from being his friend to his lover and was now the mother of his unborn child.

Both women genuinely loved him and wanted to be with him.

Each gave him something the other didn't.

But he could only choose one of them.

Squaring his broad shoulders, Brandon took a deep breath and stepped through Door Number Two.

Three pairs of eyes swung toward him.

"*Brandon!*" Cynthia cried, beaming with relief as she lunged from the table she'd been sharing with her parents.

"It's about damn time you got here," Bishop Yarbrough blustered, glaring at Brandon accusingly. "Where the hell have you been?"

"Joseph," his wife gently chided.

He scowled. "I'm sorry, Coretta, but the boy is almost thirty minutes late."

Brandon divided an apologetic glance between his would-be in-laws. "I'm sorry for keeping you waiting."

"No need to apologize, Brandon," Coretta assured him. "We're just glad you're finally here."

Brandon smiled briefly before shifting his gaze to Cynthia. Her long dark hair was elegantly pinned up, her makeup was flawless, and she wore a white silk dress that flattered her slender figure.

"You look beautiful," he told her.

She smiled with pleasure. "Wait until you see my *real* wedding gown."

Brandon hesitated. "Can we talk for a minute?"

Her smile faltered. She shot a nervous glance at her parents, who exchanged troubled looks.

"Everyone is waiting, Brandon," Cynthia said anxiously. "Daddy already had to pull strings to get us a private room for the ceremony, and the judge has been—"

"This is important," Brandon interrupted.

She held his steady gaze for a long moment, then swallowed visibly and nodded. "All right," she agreed with obvious reluctance. "We can talk. But we really need to hurry, or we're going to have to reschedule the ceremony."

"And that won't be happening," Joseph growled, leveling a warning glare at Brandon.

He just looked at the old man.

"Come on, Joseph," Coretta urged, steering her scowling husband from the room.

Once the door closed behind them, Brandon and Cynthia stared at each other for several moments.

"I can't do this," Brandon said quietly.

Panic flared in Cynthia's dark eyes. "Can't do what?"

"I can't marry you, sweetheart. Not today."

"Are you serious?" she whispered, staring incredulously at him. "Please tell me you're not serious."

"I'm afraid I am." His chest tightened with guilt. "I'm sorry."

"*You're sorry?* You wait until the day of our wedding to tell me you can't marry me, and all you have to say for yourself is 'I'm sorry?' "

Brandon grimaced. "I'm not saying the wedding's completely off," he explained, walking toward her. "All I'm saying is that we can't get married today."

"Why not?" she demanded. "We're already here at the courthouse. We have the marriage license. Our family and friends are out there waiting—"

"Listen to me." Brandon cupped her face between his hands, his eyes boring into hers. "You know I wanted a long engagement. I shouldn't have allowed myself to be talked into a hasty ceremony. I need more time."

"Time for what?" Cynthia challenged accusingly. "Time to change your mind about marrying me? Time to keep whoring around with Tamia?"

Brandon shook his head slowly at her. "I've never denied my feelings for Tamia. They're not going to disappear overnight just because you want them to."

"I know that," Cynthia snapped. "But I also know that we have a baby on the way, and I have no desire to be a single parent."

"You won't be, I promise." Brandon's voice gentled. "I meant it when I told you that I'm committed to making this relationship work. But a lot has happened over the past year, Cynthia. I need more time to process everything, get my head on straight. If you really love me and want to be with me, you need to be patient with me."

"*Patient?*" Cynthia repeated incredulously. "I was in love with you for two fucking years before I shared my feelings with you! Was *that* not patient? And once we were together, I was patient with you while you defended Tamia during her murder trial, even though I knew it'd come back to haunt me. Don't you *dare* talk to me about patience, Brandon Chambers, because I've been nothing but patient with you. If I were any more patient, I'd be a fucking doormat!"

Brandon slowly removed his hands from her face and stepped back. "I'm sorry for everything I've put you through, Cynthia. I really am. But I've never tried to hurt you or deceive you. From the very beginning I've kept it one hundred with you. You're a good woman, and I truly appreciate the way you've been there for me these past few years—"

"Yet this is how you choose to repay me," Cynthia said bitterly. "By jilting me at the altar."

"I'm not jilting you," Brandon corrected. "We're still engaged, and we're still getting married. Just not today."

"Unbelievable," Cynthia hissed, rapidly blinking back tears. "I should have known you'd pull a stunt like this."

Brandon grimaced, guilt gnawing at his insides as he tucked his hands into his pockets. "We need to let our guests know that we're postponing the ceremony."

"*We?*" Cynthia shrieked. "Are you crazy? I can't go out there and show my face to all those people! *You're* the one who's calling off the damn wedding, so *you* should be the one to tell everybody!"

Brandon nodded slowly. "You're right."

Cynthia stared at him as he turned and started from the room. Reaching the door, he paused and glanced back at her. "I know you don't want to hear this again," he said quietly, "but I truly *am* sorry."

She held up a trembling hand, nostrils flaring with emotion. "Just go, Brandon."

"Cynthia—"

"*GO!*"

He gave her one last look of regret, then turned and walked out the door.

Dreading the task ahead of him, he made his way to the small room where their family members and closest friends were waiting for the ceremony to begin. Cynthia's father stood at the front conferring with the judge, who was frowning as he impatiently checked his watch.

The moment Brandon appeared, all conversation ceased.

Joseph glowered at him, while Coretta offered a relieved smile that sent a sharp stab of guilt through Brandon.

Squaring his shoulders, he walked to the front of the room. Ignoring Joseph and the judge, he scanned the faces gathered before him. His parents watched him with tense expressions, as if they were bracing themselves for the worst. His younger siblings, Beau and Brooke, were smirking with suppressed laughter, while Cynthia's four brothers looked anything but amused. His best friend, Dre, was staring at him with a mixture of wariness and sympathy.

Brandon glanced away, clearing his throat before he spoke.

"Thank you all for coming and waiting so patiently. Unfortunately, Cynthia and I won't be getting married today." He paused. "I'm sorry."

As a shocked silence swept over the room, Cynthia's mother moaned, "*Help me, Lawd Jesus.*"

And then she fainted.

Chapter 3

Tamia

Tamia awakened with a hangover from hell.

Her head was pounding violently, and her mouth was so dry she tasted dust.

Groaning hoarsely, she cracked one eye open, then the other, and squinted around her large bedroom. The drapes were open, revealing an overcast sky swollen with thick gray clouds.

Grateful for the absence of bright sunlight, she reached up to massage her throbbing temple, trying to piece together what had happened last night. She remembered waiting at the restaurant, hoping and praying that Brandon would show up. Instead it was Dominic— *Dominic!*—who'd joined her at the table and tried to have dinner with her. After cussing him out, she'd stormed out of the restaurant and gotten into her car.

Tamia frowned, shaking her head.

Leaving Da Marco was the last thing she remembered. But judging by her monster hangover—and the empty bottle of Patrón on the bedside table—it was obvious what had happened. She'd tried to drink herself into oblivion to cope with the pain of losing Brandon.

He hadn't met her at the restaurant last night, so that could only mean one thing.

He'd married Cynthia.

Tamia closed her eyes, sickened by the thought of Brandon and Cynthia waking up this morning as husband and wife. It wasn't fair. She'd gone to hell and back trying to become Mrs. Brandon Chambers. But she'd failed, and now Brandon would spend the rest of his life with someone else.

As tears flooded her eyes, Tamia pulled back the covers and sat up. Instantly her stomach lurched and bitter nausea rushed up her throat. She clapped a hand over her mouth and ran to the bathroom. Dropping to her knees, she vomited into the toilet.

When she had nothing but dry heaves left, she wiped a hand across her mouth and swore she'd never touch alcohol again.

After flushing the toilet, she pushed weakly to her feet and trudged over to the sink. As she reached for her toothbrush, she caught her reflection in the mirror and grimaced.

She looked as bad as she felt. Her hair was a tangled mess and her mascara was smeared, giving her the dreaded raccoon eyes. She'd slept in her Bordelle lace bra and panties, a new set she'd splurged on just in case Brandon came home with her last night.

So much for that, she thought forlornly, shoving her toothbrush into her mouth and vigorously scrubbing her teeth.

Just as she finished, her smartphone went off.

Tamia froze, recognizing the familiar ringtone. It was Usher's "My Boo."

Brandon!

Heart thumping into her throat, she hurried out of the bathroom and raced to the bedside table, snatching up her phone right before the call got kicked to voice mail.

"Hello," she answered breathlessly.

"Hey. It's me." Brandon's deep voice was low. Subdued enough to make her nervous.

"Brandon." She swallowed tightly. "Where are you?"

"At home."

"Are you . . . alone?"

"Yeah." There was a lengthy pause. "I didn't do it."

Tamia slowly lowered herself onto her bed. "You didn't do what? Didn't marry Cynthia?"

"No."

Tamia almost wept with relief.

"Why not?" she whispered.

Another long pause. "I couldn't go through with it. I . . . wasn't ready."

Tamia moistened her dry lips. Her throbbing headache was suddenly an afterthought. "I waited for you at the restaurant. When you didn't show, I thought . . ."

"I know." Brandon let out a deep breath. "I'm sorry I didn't call you. I needed time to think. Sort things out."

"I understand." Tamia hesitated, a burning question on the tip of her tongue. "Is it over between you and Cynthia?"

In the heavy silence that followed, her heart plummeted.

"No," Brandon said quietly. "We're still engaged."

A spasm of pain shot through Tamia. Inhaling a shaky breath, she lay back against her pillows and squeezed her eyes shut.

"So you're still going to marry her?" she whispered.

He paused. "Eventually."

"What're you waiting for?"

He didn't answer her.

"Why prolong the inevitable?" she pressed, fighting the onset of hysteria. "If you really want to marry her, then just do it and get it over with. Don't drag this out any longer than it has to be. It's not fair to her *or* to me."

"Tamia—"

She sat up quickly, ignoring her throbbing skull. "Listen to me. I'm not saying that you *have* to marry her, Brandon."

He exhaled a deep, ragged breath. "She's having my baby, Tamia."

"I know that. I also know that you don't have to be with her to be involved in your child's life. You and Cynthia can share custody. And if you're worried about her feeling overwhelmed as a single mother, you can hire a nanny to help her."

Brandon was silent for several moments. "I don't want to be a part-time father, Tamia. I thought you understood that."

Guilt washed over her. She didn't want to be selfish. She knew better than anyone how devastating the absence of a father could be to a child. At the same time, she didn't want to lose Brandon. He was the love of her life, the only man who could make her happy.

Closing her eyes, she imagined him there with her, holding her, his breath warm against her ear as he whispered the words she longed to hear.

I love you, Tamia. I choose you.

"I didn't call to upset you," he said quietly. "I just wanted to let you know where things stand."

"Thank you for calling." Tamia swallowed with difficulty. "Goodbye, Brandon."

He lingered for a long moment, then hung up.

Blinking back tears, Tamia lay down on the bed and stared numbly at the ceiling.

Seconds later he called back.

She picked up the phone but didn't speak.

Neither did he.

They sat on the phone listening to each other breathe. The silence between them conveyed more than any words could have.

After several excruciating minutes, Tamia whispered, "I can't do this, Brandon."

"I know, baby." His voice was husky with pain and regret.

"I don't know what you want from me."

"Nothing . . . and everything."

Tears leaked from Tamia's eyes and rolled down the sides of her face. Her heart was breaking, and it hurt like nothing she'd ever felt before. "If we can't be together . . . then I need to move on."

Brandon was silent.

"We need to leave each other alone," she reiterated.

"That's easier said than done," he said thickly.

"I know." As more tears seeped out, Tamia shook her head slowly and confessed, "I was so miserable last night that I got completely blitzed, and now I have the worst hangover."

"I'm really sorry to hear that." Brandon blew out a deep, heavy breath. "If it makes you feel any better, I didn't sleep worth a damn because I couldn't stop thinking about us and missing you."

Tamia's throat tightened. "That doesn't make me feel better," she sniffled.

He didn't respond.

Swiping at her watery eyes, she sat up and slid off the bed. Padding across the room to her armoire, she retrieved a black silk robe and slipped it on.

Hearing her movements, Brandon murmured, "What're you doing?"

"Going to the kitchen to make some coffee."

"Oh." His voice softened. "I miss your coffee."

That brought a small, wistful smile to her face. "I miss making it for you."

He was silent for a long moment. "Do you want me to let you go?"

"You should." Tamia sighed. "But I'm not ready for you to."

"Neither am I."

Raking a hand through her mussed hair, Tamia left the bedroom and started down the hall toward the kitchen. "Since you're not on your honeymoon, what're you gonna do today?"

Brandon sighed heavily. "I don't know. I haven't thought about it. What about you?"

"I don't know. I'll probably just—" Suddenly she screamed.

"What is it?" Brandon asked in alarm. "What's wrong?"

Tamia froze in her tracks, staring into the living room.

There, reclining on her sofa with his feet propped up on the coffee table, was Dominic.

Jolted awake by her scream, he opened his eyes and regarded her in groggy confusion.

"Tamia?" Brandon prompted. "What happened?"

"I-I thought I saw a mouse," she stammered.

"A mouse?"

"Uh-huh."

Tamia and Dominic stared at each other.

Before he could utter a word, Tamia rushed over to the sofa, jumped onto his lap, and clapped a hand over his mouth.

Shut up! she silently warned.

A wicked gleam filled his eyes.

"As much as they charge for rent in that building," Brandon joked, "you'd better *not* have any damn mice."

Tamia forced a laugh. "I know, right?"

"Seriously though. Are you okay?"

"I'm fine," she quickly assured him. "I just hate rodents."

As Dominic's eyes glimmered with laughter, Tamia glared at him. Dark stubble covered his jaw, and he wore a white wifebeater over his suit pants. Black tribal tattoos wove down his thick, muscular biceps. Her mind flashed on a memory of her tongue tracing the intricate pattern as she slowly rode his dick.

As if he'd read her mind, Dominic's lips curved into a smile beneath her hand. The damp heat of his breath against her skin sent shivers down her spine. She watched as his heavy-lidded eyes lowered to her large breasts bulging from her skimpy lace bra. Feeling his dick harden between her thighs, she scowled and yanked her robe closed.

When she moved to climb off Dominic, his strong hands gripped her waist, holding her in place. She hated the way her pussy throbbed against his erection.

Will I ever be immune to this crazy motherfucker?

"Brandon"—her voice was shaky as hell—"let me call you back."

He hesitated for a long moment. "We can talk some other time."

Her heart sank like an anvil, because she knew that he was telling her good-bye. "Um . . . okay," she mumbled, blinking back tears. "Enjoy your weekend."

"You too, Tamia," Brandon said quietly. "Take care."

As soon as the call ended, Tamia slapped Dominic across the face and screamed, "*What the fuck are you doing in my apartment?*"

He stared at her like she'd lost her mind. "What the hell are you talking about? *You* invited me here!"

"WHAT? I did not!"

"Yes, you did."

"Stop lying, muthafucka!" Tamia shrieked, scrambling off his lap. "Why the hell would I invite you into my apartment when I didn't even want to have dinner with you?"

He shook his head slowly at her. "You don't remember, do you?"

Tamia stilled, her eyes narrowing on his face. "Remember what?"

Dominic frowned, lowering his feet to the floor. "When you left the restaurant last night, I was worried about you because you looked like you didn't feel well. So I followed you outside to the parking lot. When I saw you sitting in the car with your head on the steering wheel, I tapped on the window and asked if you were okay. You said you were, but I didn't believe you. So I offered to follow you home to make sure you arrived safely. When we got here, you invited me up for a drink." He pointed to the table.

For the first time, Tamia noticed the empty bottle of wine and two glasses, one bearing red lipstick on the rim.

She eyed Dominic suspiciously. "I don't remember any of that."

"I'm not surprised," he said wryly. "You had a lot to drink. You finished most of our wine, and before you stumbled off to bed, you grabbed a bottle of Patrón from the kitchen. I only planned to hang around until my buzz wore off, but I must have fallen asleep."

Tamia frowned. It bothered her that she couldn't remember a single thing about last night. She'd never gotten that drunk before.

She pinned Dominic with a glare. "Did anything happen between us?"

His eyes glinted with amusement. "Like what?"

"You know damn well what," Tamia hissed. "Did we have sex?"

He searched her face. "What do *you* think?"

"Just answer the fucking question."

He chuckled, rising from the sofa. "If we did have sex last night, don't you think I would have woken up in bed with you instead of out here?"

"Maybe you snuck out in the middle of the night so I wouldn't know what happened," Tamia challenged.

"If that were the case," he drawled humorously, "I would have just left the apartment. I wouldn't have stuck around."

Tamia glared at him. What he'd said made sense, but she didn't trust him. She had every reason not to.

He laughed softly, shaking his head at her. "Nothing happened last night, Tamia. As fine as you are, and as much as I've been feenin' for your sublime pussy, I wouldn't take advantage of you while you're drunk."

She snorted derisively. "This coming from the same man who blackmailed me for sex."

"Actually," Dominic countered mildly, "I'm *not* the same man. As you know, a lot has happened over the past several months. Losing my wife and grandfather forced me to reassess my life and realize the error of—"

"Nigga, please!" Tamia scoffed contemptuously. "Spare me your 'I'm a changed man' bullshit. You haven't changed. You're just as sneaky and conniving as you were the day I met you."

Dominic gave her a disappointed look. "Why is it that you expect Brandon to believe that *you've* learned from your mistakes, but you can't give me the same benefit of the doubt?"

"*Are you serious?*" Tamia sputtered incredulously. "First of all, our situations are completely different! I was minding my own damn business when you barged into my life and fucked everything up. *I* didn't go out of my way to hurt anyone—*you* did. So, no, you don't deserve forgiveness or the benefit of the doubt. And how dare you stand there and even speak Brandon's name to me when it's *your* damn fault that we're no longer together? Furthermore—"

"I can help you get him back."

Tamia broke off mid-rant, staring at Dominic. "What did you say?"

"I said I can help you get Brandon back."

Her eyes narrowed. "What the hell are you talking about?"

Dominic casually tucked his hands into his pockets. "Since I'm partly responsible for messing things up between you and—"

"*Partly?*" Tamia echoed in disbelief.

He gave her a knowing look. "Come on, Tamia. We both know you and Brandon were having problems before I entered the picture. Your relationship was built on lies from day one. You lied to him about where you lived, about your sister being in college instead of prison, about your past as a porn star. Yet for all your deception, you were frustrated because he was in no hurry to make more of a serious commitment to you." Dominic chuckled softly, shaking his head at her. "Like I said, love, your relationship was already on the rocks by the time you met me. Otherwise you never would have agreed to our affair."

Tamia frowned, knowing she couldn't refute anything he'd said and hating him for it.

"But since I caused you so much trouble," he continued, "the least I can do is try to repair some of the damage. For starters, I want to help you get Brandon back."

Tamia eyed him skeptically. "And just how do you propose to do that?"

He smiled wryly. "I'm sure you remember what happened the last time I came over here. When Brandon saw us together, he lost his damn mind—"

"—and fucked your ass up." Tamia smiled narrowly, savoring the memory. "You had it coming. You violated the restraining order and tried to choke me."

Dominic grimaced. "I'm not proud of my actions that night, but I had my reasons for behaving the way I did. The point is that Brandon went crazy when he thought you were sleeping with me again. If you want to get him back, make him think you're moving on." He paused. "With me."

Tamia's eyes narrowed. "If you think I'm gonna start fucking you again—"

"You don't have to." Dominic ran an appreciative gaze over her. "That is, unless you really want to."

"I don't," Tamia snapped, pulling the robe tighter around her body.

Dominic smiled like he didn't believe her. "Anyway, we only have to pretend to be involved to make Brandon jealous. Once he sees us together a few times, he'll come running back to you."

Tamia sucked her teeth. "You don't know that."

"*I* would." Dominic took a step toward her. "If I were Brandon and I knew there was a chance I could lose you to another man—especially a man I hated—I'd waste no time putting a ring on your finger. See, as long as lover boy thinks he has no competition, he can take his sweet time deciding what he wants."

Tamia was silent, pondering his words. Hadn't her best friend, Shanell, given her the same advice not too long ago? Could Shanell and Dominic be right about Brandon?

"I know how men think," Dominic drawled. "After all, I *am* one."

Tamia looked at his stubble-roughened jaw . . . his washboard abs molded by the white undershirt . . . his thick, tattooed biceps.

She swallowed hard. "How are we supposed to 'pretend' to be involved with each other?"

Dominic's eyes gleamed. "Does this mean you're interested in hearing my proposal?"

Tamia wavered, biting her lower lip. She couldn't believe she was even giving him the time of day. Hadn't she learned her lesson the first time? The man couldn't be trusted.

And yet . . .

"You've piqued my curiosity," she grudgingly admitted.

Dominic smiled. "Like I've said before," he murmured, reaching out to stroke her cheek, "Brandon Chambers is a *very* lucky man."

Tamia pushed his hand away. "Don't touch me."

He arched a brow at her. "Aren't you the one who jumped onto my lap five minutes ago?"

She scowled. "I wasn't thinking clearly. Seeing you on the sofa caught me off guard. Anyway, can we get back to the matter at hand? How are we supposed to convince Brandon that we're involved?"

Dominic smiled. "By becoming business partners."

Tamia frowned. "Business partners?"

"Yeah. Do you remember the time you told me that one of your long-term goals was to start your own advertising agency?"

She nodded.

"Well, I'd like to give you the funds to make that happen."

Tamia went still, staring at him. "Are you serious?"

"Very. If you hadn't gotten involved with me, you wouldn't have been charged with my wife's murder—which means you'd still have your job at Richards Carruth. I feel responsible for costing you so much, so I'd like to make it up to you by giving you the start-up capital for your business. That is, if you're still interested in going that route."

"I am," Tamia blurted, her heart racing with excitement. She'd always dreamed of running her own company. She'd spent seven years at one of the top ad agencies in Houston, so she already had the knowledge and experience to start her own business. And this was the perfect time to do it. Since getting out of prison, her job prospects had been practically nonexistent. She'd worked briefly as Brandon's assistant at his law firm, but once she'd learned that Cynthia was pregnant, she'd resigned from the position to spare herself the torture of seeing the couple every day at the office. Her stepfather, Sonny, had told her about a job opening where he worked, but the company had ended up hiring someone else. Though she'd been diligently sending out her résumé, she knew the odds of finding employment were stacked against her.

She needed to take matters into her own hands.

"I see those wheels turning," Dominic drawled, watching her face intently. "I know you want this."

"I do," Tamia reluctantly admitted.

"Then let me help you. Not only can I give you the money to set up your business, but I can refer some of my clients to you. I already know of several who need the services of a good ad agency. And I know you can deliver, Tamia. The work you did for my restaurant was amazing. It was just what I needed."

Tamia shook her head, raking her fingers through her hair. "I don't know, Dominic. This . . . this is a lot to consider."

"I understand." He smiled at her, then turned and walked over to the sofa to pick up his shirt. "Take all the time you need to think about my offer. I'll be waiting whenever you're ready."

Tamia nodded slowly, watching as he shrugged into his shirt and fastened the buttons. She thought of the first time they'd met, when he'd showed up at her office and blackmailed her into becoming his lover. She must be crazy for even *considering* his new proposal, which sounded way too good to be true. For all she knew, he could be setting her up again. Did she honestly believe that he'd changed? Did she dare risk trusting him after everything he'd done to her?

With doubt gnawing at her insides, she followed him to the front door. When he turned to face her, she instinctively tensed.

He took out his wallet and removed a white business card, then handed it to her.

"Whatever you decide, Tamia," he said quietly, "I want you to know that I truly *am* sorry for all the trouble I caused you. Even if you decide not to accept my money, I hope someday we can be friends."

Tamia stared at him, shaking her head in confused disbelief. "Who *are* you?"

A glimmer of amusement filled his eyes.

Without answering her question, he turned and sauntered out the door, leaving Tamia more conflicted than ever.

Chapter 4

Brandon

Gripping a basketball in one hand, Brandon aggressively charged the net, leveling his shoulder against the defender guarding him. As Cornel grunted and reached up to block his shot, Brandon roughly shoved him in the chest. Cornel stumbled backward and hit the floor as Brandon made the winning layup, drawing a round of raucous laughter and groans from the gathered spectators.

"What the fuck, Chambers?" Cornel shouted, glaring up at him. "You pushed off!"

Brandon laughed, wiping his forearm across his sweaty brow. "I don't know what you're talking about."

"Whatever, nigga." Swatting away Brandon's outstretched hand, Cornel shoved to his feet and jabbed a finger at Brandon. "I'ma let that shit slide this time 'cause I know you ain't in your right mind."

Brandon scowled. "Yo, fuck you."

"Fellas, fellas," Dre intervened, stepping between the two opponents. "The game's over. Let it go."

"Easy for *you* to say," Cornel grumbled darkly. "And just for the record, the only reason y'all won was 'cause your boy was hacking and pushing off the whole damn time."

"Aw, quit crying," Brandon taunted. "If your punk ass couldn't handle checking me, you shoulda let Justin do it."

Cornel sucked his teeth, exchanging disgusted looks with his teammate.

Cornel and Justin, along with Dre, were Brandon's closest friends. After witnessing the fiasco at the courthouse yesterday, they'd showed up at Brandon's apartment today to find him slumped in front of the television, mindlessly watching old reruns of *Sanford and Son.* Trading worried glances with one another, they'd grabbed Brandon and hauled him off to the gym so he could burn off some steam on the basketball court.

Unfortunately for Cornel, he'd borne the brunt of Brandon's foul mood.

As a new group of players claimed the court, the four friends headed over to the bleachers and sat down.

"I want a rematch," Cornel announced, swigging from a cold bottle of Gatorade. With his light skin, green eyes, and curly hair, he'd always been considered the pretty boy of the group. He was also ultracompetitive, a trait that served him well as a successful nightclub owner but not always on the basketball court.

Brandon wagged his head at him. "You don't want none of this."

"Whatever," Cornel retorted, stretching out his long legs. "That's why we shoulda let Cynthia's brothers go medieval on your black ass yesterday."

As Dre and Justin burst out laughing, Brandon grimaced at the memory of what had happened at the courthouse. After he'd announced that the wedding was off, all hell had broken loose. Cynthia's mother had fainted, and while most of the guests had been preoccupied with her, Cynthia's brothers had charged after Brandon, shouting and threatening to whip his ass for hurting their sister. He could have handled two of them, but not all four. Fortunately Dre, Justin, Cornel, and Beau had had his back.

"And what about Bishop Yarbrough?" Justin joked. "Dude was so mad, I thought he was gonna pull out a damn rifle and go straight *Scarface* on Brandon!"

As the others howled with laughter, Brandon glowered at Justin. He was tall and brown-skinned, sporting neat cornrows and an abundance of tattoos. Born and raised in Houston's gang-ridden southwest side, he now worked as chief administrator of a community organization that addressed the needs of underserved boys.

Brandon had always admired and respected Justin. So he was willing to give him a pass for making light of his predicament. A temporary pass.

"Man, that was one of the wildest non-weddings I've ever been to," Justin declared, shaking his head at Brandon. "The minute you walked into the room and I saw your face, I knew some serious shit was about to go down."

"No kidding." Cornel eyed Brandon incredulously. "I still can't believe you called off the wedding. What the hell were you thinking?"

Dre snorted. "You know damn well what he was thinking. He was thinking about Tamia."

This drew loud groans from Cornel and Justin.

"You gotta let that one go, Chambers," Cornel advised.

"For real," Justin agreed. "Tamia's fine as hell, but she's *way* too much trouble."

"And after the way she played you with ol' boy—"

"I get the point," Brandon snapped.

His three friends exchanged glances.

"Come on, B," Dre said. "You know we're just looking out for you."

"I get that, and I appreciate your concern. But my relationship with Tamia is complicated, something none of you can understand unless you've walked in my shoes. Tamia and I have been through hell together. Some of that was her fault. Some of it was mine. But it doesn't matter anymore because at the end of the day I still love her, and if things weren't so fucked up right now, I'd make her my wife. So when y'all tell me to leave her alone, just know that I really don't give a fuck what you think. So you might as well save your damn breath and worry about your own issues 'cause I know I'm not the only one who has them."

His heated tirade was met with dead silence.

He looked each of his friends in the eye, all but daring them to contradict him. When no one spoke, he clenched and unclenched his jaw, then downed the rest of his Gatorade like it was two-hundred-proof Everclear.

It was Justin who finally broke the heavy silence.

"If it's Tamia you really want—and I think you've made that pretty damn clear—you should just get her pregnant."

"*WHAT?*" Dre and Cornel exclaimed.

Brandon frowned at Justin. "What the hell are you talking about?"

"Yo, the only reason you're marrying Cynthia is because she's pregnant and you wanna do the right thing. If you get Tamia pregnant, then you could only be expected to marry one of them since, last I checked, polygamy is illegal in this country."

Dre scowled in disbelief. "So let me get this straight. You're telling Brandon to have not one, but *two* baby mamas?"

"Yup," Justin confirmed. "But only one of them gets to be wifey."

Cornel gave a disgusted snort. "Nigga, you a damn fool. That's a terrible idea."

"Is it?" Justin eyed Brandon knowingly. "Then why hasn't Chambers said anything?"

Dre and Cornel stared at Brandon.

"Please don't tell me you're actually considering this crazy shit," Dre warned.

"Of course not." Brandon brought the Gatorade bottle to his mouth before he remembered that it was empty. Frowning, he began picking at the label.

Dre regarded him suspiciously. "Don't even think about it."

Brandon scowled. "I'm not. Now can you get the fuck off my back? Damn. And since you wanna front like you're some relationship expert, let's talk about you and Leah."

Dre's face tightened as Justin and Cornel burst out laughing.

Last month Dre had been caught cheating on his girlfriend when she had walked in on him screwing Tamia's sister, Fiona. Angry and devastated, Leah had thrown Dre out of her house and changed all the locks. He'd been staying with his mother ever since, hoping Leah would take him back.

He shot an accusing look at Brandon. "Damn, bruh, why you have to go there?"

Brandon smirked. "Muthafuckas who live in glass houses shouldn't throw stones."

"I wasn't throwing stones. I was just—"

"Whatever," Brandon impatiently cut him off. "Back to you and Leah. Has she returned any of your phone calls?"

Dre sullenly shook his head. "I can't even get her on the damn phone. And when I went to the hospital to try to talk to her, she refused to see me. She instructed one of the nurses to tell me that the next time I showed up there, she'd file a restraining order against me."

"Dayuum," Justin commiserated, shaking his head. "That's messed up."

"I know."

Dre looked so miserable that Brandon couldn't help feeling sorry for him.

Cornel suffered no such compunction. "Oh, well. Guess that'll teach you not to fuck around in your girlfriend's house."

Dre glared at him. "It was a mistake."

"A *mistake?* Nigga, you were smashing that pussy while Leah was right down the hall taking a shower! That wasn't a mistake—that was some brazen kamikaze bullshit! You're lucky Leah didn't take a scalpel to your ratchet black ass."

As Brandon and Justin cracked up, Dre closed his eyes and dropped his head into his hands.

But Cornel wasn't finished. "Of all the women you could have cheated with, you had to choose a psychotic convicted felon who murdered two people, including her own grandmother."

Brandon sobered at once. "A'ight, nigga, that's enough. Damn. You just never know when to shut the fuck up, do you?"

Cornel held up his hands. "Oh, my bad. I forgot that Fiona is Tamia's little sister. Hey, if she ever gets sprung from the joint, maybe you and Dre can have a double wedding."

"Fuck you," Brandon and Dre snarled.

Cornel laughed unabashedly.

"Before shit starts popping off," Justin interjected, rising from the bleachers, "let's hit the showers and head over to Stogie's. I think we could all use a drink."

"Good idea." Cornel grinned. "Chambers is buying."

"What? Why the hell should *I* pick up the tab?"

" 'Cause you got the most money," Cornel reasoned. "And after the way we rescued your black ass from Cynthia's brothers, the least you can do is buy us drinks."

Dre and Justin grinned. "He *does* have a point."

Brandon scowled, shaking his head at them. "I need some new friends."

The fellas just laughed.

★ ★ ★

Later that night, Brandon was awakened by the sound of Cynthia quietly entering his bedroom. He lay completely still, listening to the soft rustle of her clothes hitting the floor before she padded over to the bed and slid beneath the heavy covers.

She settled onto her back, silent and unmoving in the near darkness.

Brandon watched her, waiting for her to speak.

"I couldn't stay away," she whispered.

He said nothing.

"God knows I wanted to," she continued. "After the way you humiliated me yesterday, I wanted to throw your ring back in your face and tell you I wouldn't marry you if you were the last man on earth. I wanted to get as far away from you as possible." She shook her head at the ceiling. "But I couldn't. Because I'm a fool. A weak, pathetic fool."

Guilt settled over Brandon like a lead blanket. "Cynthia—"

"I spent the whole day at my parents' house. You would think I was on suicide watch the way my family hovered around me—making sure I ate, keeping sharp objects out of my sight, tracking my every move. I practically had to ask permission to use the bathroom, and if I took too long, someone would knock on the door to check up on me. But that's not even the worst part, Brandon. The worst part is that you didn't even bother to call or send a text to see how I was doing. You dumped me at the altar, then simply went about your business like nothing had happened."

Brandon grimaced. "I didn't think you wanted to hear from me so soon."

"I didn't. But that shouldn't have stopped you from making the effort to reach out to me. A woman who gets jilted on her wedding day deserves the courtesy of at least *one* groveling phone call from her contrite fiancé."

Brandon pushed out a deep, weary breath and rolled onto his back. "I don't know what you want me to say, Cynthia. I knew you were angry and hurting. I didn't want to make matters worse."

"I bet you would have called Tamia," Cynthia said bitterly. "But then, you wouldn't have canceled the wedding in the first place if *she* were the one carrying your child."

Brandon was silent, Justin's words echoing through his mind. *If you get Tamia pregnant, then you could only be expected to marry one of them. . . .*

"I hate her," Cynthia hissed.

Brandon frowned. "Cynthia—"

"I know the Bible tells us to love our enemies, but I can't do that with Tamia. I hate her fucking guts. I wish you hadn't gotten her acquitted. I wish she'd been found guilty and received a life sentence. Hell, I wish one of the other inmates had gotten to her before the trial even started."

Brandon's blood ran cold. "You don't mean that."

"The hell I don't! I hate that bitch!"

"Shh. Stop this." Brandon turned and gathered her into his arms, spooning her body. As she burst into tears, he murmured soothingly, "Come on, sweetheart. All this negative emotion isn't good for you or the baby."

"I know," she sobbed, "but I can't help the way I feel. All these setbacks we've been having . . . I just feel like everything would have worked out if she hadn't been in the picture."

Brandon sighed deeply. "Tamia isn't the cause of your unhappiness. I am."

"Only because of *her!*"

"She didn't force me to postpone our wedding. That was on me. It wasn't an easy decision, but I honestly believe it was the right one. I know you're upset right now, but blaming Tamia isn't going to change anything. You're here with me, and we're going to have a baby. Nothing else should matter."

Cynthia sniffled into her pillow.

Pulling her closer, Brandon reached under her T-shirt and placed his hand against her flat stomach. "I wonder how long it'll be before you start showing," he murmured.

"Probably not for a while," she asserted. "I'm not that far along, and my mother says she didn't show with my oldest brother until she was well into her second trimester."

Brandon nodded slowly, trying to envision how Cynthia would look several months from now. But images of Tamia were what flooded his mind.

Tamia . . . her face glowing and radiant . . . her luscious breasts growing even fuller as her stomach swelled with child.

His child.

Theirs.

He saw her rubbing cocoa butter all over her beautiful caramel skin to fend off stretch marks. She'd rock designer maternity clothes, and she'd insist on wearing high heels until her sexy strut became an adorable waddle. She'd eat pickles with hot sauce while he gave her back rubs and foot massages. And they'd cuddle in bed every night and talk until one of them fell asleep.

"You're right, Brandon," Cynthia said resolutely, interrupting his sweet reverie. "We're together now, and we're having a baby. Nothing else matters."

"That's right," Brandon murmured, closing his eyes as a painful ache spread across his chest.

God, please give me the strength to get through this.

Chapter 5

Tamia

On Sunday morning, still suffering the effects of a broken heart, Tamia dragged herself out of bed, showered, and threw on some jeans, then headed downstairs to the gourmet grocery store located inside her apartment building.

She felt listless as she wandered down the aisles, absently adding items to her cart as cheery Christmas carols wafted through the store. The Phoenicia was shiny and new, boasting a wide selection of international foods, a salad and olive bar, a pita counter, a large wine collection, and a restaurant.

As Tamia rounded the corner of the spice aisle, she nearly collided with another shopper.

"I'm sorry," she mumbled quickly to the attractive black man behind the other cart.

"No, it's my fault. I wasn't watching where—*Miss Luke?*"

Tamia was surprised to find herself staring into the smiling face of Lester McCray, one of the jurors from her murder trial.

"Mr. McCray . . . um, hello."

"Miss Luke. Didn't we just run into each other last month?"

"We did. Imagine that."

Lester smiled warmly. "As I mentioned before, I live nearby. So I just had to come over and check out the new grocery store everyone's been talking about. It's great. Really impressive."

"I think so, too," Tamia said. "I'm glad it's here."

"It's definitely a welcome addition to the neighborhood."

Tamia smiled, but she was pondering the odds of her running into Lester McCray not once, but twice in the span of a month. If she didn't know better, she would think he was stalking her.

The thought sent a chill through her.

Lester's eyes roamed appreciatively across her face. "So how are things going? Are you working again?"

"I was. Briefly." Tamia tucked her hair behind one ear. "It didn't work out."

"I'm sorry to hear that," Lester said sympathetically.

"It's all right. It was for the best."

He nodded. "Don't get discouraged. Something better will come through."

Tamia smiled wanly. "I'm counting on it."

Lester hesitated, glancing around as if to make sure no one was standing nearby before he said quietly, "I have to admit I was shocked to hear that your sister was responsible for . . . what happened. I can't even imagine how devastated you must have been."

Tamia's muscles tightened, heat washing over her face. "I *was* devastated," she said tensely. "But I'm really trying to put all that behind me."

"Of course. I'm sorry. I shouldn't have brought it up." Lester gave her a rueful smile. "I guess I've just blown any shot at convincing you to have coffee with me."

She shook her head. "I don't think that'd be a good idea."

"I know. I was one of your jurors, so it's a conflict of interest." Lester sighed. "I guess I was hoping you'd changed your mind about that."

"I'm afraid not." At that moment, Tamia's smartphone rang. Grateful for the interruption, she flashed a smile at Lester. "It was nice seeing you again, Mr. McCray. Take care."

"You too, Miss Luke."

Tamia pulled her phone out of her pocket as she walked away, pushing her shopping cart. Just as before, she could feel Lester Mc-Cray's eyes following her, raising the fine hairs on the back of her neck.

She answered the phone. "Hello."

"Hey, Tamia." It was her friend Honey, whom she'd met last month at the homecoming party to celebrate her acquittal. A week later, Honey had showed up on Tamia's doorstep with a black eye and a busted lip, courtesy of her boyfriend, Keyshawn.

"Girl, you have perfect timing," Tamia said.

"Why? What's going on?"

"Long story. I'll tell you later. Where have you been? I called yesterday to see if you were back from New Orleans yet, but you didn't answer the phone."

"I know. I meant to call you back but . . ." Honey trailed off.

Tamia frowned. "Where are you?"

Honey hesitated for a long moment. "I'm back home. With Keyshawn."

"*What?*"

"It's okay," Honey hastened to assure her. "He wasn't mad. He was happy to see me. He said he missed me."

Tamia sucked her teeth in disgust. "Have you forgotten the reason you left him in the first place? He gave you a black eye and threatened to kill you!"

"I know, and he apologized for that. When he found the diamond bracelet that Bishop Yarbrough gave me, it just set him off. It made him jealous because he knows he can't afford to buy me expensive gifts—"

"Whatever," Tamia spat, impatiently tossing a bag of pasta into her cart. "Abusive men always have some sorry excuse for their behavior. It doesn't mean a damn thing."

Honey heaved a resigned breath. "I hear what you're saying, Tamia, but I *had* to come back home. I couldn't let Keyshawn go to the media about me and Bishop Yarbrough."

Tamia scowled, but she knew Honey was right. She had everything to lose if her secret affair with the megachurch pastor went public. At the same time, staying with her violent boyfriend could get her killed.

Tamia clenched her jaw, hating the sense of helplessness that had gripped her. It reminded her too much of her childhood and the terrible fights she'd witnessed between her mother and her stepfather.

"Where is he?" she gritted through her teeth.

"Keyshawn? He went to work this morning." Honey paused. "He expects me to be here when he gets back."

"So you're his fucking prisoner now?"

"Apparently." Honey sighed in defeat. "None of this would have happened if Bishop Yarbrough hadn't given me that damn bracelet. And do you know he had the nerve to call me while I was in New Orleans? Here I am trying to spend time with my family, and he's blowing up my phone wanting to know when I'll be back because he can't wait to see me again."

Tamia scowled, shaking her head. "That man is the biggest fucking hypocrite."

"I know, girl, but he's one of my best clients. Anyway, I told him we have to lay low for a while because Keyshawn's been acting jealous and suspicious. But I promised to call him tonight to get him off before he goes to bed."

Tamia rolled her eyes in disgust. "TMI, heffa."

Honey laughed. "I'm heading out to run some errands, but what're you doing tomorrow? Are you free for lunch? You need to catch me up on what's been happening in the world of Tamdon."

"Tamdon?"

Honey chuckled. "That's my nickname for you and Brandon."

"Oh." Tamia's throat tightened. "I'll fill you in tomorrow."

"Cool. I'll call you when I'm on my way to your apartment."

"Okay." Tamia disconnected and stuffed her phone back into her pocket, then headed for the checkout counter. She hadn't been waiting in line long when she saw Lester McCray. He got in the same line, standing behind two other customers.

When Tamia met his gaze, he gave her a smile that made her skin crawl.

She paid for her groceries, grabbed the two bags, and quickly left the store. As soon as she boarded the elevator to return to her apartment, she pulled out her phone again. Without thinking twice, she sent a text message to Brandon: I need a favor.

By the time she stepped off the elevator, he was calling her.

She picked up, her pulse thudding. "Brandon."

"Hey, baby," he murmured.

Her knees went weak. Closing her eyes, she said quietly, "You can't call me that anymore."

"I know. I'm sorry." There was an ache in his voice that matched the ache in her heart.

She swallowed hard, fumbling out her keys as she reached her front door. "I didn't want to call your phone in case you were at church with Cynthia."

"She went without me."

"Oh."

Silence.

"I just got your message," Brandon said. "What do you need?"

Tamia let herself into the apartment and closed the door. "Would you happen to have the home addresses of the jurors from my trial?"

"Their home addresses?" Brandon repeated, sounding puzzled.

"Yeah. As an attorney, don't you have access to jurors' personal information?"

"Only if the judge releases it, and it has to be for a good reason."

"Oh," Tamia murmured, carrying her bags into the kitchen and setting them on the granite counter. "Never mind, then."

"What's going on, Tamia?"

She hesitated, debating how much she should tell him. She didn't want to sound any alarms before she had to. *If* she had to. "Do you remember juror number eight?"

"The brotha who couldn't keep his eyes off you during the trial?" Brandon chuckled dryly. "Yeah, I remember him. Why?"

"I've run into him a couple times," Tamia explained, striving to sound nonchalant. "So I was just wondering if he lives around here."

Brandon was silent for a long moment. "What aren't you telling me, Tamia?"

"Nothing. I'm sorry. I shouldn't have called you. I was just curious, but I should have realized you wouldn't have Lester McCray's address."

"Just because I don't have it doesn't mean I can't get it."

Of course he could. Brandon was one of the most powerful attorneys in Houston. He had more connections than there were stars in the universe. And he'd have no trouble persuading some court clerk to give him the information he wanted, no questions asked.

"I don't need his address," Tamia clarified. "I just want to know if he lives around here."

"All right. Give me a day to find out and get back to you."

"Okay. Thank you, Brandon."

"You don't have to thank me. Just promise me you're not keeping anything else from me."

"I'm not."

After several moments, Brandon said slowly, "All right." He clearly didn't believe her.

Tamia leaned back against the counter, wrapping an arm around her waist. "You should have gone to church with your fiancée."

Brandon sighed. "Why?"

"Because it would have been less humiliating for her to have you by her side two days after you . . . postponed the wedding."

There was a long silence.

"Did you have a better night?" Brandon asked quietly.

Tamia closed her eyes. "I'm not gonna answer that."

"Why not?"

"Because there's no right answer. If I tell you that I slept horribly, you'll feel guilty or, worse, you'll feel sorry for me, and the last thing I want is your pity. But if I tell you that I slept like a baby . . . well, you might think I've already gotten over you. And nothing could be further from the truth."

Brandon exhaled a ragged breath. "Tamia—"

"I have to go, Brandon," she said softly. "When you get the information I asked for, you don't have to call. You can just send me a text."

He said nothing.

She swallowed tightly. "Good-bye, Brandon."

Before he could respond, she ended the call and set the phone down on the counter. Her eyes burned with tears, but she refused to let them fall. She had to be strong. Stronger than she'd ever been. It was the only way she'd be able to move on with her life.

Releasing a shaky breath, Tamia forced herself to unpack and put away the groceries.

Just as she finished the task, her phone rang. She picked it up and checked the display screen. When she saw the number to the Christina Crain women's prison, her heart thumped into her throat.

Fiona.

She hadn't seen or spoken to her sister since the harrowing night that Fiona had confessed to murdering their grandmother ten years ago. After she'd been taken into custody, she'd refused to have contact with anyone. Against the advice of the public defender assisting her, she'd waived her right to a jury trial and was now waiting to be sentenced by a judge.

Tamia stared at the ringing phone, grief and fury pumping through her veins. Not only had Fiona murdered their grandmother; she'd killed Dominic's wife and let Tamia take the fall.

Was it any wonder Tamia wanted absolutely nothing to do with her?

Your sister needs you, Mama Esther's voice whispered through her mind.

Tamia's fingers tightened around the phone. She paced over to the breakfast counter, then reluctantly pressed the talk button and agreed to accept the collect call from her sister.

Seconds later Fiona's small, tremulous voice came on the line. "Hey, Tamia. How're you doing?"

"I have nothing to say to you, Fiona," Tamia said coldly.

"I know. And I wouldn't have called unless it was really important. I . . . I need you to do something for me."

"What the hell makes you think—?"

"I'm pregnant."

Tamia froze, the blood draining from her head. "Wh-what did you say?"

"I'm pregnant," Fiona repeated in a low whisper.

Reeling with shock, Tamia sat down hard on the nearest bar stool. "When . . . ?"

"I found out a week ago. I've been trying to get in touch with Dre—"

"Dre?" Tamia interrupted faintly. "Dre who?"

"Dre Portis."

Tamia's eyes widened. "Brandon's best friend?"

"Yeah."

Tamia nearly fell off the stool. "Are you telling me that you and Deondre Portis *slept together?*"

"Yes." Fiona sounded annoyed. "Why is that so hard for you to believe?"

"Because he has a girlfriend! And they've always seemed like the perfect couple."

Fiona snorted. "They weren't. Leah wasn't handling her business, so I did it for her."

"And got yourself pregnant." Tamia frowned. "Are you sure it's Dre's baby?"

"What's that supposed to mean?"

"Have you been with anyone else recently?"

Fiona hesitated for a moment. "The only other dude I was messing with was one of my professors. And he always wore a condom. Dre didn't."

Tamia shook her head slowly. "Unbelievable."

"You think I'm happy about this?" Fiona burst out. "I'm not! I'm in prison, Tamia, and I'll probably be here for the rest of my life. I'm depressed and scared as hell, and I keep having nightmares about Mama Esther. Bringing a baby into the world is the *last* thing—" Fiona broke off abruptly, her voice choking on a muffled sob.

Tamia's heart softened with compassion.

"What do you need me to do?" she asked in a gentler tone.

Fiona sniffled. "Dre won't take any of my phone calls, and he returned the letter I sent him. I know he thinks I'm crazy and he regrets what we did, but he needs to know that I'm carrying his baby. Since I can't reach him, will you tell him for me?"

Tamia swallowed hard, then nodded slowly. "I'll tell him."

"Thank you, Tam-Tam," Fiona whispered meekly. "Will you let me know what he says?"

"Of course." Tamia stared down at the hardwood floor. Suddenly her own problems seemed small and trivial. "If he doesn't want the baby, Fee, you know I'm here."

"I know, and I appreciate that. But I want the baby to be raised by Dre." Fiona paused, then added sadly, "I'm living proof of what can go wrong when a child doesn't have her father around. I want better for my baby."

Tamia closed her eyes, sorrow and regret twisting inside her.

"I'll talk to Dre," she promised. "He'll do the right thing."

She'd make damn sure of it.

Chapter 6
Brandon

Brandon stared broodingly out the windows of his downtown office.

The winter sky was gray, making the steel and glass skyscrapers look dull and smudged.

He had paperwork to complete, phone calls to make, client meetings to schedule. But he couldn't tackle any of those tasks because his concentration was shot to fucking hell.

He couldn't stop thinking about Tamia.

After she got off the phone with him yesterday, he'd laced up his Timbs, grabbed his car keys, and headed out the door bound for her apartment. He'd needed to see her, hold her, be with her.

He'd gotten halfway across town before he came to his senses, turned around, and went back home.

He'd been miserable ever since.

Brandon sighed, surveying the downtown landscape from his forty-ninth-floor vantage point.

He was one of the top rainmakers at Chernoff, Dewitt & Strathmore, and he'd only been partner for four months.

He made more money than he could ever spend in a lifetime.

He had the POTUS on speed dial.

Everywhere he went, people knew him and bent over backward to accommodate him.

He could have anything he wanted . . .

. . . except the woman he loved.

"Well, well, well," a mocking voice interrupted his tortured musings. "Isn't *this* a surprise?"

Brandon frowned, muscles tensing.

Resenting the intrusion, he turned slowly to regard the man who stood in the doorway of his corner office.

With impeccably coiffed hair and arctic-blue eyes, Russ Sutcliffe was one of the firm's senior partners and the only one who'd voted against Brandon's promotion that summer. Though his beef with Brandon stemmed from his longstanding hatred for Brandon's father—whom Russ had unsuccessfully tried to keep out of office— he and Brandon had developed their own feud over the past eight years.

"I wasn't expecting to see *you* here this week," Russ drawled tauntingly. "Aren't you and Miss Yarbrough supposed to be on your honeymoon?"

Brandon was in no mood for the man's bullshit. "What do you want, Russ?"

He laughed, shaking his head at Brandon as he wandered into the large room. "No need to get testy with me just because you felt compelled to call off your wedding. Speaking of which, I'm sure that didn't go over too well with Miss Yarbrough and her family. Aren't you and your father supposed to be campaigning with Bishop Yarbrough starting this month?" Russ smirked. "Talk about *awkward*."

Brandon just looked at him. "Are you finished?"

Russ ignored him. "Poor Cynthia. It must gall her to know that you couldn't bring yourself to marry her because you're still hung up on a trashy porn star. What does the poor girl have to do to win your love and devotion? Get knocked up?" Russ paused, his eyes gleaming with malicious satisfaction. "Oh, but wait. She's already done that, hasn't she? Why else would you have arranged a shotgun wedding at the justice of the peace?"

Brandon smiled narrowly. "If I were you, Russ—meaning if I were a pathetic has-been whose colleagues call him a joke behind his back—I'd spend less time gossiping and more time worrying about how to generate revenue for this firm before you're tossed out on your freeloading ass."

Russ's face reddened with fury. "Who the hell do you think you're talking to?"

Though he didn't say it, the word *boy* hung between them like a grenade with an unlit fuse.

"Careful, Russ," Brandon warned softly. "I'm gonna run this town one day, so you'd be wise not to say anything that could come back to haunt you when you have to come begging me for a job."

Russ was speechless, his face going from red to an apoplectic purple.

"Good ol' Russ," drawled an amused voice from across the room. "You never did know how to quit while you're behind."

Brandon and Russ glanced sharply toward the doorway. Brandon smothered a groan when he saw his father standing there with Iris, the receptionist, who was beaming with excitement.

"Brandon," she gushed, "you have a visitor."

He could see that. "Thanks, Iris."

"I'll bring you and the lieutenant governor some coffee." She winked at Bernard. "And I'll keep your security boys entertained while they wait for you."

"Thank you, Iris," Bernard said with a good-natured chuckle. "If anyone can get them to loosen up, you can."

As Iris bustled away, Brandon smiled at his father. "Hey, Dad. I thought you'd be on your way to the capital by now."

"I wanted to stop by and see you first." Stepping into the room, Bernard Chambers divided an amused glance between Brandon and Russ. "I apologize for interrupting."

"No apology necessary," Brandon drawled. "Russ and I were just talking shop."

"Is that right?" Bernard's dark eyes glinted with humor as he nodded to Russ. "Mr. Sutcliffe."

"Lieutenant Governor Chambers," Russ said, his voice dripping with smug condescension. "So nice of you to grace us with your presence. How's your lovely wife?"

"She's well. And yours?"

"Never been better." Russ smiled thinly. "Speaking of wives, I wanted to congratulate your son on his recent nuptials, but I understand the ceremony didn't go off as planned. I hope that won't cause a rift between you and Bishop Yarbrough. I know how much his support means to your campaign."

"It does," Bernard smoothly agreed. "But Joseph Yarbrough believes in my candidacy, so I'm not at all worried about losing his support. Now if you don't mind, Russ, I'm on a tight schedule, so I'd like a few minutes with my son so that he can get back to work and you can get back to doing . . . whatever it is you do around here."

Russ's face flushed with anger and humiliation. Clenching his jaw, he shot one last glare at Brandon before turning and stalking out of the room.

Bernard and Brandon looked at each other and grinned. Nothing bonded father and son more than putting Russ Sutcliffe in his place.

After Iris brought their coffee and closed the door behind her, Brandon lowered himself into his chair and offered, "Why don't you have a seat, Dad?"

Bernard was already striding forward, radiating enough power and authority to make the enormous room seem smaller. He was a tall man, dark and distinguished. Today he wore a custom-tailored William Fioravanti suit and impeccably polished Italian loafers.

Ignoring both visitor chairs, he sat down on the sleek leather sofa near Brandon's desk and smoothly crossed his legs. As he raised the cup of coffee to his mouth and took a deliberate sip, his eyes never left Brandon's face.

Brandon waited. He knew what was coming.

"Your mother and I have been trying to reach you since Friday," Bernard said reproachfully. "You've been avoiding our calls."

Brandon didn't bother to deny it.

"What you did at the courthouse was a mistake—one that we expect you to rectify."

Brandon was silent, staring into the dark contents of his own coffee cup.

"Is Cynthia pregnant?" Bernard asked bluntly.

Brandon didn't blink. "No."

Bernard shook his head. "Boy, you must think I was born yesterday. For whatever reason, you and Cynthia have been denying that she's pregnant. But your mother and I both know that's the only reason you were getting married on Friday. And Russ knows it, too. Which is why he and my opponents are going to seize the opportunity to use this latest stunt of yours against me."

Brandon sighed. "Dad—"

"It's bad enough that we're still doing damage control from the ad they ran about Tamia and her deranged sister. You've just given them new ammunition by refusing to marry your pregnant girlfriend."

"I'm not refusing to marry her," Brandon said evenly.

His father snorted. "Sure as hell looked like it to me and everyone else who was there. I've never seen Joseph so mad. You know he's a card-carrying member of the NRA. If he'd been armed on Friday, your mother and I would be making your funeral arrangements right now. Even if he doesn't pull his support, I know he won't be too eager to campaign for me until you do right by his daughter."

"I plan to," Brandon bit off tersely. "But with all due respect, Dad, this is a private matter between me and Cynthia."

Bernard shook his head in angry exasperation. "How many times do I have to remind you that everything you do reflects upon me? As long as I'm running for governor, you can't go around impregnating women and jilting them at the altar. You have to set a better exam—"

"I know, Dad," Brandon snapped, slamming his cup down on the desk and splashing coffee onto the blotter. Ignoring the mess, he shoved to his feet and stalked to the windows. Jamming his hands into his pockets, he glared outside as anger and frustration pumped through his blood.

He heard the soft creak of leather as his father rose from the sofa and walked over to him.

"We all have to make sacrifices, son. Short-term sacrifices for long-term goals."

"Whose goals?" Brandon challenged. "Yours or mine?"

His father gave him a disappointed look. "You used to know what was important. You used to care."

"I still do. But my definition of what's important isn't the same as it used to be."

Bernard held his defiant gaze for a long moment, then turned to stare out the windows. In silence, father and son contemplated the gray skies that blanketed the city their ancestors had helped build.

Bernard said quietly, "You were absolutely right when you told Russ that you'd run this town someday. You will—without a doubt. But it won't stop there. You're Brandon Everett Chambers. The day you were born, your mother and I looked into your eyes, and we knew with unshakable certainty that you were destined for greatness. Not just because of your lineage, but because of who *you* are."

When Brandon said nothing, his father continued, "I know you resent my interference in your life. You think I'm pushing you into a political career, and you think that's not what you want. You want to be your own man, carve out your own path. And there's nothing wrong with that. But if you ever mistakenly believe that you can just settle for anything—if you ever forget how ruthlessly ambitious you are—look around this office. Think of all the attorneys you out-gunned and outworked to make partner. Think of the opponents you routinely demolish in the courtroom. And remember that it was *you* who told Russ you'd run this town one day. Those were your words, Brandon. Not mine or your mother's. *Yours.*"

Brandon remained silent, a muscle throbbing in his jaw.

"Tamia Luke doesn't belong in your world, son. I know that's not what you want to hear, but it's the truth. A woman like her will only cause you heartache and keep you from fulfilling your potential."

"You're wrong," Brandon said flatly. "When Tamia and I were dating, she was nothing but supportive of my career goals. She was my sounding board at the end of a long day, she dropped everything whenever I needed her to, and even though I canceled more than a few dates to work late, she never once complained."

Bernard gave him a mocking look. "So now you're trying to whitewash your relationship with Tamia."

"I'm not trying to whitewash anything. I'm just telling you that everything wasn't always bad between us. If that were the case, we wouldn't have been together for nine months. But you know what, Dad? I'm tired of defending our relationship to you and everyone else, so can we just move on?"

"I don't know, Brandon. *Can* we move on? Can *you*?"

They stared each other down until Brandon looked away, clenching his jaw.

Bernard shook his head. "You think I don't know that you're suffering? I know a heartbroken man when I see one. Tamia's the woman you want, but she's not the woman you need. Cynthia Yarbrough is. And if she's carrying your child, honor and decency demand that you do the right thing and marry her. The sooner, the better."

Brandon didn't respond.

Staring out the windows, he wondered if his father would have issued the same order if Tamia, not Cynthia, were pregnant.

But he already knew the answer.

Chapter 7
Tamia

Tamia strode through the glass doors that fronted the administrative offices of Pinnacle Sports Group, a sports management agency co-owned by Brandon, his brother, Beau, and Dre. Her stiletto boot heels sank into plush carpeting as she crossed to the large reception desk, which was manned by a dark-skinned beauty with a glossy weave down to her ass—eye candy for the athletes who were represented by the agency.

A look of surprised recognition crossed the receptionist's face when she saw Tamia. "Hello," she greeted her. "Can I help you?"

"I'm here to see Dre. The clerk down at the wellness center told me I could find him up here."

"Yes, he's in his office. Is he expecting you?"

"No, but I need to speak to him."

"You don't have an appointment?"

"No."

"Um . . . okay." The girl reluctantly reached for the phone. "Let me see if he's avail—"

Tamia lost her patience. "You know what?"

As she marched past the desk, the receptionist sputtered indignantly, "If you'd just wait—"

Ignoring the girl's protests, Tamia left the reception area and started toward the back. As she strode down the hall, she heard the familiar sound of Dre's laughter coming from an open doorway.

Reaching the office, she saw him seated behind the desk with his booted feet propped up as he chatted on his phone.

"Didn't I tell you that Foster's a stud?" he declared, gloating about the Houston Texans' star running back, who'd led his team to an impressive victory yesterday. Dre, who had a PhD in sports medicine, was the athletic trainer for the Texans.

"Don't sleep on us. We could go all the—" Dre broke off abruptly, his eyes widening at the sight of Tamia standing in the doorway.

When she arched a brow at him, he swung his legs down from the desk and mumbled into the phone, "Let me holla at you later, my brotha."

As he ended the call, the receptionist blurted out, "I'm so sorry, Dre. I tried to stop her—"

"And you failed." Tamia closed the door on the flustered girl and looked at Dre. "We need to talk."

He frowned. "I'm kind of busy right now—"

"Didn't look that way to me." Tamia strode to the visitor chair across from his desk and sat down. As she crossed her legs, she didn't miss the way his eyes lowered to her thick, denim-covered thighs. Remembering that he used to jerk off to her porn videos, she suppressed a shudder.

As he leaned back in his chair, his gray pullover stretched taut across his muscular chest. With his dark skin, heavy-lidded eyes, and smooth bald head, Tamia grudgingly acknowledged that he was good-looking, though nowhere near as fine as Brandon.

"So," Dre ventured cautiously, "what do we need to talk about?"

"You and my sister."

His face tightened, eyes flickering with guilt. "What about us?"

"You need to get in touch with her," Tamia told him.

He frowned. "Look, I don't know what she told you, but I'm not interested in—"

"She's pregnant, Dre."

He froze, staring at her in shock. "Wh-what?"

Tamia met his gaze directly. "She's pregnant. And the baby's yours."

If Dre weren't so dark, Tamia would have sworn she saw the blood drain from his face.

He shook his head in stunned denial. "That's . . . that's impossible."

"Why? Have you had a vasectomy? Are you shooting blanks?"

He swallowed visibly. "No."

Tamia smirked. "Then it's not impossible, is it?"

Dre held her gaze another moment, then sat forward and passed a trembling hand over his head. He looked so devastated that Tamia couldn't help feeling sorry for him.

Until he opened his mouth again.

"How do you know the baby's mine? Fiona was always flirting with her clients at the barber shop, so I know I'm not the only dude she was messing around with."

Tamia regarded him for a long moment, then slowly uncrossed her legs and rose from the chair. Planting her hands on top of the desk, she leaned toward Dre and sneered, "Aren't you the same self-righteous motherfucker who once told me that actions have consequences? Well, guess what? Screwing my sister was an action that has a consequence. That's *your* child she's carrying, so be a man and handle your fucking business."

Dre gulped hard, staring up at Tamia. "She can't have that baby."

"That's up to her. But you need to talk to her, Dre. I'm serious. If I find out that you haven't contacted her by the end of the week, I'm coming after your black ass, and I won't be so polite next time."

With that, Tamia spun on her heel and marched out the door.

She was halfway down the hall when a deep voice called out, "Tamia?"

She stopped and turned, smiling when she saw Brandon's brother standing outside his office. "Hey," she said weakly.

"Wassup, girl." Beau sauntered toward her, wide shoulders swaying beneath his pressed white shirt, long legs covered in Armani. He looked so much like Brandon that Tamia's breath caught in her throat.

Beau smiled warmly as he reached her, diamond stud twinkling in his ear. "What're you doing here?"

"I needed to see Dre about something," Tamia answered vaguely.

"So you were just gonna leave without saying hello?"

"I didn't want to disturb you. I know you're busy with clients and . . ." Tamia trailed off lamely. She couldn't tell him the truth, that seeing him was a painful reminder of everything she'd had—and lost—with Brandon.

She was relieved when Beau tactfully changed the subject. "Hey, listen, I wanted to ask you something. Last month when you came to the wellness center, there was a woman with you. Or at least that's what Dre told me when I described her to him. He said she came with you."

Tamia smiled. "You must be talking about Honey."

"Is that her name?" Beau grinned. "Yeah, she looked like a Honey. Sweet as hell. So she's a friend of yours?"

Tamia nodded. "Yeah."

"I wanna meet her. Think you can arrange that?"

Before Tamia could respond, the receptionist called down the hallway, "Beau, I've been trying to reach you. Champ Suggs is on the phone. He said it's important."

"Tell him I'll be with him in two minutes."

As the receptionist bustled away to relay the message, Tamia raised a brow at Beau. "Champ Suggs? Pro Bowl wide receiver for the Giants?"

"Yeah. He's thinking about firing his agent and jumping on board with me."

"Wow. Look at you, Beau. You're about to sign the next number-one draft pick, and now you might land Champ Suggs as well? Go on with your bad self."

"Thanks, Tamia," Beau said with a pleased chuckle. "It's been a good year."

"And it's only been your first." Tamia grinned. "You'd better not keep Champ waiting."

"I know. Listen, before I let you go, we're having a scholarship fundraiser gala next Friday. Why don't you and Honey come?"

Tamia's grin faded.

"I'm not sure that's a good idea," she said quietly. "Your brother will be there, and I don't want anyone to think—"

"You'd be coming as my guest, not his."

"I know, but . . ." Tamia shook her head. "Honestly, Beau, I don't think I'm ready to see him again."

Beau's expression softened with sympathy. "I understand. I'm not trying to make you feel uncomfortable."

She sighed. "I know."

"Tell you what. I'll mail you two tickets in case you change your mind about coming. Which I hope you will, because I'd love to see you there." He winked. "Honey, too."

Tamia chuckled dryly. "I'll think about it and let you know."

As she turned and started away, Beau said softly, "Tamia."

She glanced over her shoulder, meeting his gentle gaze.

"He doesn't love her."

Tamia's throat tightened.

"Maybe not," she murmured, "but he chose her. So I have to accept that and move on."

Beau's eyes searched her face. "Can you?"

She smiled sadly. "I don't have a choice, do I?"

Chapter 8
Tamia

Tamia had just stepped through her front door when her smartphone rang. She dug it out of her handbag and checked the display screen, frowning at the unfamiliar number.

"Hello?" she answered warily.

"Tamia, this is Cynthia."

Tamia stiffened. "How did you get my number?"

"From Brandon's cell phone. Are you free right now? I wanted to discuss something with you."

Tamia frowned. "I don't think—"

"It won't take long. Are you at home?"

"Well, yes, but—"

"Great. I'm on my way." Cynthia hung up before Tamia could protest.

Fifteen minutes later she stood on Tamia's doorstep, looking sleek and stylish in a belted Jacquard dress with black tights and suede ankle boots. Tamia's eyes were unerringly drawn to the four-carat diamond twinkling on her left hand. The sight of the ring—and what it represented—drove a dagger through her heart.

Catching Tamia's wistful gaze, Cynthia flashed a cool, triumphant smile.

"Mind if I come in?"

Tamia minded very much, but since the heffa was already here, she might as well hear what she had to say.

She led Cynthia into the living room, where they sat on opposite ends of the pristine white sofa. Tamia watched as Cynthia looked around the lavishly furnished apartment, her gaze encompassing gleaming hardwood floors, expensive artwork, and picture windows that boasted spectacular views of downtown.

"Nice place," Cynthia remarked, her voice laced with grudging admiration. "What an upgrade for you. From prison to One Park Place."

Tamia sighed. "Yes, well, I was blessed with a generous benefactor."

Cynthia's eyes narrowed with suspicion. "Benefactor?"

"Umm-hmm." Tamia smiled slowly.

Cynthia swept another glance around, her mouth tightening with anger at the realization that Brandon had provided the fancy digs for Tamia.

"So is that what you want to be, Tamia?" she jeered contemptuously. "The kept mistress?"

Tamia smirked. "Beats being the rebound chick."

Cynthia flinched, her face flushing with humiliation. But she recovered quickly. "I'd rather be the rebound chick than the whore who wasn't good enough to marry."

Tamia snorted. "Bitch, please. The only reason Brandon is marrying you is because you claim to be pregnant."

"*Claim?* I'm not 'claiming' anything—I *am* pregnant!"

"So *you* say."

Cynthia laughed caustically. "You know what, Tamia? You're just jealous because you and Brandon were together for nine months and he didn't get *you* pregnant." She smirked. "And here I thought ghetto bitches like you perfected the art of the baby trap."

Tamia narrowed her eyes. "*I* was on the pill. Were *you?*"

"I was." Cynthia smiled smugly. "But obviously God intended for *me* to have Brandon's baby."

Tamia clenched her jaw. It was all she could do not to reach over and slap the shit out of the heffa.

Striving for composure, she said in a low, measured voice, "Why are you here, Cynthia? What do you want?"

"I want you to stay the fuck away from my fiancé," Cynthia spat. "Don't call him. Don't text him. Don't invent phony excuses to see him. Just stay the hell away from him."

Tamia remained outwardly calm, though inwardly she was falling apart.

"As long as Brandon keeps his distance," she said quietly, "I'll do the same."

"Good. Because I really don't need the stress and aggravation of fighting with you when I have so many other things on my plate—planning the wedding, preparing for the baby, going house hunting with Brandon."

Tamia congratulated herself for not breaking down right then and there.

Cynthia sighed. "Well, I'd better run," she announced, rising from the sofa. "Brandon's mother and I are getting facials and massages at her favorite day spa."

Tamia swallowed tightly. "How nice."

"Isn't it?" Cynthia let out another sigh, heading toward the front door. "Mrs. Chambers has been so good to me. So loving and supportive. We've really bonded over—"

She was interrupted by a sudden burst of music from Tamia's smartphone.

Usher crooned, *"There's always that one person that will always have your heart . . ."*

Cynthia froze in her tracks.

Slowly she turned to stare at Tamia, then at the lit-up phone on the foyer table.

She knew as well as Tamia did what the ringtone meant.

Brandon was calling.

Tamia walked over and calmly picked up the phone. "Hey."

"Hey," Brandon murmured, his deep voice flooding her ear. "How are you?"

She met Cynthia's lethal glare. "I've been better."

"Me, too." Brandon paused for a long moment. "I got the information you asked for."

"Really? That was fast. What'd you find out?"

"Lester McCray lives nowhere near downtown."

Tamia frowned. "He doesn't?"

"No. Did he tell you that?"

Tamia was silent, chilled by the knowledge that Lester McCray had lied to her. *Why?*

"What's going on, Tamia?" Brandon growled.

"Nothing. Listen, thank you for getting the information."

"Tamia—"

"I can't talk right now, Brandon. I'm walking Cynthia to the door."

Silence.

"She's over there?" Brandon's voice was chillingly soft.

"Yes, she is." Tamia looked at Cynthia, who suddenly appeared nervous. "I'll give her your warm regards."

Brandon swore viciously and hung up.

Setting the phone down, Tamia smirked at Cynthia. "I think you got some 'splaining to do."

Cynthia's eyes hardened with fury. "You are such a bitch."

"Takes one to know one," Tamia drawled.

Cynthia glared at her another moment, then spun on her heel and marched toward the door.

Tamia followed her, pulling up short when Cynthia suddenly whirled around and sneered, "By the way, you know another word for rebound chick?" She held up her left hand with the diamond ring. "*Wife.*"

With that, she turned and flounced out of the apartment.

Tamia slammed the door and leaned against it, squeezing her eyes shut.

Though she'd gotten some satisfaction from the timing of Brandon's call, Cynthia's parting shot had brought her crashing back to earth, forcing her to face the hard, cold reality that Brandon and Cynthia were getting married. Having a baby. Buying a house together. Becoming one.

And where did that leave Tamia?

Alone and heartbroken, with nothing but shattered dreams and bottomless regret to keep her warm every night.

Swiping hot tears from her eyes, Tamia lifted her head from the door and looked at her handbag on the foyer table.

Before she could stop herself, she marched over and dug through her purse until she located Dominic's business card. Snatching up her phone, she dialed his number with trembling fingers.

He answered on the third ring. "Hello?"

"Dominic, this is Tamia."

"Tamia," he drawled, sounding pleased. "I've been hoping to hear from you. Have you made a decision about my offer?"

"Yes." She resolutely set her jaw. "I accept."

Chapter 9

Brandon

Brandon paced in front of his office windows with his phone pressed to his ear, temper escalating with each ring that went unanswered.

Finally Cynthia picked up. "Brandon—"

"What the hell do you think you're doing?"

She paused. "What do you mean?"

"You know damn well what I mean," he snarled. "What were you doing at Tamia's apartment?"

"Oh, you mean the apartment you rented and furnished for her behind my back?" Cynthia jeered. "The apartment you're planning to use as your love nest?"

Brandon clenched his jaw so hard the tendons in his neck bulged. "What were you doing there?"

"What do you think?" Cynthia hissed. "I went there to have a woman-to-woman talk with Tamia."

"Stay away from her."

"I have every right—"

"STAY THE FUCK AWAY FROM HER!" Brandon roared.

Cynthia fell silent.

Chest heaving, nostrils flaring, Brandon growled menacingly, "You wanna talk? Talk to me. You wanna fight? Fight me. You go anywhere near her again and we're gonna have a serious fucking problem. Do you understand me?"

Cynthia hesitated. "Yes."

"You'd better."

"What about you?" she challenged petulantly.

"What *about* me?"

"Are *you* going to stay away from her? Because it sure as hell doesn't look that way to me. I went through your cell phone, Brandon. While you couldn't be bothered to call *me* while I was over at my parents' house bawling my eyes out, you called *her* twice on Saturday and once yesterday. And I wasn't even at her place five minutes today and you were calling her again!"

Brandon stopped pacing.

"First of all," he said, keeping his voice level, "it's not like I was calling to hook up with her. I needed to give her some information. Second, if you can't refrain from snooping through my personal things, then maybe you need to stay at your house until the wedding."

"Oh, you'd like that, wouldn't you?" Cynthia jeered. "You want me out of the way so you can bring home that filthy whore whenever you want. But guess what? I'm not going anywhere, so if you're planning to sneak around with her, it sure as hell won't be happening in the bed *we* share every night!"

Brandon closed his eyes, rubbing his throbbing temple. "I'm not planning to sneak around with Tamia. She deserves better than that." He paused. "So do you."

"So do I," Cynthia repeated bitterly. "I'm always an afterthought with you."

Brandon exhaled harshly. "What do you want from me, Cynthia? I ended my relationship with Tamia. I agreed to marry you—"

"Don't do me any fucking favors!"

He tightened his jaw, glaring out the windows. "When are you coming in?"

"I'm not."

Brandon frowned. "I think you should."

"I already took this week off for our honeymoon. Just because *you* flaked out—"

He cut her off. "You're up for partnership, Cynthia. Our colleagues already think you've been slacking for the past several months. Don't give them any more reason to believe you don't deserve to make partner."

Cynthia was silent, mulling over his words.

He hoped he'd gotten through to her.

But then she said defiantly, "I have plans with your mother. She doesn't have any court cases today, so she invited me to spend the afternoon with her. Frankly, after the weekend I've had, I need all the moral support I can get."

Brandon shook his head. "You're making a mistake."

"I'll be there tomorrow," Cynthia said curtly. "And I find it interesting that you couldn't be bothered to attend church yesterday, but you had no problem getting up for work this morning."

Brandon scowled. "Are you finished?"

"What? Why are you—"

"I have to go." He disconnected and tossed the phone onto his desk, then scrubbed his hands over his face and fired off a string of harsh expletives.

His chest burned at the thought of Cynthia showing up at Tamia's apartment and flashing her engagement ring in Tamia's face, maliciously taunting her. He knew Tamia was tough and could take care of herself. But right now she was vulnerable and hurting, and the last thing she needed was Cynthia rubbing salt into her wounds.

"*Fuck!*" Brandon swore, banging his fist against the windows.

He was tempted to call Tamia back to apologize for Cynthia's visit, but he knew that would only make matters worse. The best thing for him to do was leave her alone, just as she'd asked him to.

The sooner he let her go, the sooner they could both get on with their lives.

Or some semblance of a life . . .

Brandon struggled to concentrate on work for the rest of the day. At five o'clock he gave up, grabbed his briefcase, and rolled out.

As he strode across the underground parking garage, he dreaded the thought of going home and dealing with Cynthia. So he pulled out his smartphone and called Dre to see if he wanted to meet for drinks.

The moment he heard his best friend's voice, he knew something was wrong.

"Wassup," Brandon said, climbing into his Maybach and closing the door. "Everything all right?"

"Man." Dre pushed out a deep, weary breath. "It's been a long day."

"You sound like you need a drink. I just left the office. You up for Stogie's?"

"Can't tonight. I promised Ma we'd have dinner together. Now that I'm crashing at her place, she's been nagging me to spend more time with her. She says that I've been treating her house more like a hotel than a home."

Brandon chuckled, shrugging out of his suit jacket. "You know how moms are with the guilt trips."

"Tell me about it. You know I'd get my own apartment, but I'm hoping Leah will come around soon and let me move back home. Hey, why don't you come over for dinner?" Dre suggested. "You know Ma's always happy to see you, and I need to get your advice about something."

"Yeah? What?"

Long pause. "I'd rather talk to you in person."

Brandon raised a brow. "Damn. Sounds serious."

Dre sighed heavily. "It is."

Brandon was intrigued, and he couldn't deny that a home-cooked meal in a peaceful environment held far more appeal than spending a contentious evening with Cynthia.

"I'll be there," he told Dre.

"Great. I have to wrap up a few things at the office first, but I'll call Ma and let her know to expect you."

Brandon nodded. "Cool."

Thirty minutes later, he pulled up to a two-story redbrick house situated on a perfectly landscaped lawn. The house, along with the white Lexus parked in the driveway, had been gifts from Dre to his mother, who'd raised him on her own after Dre's father skipped out on them, along with his other baby mama. Renay Portis had worked tirelessly to support herself and Dre, even scraping together the funds to send him to a prestigious NASA youth program, where he and Brandon had met at age eleven. Because she'd made so many sacrifices for him, there was nothing Dre wouldn't do for her.

Seconds after Brandon rang the doorbell, Renay Portis opened the front door and beamed at him.

"Brandon," she exclaimed warmly.

"Hey, Ms. Portis." Brandon smiled, leaning down to kiss her smooth cheek and give her a hug. "How you doing?"

"I'm good, baby," she said, ushering him inside the house and closing the door. "It's so wonderful to see you. It's been a minute, hasn't it?"

Dre's mother was an attractive woman with light skin and dyed blond hair cut into short, stylish layers. She was medium height and had a thick, curvaceous figure. She was only eighteen when she'd had Dre, so she was often mistaken for his older sister rather than his mother.

"I'm so glad you could join me and Dre for dinner tonight," she told Brandon, affectionately patting his cheek. "It'll be like old times again."

Brandon grinned, awash with memories of childhood sleepovers—him and Dre gorging themselves on pizza and Doritos, trash talking over video games, watching kung fu movies and WWF wrestling, poring over dirty magazines after Dre's mother went to bed. Because Dre had lived in the projects, Brandon's parents had usually insisted on Dre spending the night at the Chamberses' mansion in River Oaks, which was light-years away from the poverty, crime, and violence that had plagued Dre's neighborhood. But Brandon had always preferred sleeping over at Dre's apartment because his mother had let them stay up all night and eat whatever they wanted.

Brandon smiled fondly at her. "Whatever you're making smells great, Ms. Portis."

She beamed with pleasure. "Thank you, baby. It's a new recipe. Why don't you make yourself comfortable while I bring you something to drink. Beer okay?"

"Yes, ma'am," Brandon drawled, loosening his tie as he sauntered into the stylishly furnished living room and sat down on the red sofa. The large flat-panel television was tuned to the *Real Housewives of Atlanta*, where a nasty catfight was brewing between two cast members whose names Brandon couldn't have guessed to save his life.

"Feel free to turn the channel, Brandon," Dre's mother called from the kitchen.

Brandon chuckled, already reaching for the remote control on the coffee table. He turned to ESPN to catch highlights and analyses of yesterday's NFL games.

As he settled back against the sofa cushions, his smartphone went off. He dug it out of his pocket and glanced at the display screen, frowning when he saw Cynthia's number. In no mood to talk to her, he let the call go to voice mail.

Dre's mother returned to the living room, handing him a cold bottle of beer. "Here you go, baby."

Brandon smiled at her. "Thanks, Ms. Portis."

"You're welcome," she said, sitting in the adjacent armchair and crossing her legs.

As Brandon took a swig of beer, he received a text message. Of course it was from Cynthia.

Where are you???

He calmly turned off the phone and tucked it back inside his pocket.

Renay gave him a concerned look. "Is everything okay?"

Brandon nodded, drinking more beer.

"Dre told me what happened on Friday," Renay said gently. "I can't say that I was surprised."

Brandon met her gaze. "You weren't?"

She shook her head. "You don't love Cynthia Yarbrough. Not enough to marry her, anyway."

Lowering his eyes to his beer bottle, Brandon quietly admitted, "She's not the person I thought she was."

"Women seldom are once they get what they want." Renay observed Brandon for several moments, lips pursed sympathetically. "I know you're under a lot of pressure to marry Cynthia. Your parents and hers have probably been planning your wedding forever. But you don't have to go through with it if you've had a change of heart, Brandon."

"I wish it were that simple," he said grimly.

"I know. It should be." Renay reached over and consolingly patted him on the knee. "I just want you to be happy, Brandon. You have too much going for you to settle for anything less than you deserve."

Brandon mustered a small smile. "Thank you, Ms. Portis. I appreciate your support."

"Of course, baby. You know you and Dre mean the world to me." She smiled wryly. "It's a shame you both have such horrible taste in women."

Brandon choked out a laugh. "What do you mean?"

Renay gave him a knowing look. "No offense, baby, but I saw right through Cynthia the very first time I met her. Preacher's kids are some of the most treacherous people I've ever known. As for Leah . . . well, Dre knows how I feel about *her*. She always acted as if she was doing him a favor by dating him, like she thinks she's better than him just because she's a doctor. But *he's* a doctor too, and he's just as successful in his field as she is—probably even more so." Renay sniffed. "Not only that, but my son is *way* too handsome to be settling for some skinny plain Jane. Am I lying, Brandon?"

He laughed, shaking his head at her. "You know I can't answer that, Ms. Portis. And I don't think Dre would be too happy with this conversation we're having."

"You're probably right," Renay conceded with a deep sigh. "But I just had to speak my mind. Dre's got blinders on when it comes to that girl." She paused. "Same way *you* are with Tamia."

Brandon immediately sobered. "Ms. Portis—"

"Don't worry. That's all I'm going to say for now." She smiled and patted his knee again. "Let me just check on dinner. I'll be right back."

After she left, Brandon pulled out his phone and powered it back on so he could call Dre to see if he was on his way home.

When he saw that Cynthia had left him two messages, he felt a pang of guilt. He knew he should call to let her know he'd be back late. It was the considerate thing to do. The mature thing.

But he wasn't feeling very considerate or mature where Cynthia was concerned. For that reason, he intended to put off dealing with her for as long as he could.

Still, his thoughts churned as he watched *SportsCenter*, his unfocused eyes glazing over the highlights flashing across the screen. He was so out of it that he didn't immediately register the gentle hand that settled upon his shoulders and began kneading his muscles.

"Look how tight and tense you are," a voice murmured soothingly. "You poor baby."

Brandon sipped his beer, feeling some of the knotted tension ease from his body.

Warm lips brushed his ear. "Let mama take care of you."

Brandon froze, then shot up from the sofa and whipped around. Beer spewed out of his mouth when he saw Dre's mother standing there in a black lace negligee that left absolutely nothing to the imagination.

His eyes widened in shock as he dropped the bottle, spilling more beer on the floor. "What the f—"

"Shhh," Renay whispered, putting a finger to her lips. "There's no need for you to be alarmed, Brandon."

"The hell there ain't! Yo, what are you doing, Ms. Portis? Why are you dressed like that?"

"Why do you think?" she purred, seductively running one finger along the strap of the negligee, which barely contained her large breasts. "Don't you like it?"

Brandon groaned and slapped a hand over his eyes. "Please put some damn clothes on, Ms. Portis. *Please!*"

She chuckled softly. "You don't have to worry about Dre coming home and catching us. I called him and told him to stop by the store to pick up a few things I need for dinner. So we've got plenty of time—"

"For what?" Brandon demanded, staring at her like she'd lost her mind. Which she most definitely had.

"Come on, baby." She started around the sofa, moving slowly and provocatively. "You've been wasting your time with these trifling little girls who don't know the first thing about how to treat a man. You need a real woman—"

"*A real woman?*" Brandon exclaimed, backing away from her. "You're like a second mother to me! You've known me since I was eleven years old!"

"I have," she agreed. "And I've watched you grow into a fine specimen of a man. Oh, you were always a handsome boy, but there's no way I could have known just how *scrumptious* you'd turn out to be—so sexy and virile. So much *swag.*" She licked her lips. "I've been trying to ignore my feelings for you, Brandon, but I just can't resist anymore."

Brandon shook his head, torn between incredulity and disgust. "You're out of your mind, Ms. Portis. There's no way I'm sleeping with you."

"Who said anything about sleeping?" Her eyes gleamed wickedly. "Come on, baby boy. No one has to know. It'll be our little secret."

He scowled. "Hell, nah."

As she lunged toward him, Brandon retreated around the sofa and bolted for the front door.

"Don't go, Brandon! I'm sorry. Wait—"

Brandon threw open the door and rushed out into the cool night.

Dre's mother hurried after him, calling his name.

Without a backward glance, Brandon hopped into his car, jammed his key into the ignition, and floored the gas pedal.

As he sped away from the house, he glared up at the dark sky, expecting to see a full moon.

Not even close.

It was now official.

Every woman he knew had lost her ever-fucking-lasting mind!

Chapter 10

Tamia

Tamia rocked back and forth on the rickety porch swing, resting her head contentedly on her grandmother's shoulder.

"I'm so glad you came back to me, Mama Esther. I was afraid I'd never see you again."

"Put that thought right out of your head," her grandmother soothed, gently patting her hand. "You know I'll always be with you."

Tamia swallowed tightly. "I'm sorry, Mama. I'm so sorry for what Fiona did—"

"Hush, baby. There's no use shedding any more tears. What's done is done."

"I know, but she hurt you, Mama, and I miss you so much. I don't know if I can ever forgive Fiona for taking you away from me."

"You have to forgive your sister," Mama Esther said sagely. "Not for her sake but for yours."

Tamia frowned. "What do you mean?"

"A wise man once said, 'He who cannot forgive breaks the bridge over which he himself must pass.' Releasing Fiona from the bonds of your hurt and anger will set you free as well."

Tamia was silent, absorbing her grandmother's words as the swing swayed gently in the night breeze.

"She's having a baby," Tamia whispered.

"I know," Mama Esther said quietly.

Tamia lifted her head from her grandmother's shoulder. "That's why you were knitting that baby blanket a while ago. It was for Fiona."

Mama Esther nodded, her gaze intent on Tamia's face. "She's going to need you now more than ever."

"I know." Tamia sighed deeply. "And I'll be there for her. No matter what."

"I never doubted it for a moment." Mama Esther tenderly stroked Tamia's cheek. "Your heart is heavy."

Tamia swallowed hard, then nodded.

"You think you've lost Brandon forever."

"I have lost him, Mama. He's marrying Cynthia."

"So what are you going to do about it?"

"There's nothing I can do. She's having his baby—I'm not." Hearing the bitterness in her voice, Tamia heaved a deep breath. "You know what, Mama? I'm tired of putting my life on hold for Brandon. I love him, but it's time for me to stop acting like he's the only thing that matters. He's not."

"Of course he isn't, baby. You have so much to live for, with or without Brandon. You just . . ." Mama Esther suddenly trailed off.

Tamia frowned. "What is it, Mama Esther? What's wrong?"

The old woman stared off into the distance, her face creased with worry. "You need to be careful, Tamia."

"Careful? Why?"

"Your enemies have been busy."

A chill ran through Tamia. "My enemies?"

"Yes." As Mama Esther's image began to fade, she warned urgently, "Don't let them steal your soul. . . ."

Tamia awoke with a start.

Her heart stuck in her throat, she sat up quickly and swept a glance around her dark bedroom.

She'd been dreaming about her grandmother.

Over the past several months, Mama Esther had often appeared in Tamia's dreams to deliver an exhortation or warning about the future. Tamia had spent the past two weeks wondering when—or if—she'd ever see her grandmother again. Now that she had, she didn't know what to make of Mama Esther's parting words.

Your enemies have been busy. . . . Don't let them steal your soul.

Tamia shivered, goose bumps pricking her skin. She wondered what her grandmother could have meant.

She wasn't naive. She knew she had enemies, people who hated her and wanted her to drop off the face of the earth. People like Cynthia. And Brandon's parents.

For all she knew, Dominic was still plotting against her. And the verdict was still out on Lester McCray's motives for lying to her.

Tamia frowned, wrapping her arms around her chilled body.

What were you trying to tell me, Mama Esther? She whispered into the darkness.

But there was only silence.

Chapter 11

Tamia

Dominic was waiting for Tamia when she arrived at the upscale downtown restaurant that afternoon. He stepped outside to meet her as she relinquished her Honda Accord to the valet.

"Hello, Tamia," he drawled, his gaze sweeping over her.

She'd slicked her hair back into a tight bun and donned a tailored black pantsuit with tall black heels—an ensemble that made her look cool, confident, and professional. Though she'd agreed to accept Dominic's money, she wanted to establish up front that their partnership would be strictly business this time.

"Hello, Dominic," she said smoothly.

He smiled. "I'm glad you could make it. Shall we?"

Tamia hesitated, then tucked her hand through his proffered arm.

As they walked into the restaurant together, the woman behind the hostess station smiled graciously at Dominic.

"Are you ready to be seated now, Mr. Archer?"

"Absolutely. Lead the way."

As Tamia and Dominic followed the hostess toward their table, Tamia felt a sudden tingling awareness that made her glance around.

Her heart lurched at the sight of Brandon seated at a table with two suit-clad businessmen. Sipping from a glass of scotch, he nodded in response to whatever his lunch companions were saying, but Tamia could tell that he was distracted.

As she watched, he suddenly turned his head and looked right at her. When he saw Dominic, his eyes widened in surprise before narrowing with cold fury.

Tamia's knees went weak.

She quickly averted her gaze, tightening her grip on Dominic's arm as they continued through the crowded restaurant. She was relieved when the hostess led them to a table on the opposite side of the room.

As soon as they were seated, Tamia shot an accusing look at Dominic. "Did you know he'd be here?"

"Who? Brandon?"

"Who else?"

Dominic's eyes glinted with amusement. "How could I have known where he was having lunch today?"

"I don't know. Maybe the same way you knew I'd be at Da Marco on Friday."

Dominic chuckled, shaking his head at her. "I told you I was meeting with a client that evening."

Tamia smirked. "The client who conveniently had to cancel?"

Dominic gave her a lazy smile. "What are you suggesting, love? That I've been following you *and* Brandon? That I've bugged your phones? Secretly installed GPS tracking devices on your cars?"

Tamia frowned, draping her linen napkin across her lap. "You have an uncanny way of showing up where you're least expected, Dominic, and it can't always be a coincidence."

Before he could respond, the waiter appeared to fill their water glasses and take their order.

Too agitated to peruse the menu, Tamia allowed Dominic to order for both of them. Her nerves were strung so tight she couldn't relax enough to rest her back against the chair. She swore she could feel Brandon's enraged gaze boring into her from across the room.

She didn't dare turn around.

After the waiter departed, Dominic eyed Tamia speculatively. "Why does it bother you that Brandon's here? Isn't that part of the plan? To make him jealous by letting him think we're involved?"

Tamia frowned. "That's not why I agreed to this . . . this partnership."

Dominic arched a brow at her. "It's not?"

"No. Not anymore."

"I don't understand."

Tamia gave him a level look. "I don't have the time or energy to keep chasing after something that wasn't meant to be. I need to move on with my life, and the first step is reclaiming the career that I loved. Serving five months in prison and going on trial for murder all but ruined my job prospects and wiped out my savings. I need a lifeline right now, and unfortunately, you're it. That, and that alone, is the reason why I'm sitting here. So whenever you're ready to talk business, let me know. Otherwise, let's not waste each other's time."

Dominic leaned back slowly and stared at her, his eyes gleaming with respect and admiration. "You're quite a force to be reckoned with, Tamia Luke."

She smiled narrowly. "And don't you forget it."

Dominic threw back his head and laughed, turning the heads of several female patrons who smiled and eyed him appreciatively. Tamia couldn't fault any of them for staring. Dominic was fine as hell, and he rocked Italian suits like he'd been born in one.

It wouldn't be easy for Tamia to resist her attraction to him. But that's exactly what she intended to do.

"All right, Miss Luke," he drawled. "Let's talk business."

"Thought you'd never ask." Reaching down beside her chair, Tamia retrieved her leather attaché case and removed a professionally bound document, which she passed to Dominic. "This is a copy of my five-year business plan. It's the same thing I would present to a bank if I were applying for a small business loan. Based on extensive research I've done, as well as my own knowledge of the advertising industry, I was able to calculate my startup costs, which include funds needed for stationery, brochures, marketing campaigns, computer equipment, as well as insurance and legal matters. Since I'm starting out solo, I don't have to worry about hiring and paying employees, and I don't plan to collect a salary until the agency is consistently turning a healthy profit—as outlined on page ten."

Dominic looked impressed as he perused the charts, graphs, and detailed summaries she'd included in the report. "This is very thorough, Tamia. When did you prepare all this?"

She smiled sardonically. "Let's just say I made good use of the time that I was incarcerated."

Dominic glanced up, meeting her gaze. Something like sympathy shone in his eyes as he set down the document. "I'm glad you have an opportunity to put your business plan into action."

"So am I," Tamia said quietly.

They stared at each other, the connection interrupted by the return of their waiter. He settled their plates on the table and filled their glasses from the bottle of white wine Dominic had ordered.

Once he left, Dominic picked up his glass and raised it to Tamia. "To a successful partnership."

Tamia smiled. "And second chances."

"Second chances," Dominic murmured. "I like the sound of that."

They clinked glasses and sipped their wine, watching each other across the table.

"I'll write you a check after we eat," Dominic said.

"Really?" Tamia couldn't suppress a thrill of excitement. "Don't you want to read my business plan first to make sure I'm a good investment?"

"I already know you are," Dominic drawled, reaching for his fork. "You're smart, talented, ambitious, and you work hard. I have no doubt that I'll get a return on my investment."

For the first time in weeks, Tamia felt hopeful about the future. "I'm going to pay you back as soon as I can."

"You don't have to do that."

"Yes, I do. I don't like being indebted to anyone, Dominic."

He held her steady gaze for a moment, then smiled indulgently. "We'll cross that bridge when we get to it. For now, let's just enjoy our lunch and each other's company."

Tamia picked up her fork. "I think I can manage the first part."

Dominic laughed. "You don't think you can enjoy my company? Not even for an hour?"

Tamia's lips twitched. "I can try, but I make no promises."

"Fair enough." Dominic watched as she cut into her blackened mahi mahi and took a bite. "How is it?"

"Delicious."

"I knew you'd like it." Dominic smiled, cutting into his own grilled fish. "We can have lunch at my restaurant next time."

Tamia arched a brow at him. "Next time?"

"Yeah." He met her gaze. "If we're going to be business partners, we need to meet regularly to keep each other up to date on what's going on."

It sounded reasonable enough, but . . .

"Define 'regularly.' "

"At least twice a month," Dominic replied.

Tamia considered him for a moment. She'd prefer not to deal with him at all, but since he was financing her new business, avoiding him wasn't an option.

"Okay," she reluctantly agreed. "Twice a month is fine."

Dominic smiled, his eyes glinting with approval. "I may have already secured your first client. His name's Buddy Ehrlich. He and his wife own a bed-and-breakfast on a ranch outside of Houston. It's a beautiful place, but business has been slow because no one knows they're out there. I told them about you, and they were impressed with your track record. They'd like to meet with you as soon as possible."

"Really?" Tamia said excitedly. "That's wonderful, Dominic. If you give me their contact information, I'll get in touch—"

"Tamia."

She whipped her head around to find Brandon standing at the table, his dark eyes glittering with leashed violence.

Her heart slammed against her rib cage. "Brandon," she croaked.

His jaw hardened. "I need to talk to you."

Dominic scowled, rising from his chair. "Hold up—"

"Sit the fuck down." Brandon's words were growled low—a deadly warning that made Dominic hesitate.

Tamia glanced around the restaurant, meeting the blatantly curious stares of several other diners. She had an unpleasant flashback to the day she'd gotten into a fistfight with Dominic's wife at a coffee shop. Now that she was trying to rehabilitate her image, getting banned from another establishment was the last thing she wanted or needed.

"It's okay," she mumbled to Dominic.

He frowned. "Tamia—"

"No, really. I don't want to cause a scene."

Glaring at Brandon, Dominic reluctantly sat back down.

Tamia had barely wiped her mouth on her napkin before Brandon grasped her upper arm and helped her from her chair. Her face burned with embarrassment as he steered her through the crowded restaurant. Once they were outside, he wordlessly handed his ticket to the parking attendant.

Tamia swallowed hard. "Brandon—"

He rounded furiously on her. "What the hell are you doing?"

She stared at him. "Excuse me?"

"What the hell are you doing here with that muthafucka?"

She lifted a defiant chin. "Not that it's any of your business—"

"What? *WHAT?*"

Tamia darted a nervous glance at the parking attendant, who was pretending not to watch them.

She shook her head at Brandon. "This really isn't the time or place—"

Grabbing her hand, he dragged her to the farthest end of the canopied entrance.

As they turned to face each other, Tamia couldn't help admiring the delicious perfection of his dark skin . . . the succulent fullness of his lips caressed by a manicured goatee . . . the broad expanse of his shoulders and strong chest. He looked absolutely amazing in his bespoke charcoal suit, one of five he'd had custom-tailored during their trip to Italy.

God, how she wished they could go back there and never leave.

"For the last time," Brandon growled, cold fury lacing his tone, "what are you doing here with Dominic?"

"We're having lunch," Tamia said evenly.

"Why?"

"I don't owe you an explana—"

"*Goddamn it, Tamia!*" Brandon exploded, pushing his face into hers. "After everything that lowlife muthafucka did to you, do you honestly think you can trust him? Can't you see he's just trying to come between us again?"

Tamia stared at him. "There *is* no us."

Brandon flinched, pain darkening his eyes. Blinking rapidly, he rubbed a shaky hand over his clenched jaw.

Tamia wanted to cry. Her throat ached from the effort of holding back the tears.

Shaking his head at her, Brandon whispered, "Why are you doing this?"

"Doing what, Brandon? Moving on with my life? What else am I supposed to do? Huh? What else am I supposed to do?"

"Not with him, Tamia. *Not with him.*"

She sneered. "Is that all you care about? Not losing me to your hated rival? Is that all I am to you—a fucking pawn on some chessboard?"

"*NO!*" Brandon roared, urgently grabbing her face between his hands. "You know good and damn well you mean more to me than that!"

"What I *know*, Brandon, is that you're marrying another woman and having a child with her!"

"But *you're* the one I want, damn it!"

At that moment his shiny black Maybach rolled to the curb, rims gleaming. As the valet climbed out of the vehicle, Brandon marched over, yanked open the passenger door, and glared at Tamia.

"Get in the car," he commanded.

"What?" she sputtered. "Why?"

"We need to go for a ride and talk."

Tamia shook her head. "We have nothing to talk about."

"The hell we don't," Brandon growled. "Get in the car."

"No."

"*GET IN THE FUCKING CAR, TAMIA!*"

She gaped at him. "What part of 'no' did you not understand? I'm not going anywhere with you! I was in the middle of having lunch when you interrupted, so if you don't mind—"

"I do mind," Brandon snarled, slamming the car door and stalking back toward her. "I mind very much."

Tamia stood her ground as he advanced on her, bringing their faces so close together that their breath mingled and their body heat electrified the air between them.

Tamia swallowed tightly. "You're causing a scene, Brandon."

His eyes flashed. "You think I give a fuck?"

"You should. Everyone inside this building knows who you are. You have an image to uphold, a name to protect."

"Fuck all that," Brandon growled.

Tamia smiled bitterly. "We both know you don't have that luxury."

He clenched his jaw, his pupils nearly black as he stared into her eyes.

She stared back, heart hammering violently. "Let me go, Brandon," she whispered.

"I can't do that."

"You have to."

He closed his eyes and swallowed hard, nostrils flaring. "I want you to stay the hell away from Dominic."

"That's not your call to make anymore."

"Damn it, Tamia—"

"Mr. Chambers?"

"*What?*" Brandon snapped, turning to glare at the parking attendant, who'd left his station and walked over to them.

The man gulped nervously. "Sorry to interrupt, sir, but we need to clear the driveway. If you'd like to have your car reparked—"

"No," Brandon bit off tersely. "I'm leaving."

As the relieved man backed away, Brandon gave Tamia a dark look that clearly said: *This ain't over.*

Her heart thudding, she watched as he spun on his heel and stalked over to his car at the curb. After shooting her one last glare, he ducked behind the wheel, slammed the door, and roared off.

Inhaling a shaky breath, Tamia made her way back inside the restaurant on legs that felt like melted rubber.

Dominic stood as she returned to the table and sat down.

"Are you okay?" he asked her.

Tamia nodded, taking a long sip of wine to calm her rattled nerves.

Dominic shook his head at her. "Your boy's losing it."

Tamia said nothing.

"Didn't I tell you he'd go crazy when he saw us together?" Dominic's eyes gleamed with amused satisfaction. "You might get him back even sooner than we thought."

Tamia calmly picked up her fork and cut into her mahi mahi. "Tell me more about the couple with the bed-and-breakfast. The Ehrlichs, right?"

Heeding her unspoken request to change the subject, Dominic began discussing her potential client. But as his deep voice droned on and on, all Tamia could think about was the dangerous look in Brandon's eyes before he'd left her.

She knew she hadn't seen the last of him.

And for the first time since their breakup, she didn't know whether that was good or bad.

Chapter 12

Tamia

The confrontation with Brandon haunted Tamia for the rest of the day.

As she showered and shampooed her hair that evening, she mentally replayed what had happened at the restaurant.

What gave Brandon Chambers the fucking right to be angry? *He* was the one who'd wasted no time hooking up with Cynthia after he and Tamia broke up. *He* was the one who'd been playing house with her while Tamia was behind bars, wondering if she'd ever taste freedom again. *He* was the one who'd been careless enough to get Cynthia pregnant. And *he* was the one who'd agreed to marry her!

Yet *he* had the nerve to be outraged when he saw her and Dominic together?

He had the audacity to tell *her* who to stay away from?

The more Tamia reflected on Brandon's behavior, the madder she became.

Lifting her face to the hot spray of water, she vigorously scrubbed her scalp. After rinsing the fragrant shampoo from her hair, she twisted off the water faucet and stepped out of the steamy glass stall. She toweled herself off, then stalked into the bedroom.

Suddenly the doorbell rang.

She froze, pulse thudding.

She wasn't expecting company.

So there was only one person who could be at her door at this hour of the night.

Heart hammering, she yanked on a terrycloth robe and marched to the front door, her bare feet leaving damp footprints on the wood floor.

She unlocked the front door and jerked it open.

Brandon stood there, his tie hanging crookedly around his neck and his shirttail tugged from his suit pants. His eyes were black with fury and torment.

"What the hell do you want?" Tamia demanded.

Without a word he barged inside, forcing her backward.

She slapped him across the face, needing to strike the first blow.

With a feral growl, he grabbed her face between his hands and kissed her hard, bruising her lips.

She shoved and clawed at his chest—half blind with rage, lust, and anguish.

Kicking the door shut behind him, Brandon wrapped his arms around her, pinning her hands against his chest so she couldn't move or escape.

Water dripped from her hair and slid into their joined mouths to make the kiss even wetter. Hotter.

She could feel her blood roaring in her ears, her heart thundering in her chest.

Roughly breaking the kiss, Brandon ripped the robe from her body and dropped to his knees. As he lifted her against the wall, she threw her legs around his neck, crying out as he crushed his mouth to her pussy.

He licked her slick folds, each scorching stroke of his tongue making her shiver and gasp his name. As he gently bit her clit, she mewled and grabbed the back of his head.

He sucked the swollen lips of her labia, then stabbed his tongue hotly into her pussy.

She screamed as she erupted, her toes curling until they cramped.

Brandon lapped up her creamy come, bringing her to another hard, shuddering orgasm that nearly reduced her to tears.

She'd barely unwrapped her shaky legs from around his neck when he surged to his feet and lifted her higher against the wall, knocking a painting loose. It crashed to the floor, a casualty that went unnoticed as Brandon seized her wrists and pinned them above her head.

"You bastard," Tamia hissed at him. "Let me g—"

His mouth slammed down on hers, smothering the rest of her demand.

She bit his lip hard, drawing blood.

Swearing hoarsely, he reached down with one hand and impatiently unzipped his pants. His dick sprang free, outrageously long and thick, the curved head glistening wetly with pre-come.

Brandon fisted himself, stroking upward then down.

Tamia whimpered, clit throbbing.

"Still want me to go?"

He knew she didn't. "*Fuck you!*"

His eyes flashed. "I intend to."

As he pinned her against the wall, she locked her legs around his waist. Cupping the underside of her butt cheeks, he guided his shaft between the saturated folds of her sex and plunged into her.

Tamia wailed with pleasure as her pussy clenched around his dick, gripping him so tightly that he groaned, the sound both tortured and erotic.

Staring into her eyes, he began rocking against her, the muscles of his ass flexing furiously.

There was no finesse. No gentle thrusting or stroking. The way he fucked her was raw and primal, as if his very salvation depended on how far and deep he could lose himself inside her.

Gazing into her eyes like he could see into her wounded soul, he whispered fiercely, "You belong to me."

"No—"

"*YES, YOU DO,*" he thundered. "You belong to me, Tamia. And you always will—*no matter fucking what!*"

She squeezed her eyes shut as tears coursed down her face. Tears of denial that bled into tears of defeat. He was right. She would always love him, would always want him. Knowing she could never have him was unbearable.

She moaned and sobbed helplessly as he rammed his dick in and out of her, making her completely his.

Seconds later they exploded, one right after the other.

They screamed each other's names as Brandon's cock pumped furiously, his come scalding her insides. Her body clenched tightly as he shot his load, groaning harshly as he emptied every ounce of semen into her.

When it was over he collapsed against her and dropped his head, panting heavily against her neck.

Caught somewhere between anguish and euphoria, Tamia began to laugh. Softly at first, then louder and longer as hysteria took hold.

Brandon lifted his head and stared at her like she'd gone crazy. "Baby?"

As her manic laughter dissolved into tears, Brandon drew his arms around her, gathering her close.

"I hate you," she sobbed against his chest. "*I fucking hate you!*"

"Come on, baby. Don't say that," he pleaded raggedly.

"It's true! Why'd you have to come here? What the hell do you *want* from me?"

He didn't respond, tenderly rubbing his cheek back and forth against her damp hair.

She wanted to cling to him, wanted them to stay locked together with his thick shaft entombed deep inside her. But she knew that would only be prolonging the inevitable.

So she dug deep within herself to find the strength to say: "Put me down, Brandon."

"Tamia—"

"*PUT ME DOWN!*"

He reluctantly eased out of her, then lowered her legs to the floor and stepped back. She wrapped her arms around her stomach, feeling instantly bereft without the heat of his body.

He zipped up his pants, then knelt down to pick up her robe. She watched as he brought it slowly to his nose, closed his eyes, and breathed deep.

The look on his face . . . it was almost too much for her.

After an agonizing moment, he got up and gently helped her into the robe, covering her nudity. She knotted the sash tightly and swiped the tears from her cheeks.

Brandon was silent, but his tortured expression spoke volumes.

Summoning the tattered remnants of her composure, Tamia walked to the door and opened it. "It's time for you to leave."

Brandon stared at her, nostrils flaring with emotion.

She held her ground.

He started forward slowly, as if he were trudging through wet cement.

Reaching the door, he looked deeply and sorrowfully into her eyes. "I love you, Tamia."

"Then do something about it," she spat coldly. "Until then, leave me the fuck alone."

He held her gaze a moment longer, then turned and walked out.

She slammed the door and leaned against it, hearing his footsteps retreat down the hall . . . taking the broken pieces of her heart with him.

Chapter 13

Brandon

When Brandon arrived home, Cynthia was waiting for him by the front door, her arms folded across her heaving chest.

"Where the hell have you been?" she demanded accusingly. "This is the second day in a row you've come home late."

Barely sparing her a glance, Brandon closed and locked the door. "Not tonight, Cynthia," he mumbled.

"*Excuse me?* Are you out of your damn mind? You have the nerve to come waltzing in here at this late hour and all you have to say for—" She broke off abruptly, staring at his mouth. "What the hell happened to you?"

Brandon reached up, absently touching his split lower lip. "Nothing."

"*Nothing?*" Cynthia echoed incredulously. "Sure as hell doesn't look like *nothing* to me."

"Well, it is."

As Brandon moved to stalk past her, she grabbed his arm. "I want the tru—"

He rounded furiously on her. "Damn it, woman!" he shouted into her face. "Leave it the fuck alone!"

She recoiled, staring up at him as if she'd never seen him before. "Look at your eyes, Brandon. I don't even know who or what you are anymore. You're possessed, that's what you are. You need a fucking exorcism, and I know just how to give you one!"

With that she spun on her heel and stomped into the sunken living room. As Brandon watched, she grabbed the remote control off the coffee table and clicked on the television.

The huge screen was filled with a high-def image of Tamia having sex with two men. She was kneeling on the floor, her mouth wrapped around one brotha's dick while the other fucked her from behind.

Hot bile rushed up Brandon's throat and filled his mouth. As the room spun, he slammed his eyes shut and whispered hoarsely, "Turn it off."

"No!" Cynthia stubbornly refused. "You need to see the *real* Tamia Luke. Watching this should cure your obsession once and for all. God knows nothing else has worked."

A sudden black rage swept over Brandon, obliterating all thought, reason, and restraint. Charging toward Cynthia, he roared at the top of his lungs, "TURN THAT FUCKING THING OFF RIGHT NOW!"

Cynthia's eyes widened with terror.

Frantically she fumbled with the remote control, but Brandon was already upon her. He snatched the remote out of her hand and viciously threw it at the television, destroying the plasma screen.

But it wasn't enough for him.

Heart pounding violently, he stormed across the room, ripped the mounted TV off the wall, and hurled it to the floor. The loud crash drowned out Cynthia's startled cry.

Blood roaring in his ears, Brandon turned and swept an arm across the coffee table, sending the stack of porn videos flying through the air.

As he savagely upended the table, Cynthia screamed, "Stop it! Are you crazy?"

As Brandon whirled on her, she whimpered fearfully and stumbled backward, retreating from him as he stalked her step for step.

"Are you satisfied?" he snarled ferociously. "Is this the reaction you were hoping for?"

She jerked her head from side to side.

Brandon shoved his face into hers. "Don't you *ever* pull a stunt like that again, or so help me God—"

With a strangled sob, Cynthia turned and fled the room, her bare feet slapping against the wood floor. Moments later, the bedroom door slammed shut.

Having spent his fury, Brandon sank down on the sofa, dropped his pounding head into his hands, and closed his eyes.

He could still taste Tamia, could smell her on his clothes and skin. He'd been going out of his fucking mind ever since he saw her at the restaurant with Dominic. The sight of them together—the mere thought of them reuniting—had pushed him over the edge. When he'd left the office that night, he'd had only one destination in mind, and he couldn't get there fast enough.

If he'd had his way, he would have spent the entire night making love to Tamia, burying himself inside her . . . over and over and over again.

But he'd had to go home and face the music.

Lifting his head from his hands, Brandon grimly surveyed his trashed living room. When his gaze landed on one of the DVDs strewn across the floor, his gut tightened with fresh anger.

He got up and headed to his bedroom, where he found Cynthia curled up on her side beneath the covers. Though her eyes were closed, he knew she wasn't asleep.

He walked across the room and sat down on the edge of the bed. Leaning forward, he clasped his hands between his legs and began in a low voice, "I'm sorry you were frightened by my behavior. I didn't mean to upset you, but you were dead wrong for coming at me like that."

She whispered, "I did it because I love you."

"That wasn't love, Cynthia. Love isn't petty or vindictive. You deliberately tried to hurt me by playing that video. You wanted me to watch it and become so disgusted with Tamia that I'd never want to see her again. But it doesn't work that way. My feelings for Tamia can't be cured with shock therapy, or whatever the hell it is you thought you were doing."

Cynthia was silent.

"I'm trying like hell to make this relationship work, sweetheart, but you have to help me out. Harassing Tamia, digging up her Mystique videos, snooping through my phone—all that's gonna do is push me away. And once you push me too far, there's no bringing me back."

A single tear rolled down Cynthia's face.

Brandon rose to his feet, then leaned down and gently kissed her forehead. "Have a good night."

She eyed him anxiously. "Where are you going?"

"To sleep in the guest room."

Where he could be alone with his thoughts and fears . . . and his secret hopes for tomorrow . . .

Chapter 14

Tamia

For the first time since the harrowing night of Fiona's arrest, Tamia returned to her childhood home in the Third Ward.

Her footsteps were heavy as she climbed up the porch and approached the small house with the peeling white paint. She took a deep breath, turned the key in the lock, and stepped inside.

Closing the front door behind her, she glanced around the empty living room. She'd moved out last month, taking all of the furniture with her to punish Fiona for her unspeakable betrayal. Fiona hadn't bothered to refurnish the place, as if she'd known that her days of freedom were numbered.

Tamia frowned at the thought.

As she wandered slowly through the old shotgun house, the bare walls echoed with voices . . . ghosts from the past.

Who is she, Sonny? Who's the whore who keeps calling and hanging up on me?

Woman, who the hell you think you talking to?

Take your fucking hands off me!

It's just a bruise, Tamia. It'll heal.

Stop all that damn crying, Fiona! Your worthless daddy ain't coming back!

College? Who the hell has money for college, Tamia?

Someone killed Mama Esther! Why, God? Why?

Tamia swallowed tightly, shaking her head at the haunting memories.

These walls had borne witness to so much pain, suffering, and misery. But there'd also been rare moments of laughter and joy.

She remembered racing through the front door with Fiona, squealing excitedly because the ice cream truck was coming down the street. She remembered them giggling hysterically as their mother boogied around the living room after receiving a bonus at work. She remembered curling up on the sofa with Mama Esther every summer afternoon to watch *All My Children, One Life to Live,* and *General Hospital* followed by *Oprah*, because after watching soaps all day, Mama Esther had deemed it important for them to fill their minds with substance.

Reaching Fiona's bedroom, Tamia stood in the doorway and looked around. It was smaller than the room she'd occupied when she'd lived there. The space was dominated by a king-size bed and a matching dresser. On the floor was the suitcase Fiona had packed on the night of her arrest. She'd planned to skip town to avoid going back to prison, but her father had stopped her.

Tamia hesitated, then slowly entered the silent room.

Even as a child, Fiona had been compulsively neat, always putting away her toys and making her bed. For years, she'd believed that if she kept her room clean, ate her vegetables, and did her homework every night, her father would never leave her.

But Sonny did leave . . . and he never came back.

Until that fateful night.

Crossing to the dresser, Tamia picked up a framed five-by-five photograph of her and Fiona with their mother. She and Fiona were little girls. Their hair had been freshly pressed and braided, and they wore matching pink dresses with shiny black Mary Janes. Fiona sat on their mother's lap while Tamia stood close beside them, her small hand resting on Lorraine's shoulder. All three of them wore big smiles as they beamed into the camera.

Look at Lorraine and her pretty girls, the neighbors used to whisper and point from their porches. *Damn shame she can't keep their daddies around.*

Tamia stared at the photo, gently tracing her fingertips over her mother's face. She'd been a beautiful woman whose weakness for good-looking scoundrels had been her ultimate downfall.

Tamia wondered what Lorraine would think if she could see her daughters now—one pining over a man who'd never loved her enough to make her his wife, while the other had gotten herself knocked up by a man who wanted nothing to do with her.

A wave of anger and shame washed over Tamia, bringing hot tears to her eyes.

"I'm breaking the cycle, Ma," she whispered determinedly. "I'm done waiting for a man to love and accept me for who I am. From now on, I'm living for me and me only."

She stared down at the photo another moment, then carefully tucked it inside her handbag and strode from the room.

With Fiona behind bars—perhaps for the rest of her life—Tamia needed to decide what to do about their childhood home. Since she had no intention of ever living there again, the only other option was for her to put the house up for sale. Now that the neighborhood had been designated a historic landmark and would be undergoing gentrification, Tamia felt optimistic that she could find a buyer.

Making a mental note to ask her best friend, Shanell, for the name of her Realtor, Tamia started across the living room, suddenly eager to escape the oppressive silence of the house.

She opened the front door—and let out a startled shriek.

There was a man standing on the doorstep.

A man with short black hair, dark sunglasses, and a tattooed serpent crawling up the side of his neck.

Tamia stared in shock. "*Lou?*"

"Hey, Tamia." He slowly removed the sunglasses, his piercing hazel eyes settling on her face.

Tamia expelled a relieved breath. "You scared the hell out of me!"

"I'm sorry. I didn't mean to."

She shook her head at him. "I didn't even recognize you. You cut off your hair."

"I did." Lou smiled. "What do you think?"

Tamia reached up to touch the soft, thick hair that skimmed the collar of his shirt. "I like it. But it makes you look different."

Lou's smile deepened. "That was the point. I'm in a new line of work now, dealing with elite clientele. I figured it was time to retire the ponytail."

Tamia nodded distractedly. "How did you know I'd be here?"

"I was on my way to your apartment when I saw your car. I followed you and waited in the truck." He gestured to the white Escalade parked at the curb. "I thought you were just picking up something you'd forgotten to take when you moved out. But after a while, I decided to see if you were okay." His eyes searched her face. "Are you?"

"I'm fine." Tamia mustered a wan smile. "I'm just feeling nostalgic. I have to sell the house now that it's . . . empty."

Lou's expression softened. "I heard about what happened when I got back from Puerto Rico. I'm sorry, *mamacita*. I know how much your grandmother meant to you. To find out that . . ." He trailed off, shaking his head. "I'm sorry."

Tamia swallowed tightly, raking trembling fingers through her hair.

Lou shifted from one booted foot to the other. For the first time since Tamia had known him, he seemed nervous. "Can we talk for a minute?"

"Sure." Tamia pulled the door closed behind her and followed Lou to the porch swing. After he brushed dirt from the bench, they sat down, making the rickety wood creak beneath their weight.

"I owe you an apology for the way I acted that night at your apartment," Lou began.

"It's okay—"

"No, it's not. I shouldn't have put you on the spot like that. I should have realized you weren't ready to hear how I feel about you." Lou paused, staring down at his hands on his lap. "I'm in love with you, Tamia. I have been for years."

Tamia shook her head slowly. "I had no idea."

"Of course you didn't," Lou said ruefully. "I never told you because I knew you didn't feel the same."

Guilt swept over Tamia. "Lou—"

"From the moment we met, *mamacita*, I knew you were different. You were nothing like the other starry-eyed wannabes who came to audition for me, looking for instant fame or a sugar daddy. Even though you were only nineteen, you knew exactly what you wanted out of life—and that didn't include getting involved with a porn director."

Tamia didn't bother to deny it. "You know I've always thought the world of you, *papi*," she said softly.

"I know." He held her gaze, his eyes full of regret. "I just wish you could see me as more than just a friend."

"Friends are wonderful," Tamia said, reaching over and gently taking his hand. "I need as many as I can get."

Lou sighed, lacing his fingers through hers as he set the swing in motion. "You know I'm not going anywhere, *mamacita*."

"As if I'd ever let you." Tamia smiled at him. "So how was your Thanksgiving? I bet it felt good to be back home."

"It did. There's no place like home."

Tamia sighed. "Especially when home is as beautiful as Puerto Rico."

"True." Lou smiled. "You should visit sometime."

"I'd love to. But first I need to get my business up and running."

"What business?"

Tamia smiled. "I'm starting my own ad agency."

"Really?"

"Yup."

"Hey, that's great, Tamia," Lou enthused. "I know how much you loved working in advertising."

"I did, so this is the perfect opportunity for me." Since she knew how Lou felt about Dominic, Tamia saw no reason to mention that Dominic had given her the startup capital. It would only piss Lou off.

He smiled warmly at her. "Looks like things are working out well for *both* of us, *mamacita*."

"Looks that way," Tamia agreed, trying not to think about last night's painful encounter with Brandon. How could better days be ahead when she couldn't spend them with the love of her life?

Observing her troubled expression, Lou gently squeezed her hand. When she met his gaze, he smiled reassuringly. "Whatever it is, you're gonna be okay."

Tamia smiled wanly. "How do you know?"

"Because you're a survivor. Remember?"

Tamia silently mulled over his words as she surveyed the familiar street lined with old shotgun houses and shabby lawns.

Lou was right about her. She'd survived an impoverished childhood, the deaths of her mother and grandmother, her sister's devastating betrayal, and serving time in prison.

If she could survive all those things, she could survive a broken heart.

That evening, Tamia met her best friend, Shanell, for drinks at their favorite downtown bar.

Shanell and her husband, Mark, had just returned from a ten-day Caribbean cruise. Shanell's hair was beautifully cornrowed, and her skin was toasted a deeper shade of brown from romping in the sun.

Tamia smiled at her. "You're glowing."

Shanell glanced up from her margarita. "What? My face is shiny?"

Tamia laughed. "You know what I mean. You look totally happy and relaxed."

Shanell smiled. "I *am* happy and relaxed. Mark and I had a wonderful time on the cruise."

"I know. I can tell from these gorgeous pictures." Tamia scrolled through the remaining images, then sighed enviously and handed the smartphone back to Shanell. "You two did some amazing things on your shore excursions."

"We sure did." Shanell's cognac-colored eyes glinted wickedly. "But not half as amazing as what we did all over that boat. And I *do* mean all over."

Tamia shrieked with laughter. "*TMI!*"

Shanell grinned, sipping her margarita. "I brought you back a souvenir. It's in the car, so remind me to give it to you when we leave."

"Okay," Tamia said, smiling. "But you didn't have to get me anything."

"Are you kidding?" Shanell exclaimed. "After you brought me those badass shoes from Italy?"

At the reminder of Tamia and Brandon's romantic trip, the mood at the table abruptly changed, becoming tense and heavy.

Tamia lowered her gaze to her appletini but didn't take a sip. Her throat was so tight she was afraid she might choke.

Shanell eyed her with gentle concern. "How are you doing?"

Tamia exhaled a deep, shaky breath. "I've been better."

Shanell nodded slowly. "I've been afraid to ask. . . . Did he go through with marrying Cynthia at the JP?"

Tamia shook her head.

Shanell's eyes widened. "*What?* He didn't marry her?"

"No."

"Oh my God! Why didn't you tell me? Before I left for the cruise, I specifically told you to text me if Brandon changed his mind about marrying Cynthia. When I didn't hear from you, I just assumed he went through with it. What happened?"

Tamia sighed heavily. "They're still engaged."

The excitement in Shanell's eyes dimmed. "What do you mean? You just said—"

"He didn't go through with it *that* day. But he still intends to marry her." Tamia downed the rest of her martini and plunked the empty glass on the table.

Shanell shook her head slowly. "I don't understand."

"What don't you understand?" Tamia retorted bitterly. "He got cold feet on Friday, but not cold enough to make him call off the engagement. He wants to marry Cynthia and be a father to his child because, you know, it's the right thing to do, the honorable thing, and God forbid Brandon Chambers should ever do something that's not *right* or *honorable.*"

Shanell regarded her sympathetically. "I'm sorry, Tamia. I really am."

Tamia swallowed hard, blinking rapidly as tears stung her eyes.

"Let me buy you another drink." Shanell signaled for the waiter, who bustled right over and scooped up Tamia's empty glass.

"Another appletini?"

"Nah, give her something stronger." Shanell eyed Tamia. "A 'Wild Wet Dream.' Heavy on the rum."

As the waiter nodded and moved off, Tamia gave Shanell a wry look. "Don't forget I have to drive home."

"Girl, you'll be fine. You just need something to take the edge off."

After Tamia's new drink was served, she and Shanell fell silent, sipping their cocktails as they observed the crowd of young singles packed into the trendy bar. An attractive caramel-toned brotha seated a few tables away was blatantly staring at Tamia.

When their eyes met, he smiled flirtatiously and winked at her. She flashed a cool smile before looking away, not wanting to encourage his attention.

Catching the exchange, Shanell chuckled. "I bet he's gonna buy you a drink."

"I hope not." But even as the words left her mouth, Tamia saw the guy whispering to the waiter, who glanced over at Tamia and grinned.

She groaned.

"Told you." Shanell laughed, licking salt off the rim of her empty margarita glass. "That reminds me. You know Gavin's been asking Mark about you. He said the last time he spoke to you, your boss got on the phone and told him you had to work late."

Tamia rolled her eyes. "That was Brandon, acting like a jealous fool."

"I figured as much. That man is hella possessive over you. God only knows what he's gonna do when you start seeing other people again. Which brings me back to Gavin. Now that you're . . . available, maybe you could give him another chance."

Tamia sighed. "I don't know. Gavin's a really nice guy and all—"

"But he's not Brandon." Shanell smiled ruefully. "I hate to break it to you, girlfriend, but there aren't too many Brandons out there. That brotha's one of a kind—the rare total package."

Tamia glowered at Shanell. "Is that supposed to make me feel better about losing him?"

Shanell was spared from answering when the server reappeared with the drink from Tamia's not-so-secret admirer. "The gentleman wanted me to tell you that he'd love to give you another 'Wild Wet Dream'—just name the time and place."

As Shanell burst out laughing, Tamia smiled sweetly at the waiter. "Tell him the place is nowhere, and the time is never."

"Ouch." The waiter grinned before moving off.

Deliberately ignoring her admirer's hopeful gaze, Tamia slid the new drink across the table to Shanell. "Knock yourself out."

Shanell laughed. "You are a mess."

Tamia snorted. "Can you believe he came at me with that weak-ass shit? Nigga got no game."

"You ain't never lied." Shanell picked up the glass and drank. "So . . ."

Tamia eyed her expectantly. "What?"

"Is that little heffa still staying with you?"

Tamia laughed. "Who? Honey?"

"Yeah. Her."

"Nah, girl, she went back to her crazy boyfriend."

Shanell harrumphed. "Good."

Bemused, Tamia shook her head at her friend. "What do you have against Honey?"

"Who says I have anything against her?"

Tamia gave Shanell a look.

She huffed out a breath. "I don't know. She seems awfully young and immature, and hood as hell."

"Hey, I resent that," Tamia protested. "*I'm* from the hood."

"True, but *you've* got class, Tamia. Honey doesn't know the meaning of the word. Remember how she approached you at your homecoming party last month? Breathing all up in your face, asking you to autograph her titties, propositioning you for a threesome?" Shanell wrinkled her nose in disgust. "Nasty-ass heffa."

Tamia chuckled. "So she was a little star-struck. Cut her some slack."

"Whatever." Shanell frowned deeply. "Honestly, I don't want her pulling you back into that life."

Tamia arched a brow. "What life?"

"You know . . . hanging around with sleazebags . . . selling sex."

"Oh, I see." Tamia grinned teasingly. "You know what I think? I think you're jealous of Honey."

"*Jealous?*" Shanell sputtered indignantly. "Why the hell would I be jealous of *her?*"

"Because you think she's trying to take your place as my best friend."

Shanell scowled. "Bitch, whatever."

Tamia threw back her head and laughed.

"I'm glad you find my concerns so damn amusing," Shanell grumbled. "I was being serious."

"I know." Sobering at once, Tamia reached across the table and placed her hand over Shanell's. "I appreciate your concern for me. Really I do. But you don't have to worry about me anymore. I have no intention of getting pulled back into my old life or my old way of thinking. I'm putting the past behind me, moving onward and upward."

Shanell studied her for a moment. "Onward and upward, huh?"

"Yup. That's my new motto."

Shanell smiled. "I'll drink to that."

As they clinked glasses, Tamia decided not to tell Shanell about her new partnership with Dominic. She knew Shanell would think she was crazy for getting involved with him again.

And the sad part was, she'd be absolutely right.

On her way home from the bar, Tamia's smartphone rang.

She picked it up and glanced at the display screen. When she saw Brandon's number, her heart skipped several precious beats.

Yesterday she'd removed Usher's "My Boo" from her phone, giving Brandon the same generic ringtone as everyone else. He wasn't her man anymore, so he didn't deserve a special song.

The phone rang again.

Tamia stared at it, pulse drumming.

Be strong, girl. Don't answer it.

Two more rings . . . then silence.

She slowly exhaled, then set the phone down and returned her attention to the road, passing shops and skyscrapers that flanked the downtown streets.

Two minutes later, Brandon called back.

Tamia frowned, her fingers tightening around the steering wheel.

Before she could stop herself, she reached over and snatched up the phone. "What do you want?" she demanded.

There was a long pause.

"So you're ignoring my calls now?" Brandon murmured, his deep voice curling through her to settle lusciously between her thighs.

She shifted on the seat. "I thought I told you to leave me alone."

"You know I can't do that."

"Can't or won't?"

He was silent.

She waited, throat dry.

"Where are you?" he asked softly.

None of your damn business, she wanted to say. But she didn't. Couldn't. "I'm driving home from the bar. I had drinks with Shanell."

"Yeah?"

"Yeah." Tamia hesitated, biting her lip. "What about you?"

"I'm still at the office."

"Oh." Tamia fell silent.

"I miss you," he told her.

She closed her eyes for a moment, praying for strength. "Don't do this, Brandon."

"Don't do what?"

"You know damn well what."

"I can't stop thinking about you," he confessed huskily. "I can't sleep without dreaming about you. I can't eat without tasting you. I can't breathe without smelling you—"

"Stop," Tamia whispered. "Just *stop*."

"I can't, Tamia. You think I haven't tried? I have, and nothing works. I'm going outta my fucking mind without you."

Tamia clenched her jaw, trying to steel her emotions against his anguished words. "You can't do this, Brandon. You don't get to have your cake and eat it, too."

"I know, damn it. I know." He exhaled a ragged breath. "Are you fucking him?"

Tamia nearly swerved into another lane. "*What?*"

"You heard me. Are you fucking Dominic?"

"How dare you? You have no right to ask me that question! You don't see me asking *you* about Cynthia—"

"I'm not sleeping with her."

That shut Tamia up for a moment.

Narrowing her eyes, she prodded, "What do you mean?"

"I'm not sleeping with Cynthia," Brandon repeated, his voice pitched low. "We haven't had sex since before we broke up."

Tamia sucked her teeth. "Like I'm supposed to believe that."

"It's the truth."

"She's your fiancée, Brandon. You're marrying her. How long do you honestly think you can get away with not sleeping with her?"

"I don't know. I can't . . ." He trailed off.

"Can't what?"

"I can't touch her without thinking about you."

Tamia's throat tightened.

"Don't do anything with Dominic," Brandon quietly implored.

Tamia shook her head, slowing to a red light. "This really isn't fair, Brandon—"

"Please, Tamia. This is the only thing I ask of you. Don't give yourself to Dominic."

"And what about other guys?" she challenged. "Am I supposed to stay celibate while you and Cynthia get your freak on all over the place? When her pregnancy hormones are raging and she can't keep her hands off you, are you gonna be able to resist the pussy?"

Brandon was incriminatingly silent.

Tamia smirked. "I didn't think so."

"One month, Tamia."

"What?"

"I'm asking you not to sleep with Dominic—or anyone else—for at least one month. Can you do that for me?"

"You have no right to ask," Tamia said curtly.

"I know," he conceded, "but I'm asking anyway."

Tamia frowned, staring at the red light until her vision blurred. When the traffic signal changed to green, she murmured, "I have to go, Brandon."

Before he could say another word, she hung up.

And slowly exhaled.

Onward and upward . . .

Chapter 15

Brandon

Brandon went to bed thinking about Tamia.

He dreamed about her throughout the long night.

When he awoke the next morning, she was still on his mind.

She stayed there as he climbed out of bed and shuffled into the bathroom to brush his teeth and take a shower. He saw her face as he stood beneath the hot spray of water, eyes closed, head thrown back as he washed himself.

He imagined the foamy clouds of soap streaming down his body were Tamia's soft lips running along his naked skin as she chased rivulets of water with her tongue.

Before long he felt himself growing hard, swelling with arousal.

Unable to resist, he reached down and wrapped his fingers around his throbbing shaft. He squeezed the base, then slowly pumped up and down, imagining the walls of Tamia's succulent pussy gripping him.

Suddenly he felt a cool draft across his skin.

"Good morning," Cynthia greeted him, stepping into the large glass stall.

Brandon quickly released his dick, feeling guilty because he'd nearly been caught masturbating to another woman.

Cynthia gently stroked his shoulders. "You've been in here a long time."

"I know," Brandon murmured. "I was making mental notes for a meeting I have this morning."

"Hmm." Cynthia slid her arms around his chest, pressing her small breasts against his back. Her nipples were hard as pebbles. "I can't get enough of seeing you naked, Brandon. Especially when you're all nice and wet. *Sooo* sexy."

As Brandon reluctantly turned around, Cynthia's eyes traveled downward—and widened.

"Oh, my," she breathed, licking her lips as water pelted her black shower cap. "Talk about morning wood."

Brandon tried to smile, but his facial muscles wouldn't cooperate.

He still hadn't forgiven Cynthia for the malicious stunt she'd pulled the other night, though he knew she'd had every right to be mad at him for coming home so late. He'd slept in the guest room that night and avoided her at the office the next day. When he'd come home that evening, she'd had dinner waiting for him. After they ate—mostly in silence—she'd humbly apologized for playing the Mystique video and entreated him to come back to their bed.

"Mmm," she purred now, curling her fingers around his heavy shaft. "Wanna fool around?"

"Can't," Brandon said apologetically. "I don't want to be late for that meeting."

Cynthia smiled, dropping to her knees. "At least let me give you a proper sendoff."

When Brandon realized what she was about to do, he shook his head. "Baby, no—"

She wrapped her mouth around his dick.

As she began sucking him off, Brandon let out an involuntary groan.

Closing his eyes, he imagined Tamia kneeling before him, milking his shaft with hot pulls of her mouth while her hand massaged his balls.

With Tamia on his mind, it didn't take him long to get off.

As he started coming, Cynthia pulled his dick out of her mouth and purred with satisfaction as white ribbons of come spurted across her breasts. She didn't like to swallow, but she loved having him ejaculate on her as if she were his property.

When he'd finished, Brandon reached up and directed the shower head toward Cynthia, letting the warm water rinse his semen from her body.

As he gently helped her to her feet, she smiled seductively, then leaned up and kissed him. Her lips were warm and slippery. "Sure you don't have time to fool around?" she purred, rubbing her slick thighs against his. "I could make it worth your while."

Brandon smiled. "I'm sure you could, but I still have to take a rain check."

"But we—hey!" she squealed in protest as he snatched off her shower cap and held it out of reach. "Give that back! You're getting my hair wet!"

Brandon laughed, passing her the plastic cap before ducking out of the shower stall.

"I am *so* gonna get you for that!" Cynthia called through the glass.

He chuckled, draping his bath towel around his hips as he strode from the steamy bathroom.

Inside the walk-in closet, he chose a pressed white shirt, a gray silk tie, and a navy suit from a collection of designer suits that lined both sides of the large space.

Returning to the bedroom, he slapped on some deodorant and hurriedly dressed, eager to be on his way so he could be alone with his thoughts again.

Cynthia emerged from the bathroom with a fluffy towel wrapped around her slender body. Humming cheerfully, she strolled over to the dresser and opened one of the drawers that she'd commandeered when she'd moved in with him.

"Do we have any plans this weekend?"

We, Brandon mused. Like they were one of those couples who were joined at the hip, who couldn't go anywhere or do anything without consulting each other first.

"Brandon?" Cynthia prompted.

He glanced up from putting on his shoes. "The prayer breakfast is on Saturday, remember?"

"Of course I remember." Cynthia smiled. "You're giving a speech, and it'll be our first time appearing together on the campaign trail. Every TV station in town will be there."

Brandon grimaced. He prayed to God that Tamia wouldn't see any of the coverage.

"Anyway," Cynthia continued, slipping on a pair of cotton

panties, "after the prayer breakfast, I was thinking we could go house hunting."

Brandon froze, staring at her. "House hunting?"

"Yes." She frowned at his startled tone. "Don't get me wrong, Brandon. I love your condo, but surely you don't expect us to stay here after we get married? We've got a baby on the way, so we need a bigger place. The sooner we move into our new home, the sooner I can set up the nursery."

Brandon's chest felt suffocatingly tight. "You're not due for several months. What's the rush?"

Cynthia snorted. "Spoken like a man who doesn't have to worry about planning the wedding of the century while harvesting another human being inside his body."

Brandon frowned. "Wedding of the century?"

Cynthia laughed. "That's what our mothers are calling it," she explained, making her way to the closet. "You should see how giddy and excited those women are over this wedding. You would think they'd never planned anything in their lives. And I swear the guest list gets longer every day."

Brandon rose from the bed and crossed to the dresser on leaden legs. As he slid on his platinum TAG Heuer watch, Cynthia kept up a steady stream of chatter from the closet.

"I'm going to ask Shanell to hook us up with her Realtor. He's absolutely amazing, Brandon. He's sold properties for a lot of celebrities who are from Houston, including Loretta Devine. Shanell says he's in such demand that he only takes referrals, but I'm sure he'd love to have *us* as clients. I mean, we're practically royalty in this town."

Brandon went still.

Cynthia's words had triggered a memory—a memory of the very first time he'd met Dominic Archer. He and Tamia had been having dinner at a restaurant when Dominic appeared at their table. After Tamia had nervously made the introductions, Dominic had given Brandon a surprised look.

Chambers . . . Any relation to our lieutenant governor and the bigwig federal judge?

They're my parents.

Your parents? Wow, man. You're practically royalty.

Brandon frowned. *We're practically royalty in this town. . . .*

Cynthia poked her head out of the closet. "So?"

Brandon met her expectant gaze. "So what?"

"Are you up for house hunting on Saturday?"

He was silent, studying her through narrowed eyes.

Her smile wavered. "Why are you looking at me like that?"

"No particular reason." Brandon calmly picked up his wallet and smartphone, then started from the room. "I'll let you know about Saturday."

"Wait, where are you going?" Cynthia called after him. "I thought we were riding to work together."

"Not today. You're not ready yet, and I don't wanna be late for my meeting."

"But—"

"I'll see you at the office." He closed the bedroom door on her protests and headed from the apartment.

A few minutes later, as he climbed into his car and started the engine, his phone rang.

His pulse quickened.

He foolishly hoped it was Tamia calling to tell him that she had no intention of sleeping with any man until she and Brandon could be together again.

But one glance at the phone's display screen dashed that hope.

It wasn't Tamia.

It was Dre's mother.

Brandon frowned. He considered ignoring her call, but he knew he'd have to deal with her sooner or later. He might as well get it over with.

Clenching his jaw, he pressed the talk button. "Hello."

"Hello, Brandon. This is Renay Portis."

"Ms. Portis," he said coolly. "What can I do for you?"

"Oh, goodness. I don't even know where to start." She let out a nervous breath. "First of all, I wanted to apologize for what happened the other night. I didn't mean to make you feel uncomfortable."

"Really?" Brandon countered sardonically. "How did you *think* I'd feel when you came on to me?"

"Well, I was hoping you'd feel flattered. Turned on."

When Brandon didn't laugh, she heaved a resigned breath. "The point is, I was way out of line for trying to seduce you. I'd had a few glasses of wine before you arrived, but that's no excuse for my behavior."

"No," Brandon agreed, "it isn't."

"It's just that . . . well, I get lonely sometimes. It's hard to meet good men nowadays—men who are handsome, confident, financially successful. *Real* men who are about something . . ." She trailed off with a wistful sigh. "Men like you don't come around every day, Brandon. But that's not your fault. I'm sorry for coming on to you. Do you think you can forgive me?"

Brandon stared out the window, shaking his head. "Please don't do anything like that again, Ms. Portis, or you gon' have me in therapy. I'm serious."

She laughed.

He surprised himself by chuckling.

After a few moments, Renay implored, "I hope you won't tell Dre about this. He'd be furious with me."

"Yeah, he would."

"You're his best friend in the world, Brandon. I'd never forgive myself for causing a rift between you two. Please promise me you won't say anything to Dre."

Brandon hated keeping secrets. He knew all too well that secrets destroyed lives. But sometimes they were necessary.

"I won't tell him," he promised.

Renay gave a sigh of relief. "Thank you, Brandon."

He nodded, though she couldn't see the gesture.

"Well, I won't keep you any longer. I'm sure you're on your way to work to make that paper." She paused for a long moment. "If you ever change your mind about my offer—"

Brandon scowled. "Good-bye, Ms. Portis."

He hung up on her naughty laughter.

Ain't that some shit?

Shaking his head in disbelief, he shoved on a pair of sunglasses and backed out of the parking space, making a mental note to stay the hell away from his best friend's horny-ass mother from now on.

Chapter 16

Tamia

Dominic met Tamia as she stepped off the elevator, sleek bob bouncing against her cheekbones, leather briefcase swinging at her side.

"Good morning." Dominic looked her over and grinned broadly. "You look amazing. Red is definitely your color."

"Think so?" Catching her reflection in the lobby's mirrored wall, Tamia smiled. She was rocking a fitted skirt suit that accentuated her curves and hinted at her plump cleavage. She looked damn good, but more important, she *felt* good—about herself and her future.

"Are Mr. and Mrs. Ehrlich here?"

Dominic nodded. "They're waiting in the conference room."

Tamia smiled. "Lead the way."

It was Thursday morning, and she was meeting her potential new clients at the downtown offices of Archer Foods International.

As she and Dominic stepped through the double glass doors leading into his company's reception area, the receptionist stared at Tamia in openmouthed shock.

"I take it you haven't told your employees about our partnership," Tamia muttered to Dominic.

He chuckled. "Not yet."

As they passed the reception desk, he said to the stunned woman, "Melody, please bring Miss Luke some coffee."

"Um, that's okay," Tamia interjected. "I've already had my morning caffeine fix."

Dominic glanced at her. "You sure?"

"Positive." The way the receptionist was frowning at her, she didn't trust the heffa not to spit in her drink.

"All right."

Dominic guided Tamia to a spacious conference room that overlooked the downtown skyline. Seated at the long table was an attractive, middle-aged white couple talking quietly and sipping coffee.

As Tamia and Dominic entered the room, the man and woman set down their cups and stood.

"Mr. and Mrs. Ehrlich, I'd like you to meet Tamia Luke."

Tamia smiled, striding forward with an outstretched hand. "Pleasure to meet you both."

They smiled affably as they shook her hand.

"Thank you for meeting with us," Grace Ehrlich said. "Mr. Archer hasn't stopped singing your praises."

"Is that right?"

Dominic gave Tamia a lazy smile. "I've only been speaking the truth."

Out of the corner of her eye, Tamia saw Buddy and Grace Ehrlich exchange knowing smiles. She wondered whether they, like most Houstonians, had followed her criminal trial. Though Tamia had been acquitted of Isabel Archer's murder, she hadn't exactly come away smelling like roses. Her scandalous affair with Dominic—a married man—had undoubtedly left a bad taste in many people's mouths. But if the Ehrlichs had a problem with her, they wouldn't be here, right?

Tamia briskly cleared her throat. "Shall we get started?"

She was surprised—and slightly annoyed—when Dominic sat at the end of the table instead of leaving. Just because he was funding her business didn't mean she needed handholding.

When she arched a brow at him, he drawled, "Don't mind me. I'm just killing time before I have to attend another meeting. Pretend I'm not even here."

Tamia eyed him a moment longer, then cleared her throat and turned her attention to the Ehrlichs.

"I had an opportunity to review your Web site," she began, removing her iPad from her briefcase. She powered it on, then propped up the portable device so that everyone had a clear view of the screen.

"The good news is that your bed-and-breakfast is gorgeous with scenic views, and the location is perfect. Being ninety minutes outside of Houston, you're far enough away to provide a welcome break from the city and make couples feel like they're on a real vacation. At the same time, they're close enough to home to be able to rush back in case of an emergency involving their kids."

The Ehrlichs nodded, absorbing her feedback.

"What's the bad news?" Buddy asked cautiously.

"Your Web site isn't as functional and inviting as it should be. The design is somewhat sterile, and it takes too much clicking around to access basic information." Tamia demonstrated on the iPad. "You're in the hospitality business, so your Web site needs to reflect that."

Grace nodded grimly. "We both retired from corporate America, so it's hard to break that corporate mentality."

"I understand," Tamia soothed. "It doesn't happen overnight. That's why I'm here—to see how I can help you. Redesigning your Web site should be one of our top priorities. But that's only one component of your business. We also need to build your presence on social media. I've worked with several companies that have successfully leveraged the power of social networking to reach their target customers. There's no reason you can't do the same."

The Ehrlichs traded hopeful glances, which further boosted Tamia's confidence. She was in her element again, doing what she loved, and it felt good.

Grace smiled ruefully. "Since Buddy and I were both successful in our careers, we underestimated how hard it would be to run our own business. When we retired and decided to open a B and B, we mistakenly subscribed to the notion 'If you build it they will come.' But that hasn't been the reality."

"It seldom is," Tamia remarked sympathetically. "Not without some help. How have reservations been this month?"

"Slow," Grace admitted with a grimace. "We figured since it's the holidays—"

Tamia shook her head. "The holidays are the busiest time of year in the hospitality industry. With Christmas right around the corner, you should be booked solid by now."

Grace sighed. "I wish."

Tamia pursed her lips, tapping her manicured nails on top of the iPad. "Since cruise ships sail out of Galveston, most Houstonians naturally think of going on cruises during the winter holidays. But what about those who can't afford one, or who only need a few days of relaxation somewhere close to home? Those are the people you want to target."

The Ehrlichs nodded in agreement.

"You can advertise on local radio and TV stations and hold contests to give away complimentary stays. It'd be great if you could also get a celebrity endorsement."

"A celebrity endorsement?" Grace repeated.

"Yes. If you had a famous couple who stayed at the B and B, they could be featured in promo ads. That would do wonders for publicity."

"I'm sure it would." Grace exchanged wistful glances with her husband. "But we don't know any celebrities."

Tamia couldn't help thinking of Brandon's friendship with Beyoncé and Jay-Z. A glowing endorsement from the powerhouse couple would have people flocking to the Ehrlichs' B and B, turning the rustic retreat into a status symbol—except regular folks would actually be able to afford it.

If Tamia and Brandon had still been dating, she might have asked him to hook her up. But that wasn't an option anymore.

Pushing the thought aside, she said to the Ehrlichs, "I'll think of something. Anyway, do you conduct guest surveys?"

"We do." Buddy grimaced. "But we've found that some people aren't completely honest with us."

Grace elaborated, "One couple gushed about what a great time they'd had and how they were going to recommend our B and B to their family and friends. Imagine our surprise when we found a scathing review from that same couple on Travelocity."

Tamia winced. "Ouch."

Grace laughed. "Tell me about it."

"I have an idea."

Everyone turned to stare at Dominic. He was leaning back in his chair, a thoughtful expression on his face as he tapped one long finger against his lips.

Tamia narrowed her eyes. It was bad enough that he'd hung around for the meeting. Now he wanted to offer suggestions?

"I'm just thinking out loud here. . . . What if Tamia and I spent the weekend as guests at the bed-and-breakfast?"

Tamia raised a brow. "Excuse me?"

Dominic smiled at her. "We could pose as an engaged couple, which would give us an opportunity to interact with other couples who are there. We all know that guests will say things to other guests that they probably wouldn't say to their hosts. If they have any complaints—big or small—we could pass them along to Buddy and Grace."

Tamia frowned as the Ehrlichs exchanged considering glances.

"You know," Buddy mused, "that's not a bad idea."

"And it'd be a great way for Tamia to personally experience the B and B," Grace added.

Tamia's frown deepened. She had no desire to spend the weekend holed up with Dominic at some romantic retreat. They'd have to share the same room . . . and the same bed.

Hell to the nah!

When three pairs of eyes swung toward her, she nervously wondered if she'd uttered the objection aloud.

"So what do you think, Tamia?" Dominic prompted.

"I don't know," she hedged, trying to be diplomatic. "Going undercover as a couple to befriend the other guests is a bit . . . unconventional."

"Come on," Dominic cajoled, his eyes twinkling with mischief. "Where's your sense of adventure?"

Tamia glared at him. If he'd been sitting closer to her, she would have kicked him under the table with the pointy toe of her pumps. Damn him for putting her on the spot like this.

"I don't think we'd be able to pull it off," she asserted. "Anyone who'd followed the trial would recognize us."

"That's what disguises are for." Dominic winked. "Come on, Tamia. It'll be fun."

She pursed her lips, darting a glance at the Ehrlichs. They were watching her expectantly. She couldn't believe she was the only one who thought this was a horrible idea.

"I'll think about it," she reluctantly conceded.

Dominic smiled, looking satisfied.

"Well, we'd better head back to the ranch," Grace announced, rising from the table. "We left our eldest daughter in charge, but we want to be there to greet the guests who are arriving later this afternoon. But before we leave"—she removed a check from her purse and passed it across the table to Tamia—"here's a retainer for your services."

Tamia wanted to do cartwheels. "Does this mean I'm hired?"

"Absolutely," Grace said warmly. "We look forward to working with you."

After the meeting, Tamia and Dominic escorted the Ehrlichs to the elevator.

As soon as the doors closed behind them, Tamia squealed and stomped her feet in excitement.

Dominic laughed. "Congratulations on landing your first client. Looks like you're officially in business."

"Looks that way." Tamia beamed with pleasure. "This is amazing."

"*You* were amazing," Dominic told her. "The way you commanded the room, the things you were telling them. You really know your stuff, Tamia. I was very impressed."

Tamia smiled, not immune to his praise. "Thank you, Dominic. For the money, for the client referral—"

He waved off her gratitude. "You don't have to keep thanking me. I wanted to do this for you, Tamia. I believe in you."

Her smile softened. "I appreciate that."

They were standing close together, closer than she'd realized. Dominic wore one of his tailored dark suits with a pinstriped shirt and a silk twill tie. The precise trim of his goatee drew her gaze to his full, juicy lips. She found herself wishing—for the millionth time—that he wasn't so damn *foine*.

"Let me take you out to dinner to celebrate."

Tamia lifted her eyes to Dominic's. "I can't. Not tonight."

"Why not?"

"I have plans," she lied.

"Cancel them."

Tamia laughed. "I don't think so," she said, pressing the elevator call button. "And I'm not spending the weekend with you, either. Nice try, though."

Dominic chuckled. "I thought it was a good idea. So did the Ehrlichs."

"Guess you all thought wrong."

"I'm sorry you feel that way." Dominic watched as she backed into the elevator and pushed the button for the lobby. "If you change your mind about dinner, you know how to reach me."

"I do," Tamia drawled. "But I won't need to."

Dominic smiled, holding her gaze. "You never know."

As the elevator doors closed, Tamia found herself smiling.

For the first time ever, she wondered what would have happened if she and Dominic had met under different circumstances. If he hadn't been married, and if he hadn't blackmailed her for sex, could things have worked out between them?

Could she have fallen in love with him?

Dangerous thoughts, Tamia. Dangerous and foolish.

Chapter 17

Brandon

The lunch crowd was in full swing when Brandon sauntered through the doors of Stogie's that afternoon. The mahogany bar and tables were occupied by men in shirtsleeves trading raucous banter while Sinatra crooned "I'll Be Home for Christmas" in the background. The atmosphere was jovial and relaxed . . . except at the corner booth, where Dre sat brooding over a glass of cognac.

Brandon slid into the plush leather seat across from him. "Wassup."

"Yo," Dre mumbled, lifting his troubled gaze from his drink. "I was starting to think you weren't coming."

"I was with a client when you called. Our meeting ran over."

Dre regarded him suspiciously. "You sure about that?"

Brandon frowned. "What's that supposed to mean?"

"I don't know, man. Seems like you've been avoiding me lately. The other night you left Ma's house before I even got there—"

"I told you something came up with Cynthia," Brandon lied.

"You told my voice mail," Dre corrected. "And you left the message the next day when you knew I'd be at football practice, like you didn't wanna talk to me directly. Since then you've been ignoring my calls—"

Brandon forced out a laugh. "Dude, you sound like my bitch or something."

Dre scowled. "I'm just saying. Where'd you disappear to?"

"Nowhere, man, so quit girlin'. I have no reason to avoid you."

*Other than the fact that your mother tried to seduce me, which fucked up my
mind for a few days.*

Dre silently assessed him another moment, then shook his head
and gulped down some of his drink.

Brandon was more than relieved when the waiter materialized,
grinning broadly as he greeted Brandon by name and took his order:
a neat scotch and a rib-eye steak with mashed potatoes.

"Nothing for me," Dre told the waiter, drawing a surprised look
from Brandon.

"What's up with you?" he demanded as soon as the server left.
"You call and ask me to meet you downstairs for lunch, but you're
not eating?"

"I'm not hungry," Dre muttered.

Brandon narrowed his eyes, studying his friend across the table.
Suddenly remembering that Dre had wanted to ask his advice about
something, he felt a sharp stab of guilt. He'd been so caught up in his
own problems—with Tamia, Cynthia, and Renay Portis—that he'd
left his best friend out in the cold.

Feeling like a selfish asshole, Brandon did the only thing he
could: apologize.

"I'm sorry for not getting back to you sooner, bruh. I've been
dealing with a lot of shit lately, but that's no excuse for ghosting on
you. I'm really sorry for that, but I'm here now. So what did you want
to talk to me about?"

Dre scrubbed a hand over his face and pushed out a heavy breath.
"I don't even know how to say it. I'm still in shock."

Brandon felt himself leaning forward intently. "What's going
on, man?"

"It's Fiona." Dre paused, swallowing visibly. "She's pregnant."

Brandon's jaw dropped. "You're kidding."

Dre scowled. "You think I'd kid about something like this?"

Brandon stared at him. "You got Fiona *pregnant?*"

"Apparently so."

Brandon leaned back slowly against the seat, shaking his head in
stunned disbelief. "How did you find out?"

"Tamia came to see me on Monday." Dre's lips twisted grimly.

"She threatened to come after my ass if I don't get in touch with Fiona by the end of the week."

Just then the waiter appeared, bringing Brandon's drink.

He downed the scotch in one burning swallow, then ordered another one before returning his attention to Dre. "So what're you gonna do?"

"I don't know, man," Dre mumbled, passing a trembling hand over his head. "This is the *last* fucking thing I need. Fiona's a psychotic killer facing life in prison. I can't be having no damn kids with her crazy ass. And there's no way in hell Leah will take me back if she finds out about this."

Brandon grimaced. "That's probably a safe assumption."

Dre shook his head. "Fiona can't have that baby."

"Are you gonna ask her to get an abortion?"

"Hell, yeah." Dre stared anxiously at Brandon. "She can do that, right? Inmates can get abortions, can't they?"

"Legally, yes. But the judge might want to have Fiona evaluated to determine whether she's mentally stable enough to make the decision to end her pregnancy."

"*What?* She ain't mentally stable enough to be *having* a baby!"

"Maybe not," Brandon grimly agreed. "But just remember that we're in Texas, which is full of pro-life judges who'd force a woman to have a baby but wouldn't bat an eye at sending a man to the death chamber."

Dre looked stricken. "So what you're telling me is that Fiona might have to keep the baby?"

"It's possible."

"*Shit!*" Dre covered his face with his hands and groaned. "I can't believe this is happening."

A grim smile curved Brandon's mouth. "Looks like we're both gonna be fathers."

Dre snorted bitterly. "At least your baby mama isn't a homicidal maniac. At least you can marry her and have a normal life with her."

Normalcy is overrated, Brandon thought morosely.

Sipping from his second glass of scotch, he glanced around the crowded restaurant. He spied one of his colleagues sitting at the bar with a group of guys who worked for an investment firm located three floors below Chernoff, Dewitt & Strathmore. Addison Vassar was one of the few female attorneys who enjoyed hanging out at the former cigar club, and it was no secret why. She was always on the prowl for fresh meat—what better hunting ground than a man cave like Stogie's?

Brandon absently watched as the guy seated next to Addison leaned over to whisper something in her ear. She tossed back her dark hair and laughed—a wicked, bawdy laugh that turned several heads.

Catching Brandon's eye, Addison winked and smiled flirtatiously.

He nodded briefly before returning his attention to Dre, who looked more miserable by the minute as he bemoaned his fate.

"This wasn't supposed to go down like this. I mean, this is the kinda shit that happens to Shavar, not me."

Dre's half brother, Shavar Portis, was a maintenance worker who had more baby mamas than Brandon could count. He was only a few months younger than Dre because their father had been messing around with their mothers at the same time, continuing the affair even after he'd married Renay. While Shavar saw nothing wrong with spreading his seed, Dre had vowed to break the cycle of breeding illegitimate children.

So much for that.

"I don't know how I'm gonna break this news to my mom," Dre fretted. "She wants grandkids but *not* like this. She's gonna lose her damn mind over this shit."

Based on her recent behavior, Brandon was convinced that Renay Portis had *already* lost her mind. But of course he kept that thought to himself.

"How the hell am I supposed to raise a child on my own?" Dre wondered aloud. "I've got a busy career. I'm on the road all the time with the team—"

"You wouldn't be the first single parent that ever lived," Brandon wryly pointed out.

"I know that," Dre snapped. "But this isn't how I envisioned becoming a father."

Brandon lost his patience. "Look, man, I'm hearing a lot of anger, blame, and self-pity, and I feel for you. Really, I do. But the bottom line is that you fucked up. Not only did you cheat on your girlfriend, but you apparently had unprotected sex with Fiona. If you didn't wanna take any risks, you shoulda wrapped that shit up. But you didn't, so now you gotta deal with the consequences."

Dre scowled. "I know *you* ain't sitting over there lecturing nobody about practicing safe sex."

"Get the fuck outta here," Brandon scoffed derisively. "At least *I* was in a relationship with the woman I got pregnant, and the one and only time I didn't wear a condom was after she started taking the pill. And last I checked, bruh, I'm handling *my* business. So I suggest you man up and do the same."

Dre dropped his eyes to the table, looking sullen and shamefaced. Several tense moments passed.

"I guess I had that coming," Dre grumbled. "I've never pulled punches with you, so why should I expect to be treated any differently when *I've* fucked up?"

"You know how we do, man. Straight talk, no chaser."

Dre nodded slowly, glancing around the restaurant as if he'd forgotten where he was. After another moment, he heaved a resigned breath and scrubbed his hands over his face. "I need to talk to Fiona, work this out with her."

"You do that."

Dre nodded again, looking like he had something else on his mind.

Brandon waited.

"I've been meaning to ask. . . Has Cynthia talked to Leah recently? I figure since they're friends, Cynthia would know what's going on with her. Has she mentioned anything to you?"

"No, but I wouldn't expect her to," Brandon admitted. "You're my best friend, so Cynthia probably assumes I'd take your side."

Dre snorted. "Little does *she* know." He drained the rest of his cognac, then signaled for the waiter. "I'ma get something to eat."

"Good," Brandon retorted, " 'cause I ain't sharing none of my food with your greedy black ass."

They both laughed.

Chapter 18

Tamia

Tamia tilted her head to one side, surveying her reflection in the dressing room mirror. She wore a strapless red Versace gown that clung to her curves and had a plunging back and a deep slit.

She did a slow turn, inspecting herself from every angle.

She knew she looked fierce, but she wanted a second opinion.

Padding across the small dressing room, she peeked out at Brandon. He was lounging in a chair nearby, patiently waiting for her to finish trying on the dress. She watched his long fingers slide across his smartphone as he scrolled through photos he'd taken since their arrival in Venice. Photos of historic churches and palaces, rare paintings and sculptures, scenic bridges and waterways, gondolas drifting lazily down the Grand Canal.

And photos of Tamia, laughing and carefree as she twirled in playful circles and blew kisses at him.

She smiled now, watching him another moment before stepping out of the dressing room.

He lifted his head. And went completely still.

Her skin heated as he slowly looked her up and down, his dark eyes glittering with admiration.

"Well?" she purred, striking a seductive pose with the gown split up to her thigh. "What do you think?"

Brandon rose from the chair. "I think you look good enough to eat," he drawled. "Which is all I wanna do right now."

"Brandon!" she gasped, blushing.

One of the Italian saleswomen hid a grin behind her hand as Brandon sauntered toward Tamia.

As she turned to escape, he caught her around the waist and pulled her back against his body. She smiled demurely as he slid his arms around her and whispered in her ear, "You look absolutely stunning in this dress, but I wanna peel it off you and lick you inside out."

She shivered, nipples hardening with arousal. "You can't do that here."

"Says who?"

She closed her eyes as his warm lips nuzzled the sensitive skin behind her ear. "You must be trying to get us kicked out of this store," she breathed.

"If that's what it takes to get us back to the hotel, then yeah."

She grinned weakly. "We can't go back yet. We haven't finished shopping."

"We can finish later."

"But—"

He was already steering her toward the dressing room.

No one stopped him as he followed her inside and closed the curtain behind them.

No one interrupted as he lowered her to the velvet bench, knelt between her legs, pushed her gown and panties out of the way, and slid his tongue into her pussy.

And when they emerged fifteen minutes later and Brandon whipped out his platinum card to pay for the twenty-thousand-dollar dress, no one— absolutely no one—complained.

"Hello? Earth to Tamia."

Snapped out of her reverie, Tamia gave Honey a blank look. "Sorry. Did you say something?"

Honey laughed. "I was asking if you plan to try on that dress or stare at it all night."

Tamia glanced down at the red satin sheath in her hand. "I don't want it," she murmured, returning the dress to the rack.

Honey eyed her curiously. She was a voluptuous young beauty with a golden complexion and a glamorous weave that flowed down her back. She'd been a rising star in the underground porn industry when Lou was forced to sell his film studio, and now she was one of his most popular escorts, commanding a thousand-dollar hourly rate.

"Are you okay?" she asked Tamia.

Tamia forced a smile. "I'm fine. Why?"

Honey frowned. "You had a faraway look in your eyes when you were staring at that dress."

Tamia shrugged. "I was just thinking about something."

"Or someone," Honey said knowingly.

Tamia pretended not to hear her as she circled another rack of clothes, her fingers wandering over designer frocks without making another selection.

To celebrate landing her first client, she'd invited Honey to meet her at the Galleria for an afternoon of shopping. Their arms were laden with bags by the time they'd headed into Neiman Marcus, vowing that this would be their last stop before they went to dinner.

Honey followed Tamia. "I know you were thinking about Brandon. He's been on your mind all day."

"How do *you* know?" Tamia mumbled.

"Girl, please. You don't think I saw the way you were admiring those badass loafers in the Louis Vuitton store? And please don't tell me you were thinking about buying a pair of men's shoes for yourself."

Tamia said nothing.

"I didn't think so." Honey popped her gum. "I still don't understand why you didn't go to the courthouse that day to stop Brandon and Cynthia's wedding. That's what *I* woulda done, 'cause there's no way I'd have let that fine-ass brotha marry another woman."

"He hasn't married her yet," Tamia sourly reminded Honey. "And do I look like Dwayne Wayne to you?"

Honey frowned. "Dwyane Wade?"

"No, Dwayne *Wayne* from *A Different World*. He crashed Whitley's wedding to stop her from marrying—Oh, never mind," Tamia broke off in exasperation. "I keep forgetting how young you are. Or how young I *suspect* you are, since you won't tell me your age."

Honey grinned unabashedly. "Don't change the subject. We were talking about you and Brandon."

Tamia sighed. "There *is* no me and Brandon."

"Which is a damn shame. Everyone knows you two belong together."

"Not everyone. Brandon apparently didn't get the memo."

"Oh, trust, he got it," Honey affirmed. "That brotha loves you, which he more than proved during your trial. Seriously, Tamia. I don't know any other man who would have risked public humiliation by defending the woman who'd cheated on him. Sorry," she added when Tamia winced. "Not trying to hurt you, boo. Just keeping it real. Brandon put his reputation and his pride on the line when he decided to represent you. He knew haters would call him a pussy-whipped fool, but he didn't care. All that mattered to him was keeping you out of prison. Unfortunately for you, he's a standup guy who wants to be *everybody's* hero. If Cynthia wasn't pregnant and if his father wasn't running for governor, you know he'd be with you. You're the love of his life, Tamia, and nothing's gonna change that."

Tamia swallowed tightly as Honey's words brought tears to her eyes.

"I hate seeing you like this, Tamia," Honey said gently. "You're my girl, and I want you to be happy."

Tamia dabbed at her eyes. "You know what would make me happy? If we could stop talking about Brandon. I'm really trying to move on, but it's hard to do that when everyone keeps rehashing what went wrong between us."

Honey grimaced. "I'm sorry. I should have realized I was only making things worse."

"Not worse. Just . . . not better." Tamia sifted disinterestedly through a row of pleated skirts, then sighed. "By the way, I've been meaning to tell you that Beau Chambers asked about you."

Honey perked up. "Brandon's brother?"

Tamia nodded. "He asked me who you were when I ran into him the other day. He remembered seeing you with me that night at the wellness center when Bishop Yarbrough showed up."

"Oh, yeah," Honey murmured.

"He wants to meet you, so he invited us to a fundraiser banquet they're having."

"Really?"

"Yeah." Tamia hesitated. "I don't wanna go. Brandon will be there, and I don't know if I can handle seeing him again. But if you really want to meet his brother . . . I'm willing to go with you."

Honey's expression softened. "You'd do that for me?"

Tamia nodded.

"When's the banquet?"

"Next Friday. Two days before Christmas."

Honey frowned. "Damn."

"What's wrong? You can't go?"

"Nah, girl. Keyshawn's off that day."

Tamia scowled at the mention of Honey's boyfriend. "Can't you just tell him you're going out with a client that evening?"

Honey sighed. "I could, but I already promised to spend the day with him. He'll get upset if I change the plans."

"And God knows you don't wanna upset *his* crazy ass," Tamia muttered darkly.

"No, I don't. I'm really trying to keep the peace so he won't tell anyone about me and Bishop Yarbrough."

"I know, but how long are you gonna let him hold that secret over your head?"

Honey didn't respond. Her eyes narrowed dangerously as she glared at something or someone behind Tamia.

Following the direction of her hostile stare, Tamia saw a Hispanic woman standing nearby. She was folding cashmere sweaters on a display table while surreptitiously watching Honey and Tamia.

"Can I help you?" Honey spat loudly.

The store employee looked startled. "Excuse me?"

Honey smacked her lips. "Is there some particular reason you've been following us around for the past twenty minutes?"

The woman's face reddened. "I-I w-wasn't follow—"

"Let me tell you something," Honey cut her off, rolling her neck. "Ain't nobody trying to steal nothing up in here. We make *more* than enough money to buy anything we want in this damn store. What about you? Even with an employee discount, you probably can't afford *shit* with your minimum-wage check."

The affronted woman gasped.

"I don't appreciate being followed around like some fucking criminal," Honey continued, "so I suggest you fall the hell back before I call your manager over here."

Sputtering with indignation, the woman dropped the sweater she'd been folding and beat a hasty retreat.

Tamia snickered, shaking her head at Honey. "You are a mess."

Honey sucked her teeth. "That bitch was working my damn nerves. And she wasn't even slick with her shit."

Tamia chuckled, wondering how someone so feisty and confrontational could allow herself to be any man's punching bag.

Tossing her long hair back, Honey cast a bored look around the department store. "I don't know about you, girl, but nothing's really catching my eye."

"Mine either," Tamia admitted.

"Good." Honey grabbed her arm. "Let's get the fuck outta here and get something to eat."

Chapter 19

Brandon

Later that evening, Brandon was reviewing court documents for one of his new cases when someone knocked on his door.

He glanced up, not at all surprised to see Addison standing in the doorway of his office. "Wassup?"

"That's what *I* should be asking you," she drawled. "Got a minute?"

"Sure," Brandon said, setting aside his paperwork. "I need a break anyway."

Addison smiled, sauntering into the large room. She was an attractive brunette with bright green eyes and long wavy hair. She was in her early thirties, like Brandon, and taller than average at five-nine. She'd removed her suit jacket at some point during the day, revealing a sleeveless cream blouse that showcased her busty cleavage.

Brandon watched as she strolled to the leather sofa near his desk and sat down. As she smoothly crossed her legs, her skirt rode up her toned thighs.

When Brandon lifted his eyes to hers, she gave him a sultry smile. He leaned back slowly in his chair. "What's on your mind?"

A suggestive gleam filled her eyes. "Do you really wanna know?"

"Only if it pertains to work."

Her smile deepened. "What else would it pertain to?"

Brandon just looked at her.

She chuckled. "I just met with Mitch," she explained, referring to the managing partner of the firm's litigation department. "He told me that I'll be reporting to a new supervisor. Imagine my surprise when he said it was you."

Brandon nodded. He, too, had been surprised by Mitch's decision. It was customary for new partners to become supervisors of less experienced attorneys. But Addison was a senior associate, one of many Brandon had beat out to make partner that summer.

"No offense, Brandon, but I honestly don't know what to make of this move," Addison admitted. "I'm either on my way out the door—or I'm being groomed to be named partner next summer."

Brandon's mouth twitched. "You're not on your way out the door."

Her eyes lit up. "Then I'm being groomed for partnership?"

"Of course you are. But so is everyone else on the partnership track. You know that."

"I know." She sighed. "I was just hoping you could give me some insight. You know, now that you're a made man and all."

Brandon chuckled. "As Mitch probably explained to you, our department is undergoing some restructuring, which involves shifting workloads. You're not the only one who was reassigned to me."

"Oh, believe me, Brandon, I'm not complaining. You're a brilliant attorney and a rock star at this firm. I know I can learn a lot from you—and I'm not just saying that to suck up."

"Thought never crossed my mind," Brandon said drolly.

Addison laughed, shaking her head at him. "This is definitely gonna take some getting used to."

"What?"

"Our new roles. Five months ago we were peers—hell, rivals—vying for the same promotion. Fast-forward to now, and you're my boss." She smiled, twirling a strand of hair around her finger. "I'll have to get used to being under you."

There was no mistaking the sexual innuendo lacing her words.

Brandon sat up, reaching for his paperwork. "Was there anything else you wanted to discuss?"

"Actually, there is." Addison's eyes were twinkling. "Do you think I'm attractive?"

"What?"

She smiled, amused by his startled tone. "Do you think I'm attractive?"

Brandon frowned. "Why are you asking me that?"

"Because I want to know the answer. Obviously."

"Why does it matter what I think?" Brandon countered.

She shrugged. "I'm a woman. You're a man—a gorgeous one, I might add. It's only natural that I'd care whether or not you find me attractive. So do you?"

Brandon sighed with exaggerated patience. "Yes, Addison, I think you're attractive."

"But not attractive enough to date."

He gave her a bemused look. "Where are you going with this? We're colleagues—"

"So are you and Cynthia, but that didn't stop you two from sleeping together. And now you're engaged."

Brandon frowned. "I'm not going to discuss my relationship—"

Addison laughed. "I'm not asking you to. I was just making the point that your lack of interest in me has nothing to do with us working together. There's another reason." She pinned him with a direct look. "You don't date white women, and I'd like to know why."

Brandon groaned. "Can we not get into this right now?"

"You don't have to worry about offending me," Addison hastened to assure him. "I'm not the sensitive type, so I can handle whatever you tell me. I just want to know."

"Why?"

"Because I'm curious. So are a bunch of other women at this firm." Addison smiled. "Humor me. Please."

Brandon heaved a resigned breath, shaking his head at her. "It's nothing personal. I'm just not attracted to . . . certain women."

"You mean white women," Addison translated.

He nodded.

"And why is that?"

Brandon gave her an amused look. "Is there a law stating I have to be?"

"Of course not. It's just unusual, given your background. You grew up in River Oaks and attended predominantly white private schools. You're the kind of black guy who's *supposed* to end up with a white wife."

He cocked a brow. "Supposed to?"

"Under the circumstances." Addison grinned. "So how did you defy the odds?"

"I don't know, Addison," Brandon drawled sardonically. "I didn't realize I was 'defying' anything just by being me."

Addison slipped off her heels, making herself more comfortable on the sofa. "Have you ever dated outside your race?"

"Once. Back in high school."

Addison eyed him knowingly. "It must have been a bad experience."

"Not really. She was cool. We just didn't have that much in common."

"So that's it? You gave up on swirling after *one* try?"

Brandon chuckled, stroking his goatee. "I didn't give up. I just realized I preferred women of my own race."

He had fond memories of the girls he'd met from Dre's high school. They'd gone on double dates to the movies, carnivals, picnics, rap concerts, you name it. Brandon had the money and the ride—a sweet black Jetta his parents had bought him for his sixteenth birthday. His tenderoni always rode shotgun while Dre kept her friend company in the backseat. The four of them would hang out at Dre's crib, watching music videos and making out on the sofa while his mother pulled double shifts at work, oblivious to all the cherry popping that was happening under her roof.

"Looks like *someone's* enjoying a stroll down memory lane," Addison observed, interrupting Brandon's reverie.

He grinned crookedly.

"Let me ask you one more question."

Brandon sighed. "One more. Then we both need to get back to work, a'ight?"

"Yes, sir." Addison gave a mock salute, making him chuckle.

"Ask your question."

"What do you love so much about black women?"

Brandon stared at her. "*Are you serious?*"

Addison blinked. "What?"

"Yo, what the hell kinda question is that?"

"What do you mean? I wasn't trying to be offensive."

"No?" Brandon challenged. "Would you ever ask a white guy what *he* loves about white women?"

"Um . . . probably not."

"Because you'd assume the answer should be obvious."

"No," Addison countered defensively. "I wouldn't ask because I really don't care. I've always been more interested in black guys than white guys. That's why I started this whole conversation with you. Hearing your perspective has been enlightening. Depressing, but enlightening."

Brandon regarded her through narrowed eyes.

After several moments, she smiled meekly. "If you'd rather not answer my question—"

"Nah, I'll answer it." The sooner he did, the sooner he could send her on her way. "What do I love so much about black women? Hmm, where do I begin? I love the beautiful shades of their skin. I love their curves and thick asses, but even when they're on the slim side, they know how to walk into a room and own it. I love their strength and courage. I love their layers of complexity—what you see ain't always what you get. I love their intelligence, whether they're dropping knowledge from the classroom or the streets. I *love* it when they carry themselves with the pride and dignity of Michelle Obama, but they know how to get down and dirty when the time's right. I love that we can chill together and watch *Good Times*, and I don't have to explain the jokes 'cause the sister's already laughing right along with me. I love knowing that whatever differences we may have, at the end of the day, no one understands me better than a woman whose ancestors slaved under the same sun as my own."

By the time Brandon had finished speaking, Addison's mouth was agape.

A long silence passed.

"Wow," she marveled, staring at him. "That's . . . quite a tribute."

Brandon smiled sheepishly. "What can I say? The sisters got me sprung."

"No kidding." Addison swallowed visibly and pursed her lips, looking discomfited as she glanced around the room.

Brandon was vaguely amused. "You all right?"

"I think so." She met his gaze, then sighed ruefully and smiled. "I haven't been this jealous since the night I overheard you and Tamia having sex in this office."

Brandon went still. "What're you talking about?"

Addison chuckled, running her hand along the leather sofa. "You don't have to play dumb, Brandon. I was here that night burning the midnight oil. I came over to ask your advice about one of my cases, but your door was closed. Before I could knock, I heard the unmistakable sounds of fucking in progress." She grinned wickedly. "The way Tamia was moaning and groaning and begging for more . . . well, let's just say my vibrator got one helluva workout that night."

Brandon frowned at her.

"Hey, baby, I'm back from my—" Cynthia strode through the door, pulling up short when she saw that Brandon wasn't alone. As her eyes raked over Addison lounging on the sofa, her face tightened with angry displeasure.

"Am I interrupting something?"

Addison purred, "Actually—"

"Not at all," Brandon smoothly interjected. "Addison was just leaving. Isn't that right?"

She met his stern gaze, then sighed dramatically. "If you insist."

"He insists," Cynthia spat.

Addison smirked at her, then swung her legs down from the sofa and bent over to retrieve her shoes, deliberately showing off her ample cleavage. She took her sweet time sliding on her pumps, provocatively sheathing one foot then the other.

As Cynthia glared at her, Brandon had a flashback to the night he'd invited Tamia to his office for a booty call. She'd arrived to find him and Cynthia huddled over his desk, laughing at something he couldn't even remember now. It had been perfectly innocent, but Tamia hadn't seen it that way. After she and Brandon got into a heated argument, she'd stormed out on him and run straight into the arms of Dominic.

Brandon frowned at the memory, watching as Addison rose from the sofa, smoothed down her skirt, and tossed her hair over one shoulder.

"I enjoyed chatting with you, Brandon," she drawled, sauntering from the office. Pausing at the door, she smiled and winked at him. "Looking forward to our weekly one-on-ones."

Cynthia slammed the door behind Addison, then rounded accusingly on Brandon. "What the hell is she talking about? What weekly one-on-ones?"

Brandon calmly began gathering his paperwork. "I'm her supervisor now."

"*WHAT?* Since when?"

"Since today."

"You can't be serious!" Cynthia burst out, marching toward his desk. "Addison has no damn business reporting to you!"

"Mitch made the call, not me."

"I don't care! You need to have her reassigned to someone else!"

Brandon frowned. She knew he didn't like being told what to do. "Listen—"

"No, *you* listen," Cynthia hissed, planting her hands on the desk and leaning toward him. "That hussy has been after you for years! You know it, I know it—hell, everyone at this damn firm knows it! Do you really think it's wise for you to become her supervisor? Do you honestly think she won't try to seduce you the first chance she gets?"

Brandon sighed. "Come on, baby. You know I ain't checking for Addison."

"Well, *she's* checking for you!"

"That's her problem, not mine."

"*Wake the fuck up, Brandon!*" Cynthia exploded. "Can't you see what's going on here? Addison's probably the one who requested the reassignment so she'd have an excuse to work more closely with you. The second you reject her advances, she's gonna turn around and accuse *you* of sexual harassment! Is that what you want?"

Brandon scowled. "Of course not."

"Then tell Mitch to reassign that bitch to someone else!"

Brandon stood. "I'm not doing that."

Cynthia sneered at him as he rounded the desk and came toward her. "Oh, I see what's going on. You must *want* her to seduce you. You must *want* to sleep with—"

Brandon leaned down and kissed her. He had to. It was the only way to shut her the hell up.

She instantly melted against him, curving her arms around his neck and parting her lips beneath his. As his tongue gently stroked hers, she shivered and moaned with pleasure.

Slowly pulling away, Brandon framed her face between his hands and murmured, "You need to stop stressing over everything. If I wanted Addison, I coulda had her a long time ago."

"I know, but—"

"But what? You know she's not even my type, so why are you tripping?"

Cynthia pouted. "Because I hate the way she's always coming on to you. It's disgusting and disrespectful. She had no business lying on your sofa like that."

"I agree," Brandon admitted. "Before you arrived I was gonna let her know that we need to establish some boundaries now that I'm her supervisor. I'll have that talk with her tomorrow, a'ight?"

Cynthia nodded, not entirely appeased. "I'd still prefer that she not report to you."

"I know, sweetheart, but you have to understand something. I may be one of the firm's top producers this year—"

Cynthia snorted. "There's no 'may be' about it. You *are* one of the top producers, which is why you just received a cool two mil." She was referring to the hefty bonus check that had been deposited into his account that morning. The firm's annual bonus pool rewarded partners who logged the most billable hours or won the biggest cases. Brandon's successful handling of a major lawsuit that year had made him two million dollars richer.

He smiled at Cynthia. "Top producer or not, I'm still a new partner. So I need to pay my dues before I start throwing my weight around and telling others what I can and can't do. And let's face it. Supervising a senior associate looks good on my résumé."

"I suppose," Cynthia grudgingly acknowledged.

"Mitch says he's grooming me to run the department someday, so he wants me to take on even more responsibility. I don't want to give him any reason to think I can't handle it. Feel me?"

Cynthia heaved a sigh of resignation. "Yeah, I feel you."

"Good." Brandon kissed her forehead. "How'd your meeting go?"

She smiled. "It went well."

"I'm glad to hear that. You can tell me about it on the way home."

"But we drove separately," she reminded him.

"Leave your car here tonight and we can ride home together."

"Really?" Cynthia's eyes lit up. "That'd be wonderful."

"Cool. Go get your stuff and meet me in the lobby."

"Okay!" Cynthia rushed off like an excited little girl who'd just been promised a trip to the zoo.

Brandon tossed some files into his briefcase, grabbed his suit jacket off the back of his chair, and headed from the room.

As he reached the door, some impulse made him pause and glance back at the sofa.

Instantly his mind was flooded with images of the night he and Tamia had made love for the first time since their breakup. They'd been frantic for each other. Insatiable. They'd started off on the sofa and worked their way around the room, fucking long and feverishly into the night.

Brandon swallowed hard, his grip tightening on the handle of his briefcase.

He wondered how long it would take him to get over Tamia.

How much time would pass before he stopped thinking about her, stopped lamenting what could have been?

Months? Years?

What if he never got over her?

Sobered by the thought, Brandon turned off the light and walked out the door.

Chapter 20
Tamia

At the end of her day of shopping and dining with Honey, Tamia stepped off the elevator and strode down the hallway toward her apartment.

As she neared the front door, she noticed a plain white envelope lying on the floor.

Balancing her purse and shopping bags, she bent down to pick up the envelope.

It was unmarked, making her wonder if it had been left on her doorstep by mistake.

She let herself into the apartment, bumping the door shut with her hip. Walking over to the foyer table, she switched on the small lamp, dropped her keys in the shallow ceramic bowl, and set down her bags.

Flipping over the envelope, she saw that it was unsealed. With mounting curiosity, she opened it and removed a piece of paper.

As she unfolded it, a prickle of unease skittered down her spine, giving her a split-second warning before she read the words printed on the page.

I SAVED YOUR LIFE, BITCH. YOU OWE ME.

Tamia gasped, dropping the letter as her heart jackknifed into her throat.

She glanced around fearfully, half expecting an intruder to pounce from the shadows.

When no one did, she hurried to the front door and yanked it open, looking up and down the hallway.

It was empty. And eerily silent.

Trembling hard, she ducked back inside the apartment, locked the door, and grabbed her phone to call the police.

Two officers arrived shortly to take her statement.

One was a stocky Hispanic man who introduced himself as Officer Castillo. The other was Officer Greene, an average-looking brotha with a neat fade and smooth brown skin.

Tamia barely registered their names, and if she'd been asked later to identify them in a lineup, she wouldn't have been able to. She was too shaken up, her mind racing with questions. Who could have left the note for her? And why?

After checking her apartment for any signs of an intruder, the police officers followed her to the living room, where she perched tensely on the edge of the armchair while they sat on the sofa. As Officer Greene took out a small notepad, she stared numbly at the patch sewn into the shoulder of his light blue uniform shirt. The patch read SPACE CITY, USA, with flight paths circling a globe to represent NASA's presence in Houston.

"You did the right thing by calling us," Officer Greene assured Tamia. "It's not uncommon for people to receive threats after they've been acquitted of crimes. This note may have been left by someone who followed your trial and didn't agree with the verdict."

Tamia nodded mutely. The same thought had occurred to her. Except the note suggested that she shared a personal connection with the sender. Someone who believed she owed him or her something.

I saved your life. . . .

Who could make that kind of claim?

"Other than this note," Officer Castillo asked, "have you received any threatening phone calls or emails?"

"No," Tamia answered.

"Have you noticed anyone following you or loitering around the building?"

She shook her head. "You should talk to the front desk. They're supposed to call us whenever we have visitors. And there are security cameras in the lobby and on every floor—"

Castillo was nodding. "We've already questioned the front desk attendant and told him we need to review the visitor log and the security tapes from today. We'll let you know what we find out."

Tamia nodded.

"The wording of the note makes me think you might know this person," Greene said, echoing her own thoughts. "Does anyone come to mind?"

Tamia hesitated, nervously moistening her dry lips. She didn't want to implicate an innocent man. But if her life was in danger, she had to explore any and all possibilities.

"One of the jurors from my trial," she began haltingly. "His name's Lester McCray. . . . I've run into him twice over the past month, and both times he's asked me out on a date. I turned him down."

Castillo and Greene exchanged speculative glances.

"How did he take your rejection?" Greene asked, scribbling in his notepad. "Did he seem angry?"

"No. I think he was more disappointed than angry." Tamia paused. "But he told me that he lives around here, and I found out that he doesn't."

Greene frowned at her. "So he lied?"

Tamia nodded.

The officers shared another glance, pondering the implications.

"Since McCray served on the jury that found you not guilty," Greene ruminated, "it *is* possible that he thinks you owe him something in return."

Tamia shifted uncomfortably in the chair. "I don't want to jump to any conclusions, but he's the only person I could think of."

Greene nodded, closing his notepad. "We'll talk to him, see what he has to say."

"All right," Tamia murmured.

After asking her a few more routine questions, the officers rose to leave.

"If you think of anything else, or if you receive any more threatening notes, please don't hesitate to call either one of us." Castillo patted the front pocket of his shirt. "Crap. I'm all out of cards."

"I have some." Greene pulled out a card and handed it to Tamia.

"Thanks." She glanced down at his name—and froze.

Keyshawn Greene.

Keyshawn . . . *Honey's boyfriend?*

It couldn't be.

"Is something wrong, Miss Luke?"

Tamia looked up, meeting Officer Greene's curious gaze. The fine hairs lifted on the back of her neck.

He frowned. "Are you okay?"

"I'm fine." She set his card down on the coffee table, then walked him and his partner to the front door. "Thanks for coming. I appreciate it."

"We'll be in touch," they promised before leaving.

As soon as Tamia locked the door, her phone rang, startling her.

Pulse thudding, she walked over to the foyer table and cautiously picked up the phone. She felt a surge of relief when she saw Shanell's number.

Exhaling a shaky breath, she pressed the talk button. "Hey."

"Hey, girl," Shanell greeted her cheerfully. "What's going on?"

"You don't even wanna know," Tamia muttered, raking trembling fingers through her hair as she returned to the living room.

"Why? What happened?"

Tamia sighed heavily. "Someone left a threatening note on my doorstep."

"*What!* What did it say?"

As Tamia relayed the message, goose bumps raced across her skin.

"What the hell is that supposed to mean?" Shanell wondered.

Tamia shook her head. "I wish I knew."

"Damn." Shanell sounded worried. "Did you call the police?"

"Yeah. They just left." Tamia picked up Officer Greene's card and frowned at it, speculating.

"You need to pack a bag and come stay at my house," Shanell told her.

Tamia smiled wanly. "Thanks, girl, but I don't want to impose. Besides, aren't your parents coming for Christmas?"

"They don't arrive until Tuesday. And you're not imposing."

Tamia glanced around the apartment. There was no use pretending she felt safe there. She didn't.

"Tamia," Shanell growled warningly. "Don't make me come after you."

Tamia needed no more convincing. "I'm on my way."

Chapter 21
Brandon

"Brandon! There you are, darling." Gwen Chambers strode purposefully through the crowded lobby of Redeemed Life Ministries. Her hair was elegantly coiffed, and she wore a string of pearls with a tailored plum skirt suit and matching pumps. Whether she was garbed in designer clothes or her judge's robe, she was always the epitome of sophistication and class.

"Hey, Mom," Brandon greeted her as she reached him and Cynthia.

"Hey, yourself." Gwen embraced him warmly and kissed his cheek, then did the same to Cynthia before drawing back to look them over. Her dark eyes gleamed with satisfaction and approval. "You two make such a beautiful couple. I can't *wait* for your wedding day."

Cynthia beamed. "That makes two of us, Mrs. Chambers."

"You mean three," Gwen corrected, deliberately smoothing a hand down Brandon's silver tie.

He gave her a brief smile before glancing around. "Good turnout."

"Good? It's fantastic. We're all very pleased."

The bustling lobby was filled with prominent politicians, business leaders, community activists, and clergymen of all faiths and denominations. Reporters roamed around interviewing attendees, snapping pictures, and feeding live coverage to their respective television stations. The event had been billed as a prayer breakfast, but everyone knew it was nothing more than a political forum to showcase Bernard

Chambers's gubernatorial campaign—which was why he'd received the honor of delivering the keynote address.

"Where's Dad?" Brandon asked, scanning the crowd.

"He and Cynthia's parents are speaking with Bishop Jakes. You know he's doing the opening prayer. Anyway, I stepped away to track you and Cynthia down. I have several people I'd like you to meet."

"Of course you do," Brandon said wryly.

"Oh, hush." His mother laughed, affectionately patting his cheek. "Thank you for showing up on time. I know I can't expect your brother and sister to do the same."

"Just be glad they're coming," Brandon drawled, knowing how much Beau and Brooke despised these social and political functions. He wasn't too crazy about them either, but he understood that they came with the territory when your last name was Chambers.

"Don't forget our holiday dinner at the governor's mansion tomorrow evening," Gwen reminded Brandon. "Your father and I want you and Cynthia to ride with us to Austin."

"We'd *love* to," Cynthia gushed before Brandon could open his mouth.

Gwen smiled with pleasure. "We're all spending the night there and returning on Monday."

Brandon shook his head. "Cynthia and I have to work on Monday."

"No, you don't. Your father already cleared it with Mort." Gwen was referring to Mort Chernoff, one of the firm's founding partners and Bernard's longtime friend.

Brandon frowned at his mother. "In case you haven't noticed, I'm not a child who needs a note from home to get out of going to school. I'm a grown man with a job and responsibilities—"

"Darling, the governor and his wife insisted that we spend the night at the mansion. It would be rude to refuse their hospitality. Besides—Oh, look, there's Congresswoman Lee." Gwen smiled warmly and waved to an attractive black woman standing across the lobby. "I'm so glad Sheila was able to make it. Let me go say hello to her while you two mingle." She patted their cheeks and smiled before moving off.

Brandon watched her leave, his eyes narrowed with annoyance.

"Your mother's right," Cynthia said. "Turning down the governor's invitation *would* be rude."

"Surprise, surprise," Brandon muttered sarcastically.

"What?"

He glared at her. "Is there anything you and my mother *don't* agree on?"

"What's that supposed to mean?"

"It means you and Gwen Chambers can bond all you want, but she's not the one you're marrying and coming home to every night, know what I'm saying?"

"No," Cynthia said archly, "what *are* you saying?"

Brandon snorted. "It's not complicated, sweetheart, so I'll let you piece that one together. Oh, and last I checked, you're an associate at the firm and I'm a partner. So if I say we're going to work on Monday, guess where we're going?"

Cynthia smirked at him. "Pulling rank, are we?"

"Yup." He cocked a brow, unapologetic.

She grumbled under her breath, "Someone's really smelling himself."

Brandon smiled narrowly, satisfied that he'd put her ass in check. He'd deal with his mother later.

From across the lobby, someone called out a greeting to him, which he returned with a nod and a smile before murmuring to Cynthia, "Time to socialize."

With Cynthia glued to his side, he moved through the crowd shaking hands, slapping backs, and making small talk with everyone who stopped him. Doing her best impersonation of Michelle Obama, Cynthia smiled charmingly, laughed at corny jokes, asked all the right questions and gave the right answers.

Eventually they made their way inside the grand banquet hall, where they were seated at the head table with their parents, T. D. Jakes and his wife, and other VIP attendees.

The catered breakfast featured a lavish selection of crêpes, eggs Benedict, French toast, omelets, and fresh fruits. Cynthia practically sat on Brandon's lap as she fed him forkfuls of food while her mother looked on with unconcealed delight. In contrast, Joseph Yarbrough watched them with a guarded expression, making it clear to Brandon that he hadn't completely forgiven him for abandoning his daughter at the altar.

Brandon knew he'd eventually have to make amends with the bishop, but right now it wasn't high on his list of priorities. Staying sane was.

During the opening remarks by some renowned rabbi, Brandon found his gaze wandering around the banquet hall. He spotted his brother and sister seated with other dignitaries at a nearby table.

Anyone observing Beau and Brooke's rapt expressions might have been fooled into thinking they were totally into what the esteemed rabbi was saying.

But Brandon knew better. Though he couldn't tell from this distance, he knew his siblings were texting each other back and forth beneath the linen-covered table.

When his own phone vibrated, he reached inside his pocket and discreetly pulled it out. He wasn't surprised to see a message from Beau.

Don't bore us to death when you get up there to speak.

Brandon smirked as he tapped out a reply. Just listen and learn, boy.

Beau wrote back. LOL.

Brandon smiled, returning his attention to the speaker.

Moments later he received another text.

Awww, look at you and wifey. Can't you just feel that chain tightening around your neck?

Brandon frowned, contemplating his brother's words.

Beau had the luxury of teasing Brandon about his pending nuptials because he didn't have to walk in his shoes. Beau would never carry the burden of being the firstborn. He'd never have to be the mature, responsible, dutiful son who nobly sacrificed his own needs and desires for some greater good. Beau's broad shoulders would never bear the full weight of their father's hopes, expectations, and dreams.

These thoughts ran through Brandon's mind as he sat there staring at his phone, anger and resentment welling inside him.

Fuck you, he typed back.

He watched as Beau received his acerbic reply and grinned, then leaned over to show the message to Brooke. She cupped a hand over her mouth to smother her laughter.

Brandon shook his head, dismissing them as he returned his attention to the phone. He was deleting Beau's obnoxious messages when the touch screen suddenly froze on him.

He frowned.

After several seconds he began pushing buttons, trying to reactivate the phone.

And then suddenly, without warning, there was Tamia.

Brandon sucked in a breath like he'd been punched in the gut.

It was a photo he'd taken of her that night in his office. She was lounging in his chair with her feet propped up on the desk, legs crossed at the ankles, wearing nothing but a sexy pair of stilettos.

Brandon swallowed tightly as he stared at the screen, his eyes tracing every inch of her smooth caramel skin, every curve of her luscious body. He felt himself drowning in her sultry beauty . . . her hypnotic gaze . . . her captivating smile.

God, that smile . . .

"What're you doing?" Cynthia hissed.

Brandon glanced up to find her glaring accusingly at Tamia's naked picture.

"Glitch," he murmured by way of explanation.

Cynthia twisted her lips, giving him the side eye.

He reluctantly clicked off the photo, turned off the phone, and stuffed it back into his pocket. As the rabbi finished speaking, Brandon grabbed his glass and downed the rest of his mimosa, wishing it were Johnnie Walker.

Before long, Bishop Yarbrough was at the podium waxing eloquent about his friendship with Bernard Chambers. Then it was Brandon's turn to get up there and address the crowd before he introduced his father as the keynote speaker.

Standing at the podium, he spoke from his heart about the man who'd raised him. He described a relentless taskmaster who'd demanded excellence from him and pushed him to be the best, because all the money in the world could only take a black man so far. He fondly reminisced about sneaking into his father's study at night and climbing into his lap to hear stories about the ancestors who'd come before him. He called Bernard the guardian of the Chamber legacy, the anchor of his family, a faithful husband and a devoted father. He talked about his accomplishments as lieutenant governor, and he spoke passionately of Bernard's vision for unifying the people of Texas and leading them into an era of unprecedented economic prosperity.

Brandon delivered the speech without notes because the words were pouring out of him, springing from a well of deep conviction.

By the time he introduced his father, the audience was on its feet cheering and clapping loudly, his mother was dabbing tears from her eyes, and Cynthia was beaming from ear to ear. Even Beau and Brooke were visibly moved.

Bernard strode toward Brandon with a broad smile on his face, his eyes glowing with pride and adoration. As he and Brandon shared a strong hug, Bernard whispered in his ear, "Don't think all this excitement is for me. You're a natural, son. You had them eating out of the palm of your hand."

Brandon merely smiled.

But then his father took to the podium and exhorted, "How about another round of applause for my wonderful son?"

The applause was thunderous. Almost deafening.

As Brandon looked out into the sea of smiling faces, he felt somewhat dazed.

His father winked at him. *Told you*, he mouthed.

Brandon couldn't get off the stage fast enough.

Chapter 22

Tamia

Tamia sat at the foot of the guest bed with her gaze riveted to the television, where Brandon had just ended his electrifying speech. Her heart was thumping, and her skin was covered with goose bumps beneath her robe.

She'd always known what a gifted orator Brandon was. She'd watched him deliver masterful closing arguments in court, including the one that had sealed her acquittal.

Last year she'd accompanied him to a glitzy bar association function where he'd given the best presentation of the night.

She knew he had the chops to wow a crowd.

But this speech had been on a whole different level.

It was the kind of speech that launched political careers and catapulted one onto the national stage.

Brandon had always insisted that he didn't share his father's political aspirations. But after his performance this morning, it was blindingly obvious to Tamia that he was born to serve in a leadership capacity that went far beyond biglaw.

She watched as the camera panned away from the podium to show Brandon returning to his table. Cynthia stood waiting for him in her silk shift dress that perfectly matched the color of his tie. As he reached her, she threw her arms around his neck and smooched him on the lips.

Tamia had seen enough.

Grabbing the remote control, she punched off the television just as a gentle knock sounded on the door.

"Tamia?" Shanell called tentatively. "You up?"

"Yeah," she mumbled.

Shanell slowly opened the door and poked her head into the room. Noting Tamia's gloomy expression and the remote control clutched in her hand, she put two and two together and sighed. "You saw the speech."

Tamia nodded.

"Damn. I was hoping you'd missed it." Shanell heaved another sigh. "It was hella good, wasn't it?"

"It was." A faint smile touched Tamia's mouth. "Brandon's always had a complicated relationship with his father, but I know he meant every word he said about him."

"I could definitely tell. If his father didn't already have my vote, that speech sure as hell would have sold me." Shanell smiled, folding her arms across her chest as she leaned on the doorjamb. She wore a satin bonnet, one of her husband's army T-shirts, and gray leggings. "I was just about to make breakfast. Got any requests?"

"Nah, girl. I'm not even hungry." Tamia pulled her legs up to her chest and rested her chin on her knees, absently studying the French pedicure she and Shanell had gotten yesterday while they'd been out running errands and doing last-minute Christmas shopping.

"Did you sleep okay?" Shanell asked.

Tamia nodded. "Better than I did the first night." Thoughts of the disturbing note had kept her awake and on edge, her mind churning out an endless loop of questions and theories.

Officer Greene had called yesterday to tell her that he and his partner were still reviewing the security tapes from the building, but so far they had no leads. He'd promised to give her another call after they questioned Lester McCray.

"Mark and I are going to Sam's Club after breakfast," Shanell announced. "Do you want anything?"

"No, thanks." Tamia hesitated. "Actually, I was thinking about heading back home."

Shanell frowned. "Why? You got a problem with my accommodations?"

Tamia laughed. "Stop it. You know there's nothing wrong with your house. Or have you forgotten that I pretended to live here while I was dating Brandon?"

Shanell snorted. "As if I could ever forget. You had me parking in the garage and hiding family pictures every time he came over. It's a miracle we were able to keep up that crazy charade for as long as we did. Anyway, you don't need to be going back to your apartment, not while some lunatic is out there sending you threatening notes."

Tamia sighed. "But I told you I don't want to impose. You need to be getting ready for your parents—"

"Girl, please. You act like I'm hosting Barack and Michelle. It's just my parents. They've been here before—they know their way around the house and they know how to ask for whatever they need. Now stop talking about leaving, put on some damn clothes, and come help me make breakfast."

With that, Shanell left, shutting the door behind her.

Shaking her head in amused exasperation, Tamia slid off the bed and trudged toward the adjoining bathroom to brush her teeth. She'd just reached the doorway when her phone rang from the nightstand.

She turned and hurried back across the room to catch the call, anxious for another update from Officer Greene or Castillo.

"Hello?" she answered.

"Good morning," drawled a deep voice. "Hope I didn't wake you."

Her pulse tripped.

Dominic.

"No. I was already awake." Tamia sat on the bed. "What's up?"

"I wanted to know if you'd had a chance to reconsider my invitation."

"What invitation?"

"To spend the weekend at the Ehrlichs' B and B. Remember, I suggested going undercover as a couple to find out what the other guests really think of the place?"

"I remember," Tamia said dryly. "I also remember turning you down."

Dominic chuckled. "I was hoping you'd had a change of heart. So are Buddy and Grace. They're even holding a suite for us."

Tamia guffawed. "They are not."

"Are, too. They liked my suggestion, and they really want you to experience the place for yourself."

Tamia bit her lower lip, wavering.

"Come on, Tamia," Dominic softly cajoled. "You saw the pictures. Beautiful rooms, scenic views. You can go to the spa and get a massage, or take a relaxing dip in the heated pool. . . ."

Tamia couldn't deny that the offer sounded tempting. And getting away for the weekend would help take her mind off her troubles.

Or make them worse.

She frowned at the thought. "If I agree to go—and that's a big *if*—we can't share the same bed. You can have the sofa or the floor, I don't care. But you're not sleeping with me, Dominic. I'm serious. Those days are over."

He fell silent.

Tamia waited, eyes narrowed.

"All right," he acquiesced with obvious reluctance. "We don't have to share a bed if you don't want to."

"I *don't* want to." Her tone was emphatic.

"As you wish. Should I tell the Ehrlichs to expect us?"

Tamia hesitated, closing her eyes. Her mind flashed on an image of Cynthia looking like the proud wifey as she'd kissed Brandon after his speech.

Brandon was going places, and Cynthia was the lucky woman who would accompany him on his journey.

"Tamia?" Dominic prompted.

She inhaled a deep breath and let it out slowly. "Yes. Tell them we're coming."

"Wonderful." Dominic sounded beyond pleased. "I'll pick you up in two hours."

Tamia didn't tell Shanell where she was going.

She knew her friend wouldn't approve, and she didn't feel like hearing a damn lecture. So she waited until Shanell and Mark left the house before she made her escape, leaving a note explaining that she had to help Honey with a personal emergency.

When she pulled into the parking garage at her apartment building, Dominic was already waiting for her, chilling behind the wheel of a pewter Rolls Royce Phantom. Tamia felt decidedly self-conscious as she parked her old Honda Accord near the five-hundred-thousand-dollar whip.

She climbed out of her car and watched as Dominic stretched from the Phantom and sauntered toward her. He wore a chocolate leather bomber, khaki trousers, and Ralph Lauren boots. His fade was smooth and tight, and his goatee was freshly sculpted.

He looked so fine and sexy that Tamia's mouth watered. *Damn, damn, damn!*

"Hello," Dominic drawled, stopping before her. "I was afraid you got cold feet."

Tamia swallowed hard, suddenly feeling as nervous as a virgin on her first date. "Sorry. I was over at a friend's house."

"Do you need to run upstairs and pack?"

"No. I'm ready."

Dominic smiled, his heavy-lidded eyes roaming over her. She wore a short fitted jacket over a V-neck sweater, skintight jeans, and peep-toe suede ankle boots.

As Dominic completed his slow perusal of her body and licked his lips, her nipples hardened.

Nothing had changed. He turned her on as much today as he had the day she'd met him. What made it even worse was that she knew what the man was working with. She knew what he could do to her with the sensual stroke of his tongue, the deep thrust of his dick.

She knew he could have her whipped all over again.

Be strong, Tamia. Keep your pussy on lock no matter what!

"Ready to go?" Dominic murmured.

She nodded, turning away to pop the trunk of her car.

Dominic transferred her small suitcase to the trunk of the Phantom, then opened the passenger door for her.

Sliding into the luxury vehicle was like slipping into a mink coat. Tamia couldn't help admiring the sumptuous leather seats, decadent wood trim, art deco lighting, and fancy navigation system. She felt the same sense of wonder every time she rode in Brandon's Maybach.

Dominic climbed behind the wheel and slanted her a lazy smile. "This is a first."

"What?"

"You've never been inside my car before."

Tamia shook her head slowly. "You're right. I haven't."

She'd always met him at his penthouse for their secret trysts. They'd never gone on any dates and had rarely been seen together in public. Their St. Croix rendezvous had been a complete disaster even before his wife caught them fucking in their hotel room shower.

Tamia grimaced, her face heating with shame at the memory.

"We're gonna have fun this weekend," Dominic told her, as if he'd read her mind. "I know we've got a lot of baggage between us, but I don't want you thinking about that. Just relax and enjoy yourself."

Easier said than done, Tamia thought, sending him a wry look. "Weren't we supposed to wear disguises so no one will recognize us?"

He nodded. "Got it covered. I brought Afro wigs, psychedelic glasses, and a fake mustache for me to wear."

Tamia laughed. "You did not!"

"Nah, I didn't." Dominic grinned at her. "No one seemed to recognize us at the restaurant the other day, so I figured we have a good shot at keeping our cover. But since we're supposed to be an engaged couple—" He reached inside his leather jacket and pulled out a black velvet box.

Tamia stilled, watching as he removed a diamond engagement ring set in platinum. When he held it up, the princess-cut solitaire twinkled in the morning sunlight.

Her stunned gaze swung from the ring to Dominic's face. "What . . . how . . ." She trailed off, at a loss for words.

Dominic smiled. "Give me your hand."

"Why?"

"So I can put this ring on your finger."

"What? Why?"

He gave her an amused look. "Because we're supposed to be engaged, remember?"

Tamia gulped a shaky breath, then reluctantly eased her hand forward. Her pulse drummed as she watched Dominic slide the platinum band onto her finger.

He smiled with satisfaction. "Good. It fits."

Tamia shook her head, staring incredulously at him. "I can't believe you just strolled into a jewelry store and bought a diamond ring."

He chuckled. "As opposed to what? Buying one from a gumball machine?"

"Seriously, Dominic. This ring had to cost tens of thousands—"

"Is that supposed to mean something to me?" he interjected, starting the ignition.

Tamia watched as he smoothly backed out of the parking space, steering the Phantom with a one-handed finesse that reminded her of the way Brandon drove.

"I realize you have money—"

Dominic gave a bark of laughter. "Damn, woman! Are you for real?"

"What?"

"You must be the only woman I know who'd have such a damn problem with receiving a ring from Tiffany. Aren't diamonds supposed to be a girl's best friend?"

Tamia smiled sheepishly. "Well, yeah, but—"

"But nothing. Yo, fo' real, darlin', you need to relax. Stop worrying 'bout how much the damn ring cost and just enjoy it. 'E look good an yo."

She blinked at the Crucian dialect. "What?"

"The ring. It looks good on you." He winked at her. "Tell me you don't agree."

Tamia could do no such thing.

"Uh-huh." Dominic chuckled knowingly. "I thought so."

Tamia grinned, admiring her new bling as she settled into her seat for the ninety-minute drive to the ranch.

As they left downtown and got on I-59, she noticed that they were heading in the wrong direction.

"Where are we going?" she asked Dominic.

"I need to make a stop first."

"Where?"

He chuckled at her suspicious tone. "I wanted to check out some model homes in Sugar Land. It's the only chance I'll get before the end of the weekend."

"I didn't know you were looking for a new house," Tamia remarked.

Dominic nodded. "I've been staying at the penthouse ever since

Isabel died. I couldn't go back to living at our house after . . ." He trailed off, his expression clouding.

Tamia lowered her gaze to her lap, awash with guilt and sorrow at the reminder that her sister had murdered his wife.

As a heavy silence lapsed between them, she stared out the window.

"Anyway," Dominic continued after a few minutes, "I wanted to see what's on the market, and I could use a woman's input. You don't mind, do you?"

How could she?

"Not at all," she murmured.

Dominic drove to Sugar Land, steering through a gated entrance to enter an exclusive subdivision that featured custom waterfront mansions.

The woman who greeted them at the door to the front office was all smiles. Because she'd seen them pull up in a Rolls, she naturally assumed that they could afford to buy a home in the upscale community.

She handed them a glossy brochure with her business card and cheerfully talked their heads off before they were saved by the arrival of new customers.

Dominic quickly ushered Tamia from the office, both of them laughing as they headed to the first model home.

The moment they stepped through the front door, Tamia's eyes widened at the sight of a grand foyer with a winding staircase and a stunning glass sculpture suspended from the ceiling.

"Wow," she breathed.

Dominic nodded, casually glancing around. "Nice."

Tamia snorted incredulously. "Are you kidding me? *Nice?*"

He grinned at her. "*Very* nice."

She laughed, impulsively grabbing his hand and leading him toward the gourmet kitchen, where they admired gleaming hardwood floors, marble countertops, ultramodern appliances, and custom cabinets.

On the second landing they entered a mammoth master bedroom suite with double chandeliers, a clotheshorse's dream closet, and a humongous bathroom outfitted with travertine marble and a luxurious spa shower.

Dominic smiled indulgently as Tamia squealed and oohed and aahed over everything, unable to contain her excitement. This mansion was beyond anything she'd ever dreamed of owning—and she'd dreamed pretty big.

As she and Dominic wandered from one opulently furnished room to another, she couldn't help fantasizing about what it would be like to call such a place home, to wake up every morning in the lap of such luxury.

And when she caught Dominic staring quietly at her, she found herself imagining that they lived there together . . . as husband and wife.

That was when she knew it was time to go.

"So," Dominic drawled, following her from the last bedroom, "what do you think of the house?"

Tamia smiled wryly. "I think it's pretty obvious what *I* think. But it doesn't matter. What do *you* think?"

"I like it. It definitely has potential."

She laughed. "Talk about an understatement!"

As they neared the top of the staircase, Tamia heard voices coming from downstairs. Peering over the wrought-iron banister, she saw that another couple had entered the house.

Not just any couple.

Brandon and Cynthia.

Her heart plummeted.

As she stumbled, Dominic caught her arm to keep her from tumbling down the stairs and breaking her neck.

Face flushed, stomach churning, she watched as Brandon and Cynthia moved through the foyer. They were with another man, presumably their Realtor. He had skin the color of butter pecan, flawlessly sculpted eyebrows, and beautiful dreadlocks pulled back into a ponytail. He was immaculately dressed in a cranberry blazer with fine wool trousers, while Brandon wore a crewneck Rocawear sweater, dark jeans, and black Timbs, his rugged masculinity even more pronounced in the presence of his ponytailed companion.

Cynthia and the Realtor walked together while Brandon followed more slowly. He seemed unfazed by his opulent surroundings—which was no surprise. He'd grown up in a palatial eight-bedroom estate in

River Oaks. As impressive as this mansion was, it couldn't hold a candle to the childhood home he would eventually inherit.

Cynthia gushed, "Look at that staircase! It's absolutely—" She broke off at the sight of Tamia and Dominic standing at the top of the landing.

Following the direction of her shocked gaze, Brandon looked up—and froze.

Tamia nervously watched as the muscles in his face tightened into a mask of cold fury.

"Well, isn't this a surprise?" Cynthia exclaimed delightedly, her voice bouncing off the high ceilings.

Tamia didn't resist when Dominic gently curved an arm around her waist. Her legs were so rubbery she didn't think she could make it down the staircase without some assistance.

It was the longest descent of her life.

As she and Dominic finally reached the first floor, Brandon glared at Dominic with barely leashed violence.

Sensing his tension, Cynthia stepped in front of him, a move so subtle Tamia was probably the only one who noticed it.

"Wassup, Brandon," Dominic drawled mockingly. "Caught your speech on TV this morning. You did Daddy proud."

As Brandon's lips curled up into a snarl, Cynthia smoothly intervened, thrusting her hand toward Dominic. "Hello. I don't think we've ever met. Cynthia Yarbrough."

Dominic shook her hand, a lazy smile curving his mouth. "Dominic Archer."

"Nice to meet you, Dominic."

"The pleasure's mine," he murmured, smirking at Brandon.

Cynthia turned to the other man beside her. He'd been watching the unfolding drama with unabashed fascination, looking so entertained Tamia half expected him to pull up a chair and whip out a bag of popcorn.

"This is our Realtor, Marcellus Tremont," Cynthia introduced him. "Marcellus, this is Tamia Lu—"

"I know who she is." The man beamed at Tamia. "Your friend Shanell told me all about you, said you were thinking about selling your old house."

"Yes, that's right." Tamia smiled, reaching out to shake his hand. "It's nice to meet—"

"Oh my God!" Cynthia squealed, grabbing Tamia's hand and staring at the twinkling diamond on her finger. "Is this what I *think* it is?"

Heat suffused Tamia's face. She'd forgotten all about the fake engagement ring.

As she discreetly attempted to withdraw her hand, Cynthia tightened her grip and exclaimed excitedly to Brandon, "Baby, look at this rock. Can you believe it? They're *engaged!*"

Brandon stared incredulously at the diamond ring, then looked at Tamia, his eyes filled with raw hurt and betrayal.

She shook her head. "Brandon, it's—" She broke off as he turned and stalked from the house, slamming the front door hard enough to rattle the glass sculpture hanging from the ceiling.

In the awkward silence that followed, Marcellus raised his eyebrows at Tamia.

She looked at Dominic, who merely smiled.

"Well," Cynthia said with forced brightness, "I guess that's our cue to move on to the next model home."

"Um, yeah, that might be a good idea," Marcellus agreed.

Tucking her arm through his, Cynthia gave Tamia and Dominic a sickeningly sweet smile. "It was a pleasure running into you two. I always thought you were just perfect for each other. Congratulations on making it official."

Tamia gritted her teeth. "We're not—"

Cynthia winked. "Happy house hunting."

As she and Marcellus headed out the front door, he glanced back at Tamia and mouthed, *Give me a call, girlfriend!*

Chapter 23

Tamia

"How long are you gonna give me the silent treatment?"

Tamia had been glowering out the window at rolling pastures dotted with cattle and horses. Hearing Dominic's question, she snapped her head around to sneer at him. "Oh, so now you have a problem with silence?"

He frowned. "What's that supposed to mean?"

"It means you had no problem remaining *silent* and letting Brandon and Cynthia assume that we're engaged."

Dominic snorted. "How is it my fault that they assumed that?"

"*Are you serious?*" Tamia waved her hand in his face. "*You're* the one who put this damn rock on my finger!"

"That may be true," Dominic conceded, "but I don't see how it was my responsibility to let them know what was really up. I didn't see *you* grabbing a bullhorn to set the record straight."

"I tried—"

"Not hard enough."

Tamia bristled, mutinously folding her arms across her chest. "That's not the point."

"What *is* the point?" Dominic challenged. "I mean, why the hell does it even matter whether they think we're engaged? *They're* engaged!"

"I know that," Tamia said tightly.

"Do you really? Because every time we run into Brandon, you

act like you have something to apologize for when *he's* the one who's marrying someone else."

Tamia shook her head, glaring through the windshield. "You don't understand."

"No? Then why don't you make me understand?"

"Why should I?" she burst out furiously. "You're not my man, Dominic! I don't owe you any fucking explanations!"

"You don't owe him any, either," Dominic shot back. "So stop acting like you do."

"I can't!"

"Why the hell not?"

"Because I don't wanna hurt him, okay? He may be engaged to someone else, but I still love him, and it kills me to cause him any pain. But I don't expect you to understand that," she said with bitter scorn. "You don't know the first damn thing about wanting to protect someone you love. You don't even know what love is."

Dominic's face hardened. "Maybe I don't." He raked her with a scathing glance. "If this is what it looks like, you can have that shit."

Tamia recoiled as if he'd slapped her across the mouth.

As he lapsed into stony silence, she glared out the window, wondering what the hell had possessed her to agree to spend the weekend with him.

"April twenty-first."

Tamia turned from the window, eyes narrowed on his face. "What?"

"That's the date of their wedding. April twenty-first."

Tamia's heart twisted.

Dominic met her wounded gaze. "I take it you didn't know."

She swallowed painfully but didn't respond.

"They were interviewed after the prayer breakfast," Dominic elaborated. "The reporter congratulated them on their engagement and asked them if they'd set a date. They have. April twenty-first." He smirked at Tamia. "Guess that gives you four months to find out if love really *does* conquer all."

Tamia glowered at him.

He chuckled.

Seething with anger and frustration, she twisted the engagement ring off her finger and unceremoniously chucked it into a cup holder.

"I'd hold on to that if I were you," Dominic advised. "Might be the only ring you get for a while."

That did it.

Tamia reached over and slapped him across the face. "Fuck you," she spat.

He grinned insolently, rubbing his jaw. "I hope you will, love. I hope you will."

The Ehrlichs' bed-and-breakfast was even more beautiful than the photos had depicted. Surrounded by rolling hills and lakes, the ranch sat on twenty acres of lushly landscaped grounds that featured rustic cottages with wraparound porches.

The Ehrlichs awaited Tamia and Dominic inside the lobby, where the wood-beamed ceilings and cozy furnishings set a warm, welcoming tone.

Tamia was impressed—and that was before she and Dominic were escorted to a luxuriously appointed suite with a private balcony that offered panoramic views of the valley. A fire glowed in the fireplace, and the mantel was adorned with potted poinsettias and glass bowls filled with frosted pinecones and holly berries.

"Wow," Tamia exclaimed, looking around the room. "This is gorgeous, Grace."

Her hostess beamed with pleasure. "Thank you, Tamia. I'm so glad you and Dominic could make it."

Tamia smiled. "Thanks for having us. We appreciate your hospitality."

"We certainly do," Dominic chimed in, standing too close to Tamia.

Grace smiled warmly at them. "Every day at three we serve fresh-baked cookies, eggnog, and hot cider in the lobby. It gives us an opportunity to mingle with our guests and answer any questions they may have. After you two get settled in, you're more than welcome to join us."

"Great," Tamia and Dominic chorused. "We will."

"Wonderful. See you then."

As soon as Grace left, Tamia wandered into the private bathroom to look around. Taking inventory of the double sinks, spa shower, and Jacuzzi, she nodded approvingly. So far so good.

Returning to the room, she found Dominic sitting on the king-size bed.

Her eyes narrowed. "Don't get too comfortable," she warned. "You're not sleeping there, remember?"

He grinned. "Come on, love," he cajoled, running a hand over the sumptuously thick duvet. "See how nice and big this bed is? There's more than enough room for both of us."

"I don't think so." Tamia pointed toward the seating area. "That sofa looks real nice and comfy—and it has your name written all over it."

"Oh, I don't know about that," Dominic drawled, leaning back on his elbows. "This bed seems to be pronouncing my name *just* fine."

"Then you need to get your hearing checked," Tamia retorted.

Dominic laughed, rising from the bed. She watched as he sauntered across the room and opened the louvered plantation doors, then stepped out onto the balcony.

She followed him.

As they stood admiring the scenic view, Dominic marveled, "This place is off da chain. I can't understand why it's not more popular."

"It's definitely a hidden gem," Tamia agreed. "We'll have to do something about the 'hidden' part."

Dominic slanted her an amused look. "Are you gonna be able to relax and enjoy yourself this weekend? Or are you gonna be inspecting everything and looking for flaws like some undercover hotel critic?"

"I won't be looking for flaws." Tamia paused. "Well . . . I *did* bring a pair of white gloves to check the furniture for dust."

Dominic gaped at her, realized she was teasing, and burst out laughing.

Tamia grinned, resting her arms on the banister as a soft breeze washed over her face. It was a gorgeous winter afternoon, balmy for December.

Dominic smiled, watching her. "I'm glad you're speaking to me again. That ride up here was the longest damn ride of my life."

"Good," Tamia retorted. "Serves you right for being such an ass."

"I know." His voice softened. "I apologize for the things I said to you. I was trying to make a point, but I didn't do a very good job of it."

"No. You didn't."

Dominic grimaced. "I'm sorry for hurting your feelings. Can you forgive me?"

Tamia silently regarded him, eyes narrowed with suspicion. "I'm not used to this."

"What?"

"Having you apologize to me. You're really serious about this whole 'turning over a new leaf' thing, aren't you?"

He smiled. "I'm very serious. I wanna be a better man, Tamia. Better than the one you met nine months ago."

She held his gaze for a long moment, then glanced away with a small smile. "Apology accepted."

"Thank you." He shifted closer to her. "I don't like it when you're mad at me."

"Oh, please," Tamia scoffed, rolling her eyes.

"It's true," Dominic insisted. "You know I've always had a thing for you."

"You had a thing for Mystique," Tamia corrected.

"I still do," he admitted, playfully bumping his shoulder against hers. "But Tamia's no slouch either. In fact, I think she's pretty damn special. If she was *my* woman, I'd never let her go."

Tamia turned her head to stare at him.

He stared back.

After a long stretch of silence, Tamia stepped back self-consciously and smiled.

"Come on, *Dexter*," she said, calling him by the alias he'd chosen, "let's go find some guests to mingle with."

He smiled. "As you wish, *Zoe*."

They headed down to the lobby, where they spent the next two hours playing the role of a man and woman who were crazy about each other. They sat together and shared a mug of hot spiced cider while a cozy fire crackled in the hearth and lights twinkled from a soaring Christmas tree. Two white couples, one from San Antonio and the other from Killeen, joined them.

They were warm and friendly, and because they didn't seem to recognize Tamia or Dominic, she found herself relaxing and enjoying their company. She asked them the typical getting-to-know-you questions, and was pleased when they expressed what a wonderful time they were having at the B and B.

When the questions were directed to her and Dominic, Tamia let him do most of the talking. She secretly marveled as he embellished details of their "engagement," improvising with an ease that reminded her what an accomplished liar he was.

But she couldn't deny that he was also funny and irresistibly charming. Nestled beside him on the sofa, she didn't mind the heavy warmth of his arm around her shoulders or the heat of his muscular thigh pressed to hers. She didn't mind the way he absently played with her hair, sifting his fingers through the tapered layers at the back of her neck. And when she offered him the mug of cider and watched him sip from the same spot where her mouth had been, it felt good.

It shouldn't have.

But, God help her, it did.

Chapter 24

Brandon

Brandon sat in the solitary darkness of his study.

He wore a wifebeater over his jeans because he hadn't changed since returning home that afternoon. His feet were propped up on the desk, his Timbs resting next to an empty bottle of Crown Royal.

His eyes were closed, head tipped back as he quietly puffed on a Cuban cigar, thinking and brooding.

Tamia and Dominic.

Engaged.

It was impossible.

Inconceivable.

Yet there they were, touring model homes together.

And there *she* was, wearing another man's ring.

The ring Brandon should have given her.

His tortured musings were interrupted by a sudden knock on the door.

"Brandon?" Cynthia called worriedly. "You've been in there since we got home. Is everything okay?"

Brandon shook his head slowly, confounded by the question. How could everything be okay when the woman he loved was marrying some worthless motherfucker who didn't deserve her?

"Brandon?" Cynthia tried the doorknob. "Baby, the door's locked."

"I know," Brandon murmured without opening his eyes. "I'm the one who locked it."

Cynthia huffed out a breath. "Well, how much longer do you plan to stay in there? It's almost seven o'clock. Your baby and I are hungry. Can we go out for dinner or pick up something?"

Brandon took a lazy drag on his cigar and blew a cloud of smoke into the air.

"Brandon?"

He shook his head slowly. "Not now, Cynthia."

"But—"

"I said not now."

He heard her muttering under her breath. Then she spun and marched away, her bare feet slapping against the floor.

Seconds later she reconsidered and came back.

"I just want you to know that you made a fool of yourself today," she fumed through the door. "You made a fool of *both* of us when you stormed out of the house like that."

Brandon opened his eyes, slowly removing the cigar from his mouth.

"She's moving on, Brandon—"

"Get away from that door, Cynthia," he warned in a low voice.

"Did you hear what I just said? She's moving on! So you need to get the hell over her. You hear me? You need to—"

"GET THE FUCK AWAY FROM THAT DOOR!"

Cynthia let out a helpless whimper of frustration before stomping off down the hallway. This time she didn't return.

But her words lingered to taunt Brandon, fueling his simmering rage.

Because he knew she was right. He *did* need to get over Tamia.

The thing was . . . he couldn't.

And he couldn't stand by and let her marry another man either. He wouldn't.

Brandon stared at the ceiling, the cigar clenched between his teeth as smoke curled around him.

He knew all about obsession. He'd seen what it could do, how it could destroy. He'd encountered many crimes of passion in his line of work—violent crimes committed by ordinary, law-abiding people who got pushed to the edge of sanity and snapped.

He never thought he'd become a victim. Never thought he'd become enslaved to a woman.

But he had.

Look at your eyes, Brandon. . . . I don't even know who or what you are anymore. . . . You're possessed. . . .

Possessed . . . possessed . . .

Brandon swung his legs down from the desk and opened the top drawer to retrieve a lone key, which he used to unlock the bottom drawer. He reached inside, his fingers closing around the butt of a Glock nine-millimeter.

He slowly pulled out the gun and laid it down on his desk. Then he sat there and stared at it for a long moment before picking it up.

Everett Chambers, his great-grandfather and namesake, had been an avid outdoorsman who'd taught Brandon and Beau how to hunt and shoot with lethal accuracy. During childhood hunting trips, he'd regaled Brandon and his brother with tales of a distant ancestor who'd become a bounty hunter after gaining his freedom from slavery. His marksmanship and bravery had been legendary.

Brandon remembered hours of trekking through the piney woods that covered the grounds of Grandpa Everett's country estate. He remembered crouching in the dense underbrush . . . peering through the scope of his rifle . . . training his sights on unsuspecting elk roaming through the forest. He remembered holding his breath, waiting for the perfect moment to squeeze the trigger.

When he made his first kill at age eleven, Grandpa Everett had clapped him proudly on the back and congratulated him on his excellent marksmanship. But when they returned to the ranch house and Brandon began boasting to everyone about his trophy kill, his great-grandfather had taken him by the shoulders, looked him in the eye, and admonished him to remember who he was and what he was to become. Chambers men were doctors, lawyers, judges, and pioneers of industry. They were intellectuals who understood the profound power of brains over brawn.

We save lives, Grandpa Everett had told him. *We protect and enrich lives. We must never take pleasure from ending lives.*

Brandon stared down at the Glock in his hand. He savored the comforting weight of metal against his palm, let his thumb stroke the trigger almost lovingly.

He thought of the GPS device he'd secretly installed on Dominic's car after he violated the restraining order and went after

Tamia. Brandon had been furious. Worse, he'd felt powerless, knowing that Dominic could get to Tamia any time he wanted. He'd installed the tracking device to ensure her safety, but in the chaos of the past few weeks, he'd forgotten all about it.

But he remembered it now.

And he realized that if Dominic and Tamia were together tonight, he could find them if he wanted.

He took a long drag on his cigar, eyes narrowed as he pondered his Glock. He pulled back the slide, checking the barrel for ammunition.

When his phone rang on the desk, he calmly set down the loaded pistol, then reached over and picked up the phone.

"Brandon?" It was his father. "How're you doing, son? How'd the house hunting go? You and Cynthia find anything you like?"

"Not quite," Brandon murmured.

"Don't worry. You will." His father rushed on, brimming with excitement. "Listen, I wanted to let you know what's been going on. You were a hit this morning, Brandon. Everyone's talking about your speech, and I do mean *everyone*."

"Hmm." Brandon puffed on his stogie, drawing the toxic smoke into his lungs and letting it flow through his bloodstream before he slowly exhaled.

"I've been on the phone all day with members of the Congressional Black Caucus," Bernard continued. "They want you to attend their next meeting in D.C. They said they'd take care of all your travel and hotel expenses. All you have to do is show up. And Barack promised to make room in his schedule to see you while you're in town. He thinks you could be the future of the Democratic party, son. Isn't that what I've been telling you all along?"

"Umm-hmm." Brandon blew out a perfect ring of smoke and watched it curl toward the ceiling.

His father chuckled. "If I were a different type of man, I might have been upset that you stole my shine at the prayer breakfast. The keynote speaker isn't supposed to be upstaged by the person introducing him. But I'm proud of you, son. So damn proud. And so is your mother. You should have seen her crying and praising God on the way home. It was a sight to behold. And she's been receiving calls from her friends all day. . . ."

Brandon closed his eyes, tuning out his father's voice as his mind traveled back to that afternoon.

He remembered how stunned he'd been to look up and see Tamia and Dominic standing at the top of the staircase. When Dominic had possessively put his arm around her, it had been all Brandon could do not to charge up those steps and tear that motherfucker limb from limb.

But that wasn't even the worst part. The worst fucking part was when he'd seen the engagement ring on Tamia's finger. He'd died a thousand deaths right then and there.

". . . about my plan to appoint you to attorney general once I'm elected," his father's voice penetrated his dark thoughts. "But I think we need to adjust our plans and shift our priorities. It's time to start preparing you for your Senate run—"

"Lemme call you back, Dad," Brandon interrupted.

"Wait, but I'm not—"

Brandon hung up and dropped the phone onto his desk, then mashed out his cigar in an ashtray.

Visions of Tamia and Dominic rolled through his mind like dark clouds gathering before a storm. He shut his eyes to block out the images, but this only amplified the voices warring inside his head.

Maybe he really loves her. Would that be so hard to believe?

Doesn't matter! If I can't have her, he can't either.

But you can have any woman you want! Why obsess over one?

Because she's the ONLY one I want!

It was that simple. That cut and dried.

Clenching his jaw, Brandon grabbed the Glock and lurched from the chair.

The room spun, and he swayed on his feet like a punch-drunk boxer.

Squeezing his eyes shut, he waited for the dizziness to pass.

When he'd regained his balance, he tucked the gun into the waistband of his jeans and headed purposefully from the room.

Chapter 25
Tamia

That evening, Tamia and Dominic dined at a quaint little restaurant tucked into the scenic hillside. They ordered lamb glazed with balsamic honey and stuffed lobster complemented by the most expensive bottle of wine on the menu.

Over the meal, Tamia teased Dominic about the tales he'd spun that afternoon. "So we met at the Houston Rodeo last year, where you were exhibiting your prize steer in the livestock show."

"That's right." Dominic's eyes danced with amusement in the candlelight. "What's so crazy about that? You saying a brotha can't be a cattle rancher?"

Tamia grinned. "Of course they can. But you're from St. Croix, so what you know about being a rancher?"

"Enough to fool dem Yankees into believin' I am one," he drawled, slipping into his Crucian dialect.

Tamia smiled, running her finger around the rim of her wineglass. "How do you do that?"

"Do wah, me darlin'?"

Her stomach quivered. *God, he's sexy!*

"How do you turn your accent off and on like that? It disappeared completely when you were talking to our new friends this afternoon."

Dominic smiled. "I bin yankin' fo' years. Practice makes perfect." He winked at her. "Want me to teach you?"

"Crucian?"

"Yeah."

She smiled. "I don't know. I don't think you *can* teach me. I've always heard that you have to grow up on the islands to learn the dialect. Besides," she added wryly, "I don't wanna get around your people, say something the wrong way and be called some posing muddascunt."

"*Muddascunt?*" Dominic threw back his head and roared with laughter.

Tamia grinned. "See? You're already making fun of me."

"No, I'm not," he insisted, wiping tears of mirth from his eyes. "I'm just surprised you knew that word. Surprised and impressed. But you shouldn't use it in public, love. It's unladylike."

"Oh, so now you're the language police?" Tamia challenged teasingly.

"Nah," he drawled. "I just think we can find better uses for that beautiful mouth of yours."

The overtly sexual remark made her nipples harden. Trying to play it off, she picked up her glass and took a long sip of wine.

Dominic watched her, eyes gleaming with wicked amusement.

She decided to change the subject. "So, Dominic—"

"Nico."

"What?"

He smiled. "I also go by Nico. That's what everyone calls me back home. You can, too."

"Nico," Tamia murmured experimentally. She thought having a nickname humanized him somehow, made him seem less fiendish and more normal. But she wasn't about to start calling him Nico. That was getting too personal.

So is spending the weekend together.

"What were you going to say?" Dominic asked her.

She eyed him blankly.

"Just now when I interrupted you," he prompted.

"Oh." She pursed her lips. "I don't remember."

Dominic nodded, then raised his wineglass to his mouth and drank.

She watched him, silently appraising.

Lowering his glass to the table, he gave her a curious smile. "Why are you looking at me like that?"

"I was just thinking."

"About what?"

"How different you seem tonight."

"In what way?"

Tamia smiled. "Well, for starters, I didn't know you could be so . . . charming."

His eyes glinted with humor. "There's a lot you don't know about me."

"I don't doubt that," she said wryly. "We didn't spend much time talking and getting to know each other when we were, um, together before."

"No, we didn't," Dominic murmured. "That's one of the many regrets I have."

They stared at each other across the table.

Several moments passed.

"Can I ask you a question?" Tamia ventured quietly.

Dominic nodded.

"Why did you cheat on your wife?"

His expression darkened. He held her gaze another moment, then shook his head and turned to look out the window. "Talk about a buzzkill."

"Sorry." But Tamia wasn't—not really. Dominic had pulled her into his marriage the moment he'd decided to blackmail her for sex. She had a right to know what the hell he'd been thinking.

He pushed out a deep, heavy breath and sat forward, broad shoulders hunched over his glass. "I'm not proud of the way I treated Isabel. We had a rocky marriage long before I ever met you."

"I know," Tamia reminded him. "Isabel told me you were unfaithful almost from day one."

Dominic grimaced. "It's complicated."

Tamia arched a brow. "How so? Did you not understand your wedding vows? Did you have trouble comprehending that whole part about 'forsaking all others'?"

"I understood my vows just fine."

"The evidence suggests otherwise."

He glared at Tamia, his jaw tightly clenched. After several moments he leaned back in his chair and stared out the window again.

She waited.

"It wasn't easy being married to Isabel," he began. "She belonged to one of the oldest and richest families in St. Croix, and they never let me forget it." He met Tamia's gaze. "I didn't come from money. I grew up in the poorest part of Frederiksted, and my parents and grandparents were laborers. When I met Isabel I was working at an oil refinery. To earn extra money I got a job ferrying tourists around the island. There were always plenty of horny-ass women lookin' to get smashed by an island stud, and they tipped generously for my, ah, services. One afternoon of tips could add up to more than a week's worth of wages from the refinery."

"Ah," Tamia murmured, nodding slowly. "So *that's* how you became a ho."

Dominic flashed her a crooked grin. "Don't hate the playa. . . ."

"Oh, no hate from me. Trust." As someone who'd done porn to put herself through college, Tamia knew better than anyone that sometimes the ends justified the means.

"Anyway," Dominic continued, "I wasn't supposed to end up with someone like Isabel, an heiress to a sugar fortune. Our paths were never supposed to cross. But one night the uptown girl was feeling adventurous, so she and her friends decided to cross the tracks to go clubbing on my side of Frederiksted. We met on the dance floor and the rest, as they say, is history."

Tamia sipped her wine, struck by the familiarity of Dominic's story. "When did things go downhill for you two? Before or after you got married?"

"Before." His lips twisted bitterly. "Her parents didn't want her to marry me. They didn't think I was good enough for her. Neither did she, for that matter."

"She must have thought you were," Tamia countered, "or she wouldn't have defied her parents' wishes to be with you."

Dominic smirked. "She had her reasons for marrying me."

Tamia nodded. "She loved you."

"She loved the way I fucked," Dominic said bluntly.

No surprise there, Tamia mused. The man was a beast between the sheets.

"I know that's not the only reason Isabel married you, Dominic. I met her. I could tell how much she loved you."

A shadow of cynicism darkened his face. "Maybe she did. Maybe I was the love of her life. It was hard to tell though, 'cause every time

I turned around she was throwing her family's wealth back in my face and telling me I wasn't shit without her." He drained the rest of his wine, then set the empty glass on the table with a hard *thunk*.

"So, yeah, I cheated on her," he concluded grimly. "I cheated many times, and I'm not proud of that. But if a man feels constantly rejected at home, he's eventually gonna look for acceptance elsewhere."

Tamia silently absorbed his words, feeling the pain and anger that fueled them. His story had struck a chord with her because she'd experienced the same sense of rejection when she and Brandon had been together. She'd been the girl from the wrong side of the tracks dating a man who'd been born into one of the most powerful families in Texas. She'd gone to extreme lengths to erase her shameful past because she'd desperately craved Brandon's love and acceptance. Yet no matter how hard she'd tried to please him and be the perfect wifey, it had still taken him nine months to introduce her to his family.

Over the past year she'd often wondered whether she would have gotten involved with Dominic if Brandon hadn't made her feel so inadequate.

She would never know.

"Seems we have a lot more in common than you think," Dominic murmured, breaking into Tamia's thoughts.

She met his quiet gaze. "Seems we do. Imagine that."

He smiled briefly, then glanced down at his platinum watch. "Let's order dessert so we can get back to the ranch. I don't want you to be late for your massage."

Tamia smiled softly. "Thank you for scheduling that for me. It was very sweet and thoughtful of you."

Dominic winked at her. "No need to thank me, darlin'. I promised you a relaxing weekend, so that's what you're gonna get."

Tamia warmed with pleasure.

She'd always believed that Brandon Chambers was the only man who could ever make her happy.

But maybe it was time to open her eyes to a new contender . . .

. . . one she'd never seen coming.

Chapter 26

Tamia

An hour later Tamia lay on her stomach, her eyes closed in dreamy languor as her masseur expertly kneaded the muscles in her back.

He was an attractive white guy with longish brown hair and blue eyes. He'd introduced himself as Seth when Tamia was escorted into the treatment room, which was aglow with flickering candles. She hadn't missed the way Seth's eyes glittered appreciatively as she'd slowly disrobed and stretched out on the table.

After pouring massage oil into his palms and rubbing them together for warmth, he'd gotten right to work, making her body melt beneath his skilled hands.

He spoke occasionally, his soothing voice barely rising above the serene music playing softly in the background.

"Are you enjoying yourself at the ranch?"

"Umm-hmm," Tamia purred. "Very much."

"That's good. Glad to hear it." He pressed the heels of his palms into the small of her back. "How long are you staying?"

Tamia's eyes remained closed. "Just till Monday."

Seth tsk-tsked. "Too bad. You'll have to stay longer next time."

"Oh, most definitely," Tamia agreed as he paused to retrieve more massage oil.

A few moments later he poured the heated liquid over her back, making her shiver with pleasure. And then his strong hands were back in place, moving slowly down her spine and sliding under the towel to massage her butt cheeks.

As a sharp coil of desire surged through her, she let out an involuntary moan.

The masseur's hands wandered lower, kneading and caressing her thighs until her nipples hardened and her pussy grew heavy with arousal.

Opening her eyes, she looked over her shoulder.

And gasped in shock.

Dominic had replaced her masseur.

His muscular chest gleamed deliciously with oil, and he wore dark shorts that clung to his strong thighs.

Tamia's mouth watered.

Pushing herself up on her elbows, she whispered, "What're you doing here?"

Dominic smiled, slow and wicked. "What does it look like? I'm giving you a massage."

"But you're not . . ." She trailed off, looking around the room. "Where's Seth?"

Dominic's eyes gleamed. "He had to step away."

"Hmm." Tamia bit her lip, her gaze lowering to the thick bulge at Dominic's crotch.

He put his hand on the back of her thigh. The heat of his touch sent a shiver to her loins. "Do you want me to finish your massage?"

Tamia licked her lips. "Depends."

"On what?"

Holding his gaze, she turned slowly on the table, the towel slipping from around her waist to reveal the smooth V of her Brazilian-waxed pussy. "It depends," she purred, "on whether you give happy endings."

Dominic stared at her exposed mound, his nostrils flaring. "I'll give you whatever you want."

Tamia smiled seductively. "Then what're you waiting for?"

The words had barely crossed her lips before Dominic grabbed her hips, spun her around, and dragged her to the edge of the table.

She closed her eyes, tilted back her head, and let her thighs fall open as his mouth descended upon her. He licked her clit and sucked her plump folds, his tongue drawing nectar out of her like a bee-keeper harvesting honey.

She moaned with pleasure, her back arching off the table as he stretched her legs over his shoulders. He groaned as he feasted on her pussy, telling her how good she tasted and how much he'd missed having her.

When her legs were shaking and her breath was coming in sharp gasps, he plunged his tongue inside her.

She cried out as her hips shot off the table. She came long and hard, her body convulsed by shudders that seemed to last forever.

When she opened her eyes, Dominic was leaning over her, lips glistening, eyes blazing with lust.

"I'ma fuck the shit outta you," he growled.

"Oh, hell yeah," Tamia panted as he flipped her over on the table and pulled her onto all fours.

She looked over her shoulder, watching as he quickly yanked down his shorts. As his thick cock bounced free, she saw that he was already wearing a condom. It should have bothered her that he'd been presumptuous enough to come prepared. But she wasn't mad—she was almost relieved that she didn't have to wait for him to wrap it up.

She trembled as he guided the dome of his dick between her pussy lips, basting himself with the silky juices that dripped out of her. Grabbing her ass with both hands, he rammed his cock inside her.

She let out a hoarse cry.

"Fuck," he groaned, shuddering so deeply her body vibrated. "Damn, this pussy be *killin'* me."

Tamia's inner muscles contracted as he pulled halfway out, then plunged back into her, his taut stomach slapping her buttocks. She grabbed the sides of the table, holding on tight as he began pummeling her sex with long, glorious strokes that had her seeing every star in the universe.

Soon, the tranquil background music was drowned out by the orchestra they were creating—guttural moans and exhortations accompanied by the sounds of Dominic's hand slapping her ass cheeks as he slammed into her.

He fucked her until she was cursing and chanting, not caring who heard her. Her heart was pounding, and every breath she took was filled with the heady musk of oil, sweat, and sex.

Dominic squeezed her bouncing breasts as she gyrated her hips, pushing her clapping ass onto his dick as they raced toward the finish line, shouting as they crossed together and exploded in ecstasy.

Dominic pulled out of her and tore off his condom, lashing her back and buttocks with hot jism. Tamia purred with satisfaction before closing her eyes and slumping weakly upon the table.

Dominic lay on top of her, his slick chest heaving against her back.

After a few minutes, Tamia murmured, "I'm not even gonna ask how or when you arranged this."

Dominic chuckled. "I wouldn't tell you anyway."

She smiled. "I just hope these walls are soundproof."

"I don't think they are," Dominic drawled. "But it doesn't matter because you were the last appointment tonight. There's no one here but us and Seth, and he says we can stay as long as we like."

Tamia grinned. "You must have paid him very well."

"Well enough," Dominic murmured, licking between her shoulder blades.

She shivered at the hot stroke of his tongue. "In that case," she purred, turning over on the table and wrapping her legs around his hips, "I guess you'd better get your money's worth."

"I already have," he whispered as he slid inside her. "I already have."

Chapter 27

Brandon

Brandon came awake slowly . . . sluggishly . . . a man struggling to surface from the depths of a black abyss.

As he opened his eyes the pain hit him—spikes of agony stabbing into his skull.

He winced sharply, reaching up to massage his throbbing temple.

Gradually he became aware of Cynthia's warm body snuggled against his side, her head resting upon his chest and her arm flung across his stomach. Her legs were curled with one knee burrowed between his thighs.

Feeling her soft pubic hair against his skin, Brandon frowned and reached down to pull back the covers.

Not only was Cynthia naked. So was he.

Shit!

Just then Cynthia stirred quietly, roused by the cool draft on her skin.

Brandon watched as she opened her eyes and lifted her head from his chest. Meeting his stricken gaze, she smiled drowsily and mumbled, "Good morning."

He stared at her. "What happened last night?"

She searched his eyes. "You don't remember?"

He swallowed hard. Shook his head.

She sighed, her morning breath gusting over his face. "What happened is that you got drunk out of your damn mind, and you tried to storm out of here before I stopped you. Which I had to."

"Why?"

She frowned at him. "You had a *gun*, Brandon."

Her words struck him like a blast of ice water.

He stared at her for a stunned moment, then swung his legs over the side of the bed and leaned forward, holding his head in his hands.

"It wasn't easy to keep you from leaving," Cynthia grumbled. "You were a man on a mission. I thought I'd have to hurl myself at your legs and hang on for dear life just to slow you down. You only stayed because I started crying and complaining about having bad cramps, like I might be losing the baby."

"You pretended to be having a *miscarriage*?"

"It was the only way to get your attention!"

Brandon closed his eyes, head throbbing as fragments of memory came back to him. The model home . . . Tamia and Dominic . . . her engagement ring . . . the weight of the Glock in his palm.

What had he been contemplating last night?

Suicide?

Murder?

Jesus.

"You were in a very dark place, Brandon," Cynthia somberly confirmed. "It scared the hell out of me, to be honest with you. I don't know what you were planning to do with that gun, but I can only assume no good would have come of it. If it's all the same to you, I don't want our child's first introduction to his father to take place inside a penitentiary."

Brandon absorbed her words in silence, his stomach roiling with nausea.

Cynthia sat up, her warm hands settling upon his shoulders. "The best thing that came out of last night was that we made love for the first time in weeks."

Brandon stiffened. "We did?"

She smiled. "Umm-hmm."

Brandon looked down at the floor, searching for a discarded condom that wasn't there.

"It was wonderful," Cynthia purred, kneading his muscles.

"How? You said I was drunk."

"You were." She chuckled. "But your dick obviously didn't get the memo."

Brandon grimaced, his head pounding harder.

"I know you have a hangover, but we need to hurry so we won't be late for church. And don't say you're not going," Cynthia added before he could open his mouth, "because you *have* to be there. Everyone's gonna want to see you and congratulate you on yesterday's speech."

"Doesn't mean I wanna see *them*," Brandon grumbled.

"Baby—"

He stood so abruptly that Cynthia wobbled and nearly fell off the bed. He glanced over his shoulder, watching as she regained her balance and flopped back against the pillows, small breasts bouncing.

"I need a shower," he muttered.

"We can take one together," she coyly suggested. "Kill two birds with—"

"I'd rather shower alone."

Cynthia pouted as he grabbed his smartphone off the bedside table and stalked to the bathroom, locking the door behind him.

Tucking the phone between his lips, he lifted the toilet seat and took a long piss, mentally praying that he'd had enough sense not to come inside Cynthia when they'd had sex. If there was the slightest possibility that she wasn't pregnant—if she was lying about carrying his child—he didn't want to take any chances.

But considering that he'd been blitzed out of his mind last night, it was highly unlikely that he'd remembered to pull out.

Frowning at the thought, Brandon flushed the toilet and closed the lid, then grabbed his bath towel. Wrapping it loosely around his hips, he sat down on the toilet and pulled up Tamia's number on his phone.

He stared at the screen, contemplating what he wanted to say to her. *I love you. I'm dying without you. Please don't marry Dominic. I'm begging you, baby. Pleeeaaase!*

Swallowing hard, Brandon sent the call through.

The phone rang twice before it was picked up.

"Hello?" The voice on the other end was deep and drowsy. Unmistakably male.

Brandon's gut tightened. *This muthafucka!*

"Where's Tamia?" he snarled.

There was a short pause.

"She's right here sleeping soundly in my arms," Dominic drawled smugly.

Brandon clenched his jaw, gripping the phone hard enough to break it. The throbbing in his head had become an excruciating roar.

Dominic chuckled. "We had a long night. Want me to take a message?"

Brandon closed his eyes . . . and hung up without responding.

Chapter 28

Tamia

Tamia slipped from the bathroom and crept toward the bed, moving quietly so she wouldn't awaken Dominic.

Sunlight streaked through the shuttered doors to cast warm puddles across the cool wood floor. It was the light, coupled with a full bladder, that had pulled her out of her comatose slumber. After the night she'd spent with Dominic, it was a miracle she'd regained consciousness before noon.

Nearing the bed, she paused to observe her lover. He slept with one arm flung over his head, the other draped across his stomach. The sheet lay tangled around his waist, and one long, muscular leg hung off the edge of the bed. Sleep softened his features, giving him a boyish appeal that contradicted the tattoos covering his biceps.

Tamia chewed her lower lip, watching the steady rise and fall of his chest. She'd expected to feel conflicted the morning after sleeping with him. She'd expected to be consumed with regret.

But she wasn't conflicted, and she had no regrets. She'd thoroughly enjoyed making love with Dominic last night. So she refused to dwell on why she should or shouldn't have.

As she stepped closer to the bed, Dominic's eyes suddenly snapped open.

She squealed as he reached out and grabbed her, pulling her onto the bed and rolling on top of her.

"You faker!" she cried accusingly. "I thought you were asleep!"

He laughed. "Gotcha."

She grinned up at him as he settled between her thighs, nothing between them but warm skin. "And here I was tiptoeing around so I wouldn't wake you up."

He chuckled, bending his head to nibble on her neck. "I'm hungry, love."

Tamia smiled. "That's why we need to get up and head downstairs for breakfast."

"I wasn't talkin' about being hungry for food."

Feeling his dick pulse against her stomach, Tamia groaned in protest. "Oh, no, not again. Nigga, you gon' wear my ass out."

He grinned. "You say that like it's a problem."

"It will be if you don't feed me soon."

"Damn. So it's like that?"

"Yup."

Dominic smiled at her.

Without warning, her mind flashed on an image of him thrusting into her, his hips pumping up and down as he gazed fiercely into her eyes and whispered, *"I'm never letting you go, Tamia. Never . . ."*

"Tamia?"

The image evaporated, leaving her staring up at Dominic uncomprehendingly. She didn't remember him speaking those words to her last night. But maybe he had. Their lovemaking was so good, there was no telling what *she'd* probably blurted out in the throes of passion.

"What's wrong?" Dominic asked, searching her face.

She shook her head. "Nothing."

"You sure?"

She nodded.

He leaned down and kissed her, looking into her eyes as he stroked his tongue against hers. "I want you to spend Christmas with me," he murmured without breaking the kiss.

Tamia went still, then pulled back and stared at him. "What?"

He smiled. "My family can't come for Christmas, and neither can yours. Since we're enjoying each other's company so much, there's no reason we should spend the holiday alone."

Tamia pursed her lips, contemplating his suggestion. It was true that she'd been dreading the thought of spending the holidays by herself. Though Shanell had invited her over for Christmas dinner, she'd declined because she didn't want to feel like an interloper, the poor guest who had nowhere else to go. She would have given anything to celebrate Christmas and New Year's with Brandon, but that ship had already sailed.

She sighed, shaking her head at Dominic. "I don't know. Spending Christmas together . . . that's moving kinda fast for me."

"I understand. I don't wanna rush you. Just give it some thought, okay?"

She nodded. "Okay."

"Good." Eyes glinting wickedly, he reached between her legs and cupped her mound.

Her breath quickened as he rubbed her slowly and sensually, watching her eyes glaze with pleasure. Her hips undulated as he dipped his finger inside her, swirling it around until she came with a throaty cry.

She was still gasping when Dominic slid down her body and planted his face between her thighs.

"What about breakfast?" she breathed.

"Let me eat first," he murmured, his warm breath on her pussy, "then you can have your turn."

On the way back to Houston the next morning, Tamia's phone rang.

She was relieved when she checked the display screen and saw that it was Honey instead of Shanell, whose calls she'd avoided all weekend.

"Hey, girl," Honey greeted Tamia. "Sorry I didn't call you back sooner. I've been working nonstop since Thursday. It's like these tricks are tryna get as much pussy as they can before Christmas."

Tamia grinned. "Well, damn, save some for Santa."

Honey laughed. "How about one of my clients dressed up as Santa and had me give him a lap dance. I'd barely started grindin' my coochie before he—"

"TMI," Tamia cut her off, wrinkling her nose in disgust. "Damn. You like sharing just a *lil* too much, heffa."

"I know." Honey giggled impishly. "I just love messing with you, Tamia. You're, like, the most prudish porn star I've ever known. Sorry—*ex*-porn star," she amended with another giggle.

Tamia frowned. "Is your ass high or something?"

"Nah, girl. Not yet." Honey sighed. "Anyway, what's up? You left me a message saying you had something important to ask me."

Tamia paused, darting a glance at Dominic. Though his eyes were focused on the road, she knew he was listening intently to her conversation.

"Tamia?" Honey prompted. "What did you wanna ask me?"

"Um, what's Keyshawn's last name?"

Honey hesitated for a moment. "Greene."

"Greene with an *e*?"

"Yeah." Honey sounded wary. "Why?"

"I met him the other day," Tamia answered. "I wasn't sure if he was your Keyshawn or a different one."

"How did you meet him?"

Tamia hesitated, stealing another glance at Dominic. She hadn't told him about the note she'd received because she didn't completely trust him. For all she knew, *he* was the one who'd sent it. So she had to come up with another explanation for how she'd met Honey's boyfriend.

"I had to call the police on Thursday to report a disturbance in my building."

"What kind of disturbance?" Honey asked.

"Some neighbors were arguing really loud and throwing shit around. You know how I feel about domestic disputes. Anyway, Keyshawn was one of the officers who responded to my call."

"I hope you didn't mention my name to him," Honey said anxiously.

"I didn't." Tamia frowned. "Why would I?"

"I don't know, but I'm glad you didn't. Keyshawn doesn't know we're friends, and I wanna keep it that way."

"Why?"

"Girl, if I ever have to stay with you again, I don't want his crazy ass to know where to look for me!"

"Of course. I understand." Tamia smiled ruefully. "I gotta say, I was surprised to see what he looks like. No offense, girl, but he's kinda average for someone like you."

"I know. That's what all my friends tell me." Honey sighed. "What can I say? Er'body can't be as foine as Brandon, or even that West Indian brotha who was blackmailing you. Humph. Nigga might have been shady as hell, but he was sexier than a muthafucka. *Dayum!*"

Tamia saw the way Dominic's lips twitched, confirming her suspicion that he was seriously ear hustling.

"I can't even say I blame you for fucking him," Honey continued. "I *know* that brotha can lay some pipe!"

Tamia blushed, watching as a wicked grin spread across Dominic's face. Wanting to teach him a lesson for shamelessly eavesdropping on her conversation, she sucked her teeth dismissively. "He was a'ight."

She almost fell out laughing when Dominic's cocky grin turned into an indignant scowl.

Honey snickered. "Bitch, whatever. You know damn well that was some good dick."

"Hmm," Tamia murmured noncommittally. Hearing a man's disgruntled voice in the background, she smiled. "Is that Lou?"

"Yeah, girl. I stopped by his crib to give him his money like a good little ho."

Tamia chuckled. "Tell him I said hey."

Honey relayed her greeting to Lou, who called back affectionately, "Hola, *mamacita*."

She smiled warmly.

"Did y'all kiss and make up?" Honey whispered into the phone so Lou wouldn't hear her.

"Something like that," Tamia murmured.

"Oh, that's good," Honey said with a sigh of relief. "You and Lou are like family to me, so I can't have you guys not speaking to each other."

"We're good," Tamia assured her.

"Cool. Oh, by the way, I think I'll be able to attend that fundraiser gala after all."

Tamia's pulse tripped. "Really?"

"Yeah. Keyshawn has to work somebody's shift this weekend. So I'm free."

"Oh," Tamia said weakly. "Great."

"Isn't it? I'm so excited. You'll have to help me find a badass dress to wear. I wanna look good for Beau."

"Um, okay." Out of the corner of her eye, Tamia could see Dominic's hand flexing on the steering wheel.

"All right, girl," she said to Honey. "I'll catch up with you later."

As she ended the call, Dominic sent her a long glance. "Everything okay?"

She forced a bright smile. "Everything's fine."

Dominic didn't look convinced.

Turning toward the window, Tamia inhaled a shaky breath and let it out slowly.

The fundraiser gala was on Friday. That gave her less than a week to prepare herself—mentally and emotionally—to see Brandon again.

God help her.

God help them both.

Chapter 29

Brandon

Brandon stood at the windows in his office, one hand tucked into his pocket, the other holding his phone to his ear. It was Monday morning, and he was having a conversation with the most powerful man in the world.

What a way to start the week.

"Yes, sir. I understand." Brandon smiled warmly. "Thank you for calling, Mr. President. Please give my warm regards to the First Lady and the girls."

Cynthia had wandered into Brandon's office while he was on the phone. Upon hearing his parting words, her eyes grew so wide they almost popped out of their sockets.

As Brandon set his phone down on the desk, she demanded excitedly, "Were you just talking to *President Obama*?"

Brandon grinned broadly. "I was."

"Oh my God!" Cynthia squealed, damn near splitting his eardrums. She hurried around his desk and perched on the corner, staring at him with fascinated curiosity. "What did he say?"

"Can't tell you," Brandon teased, dropping into his chair and clasping his hands behind his head.

"*What!*" Cynthia sputtered indignantly. "Why can't you tell me?"

Brandon winked. "It's classified."

"*Classified?*"

"Yes, ma'am."

Her eyes narrowed on his face. After another moment, she sniffed and shrugged a careless shoulder. "Fine. Be that way, then. It's not as if *I've* never met the president before. I was at the inauguration just like you were. And your father isn't the only one who's played golf with him."

Brandon grinned. "I'm still not telling you what he said."

Cynthia made a strangled sound of vexation and lunged at him. He laughed, warding off her playful blows.

"Awww," intoned a mocking voice. "Aren't you two adorable?"

Brandon and Cynthia glanced around to find Brooke Chambers standing in the doorway, watching them with a smirk on her face.

Brandon was surprised to see her. "Hey, baby girl," he said affectionately. "Wassup?"

"Oh, nothing much. Iris said I could head on back because you weren't with a client."

"That's cool. Come in."

Brooke strutted into the room as if her name was on the door—hips swinging, hair bouncing, lips smiling confidently. She was a voluptuous mahogany beauty who made no apologies for who she was and where she was going in life. An often-imitated fashionista, she wore a white pea coat over slim red pants and fur-trimmed boots. Even the small wicker basket slung over her arm looked like a fashion accessory.

"Hey, Brooke," Cynthia greeted her, lips stretched into a plastic smile. "How're you doing?"

"I'm good," Brooke drawled, lowering herself into a visitor chair. "Maybe not as good as you, though. I could hear you squealing all the way down the hall."

"Oh. That." Cynthia looked embarrassed. "I was just excited because your brother was talking to President Obama."

Brooke snorted. "Is that all? They talk all the time."

"I wouldn't say all that," Brandon interjected, partly to rescue Cynthia from his sister's ridicule. "Barack is Dad's friend, not mine."

"Same difference." Brooke gave Cynthia a look of amused condescension. "Just out of curiosity, do you spend any time in your own office anymore?"

"Brooke," Brandon said warningly as Cynthia's face reddened.

Brooke laughed. "I'm just sayin', Brandon. It seems like she's always in your office instead of hers."

"How would you know?" he countered. "Last I checked, you don't work here."

Brooke grinned. "Touché."

Brandon could see Cynthia gritting her teeth, striving for composure. He knew she wanted to tell his sister off, but she didn't want to risk offending him because Brooke was his baby girl.

That was the difference between Cynthia and Tamia. He couldn't see Tamia holding her tongue if Brooke was talking smack to *her*.

"I was on my way out anyway," Cynthia announced. "I have to meet with a client."

"Okay." Brooke raked Cynthia with the coolly dismissive look that had been perfected by Gwen Chambers. "Buh-bye."

Cynthia's nostrils flared with indignation.

Brandon stood, giving her a peck on the lips. "Have a good meeting."

"Thanks, baby." Shooting a haughty glance at Brooke, Cynthia strode from the room.

When she turned and paused at the doorway, Brooke flapped her fingers at her, shooing her off.

Cynthia spun on her heel and stormed out the door.

Brooke snorted, rolling her eyes at Brandon. "Seriously. How the hell do you get any work done around here with that leech stuck to you?"

"Watch it now," Brandon said sternly. "That 'leech' happens to be my fiancée."

"Don't remind me." Brooke sucked her teeth. "Honestly, Brandon, getting involved with you was the worst thing that could have ever happened to Cynthia."

Brandon scowled. "Gee, thanks."

"No, I'm serious. When we first met Cynthia, she struck me as a really smart, independent woman who had her shit together. She was a fellow soror, she had her law degree from Howard, she was focused on her career—the sister was on point. But once she started dating you, it's like her personality did a complete one-eighty. She went from being Miss Run the World to having her world revolve around *you*. Nowadays if you ask her about her career, homegirl is like, 'Making partner? What's that?' All she cares about is planning the perfect wedding and picking out china for your new home." Brooke snorted, shaking her head in disgust. "It's really sad, Brandon."

He grimaced, leaning back in his chair. Brooke wasn't telling him anything he didn't already know. Though he'd shared the very same concerns with Cynthia, her behavior hadn't changed. If anything, she'd gotten worse.

"Tell you what," Brooke vowed. "I'll never let any man knock *me* off my game like that."

Brandon smiled faintly. "You'd better not."

"Oh, I won't. Trust."

"Good. Now that you've gotten that off your chest," Brandon drawled wryly, "mind telling me what's in the basket?"

Brooke glanced down at her arm as if she'd forgotten what she was carrying. "Oh, yeah. I brought you something from Mrs. Jessup."

Brandon perked up at the mention of their longtime cook, who'd always been like a member of the family. "What is it?"

Brooke smiled, passing the small basket across the desk to him. "See for yourself."

He opened the basket and folded back the checkered cloth. When he saw what was inside, his face broke into a huge, delighted grin. "Oh, man. Mississippi mud cookies?"

Brooke grinned. "Yup. Your favorite."

Brandon picked up a warm cookie and bit into it, closing his eyes with an appreciative groan.

Brooke chuckled, rising from the chair. "When I stopped by the house this morning and told Mrs. Jessup I'd be seeing you today, she whipped up a batch just for you. For old times' sake, she said."

"God bless that woman," Brandon mumbled around a gooey mouthful of chocolate and marshmallow. He killed the cookie in two more bites and reached for another one.

Looking immensely pleased with herself, Brooke perched on the corner of the desk and started swinging her legs back and forth. It reminded Brandon of the way she used to skip into their father's study, hop onto his desk, and hand him a pretty flower she'd picked from the garden—buttering him up before she asked for a new doll, or whatever it was she'd been coveting.

Brandon paused mid-chew, his eyes narrowing suspiciously on his sister's face. "What do you want?"

She blinked innocently. "What do you mean?"

He snorted. "Come on, Brooke. Do you honestly expect me to

believe you just dropped by in the middle of the workday to deliver some homemade cookies? We both know you obviously want something."

"I don't know what you're talking about," Brooke insisted, batting lashes and all.

Brandon laughed. "I can't believe you tryna play me. Have you forgotten who you're talking to? You know you can't get anything past me, so why even try?"

Brooke took umbrage. "Why are you being so paranoid? Why do I have to have ulterior motives for bringing you a special treat from home? You've been so damn depressed lately, maybe I just wanted to cheer you up."

"Uh-huh." Brandon eyed her skeptically as he polished off the cookie, then dusted the moist crumbs off his hands.

Brooke cast a look around the lavishly appointed room and sighed. "I don't know how you do it, Brandon. Don't get me wrong. Making partner is the ultimate, and your corner office is the bomb-dot-com. But I couldn't work here. Biglaw just isn't for me."

With a J.D. from UT, Brooke had abandoned her law career to become a consultant to Houston's power elite. She planned social events, hosted fundraisers, and was invited to every soiree that mattered.

"Everything's on track for Friday night," she announced, segueing to another topic. "The tickets are sold out, all of our VIP guests have RSVP'd, and we've had no cancellations despite the fundraiser taking place two days before Christmas. Didn't I tell you guys the date wouldn't be a problem? People love to dress up and attend glitzy parties around the holidays, especially if they're supporting a good cause. Everyone I've talked to is so excited—"

"Brooke."

She broke off, staring at Brandon. "What?"

"You're rambling."

She frowned and tucked her hair behind one ear, a nervous gesture that always gave her away.

Brandon smiled knowingly. "I'm waiting."

Brooke met his gaze, then took a deep breath and blurted, "I'm in love with Dre."

Brandon froze, his eyes narrowed to menacing slits. "Dre . . . who?"

Brooke swallowed visibly. "Dre Portis."

"WHAT?" Brandon shouted. "Aw, hell, nah!"

Brooke winced. "Just listen to me—"

Brandon shoved to his feet and marched across the room to shut the door. Stalking back over to his sister, he jabbed a finger at her. "You have lost your damn mind, Brooke."

"No, I haven't."

"You must have if you think I'ma let you get with Dre."

"*Let me?*" Brooke sputtered in outrage. "I don't need you to *let* me do anything!"

Brandon scowled. "Look here, little girl—"

"Stop calling me that! I'm not a little girl anymore, Brandon. I'm twenty-seven years old and a grown-ass woman. So I don't need your permission to date whoever the hell I want!"

Brandon snorted. "You ain't dating Dre, so you can just forget that."

Brooke heaved an exasperated breath. "I knew I shouldn't have told you. I didn't want to, but Beau's been holding it over my head and threatening to tell you himself. I wanted you to hear it from me, but I should have known you'd go all big-brother ballistic."

Brandon glowered at her. "You don't need to be checking for Dre."

"Did you not hear what I said? I'm *in love* with him. Have been for years. Now that he and Leah have broken up—"

"What? You figured this was the perfect opportunity to make your move?"

Brooke lifted her chin. "Why not?"

Brandon held her defiant gaze for several moments, then shook his head and scrubbed his hands over his face as he stalked to the windows and glared outside.

Brooke sighed. "I don't understand why you're so dead set against this, Brandon. I get that you've always been protective over me, but Dre's your best friend. You know him better than anyone—"

"Which is exactly why I can tell you that he's not right for you," Brandon growled, turning from the windows.

Brooke stared at him, searching his face. "What are you saying? That he's not good enough for me?"

Brandon clenched his jaw. "That's not what I'm saying."

"Good, because I'd hate to think you consider Dre good enough to be your best friend but not good enough to marry into your family. That's the kind of snobbery I'd expect from Mom and Dad, not you."

Brandon scowled. "You know me better than that, Brooke, so I don't even know why you went there. Look, the bottom line is that Dre's got a lot of shit going on right now—"

"Like what?"

"Don't worry about it." Brandon wasn't about to betray Dre's confidence by telling Brooke about Fiona's pregnancy. It was bad enough that she knew about his cheating—and she still wanted him.

"All you need to know is that he's unavailable, so don't even think about stepping to him. Besides, he still loves Leah and wants to work things out with her."

"But what if they don't?" Brooke challenged. "What if Leah doesn't take him back?"

Brandon shook his head at his sister. "Believe me, baby girl, you don't wanna be the rebound chick."

Brooke smirked. "Like Cynthia?"

Brandon grimaced. He couldn't even deny it.

Just then the intercom on his desk buzzed. "Brandon, your eleven-o'clock appointment is here."

"Thanks, Iris." He retrieved his suit jacket from the back of his chair and shrugged into it as Brooke hopped down from the desk. "We can continue this conversation later."

"No need," she said flippantly. "I wanted to let you know about my feelings for Dre, and now that I have, I can take the next step."

Brandon didn't like the sound of that. At all. "What next step?"

Brooke snorted. "Wouldn't *you* like to know?"

He frowned. "Brooke—"

But she had already pivoted on her heel and started toward the door.

"Wait." He caught up to her. "I'll walk you out."

"Fine. Whatever."

As Brandon escorted his sullen sister down the corridor, he knew what he had to do.

Leah Currie was a surgeon at Memorial Hermann Hospital located within The Woodlands, the community she also called home.

When Brandon stepped off the elevator on the floor where she worked, he saw her standing at the nurses' station reviewing patient charts while chatting with an attractive sister rocking neat twists.

When she glanced up and spotted Brandon coming down the hallway, she frowned, looking neither surprised nor pleased to see him.

As he reached her, she heaved an exasperated breath. "I knew it was only a matter of time before he'd send you."

Brandon grinned. "He didn't send me. He doesn't even know I'm here."

Leah sighed, shaking her head. "What do you want, Brandon? Or do I even have to ask?"

"I brought you lunch from Pei Wei," he offered, holding up a white plastic bag bearing the restaurant's name and logo. He wasn't above using Brooke's tactics.

Surprise flickered across Leah's face before her eyes narrowed with suspicion. "What is it?"

"An Asian chicken salad. Dre used to say it was your favorite."

Leah's expression softened. "And you remembered that?"

"Awww," the nurse cooed, gazing appreciatively at Brandon. "How *sweeeet*."

Brandon winked at her, and she smiled flirtatiously.

Leah accepted the bag and looked inside. "You got me spring rolls, too?"

"Yup. I know how much you like those as well."

He could see her lips twitching as she fought a pleased smile. That's when he knew he had her.

"You're lucky I just finished my rounds." She took his hand. "Come on. We can talk in the nurses lounge. It's usually quiet this time of day."

Inside the empty room, they sat at a small table. Brandon watched as Leah doused her salad with the sesame vinaigrette dressing and crispy wonton strips, then picked up the plastic fork and began eating.

She was a modestly attractive woman, which sounded better than calling her a plain Jane—as Dre's mother had done. She was light skinned with amber eyes and a freckled nose. Her tall, thin frame made her look like a clothes hanger in her baggy blue scrubs. If it were up to Brandon, she'd be eating steaks and cheese grits for lunch every day instead of salads. Looking at her, he couldn't help wondering how he and Dre had both ended up with skinny women when they'd always preferred sistas with ripe curves, luscious breasts, thick thighs, and phat asses.

"Mmm, this hits the spot," Leah murmured around a mouthful of chicken salad. "Thank you, Brandon."

He smiled. "You're welcome."

"Do you want some?"

"Nah, I'm good. I already had lunch."

Leah nodded, chewing quietly.

"So," Brandon said, clasping his hands on the table, "how you been, girl?"

She gave him a wry look. "How do you think I've been?"

Observing the deep bags under her eyes, Brandon said ruefully, "I think you've probably been better."

She grimaced self-consciously. "Do I look *that* bad?"

"Not bad," Brandon said diplomatically. "Just unhappy."

She nodded glumly.

"If it's any consolation, Dre isn't doing too well either. In fact, he's barely holding it together. He misses you, Leah."

Her lips twisted bitterly. "Guess he should have thought of that before he fucked another woman in my house."

Brandon grimaced, watching as she viciously stabbed the fork into her salad, as if she could see Dre's face floating above the lettuce. "He feels really horrible about what happened, Leah."

"Only because he got caught," she said scornfully. "If I hadn't walked in on them, he would have continued screwing Fiona behind my back. And after *she* got hauled off to prison, he would have found another side piece."

"That's not true," Brandon objected.

"How do you know?"

"Because he loves you, Leah."

She snorted derisively. "He sure as hell has a funny way of showing it."

Frowning, Brandon reached out and put his hand over hers, stopping her assault on the poor lettuce. When she released the fork and slowly lifted her eyes to his, he said quietly, "What Dre did was inexcusable, but should one bad mistake erase four years of him being good to you?"

Leah stared accusingly at Brandon. "Are you actually *defending* him?"

"Hell, no. What he did was fucked up, and I've told him that. So have Justin and Cornel. Believe me, he understands how much he hurt you and betrayed your trust. He knows how lucky he'd be to get a second chance with you."

Leah frowned, staring down at her half-eaten salad. "I don't know, Brandon. I'm not like you. I don't have the capacity to forgive cheating."

He smiled sadly. "You'd be amazed what you can forgive of someone you really love."

Leah's nostrils flared, eyes blinking rapidly.

Sensing the waterworks to come, Brandon eased his chair around the table. Seconds later when the dam burst, his shoulder was there to absorb the deluge of tears.

"I saw them," Leah sobbed piteously. "I saw them screwing while I was *right* down the hall! How could I ever forgive him for doing that to me?"

Brandon rubbed her back and murmured consolingly as she wept.

He suddenly felt guilty for coming there because he knew his motives weren't as pure as they should have been. Though he'd been debating whether or not to get involved in Leah and Dre's breakup, Brooke's confession had made up his mind. But was it fair to ask Leah to reconcile with Dre? As if it weren't bad enough that he'd cheated on her, he'd also gotten the other woman pregnant. Leah would be devastated when she found out. And who could blame her? If Tamia had gotten knocked up by Dominic, Brandon would probably be in prison right now.

After several minutes, Leah stopped crying and lifted her head from his shoulder. He grabbed one of the paper napkins and handed it to her.

She wiped her eyes and quietly blew her nose, then gave him a rueful smile. "Thanks for letting me cry on your shoulder. Hope I didn't ruin your Armani."

Brandon chuckled. "It's all good. That's what dry cleaners are for."

She laughed softly.

"I'm sorry for coming here and upsetting you," Brandon told her. "That wasn't my intention."

"I know." Leah smiled, cupping his cheek. "You're a great guy, Brandon. Sometimes I think I fell in love with the wrong friend."

"You didn't."

She sighed. "Maybe not, but I sure as hell wouldn't mind getting back at Dre by sleeping with you."

Brandon's smile evaporated. "Uhhh . . ."

Leah laughed. "I'm kidding, Brandon."

He believed her. But after the madness with Dre's mother, he wasn't taking any chances.

"Well, I'd better head back to work and let you get back to your patients," he said, rising from the table.

Leah nodded, gathering her unfinished food. "I have to scrub in for surgery soon." She smiled warmly at him. "Thanks again for everything, Brandon."

"You're welcome. At the end of the day, I just want you to do whatever's best for you."

Leah nodded. "I will."

As Brandon left the hospital, he hoped that Leah and Dre's relationship would have a better outcome than his and Tamia's.

But he wasn't very optimistic.

Chapter 30
Tamia

"Tamia Giselle Luke, you got some 'splainin' to do!"

Tamia cringed at the sound of Shanell's voice.

She'd been lazing on Dominic's plush sofa that afternoon when her phone rang. Even before she'd checked the display screen, she'd known it was Shanell. And she knew she was in for an epic tongue lashing.

"Hey, girl," she said meekly.

"Don't you 'hey, girl' me after you've been ignoring my calls for the past three days!"

Guilt swept over Tamia. "I'm really sorry about that, Shanell."

"You should be. Not only for avoiding my calls, but for lying about where you were going on Saturday when you snuck out of my house. I couldn't believe it when Marcellus called to tell me that he ran into you at a model home on Saturday. What the hell were you doing there with Dominic Archer? And wearing an *engagement ring*?"

Tamia grimaced. "It's a long story."

"I got time, heffa. So start talking."

Tamia heaved a resigned breath, then sat up and reached for the glass of wine on the ottoman. She took a long sip, stalling.

"I'm waiting," Shanell prompted impatiently.

Settling back against the sofa cushions, Tamia told her friend the whole story, starting from the night Dominic had showed up at the restaurant and ending with the romantic weekend they'd just spent together.

When she'd finished her account, Shanell was silent.

Deafeningly silent.

"Well?" Tamia prompted nervously.

"Well what?"

"Don't you have anything to say?"

Shanell sighed heavily. "I don't even know where to begin."

Tamia gulped hard, bracing herself.

"I understand needing money to start your business, and I'll admit that it was very generous of Dominic to hook you up like that. But honestly, Tamia, when you told me you were moving onward and upward, I didn't think that included getting involved with that bastard again. I thought—*hoped*—you were done with him after everything he put you through. I mean, you're a smart, gorgeous woman who can have any man you want. You already know that Gavin is totally smitten with you, and he never came close to even *sniffing* the pussy. Hell, some of the guys at Richards Carruth still ask me about you. Like I said, you a badass chick who can pull any dude you want. So I don't understand why you keep fooling around with that lowlife. I mean, is the dick *that* good?"

Tamia's face heated. "It's not about that."

"But the dick *is* good," Shanell said knowingly.

"It is," Tamia admitted. "Dominic is an amazing lover."

"Better than Brandon?"

Tamia hesitated for a long moment, thinking about the explosive passion she and Brandon shared . . . the powerful connection . . . the depth of emotion between them. It was never just fucking for the sake of fucking.

She sighed deeply. "You know, when I first started sleeping with Dominic, I thought he might be better in bed than Brandon. Being with him was new and dangerous and exciting, and I couldn't get enough of him. And I'm not gonna lie—part of me took some satisfaction in getting back at Brandon for not being more committed to our relationship."

"Is that what this is about, Tamia?" Shanell quietly probed. "Is that why—out of all the men you could be with—you're still giving Dominic the time of day? Because you subconsciously want to punish Brandon?"

Tamia frowned. "I don't think so."

"You don't *want* to think so."

"No . . . I honestly don't feel that way anymore. I don't want to punish Brandon. I think he's hurting enough."

"Girl, he must be," Shanell said grimly. "According to Marcellus, Brandon looked *devastated* when he saw that ring on your finger. Marcellus didn't know whether the brotha was gonna break down in tears or fuck somebody up."

Tamia swallowed tightly. "It was a misunderstanding."

"That's what I told Marcellus. I knew there was no way in hell you'd gotten engaged without telling me." Shanell snorted. "Little did I know you and Dominic were off having a romantic tryst at some B and B."

Tamia couldn't help smiling. "It *was* romantic."

"So you've said." Shanell sounded disgruntled. "How do you know you can trust him?"

"I don't," Tamia admitted.

"Then why even take a risk?"

Tamia didn't respond.

"Oh my God," Shanell murmured. "You have feelings for him, don't you?"

Tamia sighed, staring at the ceiling. "I don't know, Shanell. I got to know him better this weekend, and he's not the man I thought he was. What he told me about his marriage to Isabel gave me a different perspective on him. I'm not justifying his infidelity, but I could definitely relate to what made him stray."

"So now you're kindred spirits," Shanell mocked.

Tamia smiled. "Maybe we are. Stranger things have happened."

She could almost see Shanell rolling her eyes.

"So where are you now? At his place?"

"Yeah," Tamia answered.

When she and Dominic got back to Houston that morning, he'd asked her to come home with him and spend the night. She'd agreed, but only on the condition that they stop at her apartment first to pick up her car. Though she was enjoying Dominic's company, she didn't want to be trapped at his apartment if he started working her nerves.

"Oh, before I forget," Shanell said, "Marcellus wants you to call him to schedule an appointment so he can see your house. I'll text his number to you."

"Cool. Thanks. I'll get in touch with him tomorrow."

Just then Tamia's phone beeped. When she saw Officer Greene's number on the display screen, she said, "I gotta run, Shanell. Talk to you later." She pushed the button to receive the incoming call. "Hello?"

"Hello, Miss Luke. This is Officer Greene. How're you doing?"

"I'm fine." She felt uncomfortable talking to him now that she knew he was the same asshole who'd put his hands on Honey. She wanted to cuss him out, but she'd promised not to say a word.

"I wanted to give you an update on the investigation," Keyshawn said, oblivious to her simmering animosity. "We've reviewed the visitor log and security tapes, and everything seems to check out. Most tenants were at work during the hours you weren't home, so there wasn't much foot traffic. The few visitors to the building that day have been questioned and cleared. Unfortunately, there was some sort of neighborhood power outage that caused a glitch in the security system, so we lost over an hour of surveillance footage. It's entirely possible that the note was left during that time."

Tamia frowned darkly. "How convenient."

"Seems that way, but as you've probably learned, power outages aren't uncommon in that part of town with all the new construction going on. So whoever left the note just caught a lucky break."

Tamia blew out a frustrated breath. "Great."

"I know." Keyshawn sounded grim. "Our lab guy couldn't lift any prints from the note, but we'd already assumed that the perp wore gloves anyway. Also, we were able to track down Lester McCray. He admitted that he lied about living near you because he was hoping you'd go out with him if you ran into him enough times. But he told us that he was at a seminar all day on Thursday, and his colleagues vouched for his whereabouts. Now, that doesn't mean he couldn't have arranged for someone else to deliver the note for him, but it'll be harder to prove since he has an alibi."

Tamia sighed heavily. "Another dead end."

"I'm sorry. I wish I had better news for you, but these cases often take time to resolve. In the meantime, the building management has promised to beef up security, and the front desk staff is on heightened alert to report any suspicious activity. If you can crash at a friend's place for a while, that's what I'd recommend."

Tamia nodded, glancing around Dominic's expensively furnished penthouse. "Thank you for calling, Officer Greene. I appreciate the update."

"You're welcome, Miss Luke. I'll be in touch."

Tamia disconnected, then set the phone down and frowned. She didn't like being a prisoner to some unknown threat. It made her feel weak and powerless—two things she'd always detested.

She couldn't stay with Dominic indefinitely, nor did she want to impose on Shanell and Mark. Sooner or later she'd have to return home and resume her normal life.

Whatever "normal" means anymore, she mused grimly as she rose from the sofa.

After she and Dominic had made love that morning, he'd left to take care of some business at the office. Tamia had showered and dressed, then pulled out her laptop to work on concepts for the Ehrlichs' ad campaign until she became too drowsy to concentrate.

Crossing to the wet bar, she poured herself another glass of wine. As she languidly sipped her drink, she looked around the room, reliving memories of the first time she'd been summoned to Dominic's penthouse. She'd put on her Mystique costume, and she and Dominic had masturbated while watching each other. It had been hot and intense— the beginning of a dangerous affair that had nearly destroyed her.

As Tamia slowly glanced around, something lying beneath the ottoman caught her eye. Curious, she walked over and bent down to investigate.

It was a pair of women's leopard-print panties.

She recoiled, lips curled in disgust.

Instantly her mind flashed on an image of Dominic fucking some hoochie on the sofa, his ass cheeks flexing as he pounded her from behind.

Tamia scowled.

She knew she had no right to be pissed. Dominic wasn't her man, and these panties had obviously been left before he and Tamia reunited this weekend.

Her anger wasn't about feeling cheated on.

It was about not wanting to get played again.

Gritting her teeth, Tamia reached under the ottoman and picked up the underwear, using only the tips of her fingers lest she catch some fungus. She dropped the panties on top of the ottoman so Dominic would see them the moment he entered the room. Then she spun on her heel and marched to the master bedroom.

After grabbing her belongings, she bounced.

Chapter 31

Tamia

Twenty minutes later, Tamia swung into the underground parking garage at her apartment building. She'd decided to run home, pack more clothes, and head over to Shanell's house.

It was barely three o'clock, so the garage was practically deserted since most of her neighbors were still at work. Climbing out of her car, she closed the door and pressed the key fob to set the alarm, though she knew no one who lived here would ever want to steal her ride. The tenants of the luxury residence consisted of oil and gas executives, lawyers, doctors, professional athletes, and administrators from the nearby medical center. Compared to the vehicles they drove, her old Accord was a hooptie.

As Tamia started across the garage, she heard footsteps behind her.

Her skin prickled with unease.

She automatically quickened her pace, fingers closing around the compact canister of Mace attached to her keys.

As the footsteps came closer, she realized that there were two people.

A chill ran through her.

She walked faster, nerves tightening as the footsteps behind her accelerated to match her stride.

Heart pounding, she whirled around to see two figures in ski masks advancing on her.

Her blood ran cold.

Before she could raise her arm to get off a shot of pepper spray, one of the masked figures rushed her. She gasped as her keys—and the Mace—were knocked out of her hand, sending a jolt of pain up her arm.

Reacting on instinct, she swung her leg hard, kicking her attacker in the crotch.

A high-pitched scream rang out as the masked figure doubled over.

Tamia stared, stunned to realize that her attacker was a woman.

Before she could process this detail, the other assailant was upon her, viciously snatching a fistful of her hair.

"*You fucking bitch!*" a muffled female voice shouted.

Tamia started swinging, landing punches wherever she could. The woman was bigger and stronger, outweighing her by at least thirty pounds. But Tamia instinctively knew that she was in the fight of her life, so she couldn't afford to be intimidated by her opponent's size.

Keeping her head down to protect her face, she punched and clawed at her attacker, raking her nails across her exposed neck.

Screeching in pain, the woman violently shoved Tamia against the back of an SUV. Grunting from the impact, Tamia reached out and snatched off her assailant's ski mask so she could identify her.

She froze in shock when she found herself staring into the enraged face of the woman who'd screamed threats to her on the day of her acquittal.

You bitch! You're gonna burn in hell for what you did to Isabel!

So this attack was about avenging Dominic's wife?

Tamia didn't have time to speculate because the other woman had recovered from her kick and was coming toward them. When Tamia saw the glint of a switchblade flicking open in the woman's hand, panic shot through her veins, and she began shoving at the heavy body pinning her to the truck.

"Hey!" a man called out sharply. "What's going on down there?"

As the unmasked woman glanced toward the voice, Tamia took advantage of her distraction and twisted herself free just as the knife-wielding attacker lunged at her. She dodged the slashing blade and staggered backward, fear and adrenaline pumping through her blood. She could hear footsteps pounding across the pavement, rushing toward the commotion.

"Whoring bitch!" the unmasked woman spat, charging toward Tamia just as the parking attendant and two other men reached them.

The two women turned to flee, but the men chased them down, tackling them roughly to the ground as the parking attendant hurried over to Tamia.

"Are you okay?" he asked in concern.

She could only give a jerky nod, lungs burning as she gasped for breath.

Everything was a blur after that.

The police arrived, sirens blasting.

Dominic followed shortly, lunging from the Phantom. When he saw the handcuffed women on the ground, he began yelling at them and they yelled back, the angry Crucian words firing between them like bullets until the cops intervened.

Then Dominic was standing before Tamia, his hands gently cradling her face, his eyes peering worriedly into hers as he asked her questions. She stared at his mouth but couldn't make out his words above the dull roar in her ears.

Shaken by how close she'd come to getting stabbed, she didn't protest when Dominic told the police officers he was taking her home. She allowed herself to be led to his car and helped inside, grateful to get as far away from this crazy place as she could.

Later, she lay curled up in Dominic's bed as he spooned her, infusing her sore body with warmth.

"I'm sorry that Isabel's cousins came after you like that," he murmured, his voice rumbling quietly in the darkness. "If I had known what they were planning to do, I would have stopped them."

"Would you?"

Tamia felt him tense against her. "What's that supposed to mean?"

She was silent, her mind churning with suspicion and doubt. Dominic's dead wife's relatives had just tried to kill her. It wasn't that long ago that *he'd* shown up on her doorstep and assaulted her when she'd refused to tell him who had killed Isabel.

What was she supposed to believe? Who was she supposed to trust?

"Is that why you didn't tell me about the note you received?"

Dominic exclaimed in wounded surprise. "Because you thought *I* was the one who sent it?"

Tamia heaved a weary sigh. "I don't know, Dominic. I honestly didn't know *who* could have sent the note."

"It sure as hell wasn't me," he asserted. "I know you still find this hard to believe, Tamia, but I didn't come back into your life to hurt you again. I'm *crazy* about you. I'm trying to do right by you. When I came home early and found you gone, I almost lost my damn mind. I couldn't get over to your apartment fast enough. I would have been devastated if something worse had happened to you."

Tamia said nothing, wishing she could trust him. Wishing she could trust *anyone*. In the wee hours of the night, she'd even found herself wondering if Brandon could have left her the note. He, more than anyone else, could take credit for saving her life, and he might even feel that she owed him her loyalty.

But would Brandon go that far? How thin *was* the line between love and hate?

"Dashay and Jamila were like sisters to Isabel," Dominic explained, breaking into Tamia's thoughts. "They all grew up together and were practically inseparable. It's because of Isabel that Dashay and Jamila came to America. So they took her death pretty hard."

"I understand that," Tamia murmured. "But they know I didn't kill Isabel."

"But your sister did. And since they can't get to Fiona—"

"—I'm the next best thing." Tamia shook her head against the pillow. "They've obviously been stalking me, Dominic. They saw me leave your building this afternoon and they followed me back home. They know we're involved again, and they don't like it."

"That's too fucking bad."

"Really, Dominic? Those crazy bitches jumped me and tried to stab me."

"And that's why they're in jail," Dominic growled. "The whole damn thing was caught on the security camera. Add that to the threatening note they sent you, and it's a wrap."

Tamia frowned, not entirely convinced that she was out of danger. "The note still doesn't make any sense. It said, 'I saved your life, bitch. You owe me.' How does that apply to Isabel's cousins? How did they save my life?"

Dominic said nothing, contemplating the question.

As a weighted silence stretched between them, Tamia yawned softly, struggling to keep her eyelids open. She was exhausted. But she'd felt that way even before the attack. Dominic must have really worn her out over the weekend.

"I know what you saw earlier," he murmured, breaking the silence. "I know what made you leave. But that woman didn't mean anything to me, Tamia. She was just a one-night stand."

Tamia was quiet, wondering how many times he'd given the same speech to Isabel.

"Don't leave me again," he whispered urgently, his face buried in her hair. "You need to stay here for your own protection."

She sighed tiredly. "Dominic—"

"Promise me you won't go anywhere."

When she didn't respond, his arm tightened around her. "Promise me."

Tamia nodded weakly and closed her eyes, surrendering to the peaceful oblivion of sleep. . . .

Chapter 32

Brandon

"Did you forget something today?"

The question greeted Brandon as he stepped through the front door of his condo on Tuesday evening, a basketball tucked under one arm. He wore a black wifebeater, long black athletic shorts, and the newest LeBron James high-top Nikes.

After work, he'd met Dre, Justin, and Cornel for a pickup game at the gym. He'd gotten a good workout, burning off some pent-up tension. But he'd felt his blood pressure spike when he saw Cynthia curled up on the armchair—*his* armchair—watching him expectantly.

He set the basketball down, eyeing her guardedly. "What did I forget?"

"You don't remember?" The words were accusing, but Cynthia's eyes were soft and glowing with a quiet joy he didn't comprehend.

"I'm sorry," he said, starting toward the living room. "I don't remember what it is that I supposedly forgot. You'll have to help me out here."

Cynthia sighed. "I had a doctor's appointment today. You promised to go with me."

Brandon frowned. "That was *today*?"

"Yes."

He shook his head. "I'm sorry, babe. I could have sworn you told me your appointment was on Thursday. I even put it on my calendar."

"It was today at three," Cynthia countered, surprisingly calm. "I left from the courthouse and was expecting you to meet me at the doctor's office."

"Shit. I am so sorry. I must have gotten the dates mixed up."

"That's what I figured." Her lips twisted wryly. "I didn't wanna call and cuss you out in front of Dr. Kapoor."

Brandon grimaced. Reaching the armchair, he leaned down and kissed Cynthia on the forehead. "I'm really sorry I missed the appointment."

"So am I. I wanted you to be there for my first sonogram."

Brandon stilled. "Your first . . . you had a sonogram today?"

"Yup." She beamed and reached behind her back to retrieve something, which she excitedly handed to him.

It was an ultrasound photo.

"That's our baby!" she squealed.

As Brandon stared down at the black and white image, something like panic seized his chest. He felt his throat closing, felt himself being strangled by the invisible chain his brother had teased him about.

He tried to speak but no sound emerged.

Cynthia eyed him curiously. "Brandon?"

He just shook his head, staggering backward.

All this time he'd been secretly hoping . . . praying for some stroke of divine intervention. But it wasn't meant to be. The photo he held was the proof that had sealed his fate.

As the back of his legs hit the sofa, he sat down heavily.

Cynthia laughed. "Look at you! You're in shock."

"Uh . . . yeah." Brandon swallowed convulsively. His voice had gone hoarse. "Wow . . ."

Cynthia grinned. "I know. That was the first word out of my mouth when I saw the baby on the screen." Bubbling with excitement, she sprang from the armchair and rushed to his side. The ends of her hair tickled his shoulder as she leaned over him to stare at the sonogram photo. "Look at our son, Brandon. Isn't he beautiful?"

Brandon nodded jerkily, though the fetus in the grainy picture was so tiny it could have been anything. "How . . . um, how do you know we're having a boy? It's too soon to tell, isn't it?"

"Yeah," Cynthia said on a dreamy sigh. "But I just have a feeling I'm carrying your son. Call it a maternal instinct."

Brandon nodded, staring down at the photo until his eyes burned.

"He's gonna look *just* like you," Cynthia predicted, tenderly rubbing the back of Brandon's head. "Right down to your sexy dimples."

Dimples . . . did he have dimples? He'd nearly forgotten since it had been so long since he'd really smiled.

Cynthia giggled, giddier than he'd ever seen her. "Dr. Kapoor says when I'm at twenty-five weeks, we can get a 4-D ultrasound. Those are so *amazing*, Brandon. We'll be able to clearly see the baby's features and watch him move around in my stomach. I can't *wait!*"

"Yeah," Brandon murmured, "neither can I."

Cynthia kissed the top of his head. "This calls for a celebration. I stopped at Kroger on the way home and bought a bottle of sparkling cider, and I ordered dinner from our favorite delivery service. It should be here in twenty minutes."

"Sounds good," Brandon said weakly, pushing to his feet and handing the photo back to her. "Let me just, uh, hop in the shower first. I'm kinda funky."

Cynthia winked. "After we eat, we can *both* get funky."

Brandon just smiled before turning and heading to the bedroom. His heart pounded painfully as he kicked off his sneakers and shed his sweat-dampened clothes.

Once inside the bathroom, he ducked into the shower stall and twisted on the faucet, making the temperature as hot as he could take it. Bracing his hands against the tiled wall for support, he bowed his head and let the water run down his face, mingling with the bitter wetness that leaked from his eyes.

Chapter 33

Tamia

"I can't go to the fundraiser with you tomorrow," Honey blurted when Tamia answered her phone on Thursday evening.

Tamia frowned. "What do you mean you can't go? I thought you said Keyshawn has to work this weekend."

"That's what he told me, but I'm starting to have my doubts."

"Why?"

"Well, he's been acting jealous and suspicious again. When I got out of the shower this morning, I caught him going through my purse. He claimed he was looking for some gum, but I didn't believe him. He's started asking me questions about Bishop Yarbrough again, even though I haven't been on any dates with him since I got back from New Orleans. It's like Keyshawn's just *looking* for a reason to go public about me and the bishop."

Tamia frowned. "Damn, girl."

"I know. It's crazy." Honey sounded close to tears. "I think he followed me to one of my dates the other night, and he's probably planning to do the same thing if I go to the fundraiser banquet with you. So I ain't taking no chances."

"That's probably a good idea. And it just occurred to me that Bishop Yarbrough will probably be there—"

"Shit. That's right. I hadn't even thought of that." Honey sighed heavily. "Yeah, I'd better keep my ass at home."

"Yeah," Tamia grimly agreed. "But I'm sorry you won't be able to go. Beau's gonna be so disappointed."

"I know," Honey lamented. "I really wanted to meet him, but it just seems like it's never gonna happen."

"It will. Don't worry." Tamia ate her last forkful of plantain, tapping her foot to the rhythm of steel drums that transported her back to St. Croix.

"Where are you?" Honey asked curiously.

"At a restaurant," Tamia answered vaguely.

She was having an early dinner at Winston's, named after Dominic's late grandfather. The popular Caribbean-style restaurant featured an elegantly casual decor with French doors and dark leather booths contrasted with walls the color of papaya. There were beautiful watercolors that paid homage to St. Croix's white-sand beaches, stunning coral reefs, Carnival revelers in full regalia, and people wandering down cobblestone streets lined with shops.

When Tamia and Dominic arrived at the restaurant that afternoon, he'd steered her to a private corner booth and instructed the waitress to bring her a plate of curried goat, saltfish, and plantain. When her meal was served, he'd stuck around long enough to feed her a few delicious bites before he headed upstairs to conduct a business meeting with some investors.

"Are you still going to the fundraiser?"

Pulled out of her reverie, Tamia made a face and shook her head. "I don't think so."

"Why not?" Honey asked. "You could take someone else, have a fun night. I heard there's gonna be a lot of celebrities and ballers there."

Tamia scowled. "You know who else is gonna be there? Brandon and his fiancée."

"Oh, yeah," Honey mumbled sheepishly.

"Uh-huh." Tamia sipped her margarita, absently thinking it could use more tequila. She could hardly taste any at all. "Anyway, girl, thanks for letting me know about tomorrow. I'll holla at ya later."

As Tamia ended the call, she saw Dominic coming downstairs with a group of businessmen. They were laughing, chewing on cigars, and slapping backs in a manner that suggested their meeting had been a success.

After ushering the men to the door, Dominic started toward Tamia's booth in the corner. Along the way, he danced to the calypso music, moving his hips to a chorus of whistles and catcalls from his appreciative female customers. When one bodacious sista sashayed over and began grinding against him, the restaurant erupted in applause and rowdy cheers of approval.

At the end of the song, Dominic flirtatiously swatted the woman's thick ass and winked at her, making panties melt all over the place.

Watching from her table, Tamia could understand how Isabel must have felt being married to Dominic. He was a playa, a bona fide chick magnet whose irresistible sex appeal would awaken any woman's deepest fears and insecurities. It'd be impossible *not* to feel paranoid every time he was out of one's sight.

When he sauntered over to Tamia and flashed that wicked grin, she rolled her eyes at him.

He laughed, sliding into the booth beside her. "You mad?"

She sucked her teeth. "You wish."

He laughed again as the waitress hustled over, serving him a bottle of beer before scooping up Tamia's empty plate.

"Did you enjoy your food, ma'am?" she asked with a musical West Indian accent.

Tamia grinned. "Are you kidding? I licked my plate clean."

The girl beamed with pleasure. "Wait till you taste our coconut rum cake, made with the best Cruzan rum. You're gonna love it."

Tamia's grin widened. "Bring it on."

As the smiling girl moved off, Dominic leaned over and kissed Tamia's cheek.

She slanted him a teasing smile. "*You're* in an exceptionally good mood. I take it your meeting went well."

"It went *very* well," he confirmed.

"That's good."

Once Dominic had been cleared as a suspect in his wife's murder, he had been able to collect on her multimillion-dollar insurance policy and recover his frozen assets, which were considerable. Since he was no longer under a cloud of scandal, his company's profits had begun to rebound, clients returned, and customers flocked to the new restaurant, keeping it packed every night.

"I like having you here," Dominic said.

"I like being here." Tamia grinned, patting her full stomach. "So does my appetite."

Dominic chuckled. "I love a woman who can appreciate Caribbean food."

"What's not to appreciate when everything tastes so damn good?"

Dominic smiled, loosening the knot of his tie as he leaned back against the leather cushions. He took a swig of beer, eyes glinting with amusement as he watched Tamia drink her margarita. She was convinced that she'd been given a nonalcoholic one by mistake.

"Can we go home after this," Dominic drawled, draping an arm over the back of the seat behind her, "or would you like to stop somewhere and pick up more Christmas decorations? Perhaps a giant frosted sleigh to hang from the ceiling?"

Tamia's eyes narrowed. "You got jokes about my decorating skills?"

Dominic laughed. "You got my crib lookin' like a Christmas village with all those lights and shit."

"Hey, you told me I could decorate for the holidays."

"True, but I didn't think you'd go overboard. A twenty-foot tree?"

Tamia gave him an affronted look. "If you want me to take everything down—"

Dominic grinned. "Nah, you know I'm only teasin' you. I love the way you hooked up the place. It's beautiful, got me in the holiday spirit." He winked. "Just never figured my queen from da hood would have Martha Stewart tendencies."

Tamia blushed, shrugging a shoulder. "We couldn't afford much when I was growing up. I always wanted a huge tree, stockings hung from the mantel, lights on the roof—the whole nine." She grinned self-consciously. "I know that sounds corny."

"It doesn't sound corny at all. I think it's sweet."

Tamia gave him a shy smile, making him groan.

"You stealin' my heart, woman. Pullin' it right outta my chest and makin' it yours."

She laughed. "Um, okay."

When Dominic's phone rang, he scooped it off the table and glanced at the display screen. "I gotta take this call. It's business."

"Sure. Go ahead."

Tamia watched him slide out of the booth and saunter away with the phone pressed to his ear. As she picked up her glass and sipped her drink, her gaze wandered around the room before landing on the plasma television mounted above the bar. The channel was tuned to the local evening news.

Without warning, there were Brandon and Cynthia, along with their parents, serving holiday meals to the needy from the kitchen of Joseph Yarbrough's megachurch. It was the perfect photo op for the two family dynasties—the Chamberses and Yarbroughs.

As Tamia watched the news segment, it was clear to her that Brandon was the only one who wasn't performing for the cameras. As he interacted with the homeless, his smiles were full of genuine warmth, and his handshakes were firm and strong. But this came as no surprise to Tamia. She knew Brandon was the real deal. He mentored underserved boys through his friend Justin's community organization, played basketball with reformed gang members, and donated generously to many charities. She remembered the times when they'd been on dates and he'd stopped to talk to panhandlers before he slipped them a large bill or escorted them somewhere to get a hot meal. Sometimes she'd been uneasy, and she'd cautioned him to be careful so he wouldn't get taken advantage of. But he'd merely smile, shake his head, and remind her of the scripture, *To whom much is given, much is required.*

Brandon's generosity and complete lack of pretentiousness were among the many things Tamia had always loved and admired about him.

But seeing him on television with Cynthia by his side hurt like a knife sliding between her ribs to puncture her aching heart.

Returning to the booth, Dominic took one look at Tamia's wounded expression, identified the source, then called toward the bar, "Yo, somebody turn dah channel."

The command was promptly obeyed.

Dominic slid into the booth, this time sitting across from Tamia. "Sorry for keeping you waiting."

She waved a dismissive hand. "No problem. Everything okay?"

"Everything's fine. That was one of my clients. I told him I'd see him tomorrow night at the—"

He was interrupted by the waitress, who brought the coconut rum cake to Tamia and winked at her. "Enjoy."

Tamia grinned. "Oh, I know I will."

She dug into the wet slice of cake, slid the fork into her mouth, and closed her eyes with an appreciative groan. "Oh my God . . ."

"Good?"

" 'Good' doesn't even come close." Tamia ate another bite and moaned.

"Damn, girl," Dominic said thickly. "Watching you eat makes my dick hard."

Tamia choked out a laugh. "*Dominic!*"

"What? I'm just speakin' the truth. Don't believe me? Just slide your foot under this table and feel how hard I am."

Unable to resist the wicked challenge, Tamia slipped off one of her high heels and slowly eased her foot into his lap. When she encountered the granite mound of his erection, her eyes widened.

"Oh, my," she breathed, biting her lip.

His eyes gleamed. "Told you."

"Yes, you did." She smiled coyly. "Here, let me give you something sweet to go with all that meat."

She fed him a bite of cake, watching his juicy lips close around the tines of the fork. As her pussy clenched, she rubbed her foot against his bulging shaft and licked her lips, watching him swallow.

"Good?"

"Delicious." His nostrils flared. "Hurry up and finish so we can go home. I need to fuck you real good and hard."

"Mmm." Tamia's nipples tightened, heat spreading all over her body. "You certainly have a way with words, Mr. Archer."

"And you got a way with that tongue," he rumbled, watching her lick creamy frosting from the fork. "If you had on a skirt I'd be under this table doing some serious licking of my own right now."

Tamia's pussy pumped, leaking juices. "Okay, we'd better stop," she whispered, removing her foot from Dominic's crotch and fanning herself.

He chuckled, leaning back against the leather cushions to watch as she demurely ate more cake.

"I want you to go to the fundraiser gala with me tomorrow night."

Her eyes flew to his face in startled surprise. "What fundraiser gala?"

Dominic looked amused. "The one you're planning to attend with your friend Honey."

"Oh." Tamia swallowed, shaking her head. "She can't make it, so I'm not going either."

"I want you to go with me," Dominic said smoothly. "I bought a ticket a few weeks ago—before they were sold out."

Tamia frowned. "Why would you want to go to the banquet?"

He shrugged. "Some of my clients will be there, so it'll be a great networking opportunity for me. For both of us, actually. Besides," he added humorously, "it's the biggest social event of the season. Haven't you heard?"

Tamia calmly ate another piece of cake. "I don't want to go. And especially not with you."

"Why not?"

She frowned at him. "Because Brandon will be there."

"And you don't want him to see us together," Dominic surmised. "Because you don't want to hurt him."

Tamia nodded.

"Let me tell you something about that. Brandon—" Dominic stopped himself, shaking his head and rubbing his goatee. "Never mind."

Tamia eyed him curiously. "What were you going to say?"

"Forget it. I shouldn't even have brought it up."

"Brought what up?"

"Nothing. I don't want you to think I'm trying to start something. Because I'm not."

Tamia frowned. "What are you talking about, Dominic?"

He hesitated for a long moment, his eyes gently probing hers. "Remember the mayor's fundraiser dinner back in April? The one Brandon attended without you?"

Tamia's expression darkened. She remembered the night she'd gone to Brandon's office for a booty call and they'd ended up arguing after Cynthia casually mentioned that she'd see him at the fundraiser dinner. Tamia had known nothing about it because Brandon hadn't wanted to introduce her to his parents, who would be at the event.

"After I attended the dinner," Dominic continued, "you asked me whether I saw Brandon and Cynthia there together, and I wouldn't tell you."

Tamia stared at him, her breath lodged in her throat. Did she want to know? Did it make any difference at this point?

Probably not, but . . .

"Were they?" she asked, barely above a whisper.

Dominic met her gaze and nodded grimly. "They were. I don't know if they arrived in the same car or not, but they definitely spent the whole evening together. I know most people assumed they were a couple, and they seemed to be okay with that. I didn't tell you then because I didn't want to hurt your feelings."

"And now?" Tamia's throat was tight. "Why are you telling me now?"

Dominic's expression softened. "Because you're so concerned about not being seen with me to spare Brandon's feelings, and I can't help wondering why you keep giving him the same courtesy he never gave you."

Tamia stared down at the moist crumbs scattered across her plate. She felt hurt . . . betrayed.

Maybe that had been Dominic's intention. Maybe he was playing her for a damn fool by making up lies about Brandon.

But if he was telling the truth . . .

Calmly lifting her eyes to his, she announced with quiet resolve, "I'm wearing red."

A slow, approving smile spread across Dominic's face. "As I've told you before, red is *definitely* your color."

Chapter 34
Tamia

Pinnacle Sports Group's fundraiser gala was held in the grand ballroom of the ritziest luxury hotel downtown. The premier event was attended by a who's who of powerful politicians, business leaders, philanthropists, entertainers, and professional athletes. The keynote speaker was Emmitt Smith, and VIP guests included Beyoncé and Jay-Z, who'd generously contributed to the five hundred thousand dollars' worth of scholarships that would be awarded to several inner-city youth athletes.

When Tamia and Dominic arrived, the ballroom was abuzz with glamorously dressed people laughing and socializing, posing for pictures, and giving interviews to reporters. White-gloved waiters wended through the perfumed crowd serving champagne and hors d'oeuvres. The linen-covered tables were adorned with elegant centerpieces of silver candles nestled by glass ornaments and frosted pine branches. A jazz quartet was playing classic Christmas songs.

Tamia was wearing the strapless red Versace gown Brandon had bought her in Italy.

The twenty-thousand-dollar gown he hadn't been able to peel off her fast enough.

The gown that clung dangerously to her curves and had a plunging back and a deep slit up to her thighs.

It was sexy.

It was scandalous.

It was perfect.

Standing beside her, Dominic looked like a gazillion bucks in his

Brioni tuxedo. Tamia knew they made a stunning couple. When they entered the ballroom, heads turned, eyes widening with admiration.

Tamia felt a thrill of satisfaction that waned the moment she looked through the crowd and saw Brandon.

He and Cynthia were standing in a circle with Beyoncé and Jay-Z, Dre, Justin, and Cornel. Bey was as dazzlingly beautiful as ever, and Cynthia looked timelessly elegant in a midnight-blue evening gown. The brothas were immaculate in their designer tuxes, hands dipped lazily into pockets—every last one of them oozing swagger, charm, and testosterone galore.

Cynthia was possessively latched onto Brandon's arm, wearing one of those fake smiles that surfaced whenever she felt threatened by another female. Didn't matter that the female in question was a gorgeous megastar who only had eyes for her mogul husband. And it didn't matter that the gorgeous megastar and Brandon had been friends long before Cynthia ever came on the scene, to the extent that Bey had dedicated a song to Brandon and had given him cameo appearances in her videos. The warmer the camaraderie between the two old friends, the frostier Cynthia's smile became.

Tamia watched in quiet amusement as Brandon cracked a joke that had Bey punching him playfully on the arm. As he threw back his head and howled with laughter, Cynthia looked ready to lunge at the singer's bejeweled throat.

"Tamia."

She turned to see Beau sauntering toward her, dark and dashing in a custom-tailored tuxedo with his diamond stud twinkling in one ear. As his gaze shuttled between Tamia and Dominic, a muscle throbbed in his jaw. For the first time since Tamia had met him, she sensed that he wasn't pleased with her.

She smiled brightly. "Hey, Beau. Did you get my message? I called to—"

"I got it." His tone was cool, his eyes even colder.

She added nervously, "Well, like I explained in my message, Honey couldn't be here tonight. So I decided to, um, come with someone else."

"I see that," Beau said tightly. "I thought you might come with Shanell or another friend."

"Nah, she decided to spend the evening with me." Dominic

smirked, his eyes glinting with amusement as he slid his hand forward. "Nice to meet you, Brandon's brother."

Beau glared at Dominic's proffered hand like it was covered in shit.

"Everything looks wonderful, Beau," Tamia quickly intervened. "What an *amazing* turnout."

"It certainly is," Dominic agreed.

Beau raked him with a scornful glance, his lip curled up into a snarl. Just when Tamia began to worry that he might take a swing at Dominic, he shifted his attention to her. His accusing gaze made her feel like the worst of traitors.

"I need to finish greeting my guests," he said curtly.

"Of course." Tamia forced another smile. "It was good to see you."

As Beau bent to kiss her upturned cheek, he growled in her ear, "If anything goes down tonight, I'm holding you personally responsible."

Tamia gulped hard.

He pulled back and gave her a disappointed look before moving off, shaking his head as he departed.

That was the moment Tamia began to second-guess her decision to show up tonight.

Dominic offered his arm to her. "Come on, beautiful. Let's go find our seats."

She nodded wordlessly.

They started across the room, pausing frequently to speak to clients and acquaintances of Dominic's. If anyone was shocked or dismayed to see them in public together, they were too polite to let on.

Tamia and Dominic were walking behind a group of people making their way toward the front when the throng suddenly parted—and they found themselves practically face-to-face with Brandon and Cynthia.

Both couples pulled up short, as if they'd collided with an invisible wall.

As Tamia and Brandon's gazes locked, she stopped breathing.

He seemed to do the same.

Everything around them faded away as he ran his gaze over her, recognizing the gown she wore. Her insides trembled as she watched the range of emotions that flashed across his face—hurt, disbelief, bitterness, and fury.

Raising her chin, she defiantly stared him down, letting him know that this was payback.

His eyes narrowed.

Moments later, his expression went carefully blank, and he gave her a cool nod before moving on without a word of acknowledgment to her or Dominic. As he curved his arm around Cynthia's waist, she glanced over her shoulder and smirked triumphantly at Tamia.

"You okay?" Dominic murmured.

Tamia nodded, inhaling a shaky breath.

Suddenly this evening couldn't end fast enough.

Over the next three hours, she tried her damnedest to enjoy herself.

She ate with gusto, savoring the lavish meal of lobster, stuffed oyster, and braised duck. She smiled and chatted companionably with Dominic and the other women at their table, who couldn't stop complimenting her hair, makeup, and gown.

She was pleasantly shocked when Brooke Chambers made her way across the room and leaned over her shoulder to confide, "I know my brothers are on strike against you right now, but I just had to cross the picket line to tell you that you are rockin' the *hell* outta that dress. I've never been tempted to steal a bitch's clothes off her back until I saw you tonight. Watch out." She winked before strutting back to her table.

When Tamia caught Joseph and Coretta Yarbrough glaring at her, she smiled sweetly and waved, taking satisfaction in their affronted scowls.

She listened with rapt absorption to Emmitt Smith's heartwarming keynote speech, applauding sincerely at the end. She got misty-eyed watching the scholarship recipients choke back tears as they thanked their mothers, coaches, and mentors for believing in them. When the beaming youngsters posed for a group photo afterward with Brandon, Beau, Dre, and Emmitt Smith, Tamia found herself on her feet with everyone else, heart swelling with pride as she clapped and cheered.

When Brandon looked out over the crowd and made eye contact with her, a shadow of a smile softened his expression before he glanced away.

After the scholarships had been awarded and closing remarks made, many attendees lingered to socialize and enjoy more champagne as they waited for the floor to be cleared for dancing. Christmas Eve was only hours away, so the mood was festive and relaxed, and the night was young.

Dominic leaned close to Tamia and murmured, "Did you have a good time?"

She smiled. "I did, actually."

"Good." His eyes glimmered. "Ready to go?"

She nodded, pushing back her chair. "Let me use the bathroom first."

She left the ballroom and headed down the corridor toward the restrooms, her heels tapping against the gleaming marble floors. Reaching the ladies' room, she pushed the door open and strode inside.

She skidded to an abrupt stop at the sight that greeted her.

Brooke had Dre pinned up against the counter, her hands cupping his face as she kissed him ravenously.

Dre was groaning and moving his arms like he didn't know whether to push Brooke away or pull her closer.

Upon Tamia's entrance, they whipped their heads around and stared at her.

Dre looked stunned and guilt-stricken.

Brooke looked mildly annoyed. "Damn, I knew I should have locked that door."

Tamia stammered, "Uh . . . I'll just, um, come back later."

She backed quickly out the door, clapping a hand over her mouth to smother a hysterical giggle. She couldn't believe it. Dre and Brooke? Brandon would *kill* Dre if he ever found out about this!

Tamia didn't have time to dwell on the amusing scenario she'd just stumbled upon. The moment she reentered the ballroom, she was accosted by none other than Brandon's mother.

"I can't believe you had the audacity to show your face here tonight," Gwen hissed, raking Tamia with a look of blistering contempt. "Have you no shame?"

Tamia was momentarily taken aback. *No, this bitch is not trying to start some mess!*

"Actually," she said, finding her voice, "your son invited me."

Gwen's eyes narrowed. "I seriously doubt that Brandon—"

"Not him," Tamia coolly interjected. "Your other son."

Gwen's lips twisted with angry displeasure. "Beau always did have a penchant for bringing home riffraff. But it seems that even *his* standards have sunk to an appalling low this time."

The vicious barb stung Tamia like a slap across the face.

"I don't know what you hoped to accomplish by coming tonight," Gwen said coldly, "but all you've succeeded in doing is making yourself look weak, petty, and desperate. And there's nothing my son despises more than a weak, petty, and desperate woman."

"Really?" Tamia jeered. "Then why is he marrying Cynthia?"

Gwen looked outraged. "*What!* How *dare* you speak disrespectfully of Cynthia! She's not the one who made a living as a filthy porn star, then tried to cover her tracks by prostituting herself to a married man. She's not the one who lied and schemed her way into my son's life for the sole purpose of getting her hands on his fortune. For you to have the unmitigated gall to stand there and insult Cynthia shows just how utterly shameless you are. I don't care how many designer gowns or expensive jewels men shower upon you. You will never be *half* the woman that Cynthia is."

Tamia smirked. "Sorry to disappoint you, but I've never used Cynthia Yarbrough as a yardstick for ideal womanhood."

Gwen sneered. "You think you're so clever, don't you? It sickens me to think of how close you came to stealing Brandon away from Cynthia. But I now realize I needn't have ever worried. You see, Tamia, beautiful sluts like you will always be the Marilyn Monroes to the Jackie Kennedys of the world. Why? Because being a mistress and a whore is all you're good for."

Tamia didn't so much as flinch, though the venomous slurs hurt. *God*, how they hurt. But she refused to give this ruthless shark the satisfaction of smelling her blood in the water.

Gwen gave her a look of icy disdain. "If you had an ounce of pride or dignity, you'd take that whoremongering piece of gutter trash with you and leave these premises at once."

Tamia smiled narrowly. "Last I checked, Judge Chambers, this isn't your courtroom. So you have no right to dictate who stays or goes. By the way, how *are* things going on the bench these days? Offered any bribes recently?"

Gwen's face tightened at the unmistakable reference to her thwarted attempt to pay off Tamia to leave Brandon alone.

Stepping closer to Tamia, she hissed sharply, "You spiteful little bitch. Are you threatening me?"

"Not at all. I'm just reminding you that I hold some cards of my own." Tamia leaned closer. "And trust me, you haven't *begun* to see what a spiteful bitch I can be."

A flicker of alarm flashed in Gwen's eyes.

Tamia smiled sweetly. "Enjoy what's left of the evening. You can be sure I will."

And with that she spun on her heel and strolled from the room, leaving Gwen to stare after her with a look of stunned fury.

Chapter 35

Brandon

Brandon and Cynthia were making dinner plans with one of her sorors and her state senator husband when Brandon happened to glance across the ballroom. When he saw his mother and Tamia engaged in heated confrontation, his hackles went up.

"Excuse me," he muttered abruptly to his companions.

Cynthia grabbed his arm as he started away. "Where are you going?"

Brandon looked at her, saw the bright gleam in her eyes, and realized that she'd been covertly watching the showdown the whole time.

Clenching his jaw, he impatiently shook off her hand and stalked away. As he shouldered his way through the crowd, he ignored the friendly greetings that were called to him and evaded the hands that reached out to detain him for conversation.

By the time he reached the other side of the ballroom, Tamia had already departed. The affronted outrage on his mother's face told him Tamia had probably gotten the last word.

When Gwen saw Brandon charging toward her, she looked startled. "Darling—"

"Don't 'darling' me," Brandon growled. "What the hell did you say to Tamia?"

His mother let out a scandalized gasp. "How dare you take that tone with me! What on earth has gotten into you?"

"That's what I should be asking *you*! I saw you arguing with

Tamia. Aren't you the same one who abhors public spectacles? Aren't you the one who's always lecturing us about the proper way to conduct ourselves so we won't disgrace the family name?"

Gwen gave him a haughty look. "You talk as if I was brawling with that silly girl. We were having a perfectly civilized—"

"Bullshit," Brandon snarled. "There was nothing *civilized* about the way you were getting all up in her face."

Gwen's eyes flashed with anger. "How *dare* you defend her after she came here tonight to flaunt her lover in your face and make a fool of you!"

"I'm not defending her! Believe me, her presence here tonight says more about her than the scumbag she came with. All I'm saying is that you didn't have to confront her. You're always telling everyone else to take the high road, but you hardly ever heed your own damn advice."

"That's not—"

"I'm talking," Brandon cut her off.

As her eyes widened with indignation, he glared at her. "The evening's almost over but you just *had* to have your say, didn't you? You just couldn't leave well enough alone, could you? I mean seriously, Mom. What more are you after? You and Dad got what you wanted. I'm marrying your precious chosen one—"

Gwen sputtered. "Is *that* how you're referring to—"

"What the hell is going on here?" a low, controlled voice demanded.

Brandon and Gwen whirled around to see Bernard standing there, eyeing them with a look of stern reproach.

"Oh, thank goodness you're here," Gwen exclaimed, rushing to her husband's side like a frightened child taking cover behind her father's legs. "Please talk some sense into your son. He's behaving like a pure brute and using the most obscene language."

Bernard frowned at Brandon. "You been disrespecting your mother?"

Brandon smirked, bending at the waist in a mocking bow. "My humble apologies, Mother. Didn't mean to offend your delicate sensibilities."

His parents exchanged troubled glances.

"Brandon—"

He had already turned and stalked away. Angrily jerking his tie loose, he headed to the refreshment table to kill some time before he had to return to Cynthia.

He was glad that no one was over here. He wasn't in the mood for small talk.

Grabbing a crystal flute, he filled it with champagne flowing from an elaborately tiered fountain. He downed the wine in one swallow and helped himself to more, absently surveying the lavish spread of chilled shrimp, caviar, oysters, chocolate, and assorted fruits. They'd spared no expense with the fundraiser gala, and everything had turned out perfect.

Well . . . almost everything.

"Helluva party, Chambers."

Brandon automatically tensed. *Not this muthafucka.*

"Tamia and I really enjoyed ourselves tonight," Dominic drawled, sidling up to Brandon at the table. "Of course, we've been enjoying ourselves *every* night since she moved in with me."

Brandon swallowed hard, his chest tightening at the revelation that Tamia and Dominic were now shacking up.

"It was nice running into you and Cynthia the other day," Dominic commented, reaching toward the fruit tray. "What'd you think of that house we were touring?"

Brandon just looked at him.

Dominic grinned. "Oh, yeah, that's right. You had to leave unexpectedly, so you didn't get to see the whole thing." He selected a piece of pineapple from the tray, popped it into his mouth, and chewed thoughtfully. "I'm seriously thinking about buying it for Tamia. You should have seen her running from room to room, squealing so excitedly. Oh, man, she was like a little girl. Hit me right here," he confessed, patting his heart. "Made me wanna give her the sun, moon, and stars, know what I'm saying? *Anything* to keep that radiant smile on her face."

Brandon was silent. He knew all about wanting to give Tamia the world on a silver platter. It killed him to think of another man—especially *this* man—enjoying that privilege.

Dominic smiled at him. "We spent the weekend at this lovely bed-and-breakfast outside of town. Now, I realize it's not quite the same as whisking her off to Italy like *you* did, but we still had an amazing time together." As he contemplated the chocolate-covered strawberry he'd picked up, a lascivious grin crept across his face. "Like I said . . . it was amazing."

Brandon stared into the twinkling contents of his glass. "Does Tamia know?"

Dominic glanced at him. "Know what?"

"That you got a serious hard-on for me. Does she know that every time you fuck her you're secretly thinking of me?"

Dominic flushed with anger.

Brandon smirked.

Recovering his composure, Dominic chuckled and shook his head at Brandon. "Very clever, my man. Very clever. But I think we both know that when you're making love to Tamia, it's absolutely impossible to think of anything—or anyone—else." He bit into the chocolate-covered strawberry and sighed appreciatively. "Good stuff. *Nothing* tastes as good as Tamia, though." He winked. "But you already know that."

Brandon's fingers tightened around his glass until he heard it crack. Gritting his teeth, he set it down on the table and rubbed a shaky hand over his jaw. He knew he should walk away before it was too late. But he couldn't make himself move.

Dominic let out another sigh. "Yeah, I definitely think this past weekend made up for that whole debacle that happened when I flew her to St. Croix back in May. Hey, speaking of home, I'm planning to take her back there next month to meet my family. Since she's becoming such an important part of my life, it's only natural that I'd want to introduce her to my relatives."

He paused to let his words sink into Brandon's conscience, a taunt and an indictment. "A woman like Tamia needs to know that she's special, cherished, accepted. Otherwise," he added, eyes gleaming as he nudged Brandon's shoulder, "*you* know what can happen when she's not feeling the love at home."

The rage welled up inside Brandon like pools of molten lava, bubbling over in a volcanic eruption he couldn't contain.

Dominic never knew what hit him.

One moment he was cocky and smirking. The next moment he was grunting and stumbling backward, rocked by a blow from Brandon's fist.

Regaining his balance, Dominic slowly lifted his hand to his nostrils. When his fingers came away bloody, he stared at Brandon in outraged disbelief.

"Come on, muthafucka," Brandon taunted softly. "Hit me back this time."

Dominic charged forward and swung at him, his fist connecting with Brandon's jaw.

That's good, Brandon thought. He wanted a worthy opponent—or at least a good fight.

He threw a hard right hook, clocking Dominic on the cheek and knocking him backward. Before he could recover Brandon tackled him, driving him into the refreshment table.

It buckled beneath their weight and crashed to the floor.

A woman screamed.

The two brawlers rolled over platters of food. Dominic briefly landed on top before Brandon overpowered him, throwing punches with the fury of a raging bull unleashed from his pen.

Dominic gave it all he could, but he wasn't fueled by the same wrath, desperation, and despair that had been tearing away at Brandon's soul.

He wasn't a drowning man who'd been kicking against a raging current, clawing for survival.

He didn't know Brandon's heartbreak.

So he didn't stand a fucking chance of not getting his ass kicked.

Through the haze of fury swarming his brain, Brandon heard the sound of approaching voices—shocked, panicked, scandalized.

He landed three successive uppercuts to Dominic's stomach before two pairs of strong hands seized him and hauled him off the motherfucker. The hands belonged to Dre and Beau, who were shouting at him to stop before he killed somebody.

Dominic lay sprawled upon the demolished table with blood running from his nose, his busted lip, and a deep gash in his cheek.

Tamia rushed over, heels clicking rapidly against the marble floor. Her red dress pooled around her feet as she squatted down beside Dominic.

"Jesus," she whispered frantically. "Are you okay?"

Dominic grimaced, struggling to push himself up to a sitting position.

Tamia looked up at Brandon, met his lethal glare, and quickly looked away again.

Then Cynthia was there, along with his parents and hers and Brooke, all of them looking stunned and horror-stricken as they stared at Brandon like they'd never seen him before.

"WHAT THE HELL HAS GOTTEN INTO YOU?" his father thundered, breaking his own cardinal rule about not raising one's voice in public.

Brandon tightened his jaw, nostrils flaring, adrenaline pumping. Feeling a sticky wetness on his face, he reached up to touch the fresh cut on his forehead.

"Have you lost your damn mind?" his mother hissed furiously. "Have you completely forgotten who you are? *Where* you are?"

Brandon swept a hard glance around the ballroom, encountering a sea of shocked faces. Only Tamia looked grim. Almost resigned.

He gave her a coldly mocking smile, then pivoted on his heel and stalked off, the crowd parting eagerly this time to let him through.

Chapter 36

Tamia

Once Brandon departed the ballroom, all eyes turned to Tamia.

Her face burned with shame under the weight of their stares, rife with speculation and condemnation.

"Look what you've done," Gwen spat accusingly. "This never would have happened if you hadn't come here tonight, you trouble-making whore! I ought to—"

"Gwen," Bernard murmured warningly.

"*You're not welcome here!*" she raged at Tamia as her husband gently steered her away. "*Goddamn you! Leave my family alone!*"

Tamia blinked rapidly as tears stung her eyes.

As the deejay began bumping Wiz Khalifa, Justin, Cornel, and Brooke ushered the crowd over to the dance floor.

Tamia got unsteadily to her feet as Beau and Dre helped Dominic off the floor. He grimaced sharply, holding his stomach.

Dre frowned, observing him as if he were examining one of his injured athletes. "You might wanna get those ribs checked out. They might be cracked or broken."

Dominic shook his head, gritting his teeth in obvious pain. "I'll be fine."

Dre snorted. "Not for a while, you won't. And you need stitches," he added, pointing to Dominic's bleeding cheek.

"You can bring him to our first aid office," offered the hotel manager who'd been hovering nearby, waiting to be of assistance. "We've got an experienced RN on staff who can do minor sutures."

Dre nodded. "Great. Let's go."

Dominic reluctantly slung one arm over Dre's shoulder and the other around a scowling Beau.

As Tamia moved to follow them from the room, Dominic shot her a look, all wounded male pride. "Stay here," he ordered gruffly.

She hesitated. "Are you sure?"

"Yeah. I don't need a damn entourage."

Beau snickered, muttering "punkass muthafucka" under his breath as they headed off with the hotel manager.

Tamia watched them leave, then glanced around the ballroom. She spotted Cynthia standing in a corner with her parents, her arms gesturing as she vented to them.

Bracing herself for another confrontation, Tamia squared her shoulders and made her way over to the small group. When Joseph and Coretta saw her approaching, they looked so enraged that Tamia expected them to summon hellfire and brimstone from the heavens.

"Young lady," Joseph scolded, shaking his finger at her, "you are being used by the devil tonight! You need to repent and—"

"I'd like to speak to your daughter," Tamia cut through the man's sanctimonious diatribe—which was hard to take seriously when his eyes were glued to her cleavage.

Cynthia gaped incredulously at her. "*Are you serious?* We have *nothing* to say to each other, Tamia! And I can't believe you're still here! Haven't you caused enough trouble for one night?"

Tamia rolled her eyes. "How is it that *my* date got his ass kicked, but everyone's blaming me?"

"Because you're the one—"

Tamia held up a hand. "Never mind. I didn't come over here to discuss that."

Cynthia's eyes narrowed. "What *did* you come to discuss?"

Tamia glanced pointedly at Joseph and Coretta.

Cynthia hesitated, then turned and murmured to her hovering parents, "It's okay."

Joseph and Coretta frowned with displeasure.

"I'll be fine," Cynthia assured them.

Shooting a warning glare at Tamia, the bishop and his wife reluctantly moved away, but not very far.

Tamia sucked her teeth in disgust. "Damn, bitch. Are you thirty-three or thirteen?"

Cynthia scowled. "Whatever, Tamia. Now please get to the point so I can go check on my fiancé."

Tamia shook her head at her. "If Brandon were my fiancé, I would have followed him right out that door. Why are you standing here with your parents when you should be tending to your man?"

Cynthia's mouth tightened at the edges. She didn't respond.

"I understand," Tamia murmured. "I saw your face after the fight. I know you probably didn't think Brandon was capable of such violence. Or maybe you've already seen that side of him, and it kinda scares you. Brandon's a sweetheart—a gentleman through and through. But he got a lil crazy in him."

"Only because of you," Cynthia spat resentfully. "Every time I've seen him explode like that, it had something to do with you. You bring out the worst in him."

Tamia smiled sadly. "I think that's the first thing we've ever agreed on, Cynthia."

Cynthia looked surprised at the admission.

Tamia sighed. "That's what I came over here to discuss with you. I need to go talk to Brandon, but I honestly don't think he'll open the door if I show up at his place tonight. So I was wondering if you could give me the spare key."

Cynthia stared at her. "Seriously, Tamia? You're asking me to hand over the key to my man's apartment so you can have a *talk* with him?"

"That's exactly what I'm asking. And I need you to give us some privacy to really hash things out."

Cynthia snorted derisively. "Bitch, please. You must think I'm fucking stupid."

"What I think," Tamia countered quietly, "is that you're tired of having a third person in your relationship. What I think is that it's time for you, me, and Brandon to grow up and get on with our lives. So you need to let me say good-bye to him once and for all. Not over the phone. Face-to-face."

Cynthia silently regarded her, a hopeful gleam in her eyes. "You're telling him good-bye?"

Tamia nodded slowly.

"Give me the key," she said, holding out her hand, "and I promise you'll get it back for good."

Dominic was silent and sullen on the ride home from the hotel. Seated beside him in the Rolls-Royce limo he'd rented for the occasion, Tamia stared out the window, lost in her own troubled thoughts.

When they arrived at Dominic's penthouse, she helped him undress and brought him water to take the painkillers the nurse had given him for his sore ribs. After he'd crawled into bed and drifted off to sleep, Tamia took his car keys and snuck out.

Twenty minutes later, she let herself into Brandon's condo and quietly closed the door behind her. As she ventured toward the living room, she heard the sound of male voices coming from the back. She recognized each one as belonging to Beau, Dre, Justin, and Cornel.

The fellas had obviously come to do damage control or some sort of an intervention. But judging by the frustration edging their voices, they weren't making much progress.

As Tamia neared the open doorway of the study, she heard Brandon issue a low warning, "Y'all niggas need to get the fuck out."

There were rumblings of protest.

"Yo, man, you really need—"

"I said GET THE FUCK OUT!"

Tamia froze as the fellas shuffled quickly out of the room, grumbling darkly and shaking their heads.

Not one of them looked surprised to see her standing there. As they filed past her, Beau shot her an accusing *I told you so* look.

Dre's eyes were full of guilt: *Please don't tell him what you saw earlier!*

Justin's expression warned: *I wouldn't go in there if I were you.*

Cornel gave her an appreciative once-over, craning his neck to ogle her backside as he exclaimed under his breath, "Dayum! Shorty fine as hell, though."

Tamia barely registered any of it.

She was focused on the open doorway of Brandon's study. Crossing the threshold would be as insanely dangerous as wandering into a lion's den.

But she couldn't turn back now.

When she reached the door, she took a deep breath to shore up her courage and stepped into the room.

Brandon stood at the window overlooking a moonlit park. His head was bent, broad shoulders hunched, long legs braced apart, one hand gripping a glass of scotch. He'd removed his tuxedo jacket and unbuttoned his shirt, tugging it from his pants.

Without turning around, he said in a deceptively soft voice, "I thought I told you to spend the night at your parents' house."

Tamia swallowed hard. "My parents are dead."

Brandon went still, then turned slowly and stared at her.

She stared back.

He had a nasty cut on his forehead that had crusted over, and the skin around his left eye was starting to swell. But that was it.

Dominic looked worse.

Much, much worse.

Brandon's eyes narrowed menacingly. "Fuck you doing here?"

Tamia winced, stung by the harsh words.

To give herself something to do, she closed the door behind her. But it took extra courage to release the doorknob and turn around to face Brandon, especially given the way he was glaring at her.

She took a step forward. "I came to talk to you."

His lips curled into a sneer. "So now you wanna talk?"

Another step. "Yes."

He stared at her for a long moment, silent and brooding.

She swallowed nervously, watching as he set down his scotch and slowly rounded the desk. As he prowled toward her, her heart tried to batter its way out of her chest, as if it didn't want to be trapped inside her body should any harm come to her.

She briefly wondered if he still kept his Glock in the bottom drawer of his desk.

"I've been trying to talk to you for over a week, Tamia. But you ain't been trying to hear from me. So why the fuck are you here now?"

"Because . . ." *Because I came to tell you good-bye. Because your mother thinks being a mistress and a whore is all I'm good for, and apparently you feel the same.*

"Because what, Tamia?" he growled. "What did you come here to say?"

He was nearly upon her.

And her courage hauled ass.

"You're right," she mumbled, backing toward the door. "I can see this was a bad idea—"

"Nah." As she turned and opened the door his arm shot out, shoving it closed. He pressed his hard body to hers, trapping her against him. "You're here now. So let's talk."

Tamia kept her back to him, willing her lungs to expand and contract the way they were supposed to.

"Well?" The warmth of his breath on her bare back sent shivers down her spine, goose bumps pricking her skin. She could smell the barest trace of his Clive Christian cologne, a delicious scent that always drove her absolutely crazy.

"Whatcha gotta say, Tamia? I'm all ears."

She dragged in a shallow breath. "I can see that you're still mad—"

"Really?" he mocked bitingly. "What was your first clue?"

She didn't dare open her mouth again.

"Wearin' this fucking dress," he grumbled darkly, gripping a fistful of the red silk. "What the fuck were you tryna prove? Huh? *Huh?*"

She shivered hard as he began raising the gown up her bare thighs. The friction of silk against her skin . . . the scorching heat of his body . . . his barely restrained fury . . .

The nigga had her trembling like a rose petal beneath a torrential downpour.

"Answer me, Tamia," he growled in her ear. "What were you trying to accomplish by wearing this dress tonight?"

She gulped audibly, licking her lips. She couldn't speak as his hand curved between her legs, kneading the fleshy inside of her thighs. Her pussy throbbed, clit swelling.

His hand slid higher but stopped just inches from her crotch, denying her what they both knew she wanted.

"Tamia."

"What?" she whimpered.

"I asked you a question."

She squeezed her eyes shut. "I . . . I don't know, Brandon."

"Bullshit," he snarled, the word lashing her cheek. "You know. You were trying to hurt me. And I'm really trying to understand why, Tamia. Wasn't it enough that you used to fuck that scurrilous nigga behind my back? Nah. Wasn't it enough that you popped up outta the blue wearing his engagement ring? Nah. Wasn't it enough that you decided to show up on his muthafucking arm tonight? Nope, that wasn't enough for you. You had to put on *this* dress and strut your pretty ass into that ballroom to torture me all fucking night." He gave a low, dark laugh. "And now you wanna come here and *talk*."

Tamia had never been more terrified and aroused in her life. Even as alarm bells clanged in her head, her pussy was raining like a waterfall, soaking her panties through.

"Brandon—" she whispered.

"I'm tired of talking, Tamia. I really am."

Oh, God, please help me.

"Th-then I'll just g-go—"

"The hell you will." He seized her lace thong, ripping it clean off her ass. Then he picked her up and carried her over to the low black sofa against the wall. He set her down and pushed the gown out of the way, then shoved her knees apart and sank to a crouch before her.

She stared down at him as his face disappeared between her shaking thighs. And then he tasted her, licking her swollen clit before sliding his tongue down between her slippery folds. She moaned brokenly and opened her legs wider, grabbing the back of his head and pushing his face deeper into her sex. He opened his mouth and sucked her whole, taking her labia and clitoris in one hot, greedy swallow.

"*Oh, shit,*" she squealed breathlessly. "*Ohhh shit . . . shit!*"

He inserted two fingers inside her, spreading her pussy wide so he could fuck her opening with his tongue.

She sobbed with pleasure, head rocking back and forth on the sofa, pelvis twisting and bucking uncontrollably. Brandon licked her ravenously, lapping at the warm juices that gushed out of her while swearing fiercely that her pussy belonged to him and him alone.

As tears ran down her face, he curled his fingers upward and thrust his tongue all the way inside her canal.

She screamed at the top of her lungs, her hips rocketing off the sofa as she exploded, creaming all over his sexy face.

He licked her clean, then reared back and tore off his shirt and wifebeater. Her glazed eyes roamed over the ripped muscles of his chest and abdomen, watching as he frantically unzipped his pants and pulled out his curved dick. It was so thick and hard, so engorged with blood, that she gasped at the sight of it.

Grabbing her around the hips, Brandon surged to his feet, lifting her from the sofa. Tamia locked her arms around his neck and wrapped her legs around his waist as their mouths met, tongues clashing in an urgent duel of wet heat.

Brandon reached between their bodies, impatiently shoving her dress out of the way. Cupping her buttocks, he thrust upward, ramming his ten inches into her.

She screamed and arched backward, her stilettos clattering noisily to the floor.

"*Fuck!*" Brandon swore savagely, bouncing her up and down on his dick.

Tamia wailed with ecstasy, unbearably aroused by the friction of his steel-girder pipe stretching her swollen slit. He fucked her standing up, the muscles of his stomach and thighs flexing with each driving thrust.

After several intense minutes he moved to the sofa and sat down, keeping their bodies tightly joined as he pulled her on top of him. His hands dove under her gown to grip her ass cheeks as he pounded into her, doing his damnedest to knock the bottom out of her pussy.

She rode his dick hard, her breasts nearly bouncing out of her dress. Her nipples were stingingly erect, her pussy was aching, and her clit was on fire. When Brandon eased his finger inside her asshole, she almost busted a damn nut. She shuddered as he stroked her tight anal muscles with a gentleness contrasted by the ferocious pounding he was giving her pussy.

They kissed and tongued each other as they fucked, panting harshly and groaning like animals.

He lifted her hips then slammed her back down onto his cock, repeating this three more times before they both erupted, heads flung back, mouths open as they unleashed primal screams.

Panting for breath, the inside of her thighs slick with sweat and come, Tamia could only collapse against Brandon, her head falling upon his shoulder as her eyes drifted shut. He kissed her damp temple and tenderly stroked her bare back as his chest rose and fell against hers.

After a long time, she carefully climbed off his lap and stepped back on unsteady legs. As calmly as she could manage, she smoothed down the rumpled folds of her gown and patted her sweaty hair.

Brandon watched her sullenly from beneath his dark lashes. "Where you going?"

She said quietly, "I need to go home."

"No, you don't. Your home is right here."

Tamia smirked at him. "Does your fiancée know that?"

Brandon clenched his jaw, glaring at her as he angrily zipped up his pants. "So that's it, Tamia? You fuck me then run on back to that punkass muthafucka like nothing happened? Like nothing's changed?"

"Nothing *has* changed," she said tightly.

"The hell it hasn't."

"Really?" she challenged, hands on hips. "What's changed, Brandon? We had sex but you're still engaged to Cynthia, and I'm—" She broke off as he suddenly shot to his feet and pushed his face into hers.

She stared up at him, heart thumping as the scent of sweat, sex, and fury swirled potently between them.

"You're what, Tamia? You're engaged, too?" Brandon grabbed her hand. "Where's that rock you were wearing on Saturday? Don't tell me you took it off to spare my feelings 'cause you obviously didn't give two fucks about that when you showed up at the banquet tonight."

Tamia jerked her hand away.

Brandon glared at her. "So now you staying with that nigga?"

Her eyes narrowed. "He told you that?"

"Oh, yeah," Brandon jeered. "He was only *too* happy to share how wonderful things are between you two."

Tamia shook her head, bending down to scoop up her shoes. Sidestepping Brandon, she sat down on the sofa and shoved her feet into the strappy heels.

"Do you love him, Tamia?"

She didn't respond.

Brandon cupped her chin in his hand, forcing her to meet his probing gaze. "*Do you love him?*"

She pushed his hand away and sprang to her feet. "I'm leaving, Brandon."

His eyes flashed with pain and fury. "What that nigga got, huh? What he got that I can't give you and more?"

"Brandon—"

"*Answer my fucking question!*"

"Commitment!" Tamia exploded, shouting into his face. "He can give me commitment, Brandon! He can put a fucking ring on my finger and walk me down the aisle—something *you* apparently can't or won't!"

"That's not true!" Brandon yelled hoarsely. "I *do* wanna marry you!"

"Sure you do!"

"Are you even listening to me? I'm asking you to be my damn wife!"

Tamia stared at him, stunned into speechlessness.

He stared back, chest heaving, nostrils flaring with emotion. "Baby—"

She slapped him hard across the face.

"How dare you?" she hissed furiously. "*How dare you!* You don't get to decide you want me now that you're afraid of losing me to a man you despise!"

"BULLSHIT! This ain't about that sorry muthafucka! I *love* you—"

"Do you, Brandon? Do you really? Tell me something. Where was your *love* for the nine months that we were dating and you refused to let me meet your family? Where was your *love* when you secretly took Cynthia to the governor's state dinner and introduced *her* to your parents? Where was your *love* when you attended the mayor's fundraiser without me and spent the whole night cozying up to Cynthia? Where was your *love* when I called and poured out my heart to you, begging you not to marry her, *pleading* with you to choose *me* instead?" Tamia sneered, shaking her head at him. "You don't love me, Brandon. I'm a trophy that you love to possess. But guess what? I'm not yours to possess anymore. Do you hear me? Contrary to what you choose to believe, *I don't belong to you!*"

"The hell you don't!" he roared, eyes blazing fiercely. "You can tell yourself whatever the fuck you want, Tamia, but we both know the truth. You're here right now because you love me! And like it or not, you belong to me as much as I belong to you, and nothing you say or do is *ever* gonna change that!"

Tamia got into his face, trembling with outrage. "You know what your problem is? Your problem is that you've always gotten whatever you wanted, whenever you wanted, wherever you wanted. But not this time, Brandon Chambers. Not this fucking time!"

With that she spun on her heel and stormed from the room.

As she marched down the hallway she heard Brandon following her, but he didn't try to stop her from leaving.

When she reached the front door, he snarled viciously, "I don't care how good that nigga fucks you. I don't care how many different ways he can make you come and scream his name. Unless you're a whore, good pipe will only get you so far."

Tamia's face flamed.

Whirling around, she shrieked furiously, "*Go to hell!*"

Brandon laughed harshly. "Look at me, Tamia. I *AM* IN HELL!"

She held his anguished glare another moment, then turned and stormed out, slamming the door behind her.

She didn't even make it three steps before she burst into tears, sobbing so hard she doubled over.

It was only when she heard a loud crash from inside Brandon's condo that she managed to pull herself up and stumble down the hall to the elevator.

Once she was inside, she wrapped her arms around her stomach and closed her eyes, praying for the strength to get herself safely home.

But even that task threatened to be more than she could handle . . . because she didn't know where home *was* anymore.

Dominic was waiting for her when she returned.

He sat in the living room, lights from the tall Christmas tree scattering over him as he quietly toked on a blunt.

Tamia was instantly struck by a feeling of déjà vu.

This scene was hauntingly familiar. Except this time she was sneaking home to Dominic after being with Brandon.

Talk about an unexpected role reversal.

As she stepped out of her high heels and padded slowly across the floor, Dominic drawled, "So is this how it's gonna be?" His voice was slightly slurred, a result of the painkillers and the weed.

Tamia didn't answer him.

"Are you gonna be sneakin' off to meet him the moment I fall asleep every night?" he pressed. "Is this what I should expect goin' forward?"

Tamia sighed, perching on the arm of the sofa. "I can't talk about this right now, Dominic. And you should be in bed."

He snorted bitterly. "I can smell him all over you. Did you fuck him? Or do I even have to ask?"

Instead of responding, she eased the blunt from between his fingers, took a long drag, and blew out the smoke.

Dominic watched her, one eye nearly swollen shut. "You seem sad," he gruffly observed.

Her throat tightened. "I am."

"Is it over?"

She stared at Dominic for several seconds, then nodded slowly and whispered, "It's over."

His eyes probed hers another moment. Then he took the blunt from her hand and mashed it out in the ashtray beside him. "Let's go to bed."

He draped his arm around her shoulder as she gingerly helped him to his feet. As they shuffled toward the bedroom, she muttered darkly, "It'd serve you right if your ribs *are* broken. You shouldn't have provoked him like that. You know how much he hates you."

"I know," Dominic drawled, "and the feelin' is definitely mutual."

Inside the enormous bedroom, Tamia crawled beneath the covers with Dominic and held him in her arms, craving whatever masculine warmth she could get.

"You need to take a shower," he grumbled drowsily.

"I will," she promised.

"Good. Don't wanna be smellin' that nigga in my bed."

She smiled sadly. "You won't have to. Not ever again."

As Dominic cuddled closer, she gently stroked his battered face until his breathing slowed and deepened.

Long after he fell asleep with a contented smile on his lips, she lay awake staring blindly into the darkness, hearing the final door slam on her relationship with Brandon.

Chapter 37

Tamia

"Merry Christmas, Tam-Tam."

Tamia smiled softly into the phone. "Same to you, Fee. How you doing?"

Fiona sighed. "Been sick as a dog. I can't keep nothing down."

"Sorry to hear that," Tamia murmured sympathetically.

"I don't know why it's called morning sickness when it lasts all damn day," Fiona complained.

"I hear you. Remember Ma said she was really sick with both of us. But it only lasted for the first trimester, so just hang in there."

"I'll try." Fiona's voice softened. "Thank you for sending that old picture of us with Ma. I've been sleeping with it every night."

"You're welcome," Tamia said quietly. "I know how much it meant to you."

She could see her sister nodding. "If I have a girl, I hope she looks just like Ma."

Tamia's throat tightened.

The two sisters shared a mournful moment of silence.

"So what're you doing for Christmas?" Fiona asked, mercifully changing the subject. "Got any special plans?"

"Not really," Tamia answered vaguely. She didn't know how Fiona would react to the news that she was shacking up with the husband of the woman Fiona had killed. It was all so strange, so hard to wrap her mind around.

"I bet I can guess what you're watching right now," Fiona said knowingly. "The Disney Christmas Parade."

Tamia chuckled. "Yup."

Dominic had gotten her up early that morning to open presents. After they exchanged gifts—designer clothes, jewelry, matching silk robes—Tamia had whipped up some pancakes, eggs, bacon, and grits. After breakfast they'd shared a steamy shower. Not wanting to aggravate his bruised ribs by picking her up, Dominic had taken Tamia from behind, plunging slow and deep inside her as the hot water rained down on them.

Afterward, feeling lazy and listless, Tamia had curled up on the sofa to catch the Disney Parks Christmas Day Parade. She and Fiona had watched it every year when they were growing up—along with the Macy's Thanksgiving Day Parade—wishing they could be there to partake of the festivities.

Tamia picked up the remote control and muted the television. "Fee, Dre told me that he responded to your email over a week ago, but he hasn't heard back from you. What's going on?"

Fiona sighed heavily. "He wants me to have an abortion."

Tamia frowned. "Is that what he told you?"

"Not in so many words. But I know that's what he was getting at. He said we need to talk, and he's willing to come all the way out here to see me."

"That's good, Fee. At least he's accepting responsibility for getting you pregnant."

"Not if he's coming here to try to talk me out of having the baby." An edge of desperation entered Fiona's voice. "I don't want to get an abortion, Tamia. I want to keep my baby. Even though I'm locked up and I've been sick as hell, this baby has given me a reason to get up every morning. I don't want Dre or anyone else to take that away from me."

Tamia was silent, absorbing her sister's heartfelt words.

"I was hoping to put him off for as long as possible," Fiona confessed. "Maybe if I get far enough along in the pregnancy, he'll start wanting our baby as much as I do."

Tamia sighed. "I understand where you're coming from, Fee, but I don't think you're being fair to Dre. If you have the baby, he's the one who'll have to raise the child alone. Of course I'll be there for him, but ultimately he's gonna be a single parent, and we both saw firsthand how difficult that can be."

"So what're you saying, Tamia? That I shouldn't have the baby?"

"No, what I'm saying is that you and Dre need to sit down and discuss your decision together like mature adults. If he wants to come see you, you should let him. And the sooner, the better."

Silence.

"Will you come with him?" Fiona asked hopefully.

Tamia frowned. "I don't think that's a good idea. This is a private matter between you and Dre."

"I know but . . ." Fiona trailed off for a long moment. "Are you ever gonna come visit me? I know I was refusing visitors before, but today's Christmas and . . . I guess I was hoping you might have surprised me."

Guilt gnawed at Tamia's insides as she pushed out a deep breath. "I won't lie, Fiona. A lot has happened between us over the past year. The things you've done . . . I can't say that I'm completely ready to forgive you."

"I understand," Fiona mumbled.

Laying her head against the back of the sofa, Tamia stared up at the ceiling. "That said, you're still my sister and you're having a baby, and I promised Mama Esther that I'd be there for you no matter what."

"Mama Esther?" Fiona whispered.

"Yes." Tamia sighed. "So if you really want me to come down there with Dre, I will."

"Thank you, Tam-Tam," Fiona said humbly. "It would mean a lot to me."

"I know."

Long silence.

"Do you think . . ." Fiona trailed off uncertainly.

"What?" Tamia prodded.

"Do you think Brandon would come too?"

Tamia's mouth went dry. "Brandon?"

"Yeah. I really need his legal advice."

"What about the public defender who was assigned to you?"

Fiona sucked her teeth. "I don't like him. He's barely out of law school, and he doesn't know what the hell he's talking about."

Tamia frowned. "But didn't he advise you not to waive your right to a jury trial, and you did it anyway?"

"Yes, but I didn't know at the time that I was pregnant. Now that I'm having second thoughts, the public defender says it's too late. But I've been doing some research on my own. If my judgment was impaired, or if I didn't fully understand my rights at the time I waived them, they have to give me a jury trial."

Tamia's frown deepened. "When are you supposed to be sentenced?"

"Next month. If Brandon had been my lawyer, he *never* would have allowed me to waive any rights, no matter how much I insisted."

"That's true." Tamia closed her eyes, rubbing her temple. "But I don't know, Fee. I don't see how Brandon can take your case after representing me."

"I know, but maybe he can recommend someone good. Now that I'm having this baby, Tamia, I don't wanna just throw in the towel anymore. I want to know what my legal options are, and Brandon's the best person to explain them to me."

Tamia swallowed tightly. "If you want Brandon's help, you're gonna have to go through Dre. Brandon and I aren't . . . together anymore."

"I know," Fiona murmured sympathetically. "I've seen him with Cynthia on TV. If it makes you feel any better, everyone here hates that heffa."

Tamia smiled ruefully. "Thanks."

After she got off the phone, Dominic strolled into the living room and took her hand, gently pulling her from the sofa.

"What're you doing?" she protested. "I'm watching the parade."

He chuckled. "You've been watching it for over an hour. Once you've seen one float, you've seen 'em all."

"That's not true."

"Yes, it is. Come on," he said, steering her toward the front door. "Let's go downstairs."

"Why?"

"They're having a little Christmas social in the lobby. Thought we could pop in for a while and be neighborly."

"Aw, man, do we have to?" Tamia groaned. "I'm not feeling very sociable."

"Come on, love. Where's your Christmas spirit?"

She grumbled, "Back on the sofa, still watching the parade."

Dominic laughed. His face was battered, the skin black and blue. And somehow he still managed to be handsome.

As they boarded the elevator, he captured Tamia's hand and smiled down at her. "Don't look so depressed. It'll be fun."

She smiled weakly. "I'm sure it will."

But when they reached the lobby, it was empty.

Tamia frowned, glancing around curiously. "We must have missed it."

"That's odd." Still holding her hand, Dominic led her across the luxurious lobby, passing the concierge and heading toward the main entrance. The doorman grinned and tipped his hat to them. "Merry Christmas, folks."

They responded warmly in kind.

Tamia was puzzled when Dominic ushered her outside. "Where are—"

Suddenly a red Porsche adorned with a huge silver bow rolled up to the curb.

Dominic exclaimed, "Surprise!"

Tamia's jaw dropped. "What . . . Are you saying this is . . . ?"

"Your new car? Yup." Dominic grinned broadly. "Merry Christmas, darlin'."

Tamia stared in shock as the smiling valet nimbly hopped out of the car and tossed the keys to Dominic.

"Oh my God," Tamia breathed, walking slowly to the Porsche and running her hand over the sleek lines and contours. "This is too much, Dominic. I can't accept this."

"Yes, you can. I want you to have the best, Tamia, and no offense, but that hooptie you been pushin' belongs in the junkyard."

"Hey!" she protested, laughing. "There's nothing wrong with my Accord. It's just a little old and worn."

"Well, 'old and worn' ain't good enough for no woman of mine."

A thrill of pleasure ran through Tamia as he pulled her into his arms. She smiled up at him, her back against the car. "So I'm your woman, huh?"

"Damn right you are."

Her smile softened. She shouldn't have liked the sound of that. But she did.

"Seriously though, Dominic. The Porsche is amazing, but it's too much. Especially since you've already given me all that money to start my business."

His eyes glinted. "So you saying you don't want it?"

Tamia bit her lip, sliding a covetous eye over the hot little convertible. It was definitely a serious upgrade from anything she'd ever driven.

Dominic held up the keys to the Porsche, jangling them enticingly. "Wanna go for a ride?"

Tamia groaned. "You know I do."

"Then give me a kiss."

She grinned, pretending to glance up and around.

"What're you looking for?" Dominic asked her.

"I don't see any mistletoe."

Dominic smiled. "Then just close your eyes and use your imagination."

He slanted his mouth over hers, and they shared a long, deep kiss.

"Hmm," Dominic murmured. "About that ride—"

"Oh, no, you don't." Tamia snatched the keys out of his hand and raced around to the driver's side, laughing as she slid into the low-slung car.

"Oooh." She gazed around at the two-tone leather interior, inhaled the fresh new car smell, and squealed excitedly.

Settling into the passenger seat, Dominic grinned at her. "Damn. I knew you'd look hella good behind that wheel."

"I *feel* hella good." Tamia started the car, whooping delightedly as the turbo engine purred to life. "Let's take this sweet baby for a ride!"

"Yeah, let's do that. Then when we get back," Dominic drawled, winking at her, "you can take *me* for a ride."

Chapter 38

Brandon

Brandon sat alone at the mahogany conference table staring down at a yellow legal pad in front of him. The pages were blank, waiting to be filled. A cup of black coffee sat cooling beside a stack of case files.

He had no taste for the coffee, and he couldn't concentrate on reading reports or taking notes.

He couldn't concentrate on anything other than thoughts of Tamia.

Since Friday night he'd been consumed with reliving every moment of their devastating showdown. He'd proposed to her, and she'd thrown it right back in his face. True, it hadn't been one of his finer moments. There'd been no suave gallantry, no dropping to one knee and presenting her with a dazzling million-dollar diamond ring. He hadn't spouted romantic poetry or quoted lyrics from their favorite love song. He'd yelled out the words to her with all the finesse of some knuckle-dragging Neanderthal wielding a big club.

I'm asking you to be my damn wife!

It definitely wasn't the best of proposals. But his intentions couldn't have been more sincere. Though he was engaged, Tamia was the first woman he'd ever actually asked to marry him. He'd reluctantly agreed to marry Cynthia out of a sense of duty. But Tamia was the one he wanted to spend the rest of his life with, the one he wanted to keep fat with babies.

But he'd fucked around for too long . . . and now it was too late.

Since Tamia had rejected him, Brandon no longer felt like he was drowning. He'd succumbed to the raging current, sinking slowly to the bottom of the abyss. And now he felt dead inside . . . cocooned in a state of emotional anesthesia that nothing or no one could penetrate.

Though there was no partners' meeting today, he'd come to the conference room that morning for a change of scenery, and to avoid one of Cynthia's unannounced visits to his office.

They'd spent Christmas together with their families, and Brandon had never been more grateful for the buffer provided by their relatives. After attending Sunday service, everyone had converged upon his parents' house for an extravagant holiday feast. To compensate for Brandon's subdued demeanor, Cynthia had laughed louder and chattered animatedly, impervious to Brooke's rolling eyes and catty barbs.

Every time Cynthia looked at Brandon, he could see the unspoken questions in her eyes, the fear and uncertainty. She sensed something had changed. She just didn't know what.

He knew he owed her an explanation.

Sooner rather than later . . .

"Poor Mr. Chambers," intoned an amused voice. "Sitting all alone at that big table, looking like the loneliest man on the planet."

Brandon looked up to see Russ Sutcliffe standing in the doorway of the conference room, watching him with a look of mock pity.

Suppressing a weary sigh, Brandon murmured, "What can I do for you, Russ?"

"Nothing at all," Russ drawled, casually tucking his hands into his pockets as he wandered into the room. "I just came by to see how you're holding up. Not so well, by the looks of it. But I guess that's to be expected after everything you've recently been through."

Brandon calmly set down the pen he hadn't been using and steepled his fingers in front of him. He knew Russ had been salivating at the opportunity to taunt him about his highly publicized altercation with Dominic. He'd been forced to wait until Brandon returned to work today since he'd taken off the two days following Christmas.

"Ah, Mr. Chambers," Russ lamented. "Isn't it amazing how quickly the tide can turn? One day you're setting the world on fire with an electrifying speech. The next day you're the star of the most watched fight on YouTube." He tsk-tsked, shaking his head at Brandon. "Your father must have been *so* disappointed to see his heir apparent brawling like a common street thug. And your poor mother must have been just *beside* herself with shock and horror." Russ smiled, all but crowing over Brandon's plummet from grace. "So much for your Senate run."

"Really?" Brandon inquired mildly. "Why do you say that?"

"Oh, come on, Chambers," Russ guffawed. "I know you've fooled everyone around here into thinking you walk on water, but surely even *you* realize you can't run for office after the stunt you pulled last weekend. I mean, let's get real here. Do you honestly believe your esteemed mentor would have been elected president if *he'd* been caught brawling on camera? Obama has gone out of his way to be perceived as anything *but* an angry black man. But you won't have that luxury, dear boy. When voters see you throwing knockout punches on that YouTube video, an angry black man is *exactly* what they're gonna see, and you know it."

Brandon laughed, wagging his head. "Come on now, Russ," he said, affecting an exaggerated Southern drawl. "You know Texans love nothing more than a good barroom brawl. And fightin' over a woman? Well, hell, that's the stuff of country songs and classic westerns. Shoot, this whole dustup might even make me more likeable and relatable to the rednecks and cowboys who love a good display of testosterone. And the ladies . . . well, surely they won't begrudge a poor heartbroken man who let his temper get the best of him." Brandon winked, flashing his most devastatingly charming smile.

Russ narrowed his eyes and tightened his jaw. He knew there was a good chance Brandon might be right.

"Anyway," Brandon added with an unconcerned shrug, "none of this really matters unless I decide to run. And last I checked, I haven't made any announcements."

Russ scoffed in disgust. "Don't insult my intelligence, Chambers. We both know it's a foregone conclusion that you're running for the Senate next year. Ever since you gave that anointed speech at the prayer breakfast, your father's been working behind the scenes to rally support for your candidacy and get the party machine behind you." Russ smirked. "Of course, all his wheeling and dealing might all be for naught. You've got a whole lot of baggage, son. A porn-star girlfriend with a homicidal sister. A jilted baby mama. And now this—a table-clearing brawl that left hotel property destroyed and required a man to receive medical attention. Given all that, Chambers, you shouldn't be at all surprised if the party leaders decide to back a less risky candidate."

Brandon shrugged. "They might. Hell, I wouldn't blame them. Anyway, what difference does any of this make to you? Unless . . ." He trailed off, letting a surprised look sweep across his face. "Why, Russ, is there something you wanna share? Are *you* planning to throw your hat into the ring?"

Russ pressed his lips together, clamming up at once. But it didn't matter whether or not he confirmed anything. Everyone knew he had lofty political aspirations, and Brandon had heard through the grapevine that he'd be leaving the firm soon to pursue his Senate bid.

Brandon smiled narrowly. "If you're worried about going up against me—"

Russ blustered indignantly. "Don't flatter yourself."

"—we'd both have to make it through our respective primaries. With your clout and connections, I'm sure you'd have no problem sailing through the Republican primary. As for me . . . well, I certainly have the name and political connections, but as you've rightly pointed out, I have a ton of baggage. So I'd get pretty battered and bruised over the course of the campaign. But if I happened to pull off an upset and win my primary"—he winked at Russ—"watch out."

Russ's eyes narrowed.

They stared each other down, the air crackling with challenge.

"Are you giving my boss a hard time?"

The two adversaries turned to watch as Addison strolled into the room swinging a briefcase at her side, eyes bright and cheeks flushed from being outdoors.

Russ smiled thinly at her. "Miss Vassar."

"Mr. Sutcliffe." She gave him a chiding smile. "Are you harassing my supervisor? I certainly hope not, because he happens to be my favorite attorney at this firm."

Russ sneered. "A fact well known by everyone who works here."

Addison didn't miss a beat. "Now, now, don't be jealous, Russ. I'm sure you're *somebody's* favorite around here. The window washer, maybe?"

Russ's face flushed with anger.

Coolly dismissing him, Addison turned to beam at Brandon. "I just got back from the courthouse, and I had to track you down to thank you for the brilliant advice you gave me last week. Your strategy worked like a charm."

Brandon smiled faintly. "Good. Glad to hear it."

She grinned. "I'd love to tell you all about it over lunch. My treat."

"Thanks," Brandon gently declined, "but it's my first day back and I'm swamped. So I'll have to take a rain check."

"No problem. I'll be here whenever you're ready." She winked, then turned and sashayed out the door with Russ's eyes glued to her ass.

When Brandon discreetly cleared his throat, Russ whipped his head around to stare at him.

Brandon cocked an amused brow.

The man's face reddened with embarrassment.

Brandon chuckled.

"If you'll excuse me, I have work to do." Russ turned and started from the conference room. Pausing at the door, he added with a smirk, "Maybe you didn't get the memo, but the partners' meeting was canceled today."

"I know." Brandon leaned back in his chair. "I'm the one who canceled it."

Russ's eyes widened with outrage at the idea of a new partner being granted such authority.

As he stalked off in a huff, Brandon couldn't muster even a glimmer of the satisfaction he normally received from besting his adversary.

There was only one thing that could bring him any pleasure now . . . and that ship had sailed.

Chapter 39

Tamia

Tamia's heart began pounding the moment she stepped off the elevator and saw the gleaming black Maybach at the curb. Knowing that Brandon was inside the car made her break out into a cold sweat.

She hadn't seen him since the night of their explosive confrontation one week ago. When she'd fled his condo that night, she'd thought that was the last time she'd ever have to face him. So she was stunned when Fiona called to tell her that Brandon had agreed to accompany her and Dre to the prison. Her stomach had been twisted into queasy knots ever since.

She wiped her damp palms on her jeans, then took a deep breath and started across the lobby.

When she stepped outside, Dre climbed out of the car and smiled warmly at her. "Wassup, girl."

"Hey, Dre. How you doing?" She faltered as he held the passenger door open for her. "Um, I'll sit in the back."

"He wants you up front."

She frowned. "I'd rather sit in the—"

"Tamia." Dre gave her a look. "Get in the car. Please."

She bit her lip, then reluctantly slid into the passenger seat. As Dre closed the door, she braved a glance at Brandon. He wore mirrored sunglasses, a black sweatshirt, baggy jeans, and black Timbs.

Her heart beat triple time. "Hi."

He spared her a cool glance. "Good morning."

Damn, she mused. *This is gonna be even worse than I thought.*

She nervously fastened her lap belt as Brandon drove away from the Four Leaf Towers as if he couldn't leave the premises fast enough.

"Thanks for coming," Tamia told him, "but you really didn't have to."

"Your sister asked me to."

"I know, but she would have understood if you couldn't make it. You could have typed up some legal notes or—"

"It's cool, Tamia," he said tersely.

"But it's a long drive, and I know you're really busy—"

"I said I don't mind." He smirked. "Or is it that you and Dre wanted to be alone?"

"*What?*" Tamia exclaimed.

"Yo, what the fuck?" Dre shouted.

Brandon scowled.

A tense silence ensued.

After several minutes, Brandon heaved a deep breath and scrubbed a hand over his face. "I'm sorry," he mumbled. "I owe both of you an apology. That was uncalled for."

"Damn right it was," Dre growled. "I swear, nigga, you can be a mean muthafucka sometimes."

"Ain't that the truth," Tamia muttered in agreement.

Brandon looked sullen. "I'm sorry. All right?"

Tamia sucked her teeth in disgust as Dre grumbled under his breath.

Though his eyes were hidden by the shades, Tamia caught Brandon checking out her left hand, looking for the diamond ring that wasn't there. He still believed she was engaged, and she wasn't inclined to set the record straight—especially after he'd just insulted her.

The mood remained tense and somber as the threesome struck out for the Christina Melton Crain Unit in Gatesville, which was three and a half hours from Houston.

Brandon drove quietly with a stony expression.

In the backseat, Dre stared broodingly out the window. Watching him in the sideview mirror, Tamia wondered if he was thinking about Fiona and their unborn baby . . . or the forbidden kiss he'd shared with his best friend's sister.

"How was your Christmas?"

Startled by the sound of Brandon's voice, Tamia turned to stare at him. "Excuse me?"

"How was your Christmas?" he repeated with an edge.

"So *now* you wanna be civil?"

His jaw flexed. "Just trying to make polite conversation."

"Okay. I had a wonderful Christmas. How was yours?"

"Wonderful," he said mockingly.

"Good."

Long silence.

"Did you watch the parade?"

Tamia stared at him. "The . . . parade?"

"Yeah. The Christmas parade." Brandon glanced at her. "I know how much you enjoy watching it."

Her throat tightened. "You remembered that?"

"Yeah." A ghost of a smile touched his mouth. "We spent Christmas together last year—"

"It was our first."

He looked at her. "And only."

She swallowed hard. "Go on."

"You spent that week at my condo because we were going to New York for New Year's Eve—" He broke off as Tamia reached over and gently removed his sunglasses.

Dark, hooded eyes met hers.

"That's better," she whispered.

Brandon held her gaze for another moment, then looked back at the road. "Anyway, when you woke up on Christmas morning, you were more excited about watching the parade than opening gifts."

Tamia chuckled. "I was not."

"You certainly acted like it. And you sat glued to the TV until the parade was over." He glanced at her. "So did you watch it on Sunday?"

"I caught some of it," she murmured, looking out the window.

Brandon said nothing more.

As they headed down the highway, their hands ended up resting on the console, mere inches apart. Tamia could feel the heat pulsing off Brandon's skin, feeding the electricity that crackled between them.

Heart pounding, she silently willed his hand to slide closer.

It did.

And so did hers, moving in slow degrees until the back of their hands brushed.

A thrill of pleasure sang through her veins.

They softly rubbed against each other, savoring the connection both had been craving.

When her phone suddenly rang, their hands sprang apart.

Tamia reached down and checked the display screen. When she saw Dominic's number, she silenced the phone and put it away.

Two minutes later when Brandon's phone rang, he did the same thing.

Their eyes met.

After several moments Tamia blinked, breaking their stare.

As Brandon returned his attention to the road, she closed her eyes on a shaky indrawn breath.

No one spoke for a few minutes.

"Yo, B," Dre finally injected into the silence, "you know what this reminds me of?"

Brandon glanced in the rearview mirror. "What?"

"Remember our double dates back in high school? Remember how you'd always let your girl ride shotgun while I kept her friend company in the back?"

Tamia watched as a slow grin stretched across Brandon's face. The sight of his sexy dimples made her breath catch. God, she'd missed those dimples. Missed his smile.

Dre chuckled. " 'Course it's not quite the same now since I'm back here all by my lonesome. But watching that little moment between you and Tamia made me think about the old days." He paused. "Not that you and your old girlfriends ever did anything that warm and fuzzy."

Tamia blushed, glancing shyly at Brandon.

He smiled at her.

"Hey, Tamia," Dre joked, "has Brandon ever told you what a playa he was in high school?"

She grinned. "No, he hasn't."

"That's because I wasn't," Brandon muttered.

"Nigga, please." Dre guffawed. "You were and you know it."

Tamia laughed. "What was he like, Dre? You can tell me."

"No, he can't. Yo, for real," Brandon warned Dre, "don't be putting my business out there like that."

"Whatever, Brandon." Tamia waved him off. "Go on, Dre."

He laughed. "I don't know what he's told you, but B was no choirboy back in the day. He was a straight-up mack daddy, and everyone but his parents knew it. Check this out. You know he went to private schools all his life, right? Well, see, he wasn't feeling those bougie females he saw every day. He preferred down-to-earth sistas. Around-the-way girls with a lil hood in 'em."

Tamia grinned. "That's 'cause he a lil hood himself."

"I know, right? I used to tell him that he was born in the wrong zip code." Dre chuckled. "So, anyway, since Brandon wasn't tryna get with them chicks at his preppy private school, I'd hook him up with the girls from my school and my neighborhood. When I'd first tell them about Brandon, they'd be all like, 'River Oaks? Ain't no black people in River Oaks!' So I'd have to assure them that B was cool people, not some corny-ass brotha like Carlton on *Fresh Prince*. Since I played ball and was kinda popular, they figured Brandon couldn't be *that* bad if he was my boy. So they'd reluctantly agree to meet him, talkin' about how I'd owe them *big time* if he turned out to be a busta. And then B would roll up in the Jetta, waves spinning, rockin' fresh gear, showing off those dimples. *Ooo-wee!* The panties would start flying!"

Tamia laughed. "I bet they did!"

Brandon grimaced, shaking his head. "Does Tamia really need to hear all this?"

"Oh, just relax, baby. We've got two more hours to kill. Telling stories will help pass the time." Tamia blushed, belatedly realizing what she'd called Brandon. Seeing a faint smile on his face, she knew he'd caught the endearment as well.

"Please continue, Dre," she urged.

He chuckled. "I'm not gon' front. As popular as I was, I know I got *way* more play because of Brandon. Even back then this nigga could pull all *kinds* of puss—er, females," he quickly amended, not wanting to offend Tamia. "We'd go to the mall, and it was *ridiculous* how many numbers he got. See, he had game, but he got cocky with it. I tried to warn his black ass that some of these girls at my school were getting salty, but he wasn't tryna hear it. He thought he was the man. But it eventually caught up to him when these two chicks got together and decided to set him up."

Tamia was riveted, half turning in her seat to stare at Dre. "What happened?"

Brandon scowled. "I think we've heard enough."

"Nah, let him finish," Tamia insisted. "This is getting *good.*"

Dre grinned, eyes gleaming wickedly. "He made dates with them back to back, one in the morning and the other at night. When he went to pick up the first girl, both of them were waiting for him. Cold busted!"

Tamia threw back her head and howled with laughter.

Brandon shot her a disgruntled look. "I'm glad you find this so entertaining."

"I do," she asserted between hysterical giggles. "I should have known you were a ho, Brandon! It's always the ones you least suspect!"

"Hey, I was a dumbass teenager," he protested. "My youthful indiscretions shouldn't be held against me."

"You're right." Tamia playfully mushed him on the head. "But that's what you get for tryna be slick."

He grinned sheepishly.

Dre laughed. "He learned his lesson, though. Became a one-woman man after that."

"That's good."

Tamia and Brandon looked at each other and smiled.

After he put on some music, the threesome rode along, singing and bobbing their heads until Tamia's stomach started churning.

She looked at Brandon. "Could you pull over?"

He shot her a confused glance. "Why?"

She gulped tightly. "I think I'm gonna be sick."

Brandon quickly switched lanes, steering the Maybach to the side of the highway.

Tamia bolted from the car, dashed over to the grass, and dropped to her knees. Her stomach convulsed as she vomited repeatedly.

She heard car doors slamming, heavy booted feet crunching on pavement. Then Brandon was crouching beside her, his touch gentle on her back, his voice tender with concern.

"You okay, baby?"

Before Tamia could reply, her stomach heaved and she hurled again, foul chunks splashing the overgrown brown grass.

Brandon rubbed her back and murmured soothingly to her as she retched some more.

When she was finally finished, she sat back on her haunches and weakly dragged the back of her hand across her mouth.

Dre eyed her worriedly. "Damn, girl. You all right?"

Tamia nodded slowly.

Brandon gently stroked a hand down her hair. "Think you're done?"

"I think so," she whispered.

Brandon stood, then bent and swept her up into his arms. She closed her eyes as he carried her back to the car and gently lowered her into the seat, refastening her lap belt as if she were a small child.

He and Dre climbed into the car, then they were back on the road.

"I'ma stop and get you some water and anything else you need," Brandon told Tamia.

"Okay." She smiled wanly. "Thank you."

He gave her knee a gentle squeeze.

"Think it's something you ate?" Dre asked.

Tamia nodded, rubbing her queasy stomach. "Probably."

She saw Brandon and Dre trade speculative glances in the rearview mirror.

Resting her cheek against the cool window, Tamia closed her eyes and soon drifted off to sleep.

They never got to see Fiona that day.

When they arrived at the prison, they were informed that Fiona had changed her mind about receiving visitors.

Tamia was stunned.

Dre was royally pissed.

Brandon was strangely silent.

When Tamia returned home that evening, she had an email message waiting for her. It was from her sister.

Tam-Tam,

I'm sorry you came all the way out here for nothing. I guess I'm still not ready to face you now that you know what I did to Mama Esther. Seeing you makes me see her . . . so I can't see you yet.

Dre can come visit me another day. And I already talked to Brandon about my legal options, and he told me what to do.

Please don't think of today as a wasted trip. Seven hours in the car with Brandon was my Christmas gift to you. I hope you made the most of the opportunity. And I hope being together made you both realize that you can't live without each other.

Love,
Fee

Chapter 40

Brandon

Brandon lay with his hands clasped behind his head as he stared at the ceiling. Warm sunlight poured through the drapes to wash over his bedroom.

It was Saturday morning—New Year's Eve.

He had things to do, errands to run. But he made no move to get up, content to lie there and reminisce about yesterday's road trip. He replayed every moment, savoring the minutest details. He remembered the playful banter between him and Tamia, the easy camaraderie he'd missed so damn much. When they'd rubbed their hands against each other's, the butterflies that fluttered his stomach had been downright unmanly.

When Tamia got sick, he'd been worried as hell. But he'd also felt stirrings of hope. From that moment, the questions had begun whispering through his mind.

Was Tamia pregnant?

If so, was it his baby?

Or Dominic's?

Brandon stopped right there, not wanting to even contemplate the possibility of his boo carrying another man's child. It would kill him, put him out of his misery once and for all.

He swallowed hard, feeling his chest tighten.

He was glad Cynthia wasn't there to speculate about the play of emotions crossing his face. She'd left early that morning for a hair appointment. That evening they were attending a New Year's Eve party at her sorority sister's house in lieu of the masquerade ball Brandon's mother traditionally hosted. Since she'd been so busy helping with her husband's campaign and planning Brandon and Cynthia's wedding, Gwen had decided to cancel the masquerade ball this year.

Brandon was glad.

He'd had enough of wearing masks, pretending to be someone he wasn't.

He was done being a martyr who nobly sacrificed his own needs and desires for some higher purpose.

He'd made up his mind, and he knew what he had to do.

The sooner, the better.

Just then his phone rang on the bedside table. He reached over and picked it up, surprised to see Leah's number.

"Hello?" he answered.

"Brandon?" Her voice was low and tremulous. "It's Leah."

"Wassup, girl."

"I . . . I have something to—" She broke off suddenly and burst into tears.

A dagger of alarm shot through Brandon. "Leah?" He pushed himself up on an elbow. "What's wrong?"

She began sobbing and babbling incoherently.

"Hey, hey," Brandon murmured soothingly. "Calm down, take a deep breath, and tell me what's going on."

"It's Cynthia . . . ," she choked out tearfully.

Brandon tensed, his eyes narrowing. "What about Cynthia?"

"She's not . . . she's not pregnant."

Brandon bolted upright, the phone pressed hard against his ear. "What do you mean she's not pregnant?"

Leah gulped down a sob. "She made it up . . . to get you to marry her. And I . . . oh God, I *helped* her!"

Brandon swung his legs over the side of the bed, his feet hitting the floor with an urgent thud. "What the fuck are you talking about, Leah?"

"I'm so sorry, Brandon," she rushed on, her voice garbled with tears. "I thought I was being a good friend to Cynthia, and I honestly didn't think Tamia deserved you after the way she broke your heart. But I know what I did was wrong, and I never should have agreed to the idea!"

"Tell me what the hell happened," Brandon demanded.

"Cynthia came to see me one day. She was crying so hysterically I thought I'd have to give her something to calm her down! She was upset because you and Tamia were getting back together. She insisted that you really loved *her*, not Tamia, but you were just confused because Tamia had been playing mind games with you. Some of the nurses had just been talking about some stupid baby storyline on one of the soaps, and I made a joke about Cynthia doing the same thing. Oh my God, I never thought she would take it seriously! The next thing I knew, she was begging me to help her fake a pregnancy!"

Brandon clenched his jaw so hard the tendons in his neck bulged. "What did she want you to do?"

Leah hesitated. "Since I know all the ob-gyns and nurses who work at the hospital, I had access to . . . things."

"Like the sonogram photo," Brandon said tightly.

"Yes," Leah whispered. "She knew once you saw that picture, you wouldn't have any more doubts."

Brandon closed his eyes as a cold rage swept over him, pouring ice into his veins. "I spoke to her doctor on the phone. She's the one who confirmed the test results."

"That wasn't Dr. Kapoor. That was an old friend of Cynthia's. She's from India like Cynthia's real gynecologist."

Brandon shook his head, sickened and infuriated by the level of manipulation and deceit that had been perpetrated. Cynthia had even given him the wrong date for her doctor's appointment, making him feel guilty for missing something that had never taken place.

"Was she ever on the pill?" he demanded.

"No." Leah drew a deep, shuddering breath. "She'd been trying to get pregnant for months, but you always insisted on wearing protection—even when you guys had sex in the shower. It drove her crazy. Also, she was diagnosed with mild endometriosis several months ago, so that's why it hasn't been easy for her to conceive. The irony is that taking birth control pills is one of the treatment options for endometriosis." Leah sighed heavily. "She figured once you saw the proof that she was carrying your child, you'd stop wearing condoms, and she'd eventually get pregnant for real."

Brandon thought of the night he'd gotten drunk, and Cynthia had seized the opportunity to have sex with him.

Scheming bitch!

"I felt so horrible when you showed up at the hospital last week," Leah confessed in a low voice. "You brought me lunch, and you were so sweet and caring. I was already feeling guilty about what I'd done. Seeing you just made it a thousand times worse. After you left, I called Cynthia and told her she needs to come clean. But she refused, saying she'd come too far to turn back. She said I'd lose my job and my medical license if anyone found out, and she's right. I would. But I don't care anymore. I couldn't go into the New Year having this on my conscience. Words can't express how truly sorry I am for betraying your friendship, Brandon. I hope you can forgive me."

After a stony silence, Brandon hung up without responding.

It was the last day of what had been the craziest year of his life. A year filled with one betrayal after another from women he'd trusted.

His capacity for forgiveness had exceeded its fucking limit.

When Cynthia returned home that afternoon, he was waiting for her.

He sat in his favorite armchair swigging from a bottle of beer and laughing at an old episode of *The Jeffersons*, which always reminded him of the time he and Tamia had playfully sung the theme song to each other.

"Hey, baby," Cynthia greeted him, strolling into the living room.

"Hey." Brandon smiled at her. "Don't you look nice."

"You like?" She preened, patting her freshly glossed mane. "And it's *all* mine. Unlike your Queen Bey."

"Yo, don't be throwing shade at my girl."

Cynthia sniffed. "Just sayin'. I may not be an international sex symbol, but at least *I'm* not fake."

You're the biggest fake of all, Brandon thought cynically.

She sauntered over to him, sat on his lap, and looped her arms around his neck. As she leaned close to kiss him, he raised his bottle to his mouth and took a swig of beer.

Her smile wavered. "Did you run your errands?"

"Yup."

She glanced at the coffee table, noticing the arts and crafts materials he'd gathered. "What's all this?"

"Oh, I'm starting a baby album."

"A baby album?"

"Umm-hmm." He smiled, setting aside his beer. "I've been feeling really bad about missing your doctor's appointment that day. I should have been there for your first sonogram."

"That's okay," Cynthia assured him. "I know you've had a lot on your mind lately."

"Yeah, but that's no excuse. I don't want you to think I'm not supportive, so I was thinking we could start, like, a scrapbook to chronicle your pregnancy and the baby's first year of life."

Cynthia's expression softened with pleasure. "What a wonderful idea."

"I'm glad you think so," Brandon said. "I was looking up some scrapbooking ideas online. Some of the things we could include are pictures of your stomach getting bigger every month, photos of the nursery once we set it up, your baby shower invitations—'cause I know you've already picked them out," he teased.

Cynthia laughed. "You know me so well."

"Yup. I sure do." Brandon grinned. "Anyway, since the only keep-sake we have right now is the sonogram picture, I've been trying to think of other things to put in the album. Now don't laugh," he said, reaching down beside the armchair to pick up a plastic Walgreens bag, "but I thought no baby album could be complete without one of these."

Cynthia froze, her eyes flaring with panic at the sight of the home pregnancy test he removed from the bag. "Wh-what're you doing with that?"

Brandon smiled. "I thought you could pee on the stick so we can add it to the album."

Cynthia wrinkled her nose. "Um, that's kinda gross."

Brandon chuckled. "Obviously we'll wait until your pee dries be-fore we put the stick in the scrapbook. And we can toss it into a Zip-loc bag if you're that disgusted."

"Ohhkay." Cynthia snickered nervously. "This is probably why guys should leave the scrapbooking to women."

"Come on, baby. I'm trying to make an effort here. Humor me."

She bit her lip, darting an anxious glance at the home pregnancy test. "I don't have to pee right now."

"Really? I thought pregnant women always have a full bladder."

"*I* don't. Besides," she added irritably, "I told you before that those things aren't always accurate."

He held up the bag. "That's why I got four different brands. I figure at least *one* of them should come out positive, right?"

Cynthia's mouth tightened at the edges.

"Come on, baby. Do it for me." Brandon smiled cajolingly. "Please?"

She stared at him.

He stared back, expecting her to crack under the pressure.

But he was wrong.

After wavering another moment, she reluctantly took the bag from his hand, slid off his lap, and trudged from the room.

Brandon sat there drumming his fingertips on the armrest, waiting to see how far she would go to prolong the charade.

Pretty far, as it turned out.

About three minutes later, she returned to the living room, huffing an exasperated breath. "See," she complained, flapping the bone-dry plastic stick at him before tossing it onto the table. "I told you I couldn't pee. Not even a trickle."

Brandon looked at her.

She frowned and glanced away, shifting nervously from one foot to the other as she pretended to watch *The Jeffersons*.

Brandon let the silence hang between them, stretching it into a full minute before he spoke. "I can't do this."

Cynthia's eyes swung back to his face. "You can't do what?"

"This." He gestured between them. "You and me. I can't do this shit anymore."

She swallowed visibly. "Wh-what are you saying, Brandon?"

"I'm saying I'm done. *We're* done."

"You . . . you're breaking off our engagement?"

His voice was hard. "Yes."

She stared at him, then burst out shrilly, "I knew I shouldn't have let you go on that damn road trip with Tamia and Dre! The moment you told me about it, I *knew* it was a horrible idea! Just like it was a horrible idea for me to let Tamia come here that night after the banquet!"

Brandon narrowed his eyes. "What do you mean you 'let' her?"

"How do you think she got into the condo, Brandon? I gave her my fucking key because she said she wanted to tell you good-bye in person. But I should have refused because ever since that night, you've been like a complete stranger to me! What the hell happened between you two?"

Brandon calmly met her gaze. "I asked her to marry me."

Cynthia's eyes widened. "You did WHAT?"

"I asked her to marry me." He smiled grimly. "She turned me down."

Cynthia looked stunned. "She did?"

"Yup. Broke my heart, too. But that's not even the point. The fact that I proposed to her confirms once and for all that I have no damn business marrying you when *she's* the one I wanna be with."

Cynthia's nostrils flared, her eyes hardening with fury as she stood over his chair. "You can't do this, Brandon. You can't just walk away from me."

"Why not?"

"*Because I'm having your baby!*"

He gave her a coldly mocking smile. "You mean the baby that only exists in your imagination? The one you've been lying about from day one? *That* baby?"

He watched in satisfaction as the blood drained from her face.

She stared at him, shocked into speechlessness.

"That's right, sweetheart," he jeered. "I know all about the elaborate scheme you concocted to trap me into marrying you. Leah called to confess and unburden her soul."

Cynthia's eyes flashed with the wounded disbelief of someone who'd been grievously betrayed. "That bitch," she hissed.

"Right," Brandon mocked. "She came clean and told the truth, but *she's* the bitch."

Cynthia's face flushed. "Don't be fooled into thinking her motives were pure," she spat resentfully. "I've always suspected Leah has feelings for you, Brandon. I wouldn't be surprised if she 'came clean' just to break us up!"

"I don't give a fuck!" Brandon thundered, lunging from the chair. "We're not talking about Leah! We're talking about you and your shady behavior! I mean, come on, Cynthia. Faking a *pregnancy*? How long did you seriously think you could get away with that shit? What if you'd never gotten pregnant? Were you gonna start hiding your body from me so I wouldn't know you were wearing one of those fake fat suits? Were you gonna pretend to go into 'labor' while I was conveniently out of town or something? Were you gonna steal somebody's baby and pass it off as ours?"

Cynthia's face reddened with humiliation as he fired the questions at her as if she were under cross-examination.

"Answer me, damn it!" he prodded furiously. "How far were you willing to go to pull this off? Huh? How far?"

"*As far as I had to!*" she exploded.

Brandon stilled, eyeing her incredulously. "Do you know how crazy you sound right now? Have you completely lost your fucking mind?"

Tears flooded her eyes. "I didn't know what else to do, Brandon! You and Tamia were getting back together. You took her to Italy and . . ." She trailed off, chin quivering. "I love you—"

"DON'T TALK TO ME ABOUT LOVE!" Brandon roared. "You don't know a damn thing about love when you can lie to my face every day and not think twice about it! My God, Cynthia, you deceived me into believing you were having my *child*. You knew the kind of man I am. You knew I'd wanna do the right thing and marry you. You played me like a muthafucka!"

"I'm sorry," she cried piteously. "I didn't mean to hurt you, Brandon! I just wanted you to love me as much as I've always loved you!"

"By tricking me into marrying you? *That's* how you planned to win my heart?"

Tears spilled down her face. "She doesn't deserve you, Brandon. And she's not right for you!"

"But you are," he mocked scornfully.

"*Yes!* You and I were the closest of friends before you ever met Tamia! If she hadn't come along, I know you would have eventually realized that we belong together. We're good for each other, Brandon. And if you have any political aspirations whatsoever, you need *me* by your side—not that whore!"

Brandon raked her with a look of scathing contempt. "You know what? I'm done with this conversation, and I'm done with you. Have a nice fucking life."

She gasped as he shoved past her and stalked toward the door.

"Where are you going?" she taunted bitterly. "Crawling back to Tamia?"

"Don't worry about where the fuck I'm going. All you need to worry about is packing up your shit and getting the fuck up outta here before I come back."

She started forward beseechingly. "Brandon—"

"I'm dead serious, Cynthia. I want you gone. Vanished. Ghost. The front desk is bringing up moving boxes, and a driver will be here to load up a rental van for you. You got two hours to get your shit together before security shows up to escort your ass out, so I suggest you get cracking."

Shooting her one last scornful glare, he turned and stormed out, slamming the door behind him.

Two minutes later, he was climbing into his car when Dre called.

"Wassup, B."

"Yo, wassup."

"You and Cynthia still going to that party at her friend's house?"

"Nah, man. I think I'll ring in the New Year with y'all at Cornel's club."

"Word? That's cool. It's gon' be off da chain." Dre chuckled. "So what's good with you? What you up to?"

Brandon sighed. "Just taking out the trash, bruh. Just taking out the trash . . ."

Chapter 41

Tamia

"Where do you want this, ma'am?" grunted one of the red-faced furniture deliverymen who greeted Tamia when she opened the front door.

"Right this way."

She turned and led the two men through the penthouse to the bedroom, where they lowered a California king mattress onto the platform bedframe. Tamia thanked them and signed off on the delivery before seeing them to the door.

Dominic had purchased the new mattress after she told him she didn't want to continue sleeping in the same bed he'd shared with all his other mistresses. The replacement mattress, delivered on the eve of a new year, was supposed to signal a clean slate for them. A new beginning in their relationship . . . a relationship Tamia wasn't even sure she still wanted after spending time with Brandon yesterday.

I hope being together made you both realize that you can't live without each other, Fiona's words drifted through her mind.

Don't even go there, another voice warned. *It's over between you and Brandon. Stop looking back. Keep moving forward!*

Easier said than done.

Tamia frowned, returning to her laptop to finish working on promo materials for the Ehrlichs' B and B. Dre had generously secured a raving endorsement from a Houston Texans player and his wife, so Tamia was featuring the couple in an ad campaign set to launch before Valentine's Day.

When her phone rang on the breakfast counter, she reached over and picked it up.

"Hey, love." It was Dominic. "Have they delivered the mattress yet?"

"Yup," Tamia confirmed. "They just left."

"Cool." He chuckled wickedly. "I look forward to christening it tonight after we get back from the party."

"If we're not too tired."

"Come on now. You know I'm never too tired to make love to you."

Speak for yourself, Tamia mused.

She'd been exhausted lately, craving naps at all hours of the day. Her chronic fatigue, coupled with the nausea she'd been experiencing, were definitely causes for concern. But she wasn't ready to explore the suspicion taking root in her mind. There was too much to hope for . . . too much to fear.

"How are things going at the restaurant?" she asked Dominic, who was hosting a New Year's Eve bash at Winston's tonight.

"Everything's shaping up nicely. I just need to check on a few more things, then I'll be on my way home."

"Okay." Tamia smiled. "See you soon."

She had just ended the call when her phone rang again. Recognizing Officer Greene's number, she answered, "Hello?"

"Hello, Miss Luke. This is Officer Greene. How're you doing?"

"I'm fine. Do you have any new information about my case?" she asked hopefully.

"I don't, unfortunately. As you know, the two women who assaulted you—"

"Isabel Archer's cousins."

"Yes—Dashay and Jamila Ganteaume. As you know, they're both out on bail and are awaiting trial. I feel confident that they're the ones who left you the note, and this will come out during the trial."

Tamia frowned, wishing she shared his optimism. She still wasn't entirely convinced that Isabel's cousins were responsible for the note. But with no other leads to go on, there was nothing she could do but wait for the truth to come out. *If* it ever came out.

"Anyway, there's another reason I was calling." Keyshawn cleared his throat, suddenly sounding nervous. "I hope this doesn't seem inappropriate, but I was wondering . . . I mean, I know it's short notice and it's New Year's Eve, but if you don't have any plans this evening, I was wondering if you'd like to have dinner with me."

Tamia was taken aback. "Are you asking me out on a *date*?"

"Um, yeah. I don't know if you're seeing anyone—"

"I am," she cut him off. "But even if I weren't, I wouldn't go out with you. And you've got a lot of nerve coming on to me when you already have a girlfriend."

There was a startled pause on the other end. "I don't have a girlfriend," he said, sounding perplexed. "Who told you that?"

"Oh, please," Tamia scoffed, rolling her eyes. "I know damn well you've been dating my friend Honey."

"Who?"

Tamia sucked her teeth. "Why you tryna play me, Keyshawn? I know all about your relationship with Honey."

"I'm sorry, Miss Luke, but I don't know anyone by that name."

Tamia frowned. "She goes by Honey, but her real name is Halima. Halima Selvon."

"Halima," Keyshawn repeated, mulling over the name as if he was trying to jog his memory. "There was a young woman I arrested for solicitation sometime last year. The charges were later dropped, but now that I think about it, her name *was* Halima . . . or something like that. Like I said, it was a while ago."

Tamia was perched tensely on the edge of the bar stool. "So what you're telling me is that you *don't* have a girlfriend named Honey?"

Keyshawn chuckled. "I don't have a girlfriend—period. But I'd be interested to know why someone's running around claiming me as their boyfriend. I don't know whether to be flattered or alarmed."

"I'll let you know when I find out," Tamia whispered before ending the call, pulse thudding, mind racing with speculation.

Why would Honey have lied about dating Keyshawn Greene? Why would she have concocted an elaborate story about being in an abusive relationship with him? Why had she—

Tamia froze, struck by another realization.

Honey wasn't the only one who'd told Tamia about Keyshawn.

Lou had also confirmed the relationship the night he'd come to her apartment for dinner. She remembered him thanking her for letting Honey stay with her after she'd gotten into a fight with Keyshawn.

I told her what I'd do to that motherfucker if he ever hit her again. . . .
Lou had been so angry, so fiercely protective over Honey.

Either Keyshawn was lying about not knowing her—or Honey and Lou had played Tamia for a fool.

Your enemies have been busy. . . . Don't let them steal your soul.

As a surge of anger swept through Tamia, she jumped to her feet, snatched her car keys off the foyer table, and slammed out of the apartment.

Thirty minutes later, she whipped her car into the circular driveway of the large house Lou had purchased—along with an Escalade and a Beemer—after opening his escort agency.

As Tamia glared at the two-story house and luxury vehicles, she remembered what Shanell had told her on the night of her homecoming party after she was acquitted.

Am I the only one who doesn't think it's just a coincidence that Lou shut down his film studio shortly after you went to prison—and now he's living large?

Seething with fury, Tamia hopped out of her car and marched up to the front door, a baseball bat swinging at her side.

Lou answered the door, his hazel eyes widening in surprise when he saw her. "*Mamacita!* What are—"

"Where is she?" Tamia snarled.

"Where's who?"

"You know damn well who." Tamia shoved her way past him, barging into the house and looking around. "Where the fuck is she?"

Lou closed the door behind her. "What's going on, Tamia?"

"That's what I came to ask you," she spat, rounding accusingly on him. "You and that lil bitch got some explaining to do, so go get her or I will!"

"Tamia—"

"*GO GET HER!*"

"Whoa!" Lou leaped back as she swung the bat in warning. He held up his hands in surrender, eyes wide with alarm. "Damn, *mamacita!* Easy with that."

"I want some fucking answers, *papi*, or muthafuckas gon' start droppin'!"

"Come on, Tamia—"

"She's right," spoke a quiet, resigned voice. "She deserves answers."

Tamia whirled around.

Honey stood across the living room toking on a blunt, watching Tamia through a veil of smoke. Her hair was tousled, and she wore one of Lou's dress shirts that hung down to her thick thighs.

She sighed, shaking her head at Tamia. "I knew this day was coming when you told me you'd met Keyshawn."

Tamia's eyes narrowed menacingly. "Why the hell did you lie about dating him?"

Lou and Honey exchanged guilty looks.

"Somebody better start talking!" Tamia shouted, tightening her grip on the baseball bat.

Honey gestured nervously to the sofa. "Why don't we sit down?"

"I don't wanna sit down," Tamia spat, stalking toward the living room.

Lou darted around her, using himself as a barrier between her and Honey. Tamia scowled as Honey lowered herself onto the sofa, flashing leopard-print panties that reminded Tamia of the pair she'd found at Dominic's apartment.

Her eyes narrowed as she watched the girl tuck her legs beneath her and take a deep drag on the blunt.

"Could you put that shit out?" Tamia snapped. "The smell's making me sick."

Honey quickly complied.

As Lou went and stood beside the sofa, Tamia began pacing back and forth, the bat swinging at her side as she glared at Honey.

"Keyshawn called and asked me out on a date," she explained. "I turned him down and told him off because I *thought* he was dating my so-called friend. Imagine my surprise when he told me he didn't even know you."

Honey swallowed visibly. "I needed him for my cover."

"Your cover for *what?*"

"To get into your life . . . to spy on you."

Tamia froze, a chill running through her. "To *spy* on me? For who?"

"Bishop Yarbrough." Honey paused. "He's the one who told Dominic that you were Mystique."

Tamia stared at the girl, reeling with shock and outrage. "*Bishop Yarbrough?*"

"Yes." Honey looked her in the eye. "And I'm the one who told him who you were."

"WHAT?"

As Tamia lunged at Honey, Lou moved quickly, knocking the bat out of her hand and holding her back as she struggled furiously in his arms.

"Calm down, *mamacita*," he urged. "Just hear her out. Please—"

"*I can't believe you betrayed me like that!*" Tamia screamed at Honey. "I took you into my home! I treated you like my own damn sister! I TRUSTED you!"

Honey's nostrils flared, tears springing to her eyes. "I'm sorry, Tamia. I never meant to hurt you. You have to believe me—"

"I *don't* believe you!"

Honey sniffled, dragging a shaky hand through her hair.

Chest heaving with fury, Tamia viciously jerked free of Lou's grasp and retrieved her bat from the floor, then sat down in the nearest armchair. Resting the bat beside her, she crossed her legs, folded her arms, and glared at Honey.

"Start talking, bitch."

Honey inhaled a deep, shuddering breath. "When I found out that Lou's studio was losing money last year, I started moonlighting as an escort to make some extra money. I told you before that I've been trying to save up enough to bring my family here from New Orleans—"

Tamia sneered. "How do I know *that* wasn't a lie?"

"It wasn't. I swear to you that everything I told you about my family—even my grandmother's bad heart—was true."

Tamia gritted her teeth. "Go on."

"Working as an escort is how I met Bishop Yarbrough. One night I was waiting outside for him when Officer Greene showed up and arrested me for solicitation. Since I kept my mouth shut and didn't tell the cops that Bishop Yarbrough was my client, he pulled some strings to get the charges dropped against me. That's when I started thinking of other ways we could help each other."

Honey paused, nervously moistening her lips before she continued. "We spent a lot of time talking about his family, especially Cynthia. She was his princess, his angel, and she could do no wrong. Honestly," Honey added, wrinkling her nose in disgust, "at one point I thought there might be some incest going on, that's how attached he is to her. It was clear to me that he'd do anything for her."

Tamia frowned, remembering how Cynthia's parents had behaved at the fundraiser gala, hovering over her as if she were a child.

Honey shook her head, heaving a deep sigh. "What Cynthia wanted more than anything, of course, was Brandon. She loved that brotha like crazy, but he wasn't checking for her like that. Then he met you, Tamia, and Cynthia *really* didn't stand a chance. She confided in her parents about everything, and it made Bishop Yarbrough kinda mad that she was so hung up on Brandon. He didn't think anyone was good enough for his little girl, and I think he even felt a little jealous of Brandon. But he wanted Cynthia to be happy, and he also wanted her to marry Brandon so their two families could be even more powerful. He always referred to them as the black Kennedys and Rockefellers."

Honey paused, glancing apologetically at Lou. "One night after Lou and I slept together, we got really high. I was joking about Mystique, asking Lou if I was a better fuck than she was. He said he didn't know because he'd never fucked her. And then he slipped up and said your real name." Honey bit her lip, shaking her head at Tamia. "I couldn't believe you were the same Tamia Luke who'd been causing Bishop Yarbrough's daughter so much misery."

Tamia sat forward slowly, her eyes narrowed on Honey's face. "So you sold me out."

The girl swallowed hard, then nodded. "For my next date with the bishop, I brought one of your *Slave Chronicles* videos for us to watch together. After we fucked to it, I told him that I knew who Mystique was and I could arrange a threesome with her. He got all excited, but I told him he had to pay to play. Since Lou was the one who'd given me your identity, I thought it was only fair to cut him into the deal as well. Bishop Yarbrough agreed to pay whatever I asked. Once I told him who you really were . . . it was like he'd hit the mega jackpot."

Tamia felt sick to her stomach. She didn't want to hear any more, but she had to know how this betrayal had unfolded—from beginning to end.

"Dominic and his wife had visited Redeemed Life a few times," Honey explained, "which is how he and Bishop Yarbrough met. They did some investment deals together, and apparently the bishop found out that Dominic had embezzled a ton of money several years ago. Once the bishop decided on a plan, he went to Dominic and basically made him an offer he couldn't refuse. If Dominic didn't agree to it, the bishop was gonna turn him in to the feds."

Stunned, Tamia stared at Honey, trying to process what she'd just heard. Dominic had been blackmailed into blackmailing *her*?

Honey smiled ironically, interpreting her thoughts. "Did you honestly think a man like Dominic Archer would have to force any woman to have sex with him? Hell, no. The bishop has dirt on a lot of people, but he chose Dominic because he knew you wouldn't be able to resist him."

Tamia's face heated with shame as Honey continued, "Dominic resented the hell out of being blackmailed, especially over something he considered so trivial. He thought Cynthia was desperate and pathetic, and he thought Bishop Yarbrough was crazy for going to such lengths just to get a man for her."

Tamia frowned, remembering the comment Dominic had once made to Brandon. *You got some interesting taste in women.* Now it made sense.

"Sometimes Bishop Yarbrough worried that Dominic might renege on the deal," Honey said. "But he kept his mouth shut, even during your trial when Brandon put him on the stand and interrogated the hell out of him."

This didn't surprise Tamia. She'd long ago realized that in some twisted way, Dominic enjoyed being punished by Brandon almost as much as he enjoyed making Brandon suffer.

"All of them were hoping that you'd be found guilty of Isabel's murder," Honey grimly continued. "When Brandon got you off, I thought the bishop was gonna kill somebody. And Cynthia was absolutely devastated. She was worried that you and Brandon would get back together. That's when her father decided that I needed to keep a close eye on you so I could report back on everything you and Brandon were doing. It was his idea for me to become your friend."

Tamia shook her head in disbelief. "So it was all a setup. The night you came to my apartment after you'd supposedly gotten into a fight with your boyfriend, it was just a fucking ploy to get you in the door."

Honey nodded slowly. "I had followed your trial. You testified about your childhood, how your mother was abused by your stepfather—"

"So you knew that was my soft spot," Tamia said bitterly. "You knew I'd be sympathetic toward you."

Again, Honey nodded.

"Who really gave you that black eye?"

The girl bit her lip, glancing at Lou.

Tamia eyed him incredulously. "*You* hit her?"

He looked shamefaced. "It was her idea," he mumbled.

"Dear God," Tamia whispered, shaking her head at him. "How *could* you, Lou? How could you have agreed to any of this?" She pointed at Honey. "*That* bitch didn't know me, but *you* were supposed to be my friend! You didn't have to be a part of this. You could have told her you weren't interested! My God, Lou, I still remember the night you came to tell me that Dominic had supposedly showed up at the studio asking questions about Mystique. You acted all concerned for me, promising to get to the bottom of who'd outed me. But you knew all along because *you're* the one who sold me out!"

"What else was I supposed to do?" he burst out defensively. "The studio was losing money! I was facing bankruptcy! *You'd* moved on with your life a long time ago, Tamia. You didn't care about me or the studio when you decided to walk away. You did what was best for *you*, and I had to do what was best for *me!*"

"Really?" Tamia jeered, gesturing around the garishly furnished house. "Well, I hope it was worth it!"

He clenched his jaw, dropping his guilty gaze to the floor.

Tamia sneered at Honey. "By the way, you seem to be *awfully* familiar with the inner workings of Dominic's mind. Did Bishop Yarbrough tell you how Dominic was feeling about all this? Or did he tell you himself during pillow talk?"

Honey's face reddened as Lou shot her a stunned look. "*Puñeta coño!* You were *fucking* that asshole?"

"Oops." Tamia smirked. "Didn't mean to let the cat out of the bag. Speaking of cats, nice panties, bitch. Did you mean to leave them behind at Dominic's crib so I'd find them? When you called me that morning when he and I were driving back to Houston, did you already know I'd be stupid enough to go home with him?"

Honey shook her head quickly. "No, I didn't."

"*Liar!*"

"I'm not lying, Tamia! I didn't even know you and Dominic had spent the weekend together because I hadn't spoken to him in weeks! The last time I'd seen him was the night he showed up at your apartment and—"

Tamia gasped. "*You're* the one who let him up, aren't you? You left for a date, and the next thing I knew, he was standing on my doorstep. He wasn't let up by some woman who lives on the same floor as me!"

"No, he wasn't," Honey confirmed, looking guiltier by the moment. "He paid the front desk clerk to tell you that story. It ended up costing the guy his job—in case you were wondering where he's been. Anyway, I don't even know why Dominic was there that night. Once you went to prison, he told Bishop Yarbrough he was done with the whole scheme. He'd kept his end of the bargain and wanted nothing more to do with any of us."

Tamia sneered. "Yet he kept fucking you. No wonder you told me you didn't blame me for sleeping with him. As you rightly said, the brotha can lay some pipe!"

Honey shot a remorseful glance at Lou, who looked hurt and disgusted. "Like I said, I hadn't spoken to Dominic in weeks. The day after you and I went shopping together, I went to his apartment to see him—"

"Feenin' for the dick, huh?" Tamia taunted.

Honey blushed, biting her lip. "I didn't leave my panties there on purpose. After we . . . were done, he kinda hustled me out the door, didn't really give me a chance to get all my shit together."

"Made you feel cheap and used, didn't it?" Tamia smirked, relishing the girl's humiliation. "That's what men like Dominic do. They use you, then they toss your ass out when you've served your purpose or they've grown bored with you. Guess being the bottom bitch ain't all it's cracked up to be, is it?"

Honey sniffled, scraping tears from her eyes with the heel of her palm. "I know you don't wanna hear this, Tamia, but I've always admired you. I can't tell you how many times I watched your Mystique videos and took notes. You were a badass bitch, the best in the business as far as I'm concerned. And I respected the way you did your thing and made your paper, then got out the game after you earned your college degree. Honestly, I jumped at the chance to live with you because I really liked you and I *wanted* to get closer to you. I didn't have to pretend to be your friend. I *am* your friend."

"Some friend," Tamia spat bitterly. "With friends like you and Lou, who the fuck needs enemies?"

Tears leaked from Honey's eyes. "Tamia—"

"This is CRAZY!" she exploded, slapping her palm against the armrest. "I'm running out of muthafuckas to trust!"

Lou swore under his breath in Spanish, his voice hoarse with shame and regret. "I'm sorry, *mamacita*. I'm so—"

"*Save your fucking sorry!*" Tamia screamed, jumping to her feet. She snatched up her baseball bat, then spun on her heel and marched toward the front door.

Lou caught up to her, grabbing her arm to detain her.

She whirled around, shoving at his chest hard enough to knock him backward.

"I love you, Tamia," he fervently declared. "If I could go back and make a different choice, I would in a heartbeat!"

Tamia sneered contemptuously. "When Dominic showed up at my office and called me Mystique, I didn't know who could have sold me out. My first instinct was to question everyone—including you. I should have trusted that instinct. Lesson learned."

Lou flinched, pain darkening his eyes.

Without sparing Honey another glance, Tamia turned and strode out the front door.

Instead of returning to Dominic's penthouse, she drove straight home, seething with pain and fury.

When she arrived at her building, she relinquished her Porsche to the valet, wisely taking advantage of the complimentary service so she wouldn't have to go anywhere near the parking garage.

After letting herself into her apartment, she tossed down her keys and crossed to the windows, fuming as she glared out at the downtown skyline that would be ablaze with fireworks at the stroke of midnight.

Honey and Joseph Yarbrough had ruthlessly conspired against her, setting her up for a fall she'd never seen coming. Since they'd thought nothing of destroying *her* life, she'd gladly return the favor.

Pulling out her phone, Tamia scrolled through her contacts until she found the number she was looking for.

Ten minutes later she'd placed her phone call, setting the avalanche in motion.

Staring out the windows, she smiled narrowly.

Payback is a straight-up bitch!

Chapter 42

Brandon

Everyone was already gathered in the sun-drenched solarium when Brandon arrived at his parents' house for the family's traditional New Year's Day breakfast. They sat around a long table adorned with fresh-cut flowers from the garden, fragrant platters of food stretching from one end to the other. Laughter and conversation flowed over the pleasant tinkle of crystal and silverware.

It was all so perfect and idyllic. Like a picture out of one of those home-decorating magazines.

This year's familial gathering included Joseph and Coretta Yarbrough and their four sons. Cynthia was conspicuously absent.

As Brandon entered the solarium, his mother beamed at him from her throne at the head of the table. "Hello, darling! We didn't expect to see you or Cynthia this morning. She called and said you two wouldn't be able to make it to church or breakfast because you'd had a late night ringing in the New Year."

"Did she, now?" Brandon drawled, stopping beside his mother's chair to survey the feast on the table. "Did she also tell you that we rang in the New Year separately?"

Gwen's smile faded as the others exchanged speculative glances. "No, she didn't tell me that."

Brandon smirked. "Then I guess she also didn't tell you that I broke off our engagement yesterday."

This drew exclamations of angry protest from his parents and Cynthia's family.

"Why on earth did you do that?" Gwen demanded.

"It's kind of a blur now," Brandon mused, thoughtfully stroking his goatee, "but it might have had something to do with me finding out that she's been faking her pregnancy for the past month."

Shocked gasps went around the table, his mother's being the loudest and most scandalized. One look at Coretta Yarbrough's flushed face told Brandon that his bombshell announcement wasn't news to her.

"Coretta," Gwen coolly inquired, biting off each syllable, "what is the meaning of this?"

Coretta nervously picked up her glass and gulped down her mimosa as her husband gaped incredulously at her.

Beau and Brooke bowed their heads, their shoulders shaking with silent laughter.

Their father looked outraged.

Cynthia's brothers looked like they wanted to be raptured away.

"Call me old-fashioned," Brandon continued sardonically, "but if I'm gonna be forced into a marriage of convenience, I expect to get a real baby out of the deal." He sighed, shaking his head as he snagged a powdered beignet from a silver tray on the table. "Anyway, I'm afraid I can't stay for breakfast. But Mrs. Jessup, God bless her, is fixing me a plate to go. So you folks enjoy the rest of your meal."

He moved to leave, then snapped his fingers and turned back. "Oh, yeah, that's the other thing," he said, addressing Bishop Yarbrough. "I was listening to the radio on my way over here, and they were talking about you. Apparently some story just broke about you paying escorts for sex?"

As a shocked silence swept over the room, the bishop looked like he was about to have a stroke.

Bernard glared furiously at his campaign surrogate, a vein throbbing at his temple.

Coretta burst into tears, sprang from her chair, and fled the room.

Darting a shamefaced glance around the table, Joseph got up and hurried after his distraught wife. Their sons weren't far behind.

In the deafening silence that followed the Yarbroughs' departure, Brandon kissed his mother's forehead, smiled into her eyes, and drawled, "Guess we really dodged a bullet, huh?"

As her mouth flapped open and closed, Brandon bit into the

warm beignet and hummed appreciatively, then glanced around the table at his family.

"Happy New Year, everyone." He winked, then turned and sauntered out as Beau and Brooke erupted into laughter.

Later that evening, Brandon sat alone in the shadowy darkness of his living room. He was nursing a glass of scotch as he broodingly contemplated a DVD in his hand. He read the title scrawled in marker across the plastic cover. *Mystique Slave Chronicles: Pussy Sublime, Volume One.*

He remembered the first time he'd ever laid eyes on the DVD at Dre's apartment. He'd casually pulled it out of a moving box, never suspecting that the video held a secret that would turn his whole world upside down.

Brandon stared at the disc, tapping it slowly against his thigh.

Then he glanced up at the television—a huge high-def flat-panel TV he'd bought to replace the one he'd destroyed during an argument with Cynthia.

Watching this should cure your obsession once and for all. God knows nothing else has worked.

Brandon tossed back the rest of his scotch, then set the glass down on the table.

Chest burning, heart pounding, he opened the plastic case and removed the disc, then got up and slowly made his way over to the DVD player. . . .

Chapter 43

Tamia

Tamia sat curled up on her sofa, her legs drawn up to her chest. She was staring at a plastic stick gripped between her fingers, struggling to absorb the magnitude of what the colored lines meant.

Her phone rang beside her on the sofa cushion.

She glanced down, showing no reaction when she saw Dominic's number on the display screen. He'd been calling her since yesterday, starting from the moment he'd returned home and found her gone. She'd let his calls go to voice mail, not bothering to listen to any of the messages he left.

She'd been in a state of numb shock since learning about his involvement in Bishop Yarbrough's conspiracy plot. The fact that Dominic had been blackmailed didn't absolve him of blame, though Tamia could understand why he'd agreed to the scheme. She didn't know too many people who *wouldn't* have if given the choice between extorting sex from a stranger or going to federal prison. Dominic had done what was best for him, just as *she'd* done what she thought was necessary when she'd allowed him to blackmail her.

What bothered Tamia more than anything was that he'd been sleeping with Honey the whole time they'd been conspiring against her. When Tamia found Honey's underwear at Dominic's apartment, he'd told her that the panties belonged to a one-night stand, when in actuality he'd been screwing Honey for months. How could Tamia ever believe a word that came out of his lying mouth? She couldn't, because he'd proved to be downright shady and untrustworthy. With him, the next betrayal was always right around the corner.

When the phone stopped ringing, Tamia calmly picked it up and stared at the display screen: 32 Missed Calls.

She heaved a resigned sigh. It was clear that Dominic would keep calling until he'd spoken to her. Knowing that she couldn't avoid him forever, she reluctantly proceeded to listen to his messages.

In the first one, he sounded concerned but annoyed: *"Where are you? Is everything okay? You didn't say anything about having to run out. We can't be late to our own party tonight, so hurry the hell up and get home."*

The second message was all concern: *"All right now, Tamia, I'm getting worried. Where the hell are you? Do I need to call the police? Call me back or I'm doing a drive-by on Dashay and Jamila."*

By the third message, he'd obviously spoken to Honey and gotten a heads-up that he was busted. *"Tamia . . . I'm sorry. I don't even know what to say. I know I should have been truthful with you, love, but I couldn't. . . . I had no other choice. I was as much a victim as you were. Come home so we can talk about this. Please, love. Come home."*

This morning, while Tamia was in the bathroom puking her guts out, he'd left her a fourth and final missive: *"So you kickin' me to the curb but keepin' the fuckin' car I gave you, bitch?"*

Tamia scowled, angrily deleting all of his messages.

When he called back a few minutes later, she picked up the phone but didn't say a word.

"Tamia?" He sounded relieved. "I'm glad you finally answered your damn phone. Listen, baby, I know you're upset and you have every right to be. But you need to give me a chance to explain. It wasn't my idea to blackmail you! And if you're mad about that little jump-off, don't be. She don't mean shit to me. *You're* the only woman who matters. In fact, the reason I bought you that engagement ring is 'cause I wanted you to get used to wearing it. I wanna marry you, Tamia."

She stopped breathing for a moment.

Dominic sighed heavily. "Fuck. This isn't the way I wanted to propose. We need to talk, love. Face-to-face. I just pulled up in front of your building—the valet's about to park my car. Can you come downstairs and get me? You know they've been extra tight with security because of that note you got. So come down and get me so we can talk. All right?"

Tamia nodded slowly and whispered, "All right."

She hung up and sat there, silent and unmoving. The plastic wand with the double pink lines was still clutched between her numb fingers.

Three minutes later, her phone rang again.

When she saw that the front desk was calling, she picked up.

"Miss Luke?"

"Yes," she said tonelessly.

"Brandon Chambers is here to see you."

Tamia's heart lurched into her throat. *Brandon is here. . . . Brandon is here. . . .*

"Miss Luke?" the attendant prompted. "Should I tell him you're coming down?"

Tamia closed her eyes and lay her head back against the sofa.

The attendant hastened to explain, "Even though Mr. Chambers's name is on the lease, we're under strict orders not to allow any visitors upstairs without proper clearance. It's for the safety of our residents."

"I know." Tamia swallowed tightly and opened her eyes. "I'm coming."

She pushed to her feet and dragged herself to her bedroom. After tugging on a blue V-neck sweater and black leggings over thick socks, she padded to the bathroom to brush her teeth and gargle with mouthwash to remove the nasty taste that still lingered hours after she'd last vomited. Surveying her reflection in the mirror, she grimaced at her disheveled hair and puffy eyes. A good combing fixed one problem, but there was nothing she could do about the other.

Gnawing her lower lip, she contemplated the home pregnancy test she'd set on the counter. After a few moments, she picked it up and stuck it inside the cabinet beneath the sink. Turning off the light, she left the bathroom and headed from her apartment.

When she reached the lobby, she saw Brandon and Dominic glowering at each other from opposite ends of the reception desk. Brandon had his black gym bag slung over one shoulder, feet braced apart in a dangerously aggressive stance that dared Dominic to come closer for another ass whipping.

The security guard had positioned himself between the two enemy combatants, his hand resting warningly on the butt of his weapon.

Hearing the *ding* of the elevator, Brandon and Dominic swung their gazes around.

Tamia froze, and for one cowardly moment she was tempted to haul ass back to her apartment.

Taking a deep breath to shore up her resolve, she stepped off the elevator and began walking toward her two lovers.

They watched her intently, jaws clenched, postures tense as they waited to see who would be returning upstairs with her.

When she walked up to Dominic, his eyes gleamed with smug triumph. She took his hand and turned it over, then dropped the keys to the penthouse and the Porsche into his palm.

As he stared down at the keys in stunned disbelief, Tamia moved on to Brandon. He gazed tenderly at her as she took his hand and wordlessly led him toward the elevators.

"Tamia!" Dominic blustered in protest. "What the fuck are you doing? I told you we need to talk! *Tamia*—"

She and Brandon ignored him, staring at each other as they boarded the elevator.

The moment the doors closed behind them, Brandon dropped his bag to the floor. They pounced on each other, mouths clashing voraciously. Brandon lifted Tamia, and she wrapped her legs around him as her back hit the wall. He sucked her tongue and ground his hips against hers, making her pussy throb.

Gasping, she tore her mouth from his. "Wait, damn it. *Wait*."

He stared at her, nostrils flaring, eyes glittering fiercely. "*I missed you.*"

The aching words, the raw need, the low register of his deep voice—they were enough to have her dropping to her knees, unzipping his pants, and swallowing him down her throat.

Somehow she managed to look him in the eye and say firmly, "We need to talk."

He nodded. "We do."

When the elevator arrived on her floor, he bent to pick up his bag without setting her down.

They gazed intently at each other as he carried her down the hallway. It was only when they reached her door that he reluctantly put her down, then stood close behind her as she fumbled to unlock the door.

He followed her inside, shutting the door behind them and dropping his bag by the foyer table.

As Tamia backed toward the living room, he stalked her step for step.

When she came to a stop, he stopped just inches away, so close that their breath mingled warmly and their heartbeats synced up.

His dark eyes roamed across her face, missing no detail. "You're still not feeling well," he gently observed.

Tamia smirked. "Is that your polite way of telling me I look like shit?"

"Nah." He smiled softly. "And you could never look like shit."

She snorted. "Shoulda seen me this morning."

He frowned, tenderly cupping her cheek in his hand. "What's wrong, baby?"

Her throat tightened at the endearment. Resisting the urge to rub her face against the warmth of his palm, she took a step backward and folded her arms across her chest. "Why are you here, Brandon?"

He stepped forward, closing the space she'd just created. "I came to see you."

"Why? Because of the scandal involving Cynthia's father? Are your parents suddenly rethinking that whole family alliance?"

Brandon grimaced. "They are," he admitted, "but that's not why I'm here. I would have come regardless of that story breaking."

Tamia's eyes narrowed. "Does Cynthia know you're here?"

"It doesn't matter." Brandon held her gaze. "I broke off our engagement."

Stunned, Tamia stared at him. "You . . . broke up with her?"

He nodded. "For good this time."

Tamia held his gaze another moment. As a choked sob rushed up her throat, she cupped a trembling hand over her mouth.

When Brandon reached for her, she tossed up her hand, stopping him. "No," she whispered shakily. "Don't touch me."

A shadow of pain crossed his face. "Baby—"

"I've waited so long. . . . I've waited forever. . . ." She inhaled a shuddering breath, looking at the ceiling and slowly shaking her head. "I've put myself through *so* much to have you, Brandon. And I just don't know . . ."

"You don't know what, Tamia?" His voice was husky with fear. "You don't know if I was worth the wait? You don't know if you still love me? What don't you know?"

She looked at him, tears blurring her eyes.

"Please don't do this to me, Tamia," he whispered raggedly. "*Please.*"

She gulped hard. "I just need—"

"Hold on. Don't say another word."

Tamia watched as he pivoted on his heel and marched back to the foyer. He knelt, unzipped the gym bag and pulled out a stack of DVDs and a small metal pail, the kind guys used to put beer on ice.

Puzzled, Tamia frowned. "What're you doing with all that?"

Brandon strode toward her, jaw set with steely determination. "Come with me," he growled, grabbing her hand.

He tugged her across the living room to the sliding glass door that led to the balcony. He unlocked and opened the door, then pulled her outside with him.

Her eyes swept over the glittering night skyline before she looked at him. "Brandon—"

When he set the metal pail and the stack of DVDs on top of the small table, a chill ran through Tamia that had nothing to do with the cool evening temperature.

"Why did you bring the Mystique videos?" she asked faintly.

"Because I realized something tonight." Brandon met her gaze. "Long before Dominic or Cynthia ever came between us, these videos were a tumor in our relationship, always festering beneath the surface. Because of these videos, Tamia, you were ashamed to let me know the *real* you. You convinced yourself that even if I could 'accept' your humble beginnings, I could never accept that you used to be a porn star. Because of these videos, you were determined to hide your past from me at any and all costs. And it cost you dearly, sweetheart. It damn near cost you your life." He picked up a DVD from the stack and held it up. "Because of these fucking videos, I was afraid to completely trust you because I was afraid of finding out something else you might have kept from me. But that's not your fault, baby. That was on me. Because *I'm* the one who made the mistake of letting you walk out of my life when you're the best damn thing that ever happened to me."

"Oh, baby," Tamia whispered as tears brimmed in her eyes, threatening to spill over. "I love you so much."

"I love you, too," Brandon said fiercely, nostrils flaring as he cupped her cheek. "I love you and I need you in my life. So don't go no damn where."

"I won't. I'm not." She gave him a teary smile. "So what're you gonna do with the videos?"

"What I shoulda done a long time ago." He scooped up the DVDs and dumped them into the pail, then whipped out a canister of lighter fluid from his back pocket and doused the stack of discs.

Tamia stared as he struck a match and gently warned, "Move back."

When she obeyed, he tossed the lit match into the pail. The DVDs caught on fire with a soft whoosh and a flash of orange.

As thick smoke curled into the night air, Brandon stepped back, wrapped an arm around Tamia's waist, and kissed her temple. Together they stood staring into the crackling bonfire, watching the Mystique videos burn.

Tamia asked quietly, "Did you watch them?"

Brandon shook his head. "I couldn't get through ten minutes of the first one," he admitted darkly. "But not because I was mad or ashamed of you. I couldn't finish watching it because I don't wanna see my baby fucking other men. Period."

Tamia nodded, enjoying the warmth of the flames washing over them. "I'm glad you're here, Brandon. I'm glad you came."

"I couldn't stay away any longer." He turned her in his arms and framed her face between his hands, his eyes boring into hers. "It's a new year, sweetheart. A new day. That means no more secrets between us. No more ghosts from the past. From now on, the only two people allowed in this relationship are you and me. You feel me?"

Tamia laughed softly. "I feel you. *God*, I feel you."

Brandon smiled, resting his forehead against hers and staring into her eyes. "I promised myself I'd do this right if I ever got another chance."

Tamia stared at him. "Do what?"

He reached into his pocket and pulled out a small velvet box. As

Tamia watched, her heart pounding wildly, he lowered himself to one knee and opened the lid.

Her eyes flew wide as she found herself staring at the most stunningly exquisite ring she'd ever seen. It was at least six carats, with one huge oval-cut diamond surrounded by smaller diamonds set on a platinum band.

"Oh my God," she breathed. "What an *amazing* ring."

Brandon smiled softly, taking the ring out of the box. "It belonged to my great-grandmother."

Tamia stared at him, struck by the realization that he hadn't given the ring to Cynthia when he'd proposed.

As if he'd read her mind, Brandon murmured, "Mother Chambers made me promise to give it to the woman I loved and only her."

Tears welled in Tamia's eyes. "Oh, baby . . ."

Brandon gazed up at her, his eyes probing hers. "This is another thing I should have done a long time ago," he said with quiet intensity. "I can't live without you, Tamia, and I'd be a damn fool to try. I wanna be your husband, and I desperately need you to be my wife. So will you marry me?"

"Yes." Tamia nodded vigorously. "*Hell*, yes!"

Brandon grinned broadly, sliding the ring onto her finger. It was a little loose, but still perfect in every way.

"We'll get it resized," Brandon said. "If you want it."

"*Are you kidding me?*" Tamia whispered, choked up with emotion. "Of course I want it! It's absolutely *beautiful*, Brandon. And it's a family heirloom, so that makes it even more special."

As Brandon rose to his feet, she threw her arms around his neck. Laughing, he lifted her off the ground and swung her around. She squealed ecstatically, her head flung back as the city lights flashed around them in a dazzling kaleidoscope.

Gently putting her down, Brandon cupped her face and slanted his mouth over hers. They kissed passionately, their lips fusing, tongues stroking between whispered endearments.

As Brandon began backing Tamia toward the glass door, she reminded him, "What about the fire?"

"It'll burn out." His eyes glittered. "Now let's go start another one."

He swept her up into his arms and carried her back inside, moving purposefully to the bedroom. He turned on the lamp and set her down by the bed. Gazes locked, they slowly undressed each other as though they were unwrapping the most precious gifts they'd ever received.

Brandon lowered Tamia to the bed, then proceeded to make love to her as if they'd just met, as if her body were a revelation to him. He kissed every part of her, leaving no area of skin untouched. She trembled as he slowly ran his lips over her tender breasts and sucked her swollen nipples, sliding lower to kiss her quivering stomach, where his child grew inside her. He lingered there as if he knew, whispering husky words of love and adoration that brought tears to her eyes.

He kissed the inside of her thighs, setting off explosions of sensation that had warm juices seeping out of her to soak the bed. He rasped his tongue across her slit, each lick sending jolts of raw pleasure through her. She whimpered breathlessly, her fingers clenching the covers beneath her as he kissed his way downward. He kissed her knees, lifting them so his lips could caress her supple calves. He sucked her curling toes until she moaned, her body arching upward.

By the time he rose above her to enter her body, she was already weeping softly, whispering his name like a fervent prayer. "*Brandon . . . Brandon . . . Brandon.*"

They gazed into each other's eyes as he eased his thick shaft inside her, feeding her ever so slowly. She wrapped her arms around his muscled back and clamped her thighs around his hips.

He began stroking into her . . . slow . . . deep . . . the curved head of his cock shooting spasms of pleasure to her cervix. She moaned, biting her lip so hard she tasted blood. Together they looked downward, watching him slide in and out of her pussy. And then they looked at each other with the same sense of awed wonder.

She ran her hands over his back and his round butt, the muscles flexing and denting as he slowly pumped into her. Back and forth, up and down. He kept a measured pace, never pounding, just stroking and letting their joined bodies heed their own natural rhythm and flow.

It was lovemaking like Tamia had never imagined. It was beautiful, healing, profoundly powerful.

And when they came explosively together she was crying, and so was he, their warm tears blending as they kissed.

★   ★   ★

Long afterward, Brandon held Tamia close as she stroked his chest, packed with muscle.

She sighed dreamily. "I could stay right here forever."

"Me, too," Brandon agreed. "I missed the hell out of you, Tamia."

"I missed you too, baby. These past five weeks have been pure hell without you. I'd just about given up on us."

"I'm glad you didn't." Brandon kissed her forehead. "Don't *ever* give up on us."

"I won't," she promised, snuggling closer to him. "And you'd better not either."

"Are you kidding? You're stuck with me, woman."

Tamia smiled. "You won't hear me complaining."

"Good."

As Brandon gently stroked her hair, she held up her hand to stare at her ring, admiring the way the diamonds sparkled in the warm lamplight.

She sang softly, "*If you liked it then you shoulda put a ring on it . . .*"

Brandon laughed. "Point taken."

Tamia grinned unabashedly. "Think she could sing at our wedding?"

"I don't know. Want me to ask?"

"Please?"

"Anything for you."

Tamia smiled, kissing his chest. "I can definitely get used to this."

Brandon chuckled. "Speaking of our wedding, we need to set a date. And it needs to be soon, like yesterday."

Tamia wanted to pinch herself. Was this really happening? Was she really on the verge of becoming Mrs. Brandon Chambers?

"How about April?" she suggested. "I mean, since you were already planning to get married that month anyway . . ."

Brandon searched her face. "Would that be okay with you?"

She nodded. "I like April. The wildflowers are in bloom, the weather's not too hot yet. It's a perfect month for a wedding."

Brandon's expression softened. "Any month would be perfect to marry you."

Tamia smiled, her insides warming with pleasure. And something else.

"Be right back," she said, slipping from the bed.

"Where you going?" Brandon asked.

"I have to pee."

As she started toward the bathroom, Brandon propped his head on his hand to watch her saunter away. "My, my, my. All that ass."

Tamia grinned. She clapped her round buttocks like a stripper and slapped one cheek, then winked and strolled off as Brandon groaned laughingly and fell back against the pillows.

Once inside the bathroom, Tamia perched on the toilet to empty her bladder. She didn't realize how long she'd been sitting there until Brandon called teasingly from the bedroom, "Damn, girl, how much water did you drink today?"

Tamia giggled. "Don't be listening to me piss!"

He laughed. "Just sayin', babe. You peeing like a camel in there."

I know, Tamia mused. She'd read that frequent urination was another early symptom of pregnancy. Something about hormones causing blood to flow more quickly through the kidneys, resulting in the bladder filling more often.

After flushing the toilet and washing her hands at the sink, she retrieved the home pregnancy test she'd hidden in the cabinet earlier. Now that she and Brandon were engaged, she was excited to share the good news with him.

When she emerged from the bathroom, Brandon lay with his hands clasped behind his head as he stared at the ceiling with a look of blissful contentment.

Keeping one arm behind her back, Tamia padded over to the bed and climbed onto Brandon.

He smiled up at her, lazily running his hands up and down her thighs straddling him. "You finish handling your business?"

"Yes." She smiled. "I have something to tell you."

"What?"

She brought her arm from behind her back, holding up the plastic applicator.

Brandon sat up slowly. "You're . . . pregnant?"

She nodded. "That's why I've been so sick."

He took the stick from her hand, staring incredulously at the double pink lines before he lifted his eyes to hers. "We're having a baby?" he asked hopefully, reminding Tamia of a little boy who was afraid to be told that Santa Claus wasn't real.

Her heart melted. "Yes, baby. We're having a baby."

His eyes lit up, and a broad grin swept across his face, dimples on full display. "When did you find out? Is that what was taking you so long in the bathroom?"

"No, I took the home pregnancy test this morning. I guess I shouldn't have been shocked by the results. I was on birth control when we were dating, but I stopped taking the pill after I went to prison. Anyway, since today is Sunday, I have to wait until tomorrow to call my doctor to schedule an appointment. But these home tests are pretty accurate, and my body's certainly *acting* pregnant."

Brandon smiled, but Tamia could see the unspoken question in his eyes, the fearful uncertainty.

"The baby's yours, Brandon," she assured him. "I haven't had un-protected sex with Dominic. Only you. It must have happened the night you came to my apartment." Her eyes narrowed with suspicion. "Were you *trying* to get me pregnant?"

A sheepish look crossed his face.

Tamia stared at him. "That's why you asked me not to sleep with Dominic or anyone else for a month, isn't it? If you got me pregnant, you wanted to make sure there'd be no question whose baby I was carrying."

Brandon's mouth twitched. "I didn't go to your apartment that night to get you pregnant. Not consciously anyway. I was mad as hell and I needed to see you. But right after I left, yeah, it did occur to me that we hadn't used protection. And, yes, I've been hoping and pray-ing that I'd answer the phone one day and hear you say what you just said: 'We're having a baby.' And I—" He broke off suddenly, staring at her with an awestruck expression. "Damn. You really *did* just say that, didn't you?"

Tamia grinned. "Yes, I did."

Brandon laughed and crushed her to him, holding her tight as he rocked back and forth on the bed.

"Thank you," he whispered against her heart, making Tamia wonder whether he was thanking her or God.

It didn't matter. There was plenty of gratitude to go around.

As Brandon lifted his head, she stared down at him, loving this man more than she'd ever loved anyone in her life. She tenderly cra-dled his face between her hands and lowered her mouth to his for a deep, soulful kiss, lips brushing and exploring, tongues meeting and twirling in a sensual slow dance.

It wasn't long before Tamia felt her folds growing slick, felt Brandon's shaft thickening against her mound.

"Lie down," she whispered, pushing him back against the pillows.

When he was stretched out on the bed, she slid off his lap and knelt between his parted legs. She licked the muscled flesh that defined his hard thighs, smiling when he jerked sharply. He stared at her as she wrapped her hand around his engorged dick and leaned down, aroused by the scent of his musk mingled with hers.

He moaned gutturally as she licked the smooth underside of his meat, tracing the dark line that ran down to his heavy scrotum. He shuddered as she licked underneath his balls, watching his stomach muscles clench as she tongued his perineum.

Looking into his heavy-lidded eyes, she slowly took his shaft into her mouth. He was so thick and firm and hot, an extra-long chocolate bar melting on her tongue.

"Umm," she purred on a throaty moan. "*Love, love, love* this big-ass dick."

Brandon groaned as she sucked the mushroom crown, worshipping her king as he rewarded her with sweet drippings of pre-come. She slurped him down the back of her throat, swallowing as his steely girth hit her tonsils.

"*Fuuuccckkk,*" he swore loud and long, his fingers tangling in her hair.

Tamia pumped her hand up and down as she licked and sucked his dick, her lips sliding from top to bottom. When she felt his balls tighten, she knew he was close.

"*Ahhh, shit,*" he groaned. "Tamia . . . baby . . . *damn . . .*"

She hollowed out her cheeks and gave him one last hard suck. As his cock exploded in a hot river of come, he grabbed the back of her head with both hands, shouting hoarsely as he shot deep into her throat. She swallowed and swallowed as he spurted repeatedly, his semen running out the corner of her lips and down her chin.

When he had nothing left to give, she slowly eased him out of her mouth, staring at him in fascination. His eyes were squeezed shut, his head flung back as he gasped for breath.

Tamia smiled, wiping her mouth with the back of her hand.

Then she slid back up his body, tenderly kissing his closed eyelids and licking his dimples when he smiled. He gathered her close as she settled contentedly in his arms.

This was where she belonged. This was home.

Chapter 44

Brandon

Warm sunshine poured into the room, washing over the bed where Brandon lay on his elbow with his head propped in one hand.

It was Monday morning. He should be up and about getting dressed for work. But he couldn't make himself leave the bed, not with Tamia in it. He'd been awake for the past half hour quietly watching her sleep. She was so beautiful, he couldn't get enough of staring at her.

She looked innocent in sleep, almost childlike. But that had always been part of her allure . . . the contradictions. On one hand she was a sultry vixen who could set him on fire with one hot glance. On the other hand she was an ingénue who got weepy over romantic comedies and cooed about parades and lunar eclipses.

Brandon loved damn near everything about her. He'd been crazy to think, even for a second, that he could ever settle for another woman. Tamia was his soul mate, his true ride-or-die chick. And knowing that his child was growing inside her . . . it was enough to make him wanna bawl like a straight-up punk.

He couldn't wait to spend the rest of his life with Tamia, couldn't wait to wake up beside her every morning.

Unable to resist, he leaned down and gently nibbled her plump lower lip.

"Mmm," she purred contentedly without opening her eyes. "So yesterday *wasn't* just a dream."

Brandon smiled. "Nope. You're still stuck with me."

"And I'm still not complaining." As she stretched languorously beneath the covers, Brandon's groin heated at the sight of her large, luscious breasts with those mouthwatering dark caramel nipples. He bent down and wrapped his lips around one of them, making Tamia moan softly with pleasure.

Gently sucking her nipple, he curved his hand against her smooth, flat stomach. "How you feeling?"

She sighed. "Not great. But at least I'm not throwing up—*yet*."

Brandon grimaced. "I'm sorry you have to go through this," he murmured sympathetically.

"Me, too." She smiled, affectionately rubbing his head. "But it's so worth it."

Brandon smiled, feeling his chest swell. He gathered her protectively in his arms, spooning her warm body. "I'm gonna call Mrs. Jessup—"

"Your family's cook?"

"Yeah. I'll see if she has any remedies for morning sickness. She's got a cure for everything else, so why not that?"

Tamia sighed deeply. "I hope she does. I'd be *ever* so grateful."

Brandon kissed the nape of her neck, moving from bare skin into her hair. "Let me know when your doctor's appointment is. I wanna go with you."

Tamia looked over her shoulder at him. "Really?"

"Yeah. I wanna go to all of them if I can." He searched her face. "You don't mind, do you?"

Her eyes softened. "Of course not. I'd love to have you with me every step of the way."

"And that's where I plan to be."

Tamia smiled tenderly as he brushed his lips across hers.

"Are you going to work today?" she whispered.

"Nope. Staying right here." He didn't want to be apart from her. They'd spent more than enough time separated.

Visibly pleased, Tamia turned in his arms, draping her luscious thigh across his hip. Her eyes were twinkling with amusement. "By the way, you looked a *lil* too comfortable setting that fire last night," she teased. "Lemme find out you were a pyromaniac as a child."

Lowering his lashes over his eyes, Brandon drawled mysteriously, "I'll never tell."

"What?"

"Yo, I'm like Bruce Wayne. You can't be knowing all my secrets."

"Stop playin'!" Tamia laughed, playfully bumping her pelvis against his.

"Oh, my damn," he groaned as his dick swelled against her stomach. "Keep that up, woman, and I'm never letting you outta this bed."

"You have to."

"Why?"

" 'Cause I have to pee!"

Brandon laughed. "So do I!"

He chased her into the bathroom, where they took turns using the toilet before brushing their teeth together. Brandon had expected Tamia to comment on how he'd presumptuously packed an overnight bag, but she hadn't said anything.

As they stood at the double sink watching each other in the mirror, he was struck anew by how natural it felt to share a bathroom with her. He'd enjoyed their closeness when she'd lived with him before, but it had been different with Cynthia. He'd often felt like she was intruding upon his space. Even when she sat in his favorite armchair, he'd been irked.

Tamia rinsed out her mouth, then hopped onto the gleaming counter and grinned at Brandon as he dropped his toothbrush into the cup with hers.

"Bruce Wayne, huh?"

"Yup."

"Hmm." She considered him. "Handsome, debonair bachelor. Super-rich humanitarian. Wealthy, influential family. Grew up in a mansion with servants. Killer fighting skills." A slow grin curved her mouth. "Okay. I'ma start calling you the Dark Knight."

Brandon laughed. "I like that. Has a nice ring to it."

Tamia sighed. "Batgirl was lame, so I guess I'll have to become Catwoman."

Brandon grinned. "You'd make a *sexy ass* Catwoman."

She chuckled. "Well, I was already used to disguising myself with leather masks—" She broke off, blushing self-consciously.

It was the first time she'd voluntarily referenced her former alter ego, and she was embarrassed.

Brandon gently tipped her chin up. When her eyes met his, he smiled and winked. "Mystique was sexy as hell, too. Which is why I'm keeping her to my damn self from now on."

Tamia gave him a sweet, grateful smile that sucker-punched him in the chest.

Damn, I love this girl.

He affectionately tweaked her nose. "Since I'm playing hooky today, whatcha wanna do? You already got plans?"

"Not today. I'm meeting with Shanell's Realtor tomorrow to show him my old house."

Brandon's expression softened. "You sure you're ready to sell it?"

She nodded. "It's time."

"Okay." Brandon touched her cheek. "Well, let me know if there's anything I can do. If you need to make repairs to the house or anything, I got you. And let dude know you and I need to go house hunting soon."

Tamia's eyes lit up. "Really?"

"Really." He smiled. "We need a bigger place now that we're starting a family." He thought fleetingly of Cynthia, remembering how *she* was the one who'd been making all the plans. If she could see him now, she'd probably kill him.

"I'll see when Marcellus is available to go with us," Tamia said.

"Cool. And we can always do some exploring on our own."

"I'd like that very much."

They smiled warmly at each other.

"I want to hear all about your new ad agency," Brandon said.

"Okay. I'll tell you about it. But first," Tamia said quietly, "there's something else I have to share with you."

Brandon instinctively tensed. "What is it?"

Her gaze was intent on his face. "In the spirit of new beginnings and not keeping secrets from each other, you should know that I'm the one who leaked the story about Bishop Yarbrough to the media."

Brandon stared at her. "*You* outed the bishop?"

"Yes."

"Why?"

"Not to break up you and Cynthia, if that's what you're thinking."

He frowned. "I wasn't."

"Good. Because that wasn't even on my mind." Tamia's expression hardened. "I did it because I wanted to make Bishop Yarbrough pay for what he did to me."

Brandon's eyes narrowed swiftly. "What did he do to you?"

"He's the one who told Dominic that I was Mystique."

"WHAT?"

Tamia's eyes flashed with anger. "After the bishop found out from Honey, he blackmailed Dominic into blackmailing *me* for sex. Apparently he knew that Dominic had embezzled money in the past, so he used it against him. He even bought off Honey and Lou."

Brandon was seething with fury. "I *knew* there was a reason I never liked that self-righteous muthafucka," he growled.

Tamia scowled. "It was all an elaborate scheme to get me out of the way so that Cynthia could sink her claws into you. It worked out even better than they'd hoped when I went to prison for murder."

Brandon scrubbed a hand over his face, striving to keep his temper in check. He couldn't believe this shit!

"I've known about Bishop Yarbrough hiring escorts for a while," Tamia grimly admitted. "I know I could have told you to warn your father, but I promised to keep Honey's secret. And no offense, Brandon, but your parents haven't exactly done anything to warrant my loyalty."

Brandon grimaced. "That's true."

"So I kept my silence, thinking I was being a good friend. But once I found out how they'd all played me, I wanted revenge. If that makes me a vindictive bitch, so be it."

Brandon frowned. "It doesn't make you a vindictive bitch. It makes you human. I'd be lying if I said I'm not thinking about ripping Yarbrough's throat out so he can never stand behind another pulpit spewing his sanctimonious bullshit."

Tamia snickered. "You'd certainly be doing the world a favor, but the bishop's days of sermonizing may be numbered anyway. I heard the feds will be investigating his finances to see whether he used church funds to pay for the escorts and a number of other questionable things. Looks like his empire is crumbling fast."

"Serves that muthafucka right." Brandon stared at Tamia, his eyes narrowed with suspicion. "Did Cynthia know about this scheme?"

"I don't think so," Tamia grumbled. "But considering how many other people were involved, it wouldn't shock me in the least if Cynthia was in on it, too."

"Wouldn't shock me either," Brandon muttered darkly.

Tamia frowned, searching his face. "You never did tell me why you broke up with Cynthia."

"I broke up with her because I don't love her and I wanna be with you. I had already made up my mind to end the engagement before I found out that she'd been lying about being pregnant."

Tamia's jaw dropped. "WHAT?"

Brandon scowled. "She was faking her pregnancy so I'd marry her."

"Oh. My. God." Tamia stared at him in disbelief. "I had my suspicions, but then I told myself I was just being jealous. Which I was. I *hated* the idea of her having your baby, Brandon."

"Well, it ain't happening, so you never have to worry about that again."

Tamia slowly shook her head. "Poor Cynthia. She must be absolutely devastated."

"I'm sure she is, but that's not my concern anymore." Brandon cupped Tamia's face, his eyes boring into hers. "There's something else I'd like to discuss with you."

She eyed him curiously. "What?"

He glanced around, suddenly remembering that they were still in the bathroom. He scooped Tamia off the counter and carried her back into the room. After they climbed into bed, he drew the covers up to their waists.

When they lay on their sides facing each other, Brandon announced, "I'm running for the Senate this year."

Tamia's eyes widened. "*You are?*"

He nodded, closely observing her face to gauge her true reaction.

She beamed. "That's wonderful, Brandon! After you gave that speech at the prayer breakfast, I knew it was only a matter of time before you'd be throwing your hat into the ring."

Brandon shook his head slowly. "When I was standing up there talking, something came over me. . . . It's hard to explain. Afterward, Dad told me he knew I'd been speaking from the heart because the vision I described for Texas is nowhere to be found on his Web site or strategic initiatives report." Brandon chuckled. "His campaign manager has already adopted the language I used."

Tamia grinned. "Biter."

Brandon laughed.

Tamia touched his face. "Seriously, baby, I'm glad you've decided to heed your calling."

Brandon grimaced. "I don't know about all that. A 'calling' sounds so lofty . . . but maybe it's more accurate than not."

Tamia smiled softly. "You seem surprised. You *are* a Chambers."

"I know, but that's not why I'm running. I know it sounds like a cliché, but I honestly *do* wanna make a difference and serve the people of Texas."

"I think you'd make a wonderful senator," Tamia said proudly. "The people of Texas—myself included—would be very lucky to have you representing our interests."

Touched by her words, Brandon leaned down and tenderly kissed her forehead. "Thank you for saying that."

"I meant it."

"I know. That's why I appreciated it so much." He stroked her hip. "But make no mistake about it, baby, this ain't gonna be a cakewalk. They're gonna throw the kitchen sink at us. Everything about our lives will be dissected and raked over the coals. Nothing—absolutely nothing—will be off limits. So that means they're gonna try to put your porn career front and center. You understand that?"

Tamia swallowed visibly and nodded.

"They're gonna comb through our school records and pore over the cases I've litigated over the years. I didn't play for the good guys—I'm a defense attorney, so my methods have been far from squeaky clean. If there's dirt to be found, my opponents will find it and exploit it. For real, baby girl, we might not make it out of the primary with our skin intact. The odds are seriously stacked against us."

Tamia smiled quietly. "When *haven't* they been? Yet here we are."

Brandon held her gaze for a long moment. "That's true."

"If you really want this, Brandon, I support you one hundred percent and I'm willing to do whatever it takes to help you win. I'm ready to roll up my sleeves and get to work creating campaign materials, scheduling press appearances, planning rallies—whatever you need, whatever you want." She searched his face. "Do you want this?"

"I *do* want it," Brandon asserted, gazing intently into her eyes. "But I want you more."

Her expression gentled. "Oh, Brandon . . ."

"I'm dead serious, Tamia. If I have to choose between you and becoming a senator, it ain't gonna be a hard choice for me. I've already let too many external things keep us apart, and we've both suffered as a result. But those days are over. From now on it's just you and me, and fuck er'body else."

Tamia gave a teary laugh. "That's right. Fuck er'body!"

Brandon grinned, then leaned down and kissed her. She sighed softly as he slipped his tongue into her mouth, gently licking and sucking hers.

When he suddenly pushed her back onto the bed, she laughed breathlessly. As he pinned her wrists above her head and laced their fingers together, she gazed up at him, her eyes shining with pure love.

Oh, hell yeah. Most *definitely* his ride-or-die chick.

"If you become senator," she mused as he bent to nuzzle her throat, "I guess we'd have to find someplace to live in Washington, D.C. while Congress is in session."

"Um, yeah, we would." Brandon chuckled. "I mean, that'd be a long-ass commute from Texas to the nation's capital."

Tamia giggled. "Don't make fun of me!"

"I'm not, baby. I wouldn't dare."

"Umm-hmm. *Anyway*," she said with attitude, "the reason I was making the comment is that I've never been to D.C., and I was just thinking it might be nice to live on the East Coast for a change of scenery."

Brandon nodded, settling between her warm thighs. "I think you'd really like D.C. I lived there when I was doing my federal clerkship during law school. Got some nice neighborhoods. We can live in Georgetown or Dupont Circle, or I'll buy you a big-ass house in Virginia or Maryland. We can live wherever you want, sweetheart, as long as we're together."

"Sounds hella good to me." Tamia sighed dreamily. "*Fish don't fry in the kitchen—*"

Brandon laughed, recognizing the theme song from *The Jeffersons*.

He crooned the next line as he slid into her, and they spent the rest of the day making sweet music of their own.

Chapter 45

Tamia

"Oooh, girlfriend, you are blinding me with that *rock!*"

Tamia grinned, shaking her head at Marcellus. "You need to stop."

"He's right, Tamia. That ring is *fiyah*." Shanell wistfully eyed her own modest wedding band set and harrumphed. "Mark's gonna have to give me an upgrade before I upgrade *him*."

They all laughed.

It was Tuesday afternoon. Tamia and Shanell had met for lunch, then headed over to the Third Ward for Tamia's appointment with Marcellus. After completing their tour of her childhood home, Marcellus had given Tamia a checklist of things to do before they put the house on the market.

The threesome now lingered in the empty living room chatting and laughing. It was inevitable that Tamia's engagement ring would become the topic of conversation, just as it had dominated the discussion between Tamia and Shanell over lunch.

Shanell had been stunned by the dramatic turn of events Tamia relayed to her. She'd furiously denounced Cynthia's fake pregnancy scheme, and squealed excitedly over Tamia and Brandon's engagement and baby news. When she heard about Bishop Yarbrough's conspiracy plot, she'd cursed up a storm and called her newly fired pastor everything but a child of God. Even though she'd been right about Dominic, Lou, and Honey, she hadn't said *I told you so*—which Tamia appreciated.

"Girl, I knew that man didn't love her," Marcellus was saying to Tamia. "From the moment they arrived at my office that day, I could tell Brandon was just going through the motions with Cynthia. Then when we ran into you and ol' boy at the model house? Child, please. I knew that marriage wasn't happening."

"I'm glad *you* were so confident," Tamia said wryly.

"Are you serious? After the way Brandon reacted to seeing you with another man, how could *you* have thought he'd still go through with marrying Cynthia?" Marcellus snorted, shaking his head. "Anyway, I'm glad he came to his senses. I'm a good judge of people, and Cynthia gave me bad vibes from the jump. But *you*, on the other hand"—he winked at Tamia—"I liked you right away."

Tamia smiled. "Did you?"

"Umm-hmm. I took one look at you and thought, 'Now *this* is a real sista I can bond with.' And I must say, girlfriend, you got some badass cheekbones."

Tamia cupped her face. "I do?"

Marcellus guffawed. "Don't be coy. You know you do. Who's doing your makeup for your wedding? I know an amazing makeup artist who'd *love* to do the honors."

Tamia laughed. "I haven't thought that far ahead yet."

Marcellus raised a brow. "I don't know why not. You only happen to be marrying Houston's most eligible bachelor. Any other chick in your shoes would already have everything planned down to the last detail. Tell her, Shanell."

Shanell, who knew the trials and tribulations Tamia had endured over the past year, smiled quietly and reached for Tamia's hand. "This wedding has been a long time in the making. Trust me, Tamia will be more than ready when it's time to say I do."

After parting ways with Shanell and Marcellus, Tamia drove to the Four Leaf Towers. She'd mailed Dominic a full refund for the business loan he'd given her. After receiving the check, he'd called and left her a terse message instructing her to pick up her things while he was at work. He'd left the key for her at the front desk, and the concierge was on standby to help her carry her suitcase to her car.

As Tamia entered the silent penthouse and headed to the bedroom to pack her belongings, she was glad she wouldn't have to deal with Dominic. After the way things had ended between them, she hoped she'd finally seen the last of him.

She should have known better.

"I understand congratulations are in order."

She whirled around, startled to see Dominic standing in the bedroom doorway with his hands casually tucked into the pockets of his suit pants.

She swallowed nervously. "I thought you weren't going to be here."

"I know." He smiled narrowly. "I only told you that because I knew you wouldn't come otherwise."

A whisper of foreboding snaked down Tamia's spine.

"Well," she said, wheeling her suitcase toward the door, "I was just about to leave, so—"

As she tried to move past Dominic, he stepped into her path, blocking her escape.

She felt a moment of panic as she stared up at him. "What do you want, Dominic?"

He smirked. "I heard through the grapevine that Brandon finally popped the question. Looks like you're gonna get the fairy-tale wedding you've always wanted. Congratulations."

Tamia just looked at him.

"So how you been feeling? You look great—your skin is glowing." He smiled slowly. "Pregnancy really agrees with you."

Tamia froze, staring at him. How the hell did he know about the baby? Shanell was the only person she'd told. Brandon hadn't even shared the news with his family yet.

Dominic chuckled, as if he'd read her mind. "I've suspected for a while now that you were pregnant. Why do you think I instructed my waitress to give you a virgin margarita that night at my restaurant?"

Tamia tensed as he reached out, stroking his hand down her cheek.

"Brandon must be so thrilled about the baby."

"He is," Tamia said tightly. "We both are."

"That's good." Dominic paused. "There's just one thing though. . . ."

"What?"

"He might not be the father."

The words sent a jolt through Tamia. "Wh-what are you talking about?"

A cunning gleam filled Dominic's eyes. "Remember the night I met you at the restaurant when you were waiting for Brandon to show up? The next morning at your apartment, you asked me if we'd had sex because you couldn't remember a thing. Well, there's a reason you couldn't remember." He smirked. "You weren't supposed to."

A chill ran through Tamia.

She suddenly recalled the flashback she'd had the morning after they slept together at the bed-and-breakfast. In the vision, Dominic had been thrusting into her as he whispered, "*I'm never letting you go, Tamia. Never . . .*"

The room spun.

Reeling with shock and horror, she stared at him as white dots danced before her eyes. "You . . . *raped* me?" she whispered.

He made a pained face. "*Rape* sounds so criminal."

"You drugged me and had sex with me! That *is* rape—and it *is* criminal!"

"I disagree," he said mildly. "I prefer to think of what I did as seducing you."

"*Seducing?* You slipped something into my drink while I was in the bathroom!"

His eyes gleamed. "And then I drove you home and had your car towed back because you were too out of it to drive. Thankfully no one batted an eye at me carrying you from the garage up to your apartment. If anyone had asked, I would have simply told them you'd had too much to drink."

Aghast, Tamia slapped him across the face as hard as she could. "*You son of a bitch! How could you?*"

A slow, satisfied smile curved his mouth. "You didn't complain or tell me no, Tamia. You thoroughly enjoyed our lovemaking that night. We both did."

She eyed him incredulously. "You're *sick!*"

"Not sick," he countered. "In love."

"*In love?* This isn't love, Dominic! It's obsession!"

"Maybe," he conceded. "Or maybe it's both. Whatever it is, I can't let you go, Tamia."

"I'm not yours!"

"Maybe not," he agreed, "but that baby inside you might be."

"Oh my God." Tamia pressed a trembling hand to her stomach, rocked by the realization that she might not be carrying Brandon's child.

"Once you got out of prison," Dominic calmly explained, "I knew it wouldn't take you long to find your way back to lover boy. You'd only been home two weeks before he whisked you off to Italy. But once he got engaged to Cynthia, I realized I'd have another chance with you. Honey bugged your phone for me, so that's how I knew you'd be at Da Marco waiting for Brandon that night. I had to act quickly, and there was only one way for me to keep you permanently in my life."

Tamia stared at him in horrified disbelief. "By getting me *pregnant?*"

"Of course. If the baby trap works for women, why can't it work for men?" He struck a thoughtful pose, lips pursed as he stroked his goatee. "So let's see . . . we made love on December ninth. When did you and Brandon hook up?"

December thirteenth echoed through Tamia's mind. She'd counted back to the date when she'd realized her period was late. So that meant she'd had sex with Dominic and Brandon within four days of each other—too close for any doctor to accurately pinpoint when she'd conceived.

Dominic grinned, watching her do the mental calculations. "Since my boys were in the pool first," he drawled, "you'd better hope they aren't strong swimmers."

Tamia stared at him, her stomach roiling with nausea and dread. "I was crazy for ever thinking I could trust you. You haven't changed. You're the same evil, conniving muthafucka you were the day I met you!"

He flinched. "You're wrong. I *have* changed. Why? Because I found a woman worth changing for. We can be good together, Tamia—"

"*Are you insane?*" she shrieked. "I want nothing to do with you!"

Dominic smiled slowly. "If that's my baby you're carrying, you won't have a choice in the matter. You *will* deal with me whether you want to or not."

Their stares locked.

As he let out a soft, menacing laugh, Tamia shoved past him and ran out of there as if the devil were on her heels.

No one could tell her he wasn't.

Chapter 46

Brandon

That afternoon, Brandon met Dre for lunch at Stogie's and told him everything that had happened between him and Cynthia.

When he'd hung out with the fellas on New Year's Eve, he'd just wanted to chill and put everything out of his mind for the evening—not that a thumping nightclub packed with drunk revelers was an ideal environment for sharing confessionals anyway.

By the time he'd finished his account over lunch, Dre was flabbergasted.

"Yo . . ." He breathed, shaking his head at Brandon. "That's some coo-coo for Cocoa Puffs shit right there."

"Tell me about it," Brandon muttered darkly.

"Damn, bruh. Lemme find out you almost married Sybil."

Brandon couldn't help laughing.

"Yo, seriously. Cynthia's ass is straight-up psychotic. But you know what? Honestly—and this might sound bad—I'm not even surprised that she went there. You know she was determined to lock you down one way or another."

Brandon scowled. "Yeah, but faking a *pregnancy*? That's beyond fucked up."

"I hear you, man. But women do that shit all the time, unfortunately. What *I* can't believe is that Leah went along with it. She's always riding on her moral high horse, preaching the importance of integrity and doing the right thing. And here *she* is doing some shady

shit like this." Dre shook his head in angry disgust. "You think you
know a person."

Brandon snorted. "Right."

"What I did to Leah was wrong—no doubt. But damn, bruh, she
was gonna let you marry Cynthia based on a fucking lie. That's just
foul, man. Just wrong on every level." Dre wagged his head again, taking a swig of beer and wiping his mouth with the back of his hand. "I
didn't tell you that she called me on New Year's Day. Said she was
ready to talk about how we can fix our relationship."

"Word?"

"Yeah, man. But I don't know if I even *want* her ass back after she
pulled this kind of crazy stunt."

Brandon grimaced, sipping his beer. "It's your call. If I could forgive Tamia for cheating, you can forgive Leah for this."

Dre grunted. "Maybe."

As silence lapsed between them, Brandon glanced around and
noticed that all eyes were glued to the television mounted above the
bar. Joseph and Coretta Yarbrough could be seen scurrying from a
pack of reporters hurling questions at them. The bishop's sex scandal
had been dominating national headlines since the story broke on
Sunday. Tamia's ex-friend Honey—the escort at the center of the
controversy—had also been mercilessly hounded by the press, who'd
followed her home to New Orleans after she'd skipped town to hide
out with her family. The harassment she was receiving was her just
due for betraying Tamia.

All around Stogie's, heads were shaking, tongues were wagging,
and raunchy jokes were being cracked. Brandon had caught more
than a few amused glances.

"Looks like you really dodged a bullet, Chambers!" someone
called out, drawing raucous laughter and rumblings of agreement.

Brandon could only chuckle and shake his head.

"Fucked-up situation right there," Dre commiserated. "How's
your Dad handling it?"

"Not well," Brandon said wryly. "His campaign is in full damage-
control mode, trying to distance him as much as possible from
Yarbrough."

"I know." Dre snickered. "I caught a few sound bites from his
press conference this morning. He even made a point of announcing

that you had already 'parted ways' with the bishop's daughter before everyone found out about her father. He called Cynthia 'unsuitable' for you." Dre laughed, slapping the table. "Pops ain't playing—he's throwing the whole damn family under the bus!"

Brandon smirked. "How quickly the tide turns," he drawled, thinking of the conversation he'd had with his mother yesterday.

I liked Cynthia, but I was starting to have my doubts about her, Gwen had confided. *Once she started dating you, darling, she didn't seem all that interested in being a lawyer anymore. Now you know Chambers women are not ornamental housewives!*

"With all the madness that's going on," Dre observed, breaking into Brandon's thoughts, "you seem so calm and Zen-like. Happy, even."

"I am happy." Brandon smiled. "I asked Tamia to marry me, and she said yes."

Dre's eyes widened. "*Whaaat?* You proposed?"

"Sure as hell did."

"Wow." A broad grin stretched across Dre's face. "Congratulations, man. I'm really glad to see you and Tamia back together."

Brandon shot him a surprised look. "You are?"

"Absolutely." Dre made a wry face. "You know I haven't always been Tamia's biggest advocate. But after seeing you guys together on that road trip . . . *man.* It was so damn obvious that y'all belong together, I don't know how I could have ever doubted it." He smiled warmly. "You my boy, B, so I want you to be happy. It's clear that Tamia does it for you, so that's all that matters."

Brandon's expression softened. "Thanks, man. I really appreciate your support. Just for that, I might make you my best man."

"All right, nigga," Dre said gruffly. "Don't go getting all sentimental on me and shit."

They both laughed.

"If not best man," Brandon drawled, "definitely godfather."

"Godfather? What . . ." As comprehension dawned, Dre stared at Brandon in openmouthed shock. "Tamia's *pregnant?*"

"Yup." Brandon was grinning from ear to ear. "I got the baby mama I wanted."

Dre threw back his head and roared with laughter as Brandon grinned harder.

"This calls for another round of drinks," Dre declared, signaling for the waiter before shaking his head at Brandon. "You've been a busy man, haven't you?"

Brandon chuckled. "You have no idea."

"Oh, I think I do. I still remember the day Justin suggested you get Tamia pregnant so you could marry her. Your black ass got *real* quiet, and we could all see the wheels turning." Dre grinned, raising his beer to Brandon. "To schemes and dreams that turn out the way we please."

The two friends clinked bottles, then shared another warm laugh.

Sobering after several moments, Dre leaned forward, his hands clasped on the table. "Listen, bruh, there's something I wanted to—"

Suddenly Brandon's phone vibrated with an incoming text. He held up a finger, signaling Dre to wait while he checked the message, hoping it was from Tamia.

When he saw the photo that popped up on his screen, he almost choked on his beer.

Renay Portis had sent him a picture of herself posing provocatively in skimpy black lingerie. *"What the fuck?"*

Dre eyed him curiously. "What's wrong?"

Brandon shoved the phone into his friend's face.

Dre spat out his beer, his eyes bugging out. "WHAT THE—"

Brandon scowled. "Yo, man, I didn't wanna tell you, but your moms came on to me that night I went to her house for dinner. That's why I left before you got back. She had on a negligee and everything. Shit was crazy. She called a couple days later to apologize, so I figured that was the end of it." He pointed to the photo. "You need to handle that—or I will."

Dre was already scrambling out of the booth, his phone pressed to his ear as he charged furiously away. "Ma," he shouted, "why the hell you sending butt-naked pictures to Brandon?"

Several people at nearby tables burst out laughing.

Even Brandon had to chuckle as he deleted Renay's scandalous photo. It had definitely shocked and annoyed him.

But he was feeling so damn good about his future with Tamia, *nothing* could bring him down.

Chapter 47

Tamia

Four nights later, Tamia and Brandon had dinner at a five-star restaurant overlooking the city. It was incredibly romantic with the glittering skyline, the soft candlelight, and a violinist playing quietly for them while they ate.

Seated across the table from Brandon, Tamia felt like the luckiest woman alive.

Until she thought of her dilemma involving Dominic.

Since learning what he'd done to her, she'd considered going to the police. But she had no proof, so she knew it would be her word against his.

She'd fervently prayed for Mama Esther to visit her in a dream and give her answers. But so far her grandmother hadn't appeared.

Tamia had promised to keep no more secrets from Brandon. But if she told him the truth—that Dominic had drugged and raped her—she knew Brandon would kill him. Then where would that leave her? With one man dead and the other behind bars, neither would be around to be a father to her child.

She couldn't bear the thought of spending her entire pregnancy in a state of fear and uncertainty, not knowing whose baby she was carrying. So she'd done some research and found a reputable company that performed paternity tests before birth. She couldn't be tested until her eighth week of pregnancy, but that was far better than having to wait several months. The DNA test was costly, but it was worth any price for the peace of mind and closure she would receive.

All she needed were blood samples from her and Dominic, which he'd spitefully refused to provide because he wanted her to suffer until the baby was born.

After hanging up on him, she remembered that he'd bled on her dress the night of the fundraiser gala. To her everlasting relief, the paternity testing company assured her that their lab specialists could extract Dominic's DNA from the bloodstained fabric.

So she'd carefully packaged up the gown, and now all she had to do was wait three more weeks before she could be tested.

It would be the longest three weeks of her life, but she was determined to remain optimistic about the outcome of the paternity test. Too many things had conspired against her and Brandon to keep them apart. After everything she'd already been through, Tamia refused to believe that fate could be so cruel to deny her a happy ending with Brandon.

So she pushed all thoughts of Dominic out of her mind and focused on Brandon, because he was all that mattered.

After dinner they headed to his parents' house in River Oaks to pick up the morning-sickness remedy Mrs. Jessup had left for Tamia. Brandon had sworn the excited woman to secrecy because he wanted to be the one to tell his parents that he and Tamia were engaged and expecting a baby—an announcement he'd had to postpone since Bernard and Gwen had been traveling this week, hitting the campaign trail hard to minimize the fallout from Bishop Yarbrough's scandal.

As Brandon parked in the family's ten-car garage and came around to open Tamia's door, she couldn't help remembering the last time she'd been there for his father's campaign launch party. It had been a disastrous evening that had haunted her for months.

But things were different now. Tonight she was returning to the house as Brandon's fiancée and the soon-to-be mother of his child. Even if his parents still perceived her as a leper, she would be joining their family whether they liked it or not.

She smiled as Brandon helped her from the Maybach and held on to her hand. As they made their way up the flagstone driveway toward the palatial Mediterranean-style villa, Tamia couldn't help feeling the same sense of awe she'd felt the first time she was here. She couldn't believe she was engaged to a man who'd grown up in a place like this. It was surreal.

When no butler greeted them at the front door, Tamia teased, "Where's Benson?"

Brandon laughed. "Oh, you got jokes?"

She grinned. "Sorry. I couldn't resist."

"Uh-huh. Keep playin' and I'ma leave your pretty ass standing out here in the cold."

"You'd better not!"

Brandon chuckled as he unlocked the door and gestured her inside.

Tamia entered the mansion and cast an admiring look around the grand marble foyer, noting the humongous crystal chandelier and butterfly staircases that swept to the upper level.

Yup. Just as impressive as she remembered.

Brandon closed the door. "Since my parents will be out of town until Sunday, they gave everyone the weekend off to spend time with their families."

Tamia glanced at him. "You mean there's no one here?"

"Nope. Just you and me."

Tamia grinned, then cupped her hands around her mouth and called out, "*Yo, Tamia Luke up in da hizzy!*"

As her voice echoed and bounced off the cathedral ceilings, she burst into giggles.

Brandon laughed, hauling her close and kissing her temple. "Silly ass."

She grinned unabashedly. "You can take the girl out the hood, but you can't take the hood out the girl."

"Nor would I want to." Brandon winked, capturing her hand. "Come on. Let me give you the tour I promised last time."

As they started from the foyer, Tamia's heels clicked sharply against the marble floor, the sound magnified in the cavernous house. When she paused to step out of the stilettos, Brandon grinned at her.

"I bet you're gonna wear high heels up to the day you go into labor."

"Of course. You know I gotta keep my sexy on."

They both laughed.

During her previous visit, Tamia had only seen the ballroom and the sewing room before Dre had busted her for being Mystique. She shoved that memory aside as Brandon gave her the grand tour of the rest of the house, leading her through an opulently appointed living room, an enormous gourmet kitchen, a wine cellar, a stately wood-paneled library, a media room, a home theater, a solarium, and a billiard room with a full bar. On the second floor, each beautifully furnished bedroom had a private bath and a fireplace. Out of respect to his absent parents, Brandon and Tamia didn't venture to the master suite at the opposite end of the wing.

When they reached Brandon's old room, Tamia gazed around trying to imagine him dwelling there as a child. But the space had long been redecorated, removing all traces of the teenager who'd last occupied it. Tamia lingered nonetheless, savoring this connection to Brandon's past.

"Wanna spend the night?"

Tamia glanced around, meeting his amused gaze. "What?"

"You seem like you don't wanna leave, so maybe we should spend the night."

She smiled demurely. "Why, Brandon Chambers, are you inviting me for a sleepover while your parents are away?"

His eyes glinted wickedly. "That's exactly what I'm doing."

"What kind of girl do you think I am?"

"I already know," he teased, wiggling his brows suggestively, "which is why I'm inviting you."

Tamia feigned indignation. "Well, I *never!*"

"You have"—he winked—"and you will again tonight."

"Oh, yeah?"

"Yeah."

"Well . . . you're gonna have to catch me first!" Dropping her shoes, Tamia turned and raced out of the room.

Laughing uproariously, Brandon chased her through the long corridor and down the sweeping staircase, her squeals ringing through the house. As he caught her and swung her up into his arms, she howled with laughter.

"Thought you were gonna get away from me?" Brandon taunted her playfully. "Weren't you just oohing and aahing over my trophies in the media room? Did you forget that quickly that I ran track in high school?"

"Yeah, yeah, yeah," Tamia grumbled, looping her arms around his neck and nipping his jaw. "Let's finish the tour."

Brandon carried her out to the backyard, which was unlike any other backyard she'd ever seen. Her eyes bulged as they swept over the sprawling lawn that boasted a koi pond, a tennis court, and an Olympic-size swimming pool complemented by an infinity pool and a cabana.

"Wow . . . ," Tamia breathed.

Brandon put her down and took her hand, and together they set off to roam the moonlit grounds, talking and laughing companionably as they strolled along.

Soon they came upon the pool area, which was aglow with torchlights and bordered by manicured hedges and palm trees that provided privacy from the neighboring estate. Gleaming black marble framed the shimmering infinity pool, which featured a cascading rock waterfall. It looked like something that belonged at an exotic luxury resort.

Tamia was so busy admiring her surroundings that she didn't immediately notice Brandon toeing off his shoes and socks. When he bent and picked her up, she let out a startled squeak.

As he began carrying her toward the infinity pool, she eyed him suspiciously. "What are you doing?"

A wicked gleam filled his eyes.

Realizing his intent, she warned, "Oh, no, don't even *think* about it."

He grinned. "Why not?"

"Negro, are you crazy? It's barely seventy degrees out here!"

"Warm enough for you to be walking around with no shoes on," he pointed out. "And, anyway, the pool is heated."

"I don't care! Put me down!"

"Come on, baby," he cajoled. "I think a nice evening dip sounds good."

"Not fully clothed!" Tamia wiggled in his arms but he held fast, moving unerringly closer to the pool. "I'm serious, Brandon! And we don't even have anything to change into!"

"I've got a closet full of clothes here. And you can borrow something of Brooke's since you're about the same size."

"Brandon, I swear—"

But he was already descending the steps and wading into the pool as if he were carrying her into a lake to be baptized. Tamia squealed and clung to his neck as they sank into the warm water.

"You have lost your mind!"

Brandon threw back his head, unleashing one of those diabolical movie villain laughs. "I got you now!"

Tamia couldn't help laughing. "You play too damn much!"

He grinned at her, and she grinned back.

As the heated water lapped gently around them, he drawled, "See? Doesn't this feel good?"

"It does," Tamia grudgingly admitted.

"Told you."

As he shifted her in his arms, she warned, "Don't you dare get my hair wet."

"I won't." He chuckled. "You sistas and your hair."

"That's right. We don't play that." As Brandon nuzzled her ear, Tamia smiled and gazed around the glistening pool, marveling at how one edge seemed to drop off into . . . well, infinity. "This is amazing."

"Umm-hmm," Brandon agreed. But when she looked at him, he was staring at her big breasts outlined against the sheer fabric of her dress. He licked his lips. "*Um-mmm-umph*. My own personal wet T-shirt contest."

Tamia grinned. "I was just thinking the same thing," she purred, admiring the way his soaked dress shirt clung to the chiseled muscles of his chest.

He lowered his head and wrapped his lips around one of her erect nipples. She moaned as he sucked her, the wet heat of his mouth swelling the folds of her pussy.

"We shouldn't be doing this," she breathed.

"Why not?"

She shivered as his mouth closed over her other nipple. "Someone could catch us."

"No one's home, remember?" Lifting his head, he silenced her protests with a deep, toe-curling kiss.

Tamia wound her arms around his neck as his hands slid under her dress and cupped her ass, caressing and squeezing her juicy cheeks. She didn't resist as he peeled off her silk panties and let them float away, then unzipped his pants and fisted his hard shaft.

As she wrapped her legs around him, her dress bunched around her hips. She shivered at the feel of his cock, hot and thick, throbbing against her plump folds. He pulled her onto his strong thighs so that she was half sitting on him.

Their stares locked as he slid inside her, both of them groaning with pleasure.

"Damn, baby," Brandon whispered. "I can't get enough of you."

Tamia licked at his lips. "I hope you never do."

They kissed deep and slow, mouths meshing and parting, tongues tasting and swirling. Tamia clamped her thighs around Brandon's waist, gliding up and down the granite length of his dick as the heated water sloshed against them.

They stared into each other's eyes as he gradually increased the tempo. Tamia gasped with pleasure, her toes curling tightly behind his back as he thrust in and out of her pussy. When he reached between their joined bodies and thumbed her hard clit, she flung back her head and wailed with ecstasy.

Kissing the curve of her neck, Brandon grasped her hips and drove his dick deeper and harder inside her. She sobbed his name, her body arching backward as she exploded in orgasm. He followed seconds later, groaning hoarsely as his hot come flooded her insides.

They clung to each other, shuddering and panting for breath.

They didn't hear the approaching footsteps until it was too late.

"What on *earth* is going on here?"

Tamia and Brandon whipped their heads toward the scandalized voice.

His parents stood at the edge of the pool staring thunderously at them.

Tamia gasped, slapping her arms over her chest as her face flushed with embarrassment.

Brandon was remarkably unfazed.

"Oh, hey, Mom and Dad," he murmured, slowly easing out of Tamia. "Didn't expect you back this early."

"Clearly not," Gwen spat indignantly. "We saw your car and came looking for you. What is *she* doing here?"

"If by 'she' you mean Tamia, she's enjoying a relaxing dip in the pool with me."

Gwen raked them with a look of disgust. "Looks like you were enjoying *more* than a dip."

Brandon chuckled, zipping up his pants. "A gentleman should never kiss and tell. Right, Dad?"

Bernard frowned, his eyes narrowing on a scrap of pink silk floating around the pool. When Tamia realized it was her panties, her face flamed with mortification.

Still holding her, Brandon waded through the water to reach the steps, letting Tamia climb out ahead of him. She felt self-conscious as her sodden dress clung to her hourglass body like a second skin.

Brandon's father looked her over, then quickly averted his gaze as if he'd been caught doing something he wasn't supposed to.

"I cannot believe you brought that girl to this house," Gwen hissed at Brandon.

He smiled languidly. "Well, I figured she should have a tour of the property she'll eventually call home."

Bernard and Gwen exchanged confused looks, then demanded, "What the hell are you talking about?"

"Tamia and I are getting married."

"WHAT?" Bernard and Gwen exclaimed in shock.

"We're engaged," Brandon calmly explained. "I love Tamia, and I was tired of living without her. So I asked her to marry me, and she took pity on me and said yes."

Tamia laughed softly. "I didn't take pity on you."

Brandon smiled, raising her hand to his mouth and kissing it.

"Are you out of your damn mind?" Gwen demanded furiously. "You can't marry this girl!"

"I can, and I will."

"Over my dead body!"

Brandon chuckled. "That would be unfortunate. But maybe you could stick around long enough to meet your grandchild."

Bernard and Gwen exchanged astonished glances, then stared at Brandon and Tamia. "Grandchild . . . ?"

"That's right," Brandon confirmed, gently drawing Tamia closer. "We're having a baby in September. And before you even think about accusing Tamia of getting pregnant to trap me, you should know it was the other way around. *I* got *her* pregnant because I need her in my life, and she's the only woman I've ever wanted to be the mother of my children."

As Bernard and Gwen stared at Tamia, she saw something soft in their eyes. Something like acceptance. But she must have only imagined it, for the very next moment their expressions hardened, and she felt the chill of their rejection.

"You're not thinking rationally, son," Bernard scolded.

"And you're insane if you think you're bringing *her* to live in this house," Gwen hissed.

The words hurt, but Tamia had already resigned herself to the reality that Bernard and Gwen Chambers might never accept her, and that was okay. Having Brandon's love was all that mattered.

But it was with great pride and satisfaction that she watched Brandon dismantle his parents, all without ever raising his voice above a lazy drawl.

"I assure both of you that I was of sound mind when I asked Tamia to marry me. Being apart from her is what tested my sanity. As for where she can or can't live, I'll kindly refer you to my great-grandparents' will, which grants me full ownership of this estate upon my thirty-seventh birthday as long as I have a wife and children." Brandon glanced at Tamia. "When's my birthday, baby?"

"June seventeenth," she supplied.

"June seventeenth," he repeated. "Let's see. I turn thirty-four this year. So that means in approximately three years I'll inherit this fine property, at which time I can allow my parents to stay here with us— or I can send them packing to the family's country estate."

Gwen gave an affronted gasp. "You wouldn't *dare* put us out!"

Brandon smiled narrowly at her. "Treat Tamia with the love and respect she deserves, and maybe I won't. But I can't have my wife and the mother of my children feeling like an outcast in her own home. No, ma'am, that ain't happening."

Mother and son stared each other down.

Gwen was the first to look away, silently imploring her husband to intervene.

"You need to think about your political future, son," Bernard warned sternly. "Every decision you make will have an impact on your viability as a candidate."

"I'm well aware of that, Dad," Brandon said coolly. "But your concern is duly noted."

Bernard pressed his lips together, a muscle clenching in his jaw.

"Now if you folks don't mind," Brandon drawled, possessively curving an arm around Tamia's waist, "my fiancée and I are gonna head up to my room and take a nice hot shower, then curl up in front of a cozy fire. If you'd like to join us for breakfast tomorrow morning, we should be up around, say, ten o'clock"—he winked at Tamia—"unless we keep each other up too late."

Tamia gave him a coy smile.

"You're making a terrible mistake," Gwen burst out shrilly. "She's not right for you, Brandon!"

Brandon raised a brow. "Need I remind you what happened with the *last* woman you and Dad swore was perfect for me?"

Bernard and Gwen's faces tightened.

Brandon smirked. "Don't trouble yourselves trying to find any more 'suitable' wives for me. I got this." He brushed his lips across the diamond ring on Tamia's hand and smiled at her. "Ready, sweetheart?"

She smiled softly. "Yes, my dark knight."

Brandon grinned and winked at her.

As they turned and started toward the house, Bernard let out a panicked, "*Gwen!*"

Tamia didn't have to look back to know that Brandon's mother had fainted.

Maybe if she threw a bucket of water on the bitch, she'd melt away like the Wicked Witch of the West.

Chapter 48
Tamia

One month later

The envelope was waiting for Tamia when she checked her mail at One Park Place. She no longer lived there, but since Brandon had already paid the lease up through a year, the apartment still belonged to her. So she'd had the paternity test results sent there so that Brandon wouldn't see them.

She stood in the foyer, her heart pounding violently as she opened the envelope and slowly unfolded the one-page report.

She read the results.

And burst into tears.

Her hands trembled as she picked up her phone and called Dominic.

The moment he answered, she crowed, "Your boys may be strong swimmers, but they're not stronger than Brandon's."

Dominic was silent for a moment. "What the hell are you talking about?"

"I'm looking at the results from the paternity test I ordered. The report shows a probability percentage of zero for your DNA, which excludes you from being the father of my baby."

"That's impossible," Dominic growled. "I didn't give you a blood sample."

"Actually, you did. Or rather, Brandon took one from you the night he kicked your punk ass at the fundraiser banquet. They were able to get your DNA from my dress that you bled all over."

"What is this fuckery?" Dominic raged. "You expect me to be satisfied with the results from some bullshit *CSI* test? I want a real test!"

"That *was* a real test, done by a federally certified testing company."

"So you say," Dominic jeered. "I wonder if Brandon would be so willing to take these results at face value. Maybe I should give him a call and see what *he* thinks."

The malicious threat sent a wave of fury blazing through Tamia.

"You listen to me, muthafucka," she snarled into the phone. "I'm not carrying your demon spawn. Got it? I'm having a baby with the man I love. If you ever come anywhere near me or Brandon again, I will personally call up Brandon's contacts at the Justice Department and tell them about your embezzlement problem. I may not know the specific details, but one phone call is all it would take to get them sniffing up your ass, and we both know your shit stinks. You shoulda learned your lesson the first time you fucked around with Brandon and he almost bankrupted you. If he becomes a U.S. senator, how much *more* damage do you think he can do to you? Do you really wanna find out? Keep playing with me and your black ass will *beg* to be deported back to St. Croix. I'm warning you for the last time, Dominic. Leave me and my man the fuck alone!"

With that Tamia hung up, then slowly exhaled the breath she'd been holding for weeks.

Free at last . . .

Her phone rang.

When she saw that Brandon was calling, her heart soared.

"Hey, baby," he said warmly.

She beamed. "Hey, yourself."

"What're you up to?"

"Oh, just taking out the trash."

"Why? I coulda done that when I got back from D.C."

"It's okay. I don't mind taking out the trash—especially when it's really foul."

Brandon chuckled.

"So how'd everything go with the Congressional Black Caucus?" Tamia asked.

"It went well. I'll tell you all about it when I get home."

"Okay. Where are you?"

"On my way to the airport." Brandon sighed heavily. "I don't know if I'll be able to do this after all, sweetheart. I *hate* being away from you and the baby."

"And we hate being away from you too, boo. But you're running for the Senate, so we understand that sacrifices have to be made."

"I know." His voice grew husky with emotion. "I love you, you know that?"

"I do. And I love you, too." Tamia leaned against the wall—the very same wall where their child had been conceived. "I'm missing you, and my hormones got me so wet and horny."

"Damn," Brandon groaned. "Why'd you have to tell me that? Now you gon' have me sitting on the plane with my dick all hard."

Tamia laughed wickedly. "Just get home soon."

"I will," he promised. "I'm on my way back to you."

"I'll be waiting. . . ."

Two hours later, Tamia pulled up to Brandon's building in the silver Mercedes-Benz he'd bought her for an early Valentine's Day gift.

On her way home, she'd passed a Babies "R" Us and couldn't resist sneaking inside to buy a few things to add to her growing collection of baby stuff. Shanell kept complaining that she'd have everything she needed by the time her baby shower rolled around.

Tamia chuckled at that as she let herself into the condo and closed the door.

It was the smell that alerted her to danger.

The pungent, coppery scent of blood that reminded her of the night she'd found Isabel Archer's dead body.

Turning from the door, she gasped sharply at the sight of Coretta Yarbrough lying motionless on the floor, blood pooling around her head.

As Tamia's fight-or-flight instincts kicked in, she spun around and lunged for the door.

"Don't take another step or I'll shoot."

Tamia froze, then slowly turned around and peered toward the shadowy living room.

Cynthia sat in Brandon's favorite armchair with a silenced pistol pointed at her.

Tamia's blood ran cold. "Wh-what're you doing here?"

"What do you think?" Cynthia jeered. "I came to settle the fucking score."

Swallowing hard, Tamia considered making a run for it.

"I wouldn't try it, bitch," Cynthia warned. "I used to go hunting with my father and brothers. Trust me, there's nothing wrong with my aim."

Tamia took her word for it.

Cynthia switched on the tableside lamp.

She should have looked deranged—wild hair, bloodshot eyes, foaming at the mouth. Instead, she looked as poised and polished as ever. Perfectly flat-ironed hair, designer pantsuit, kitten-heel pumps.

Just another day at the office.

"What happened to your mother, Cynthia?" Tamia asked nervously. "Did you shoot her?"

Cynthia smirked. "Well, let's see. There were only two of us in the apartment. *She's* over there lying in a puddle of blood while *I'm* sitting over here. So, yeah, it would appear that I did, in fact, shoot her. Congratulations. Your powers of deductive reasoning are amazing." She snorted. "Stupid bitch. And Brandon says you're so smart."

Tamia ignored the nasty sarcasm. "Why did you kill your own mother, Cynthia?"

"I didn't." A sinister smile curved her mouth. "*You* did."

Tamia stared at her. "What are you talking about?"

Cynthia sighed. "Mom's the one who sent you that threatening note."

"*What?*"

"When my parents came up with the idea for Dominic to blackmail you, Dad considered having you permanently removed from the picture—"

Tamia gasped.

"—but my dear mother talked him out of it." Cynthia's lips twisted. "She didn't have the balls to commit murder."

I saved your life echoed through Tamia's mind. It made sense now.

"Mom knew about Dad and that trashy escort all along. But after she caught him masturbating to your porn video one day, she started to suspect that he was screwing you, too. It made her furious, so she left you that note to scare you."

Tamia was shocked. Coretta Yarbrough was the last person she'd suspected, though in hindsight, she probably should have been among the first.

"Anyway," Cynthia continued, "Mom was feeling sorry for herself the other day, so she confessed everything to me. She says she and Dad kept me in the dark for my own good. You know, plausible deniability in case Brandon ever found out about their scheme."

Cynthia glared at Tamia, her eyes gleaming with malice. "We know you're the spiteful bitch who outed Dad to the media. After I told Mom that Brandon was out of town this week, she decided to come over here to confront you. I tagged along. Your new car wasn't here, so I told Mom we should wait inside for you. I still have a spare key to the condo, so I told the front desk that I needed to get something that I'd forgotten before, and Brandon had given me permission to drop by. The clerk was new, and since I had my mother with me, he figured I was on the level. Once we were inside, Mom started getting cold feet, saying we shouldn't be here when no one was home. When she saw that I'd brought one of Dad's guns, she freaked out and tried to leave." Cynthia sneered. "Once again, she wasn't willing to do what needed to be done. So I'm handling it for her."

Fear pulsed through Tamia's veins. If this bitch was crazy enough to kill her own mother, what chance did Tamia have?

"Look at you," Cynthia snarled contemptuously. "Who the hell do you think you are living in this condo, sleeping in Brandon's bed, fucking him every night, showering with him every morning? You don't belong here, Tamia. *I'm* the one who belongs in his life. Even though we were just friends, he was *mine* first."

Tamia shook her head slowly. "He made his choice, Cynthia. You need to live with it."

"*Fuck you!* I don't have to live with *shit!*" Suddenly Cynthia froze, her gaze locking onto the bag Tamia was carrying. "Wait a minute. . . . You went to Babies 'R' Us?"

Oh, shit. Tamia gulped nervously.

Cynthia raised her eyes from the bag to stare at Tamia. "Are you *pregnant?*" she whispered.

Tamia just looked at her.

"*Answer me!*" Cynthia screeched.

"Y-yes," Tamia stammered. "I'm pregnant."

For a moment, the gun wavered as Cynthia seemed to deflate against the armchair, nostrils flaring, eyes blinking back tears.

Tamia watched her tensely. Homegirl looked so devastated she almost felt sorry for her.

Almost.

Cynthia swiped furiously at her tears. "I bet he screwed you that night he came home late. The night he went on a rampage and destroyed the damn TV just because I asked him where he'd been." She glared accusingly at Tamia. "You fucked him that night, didn't you? That's when you got pregnant, isn't it?"

Tamia hesitated, then reluctantly nodded.

"Fucking whore!" Cynthia spat viciously, her grip tightening on the pistol.

Tamia panicked. "*I'm* the one who should be jealous of *you*, Cynthia! You have *everything* I never had! *You* have doting parents who love and adore you while my parents are dead, and I barely even knew my father. *You* grew up never wanting for anything while I grew up on food stamps. *You* didn't have to do porn to put yourself through college—"

"ENOUGH!" Cynthia exploded. "I didn't come here to hear your fucking sob story, Tamia! At the end of the day, you're getting the one and only thing I've ever wanted. As if that weren't bad enough, you're having his baby." As her face contorted with hatred, she lowered the gun to Tamia's stomach and shrieked, *"That was supposed to be MY baby! Mine and Brandon's! Not yours, you fucking cunt!"*

Tamia swallowed audibly.

"*You're* the one who repeatedly lied to him," Cynthia ranted bitterly. "*You're* the one who cheated on him. *You're* the one who broke his heart. Yet *I'm* the one he sent packing because nice girls always finish last. But not today, motherfuckers! NOT TODAY!"

Tamia's heart was racing, sweat pooling in her armpits. "How do you really expect to get away with this, Cynthia? You broke into Brandon's condo. The front desk knows you're here."

A cold, calculating gleam filled Cynthia's eyes. "I'm a defense attorney, remember? I've been called to clients' homes after they committed murder, so I know how to manipulate crime scenes to help get them acquitted. Trust me, bitch, I won't have a problem staging this scene to match my version of events."

Tamia felt chilled to the bone.

"It's a simple scenario," Cynthia said as casually as if she were explaining why the sky was blue. "I stopped by to pick up something I mistakenly thought I'd left behind. The reason I lied to the front desk is because I didn't want them to make me come back another time when Brandon was home. I didn't want to see him, nor did I want him to stop me from getting back my property. My mother offered to come with me for moral support. Unbeknownst to me, she was planning to kill you for destroying her husband's reputation. When you came home and found us here, you were understandably alarmed. While I was in the bedroom searching for what I'd come for, you snuck to the study and grabbed Brandon's gun for protection."

Cynthia held up the Glock in question, then carefully set it down on the coffee table. It was wrapped in the cloth she'd used to wipe off her fingerprints after she killed her mother. The gun would undoubtedly be placed in Tamia's hand, or near her body, once she'd been shot.

"After you came back from the study," Cynthia calmly continued, "you and my mother started arguing. It escalated to the point where you both drew your guns. As I came running out of the bedroom to see what was going on, you shot each other. I screamed and called the police. End of story."

Tamia's heart pounded with fear as Cynthia rose from the armchair and came toward her with the silenced pistol. "Enough talking, bitch. I need to put a bullet into you so that your time of death coincides with my mother's."

Tamia took a small step backward. "Don't do this, Cynthia. It's not worth ruining your life over."

Cynthia snorted harshly. "Are you fucking kidding me? *What life?* I lost my fiancé to a filthy slut who's having his baby. At the office he looks right through me like I'm a stranger, then I learned today that I won't be making partner this year. As if that weren't bad enough, my father has been publicly disgraced and shunned from the church *he* built, my brothers are ashamed of me for pretending to be pregnant, and now my mother is dead. So tell me, Tamia," she jeered, coming closer, "what do I possibly have to lose by ending your miserable life?"

Hearing voices out in the hall, Cynthia looked over Tamia's shoulder.

Taking advantage of her momentary distraction, Tamia swung the bag and knocked the gun out of Cynthia's hand.

She gasped in surprise, watching as the pistol clattered across the floor.

She and Tamia dove for it at the same time, landing near Coretta's lifeless body. When Tamia found herself staring into the dead woman's glassy eyes, there was no time for her to scream—she had her hands full with a psychotic killer.

Cynthia was skinny, but she was fueled by a maniacal hatred and fury that made her stronger than Tamia had expected. She fought like a wildcat, clawing and swinging her fists as she screamed invectives at Tamia. When Tamia wrestled her way to the top, Cynthia viciously drove her knee into her stomach.

Tamia gasped sharply, staggered by the searing pain that radiated through her.

"*Bitch!*" Cynthia yelled. "I'll see you in hell before I let you have that fucking baby!"

As she went for Tamia's stomach again, a blinding rage overtook her—the rage of a mother lioness protecting her young—and she roared into Cynthia's face, "*I'MA SEND YOU THERE MYSELF, YOU CRAZY ASS BITCH!*"

She furiously punched Cynthia in the face, then seized two fist-fuls of her hair and banged her head against the wood floor as Cynthia howled in pain.

Suddenly the front door burst open, the sound of loud male voices and heavy footsteps erupting into the apartment.

"*Tamia!*" Brandon shouted, his voice hoarse with panicked alarm as he pulled her off Cynthia.

As Cynthia rolled to her stomach and tried to crawl after the fallen gun, she was apprehended by one of the cops who'd arrived with Brandon.

"You're under arrest!" the officer barked, planting his knee firmly in her back.

Brandon swept Tamia into his arms, carried her over to the sofa, and settled her across his lap as he ran trembling hands over her hair and face. "Oh, baby," he groaned as if he were in agony. "Jesus God. What the hell did she do to you? Are you okay?"

Tamia nodded weakly, gritting her teeth against spasms of pain spearing through her stomach.

After checking Coretta for a pulse, the second cop frowned and radioed for an ambulance.

"WHAT THE FUCK DID YOU DO, CYNTHIA?" Brandon yelled as she was handcuffed and led out of the condo sobbing hysterically.

Returning his attention to Tamia, Brandon kissed her forehead and rubbed his cheek back and forth against her hair. "I'm so sorry, sweetheart," he said raggedly. "I didn't know she'd come after you. *I didn't know.*"

"Neither did I." Tamia shuddered against him. "How did you get home so quickly?"

"I caught an earlier flight. I wanted to surprise you. When I got here, the cops had just arrived. The front desk told me the neighbors heard shouting coming from the apartment, so they called the police." Brandon frantically looked her over, checking for injuries. "Are you sure you're okay?"

"I think so." Tamia closed her eyes, her hand pressed to her stomach. "Just get me to the hospital so we can make sure our baby's all right. . . ."

Chapter 49

Fiona

"Well, well, well," Fiona drawled. "Look what we have here, ladies. A new arrival."

Cynthia sat down and glanced nervously toward the end of the lunch table where Fiona sat holding court with a group of her fellow inmates.

Fiona smirked, slowly looking Cynthia up and down. No more designer threads for this bougie heffa. Orange jumpsuits all the way.

"Hello, Miss Thang," Fiona taunted. "Bet you never thought you'd end up in a place like this with the unwashed masses."

The other women cackled and smacked their lips as Cynthia ducked her head over her meal tray.

"How's your ex-preacher daddy doing?" Fiona jeered. "I heard the feds charged him with running a Ponzi scheme and swindling millions out of his dumbass parishioners. Heard they got enough evidence to lock his ass up for life, too." Fiona *tsk-tsked*. "Looks like fucking prostitutes was the *least* of your daddy's sins. But, hey, considering how ugly your mama was, I can't even blame the poor man for getting pussy elsewhere."

Cynthia's face reddened as the other inmates shrieked with laughter.

Fiona knew badmouthing a dead woman was a low blow, but she figured it couldn't be worse than what her own daughter had done to her. Hell, the psycho bitch had killed her own mother. It didn't get any lower than that.

"I saw my sister yesterday," Fiona announced. "She and Brandon came to visit me. They look so happy together. So right for each other. Their wedding plans are coming along great and they found the perfect house, so they're moving next month. Of course they couldn't stay at Brandon's condo after you turned it into a crime scene, so they've been staying with his parents. And wouldn't you know it? Mr. and Mrs. Chambers are actually starting to warm up to Tamia. Yup, Brandon's mother has been planning their wedding, so you *know* it's gonna be off da chain. Ain't that something? You tried your best to prove to Brandon's parents that *you* were right for their son, but in the end, your psychotic breakdown made them realize *Tamia* was the better woman for Brandon. Oh, by the way, their baby is doing just fine, fuck you very much."

Cynthia stared down at her untouched food, rapidly blinking back tears.

"We're all looking forward to watching Brandon and Tamia's wedding on TV," Fiona gleefully continued. "I know the local stations are gonna cover the ceremony like it's the royal wedding. You're more than welcome to join our viewing party, Cynthia. That is, if you think you can handle seeing my sister get everything you wanted."

Tears rolled down Cynthia's face.

But Fiona wasn't done. "I just gotta ask. How do you sleep at night knowing that you murdered your own mama and almost killed an innocent unborn baby?"

Cynthia's nostrils flared. "The same way *you* slept after murdering your grandmother," she retorted under her breath.

"*No, she didn't!*" the other women hissed and exclaimed, outraged on Fiona's behalf.

Fiona chuckled, calmly holding up a hand. "It's all good, ladies. Let her talk shit. Miss Thang got some spunk in her, so she just might do a'ight up in here."

Someone sucked her teeth. "You need to fuck that bitch up, Fee."

This drew hearty echoes of agreement that had Cynthia looking petrified.

Fiona smiled consolingly at her. "Don't worry, ma, I ain't gonna whip your ass," she promised, gently rubbing her swollen stomach. "You fight dirty, and while that normally wouldn't be a problem for me, I can't risk nothing happening to my precious daughter."

A look of relief flashed across Cynthia's face.

"But I can't speak for some of these other salty bitches around here," Fiona smoothly continued. "Some of them got nothing to live for, so they wouldn't think twice about shanking your crazy ass. Some of them don't care for pampered princesses who think they're better than everyone else, so they'd love nothing more than to fuck you up and knock you off your high horse. And some of them"—Fiona pointed to a butch-looking inmate with thick cornrows—"are just out to make you their bitch."

The color drained from Cynthia's face as the woman leered suggestively at her.

Fiona sighed dramatically. "Any of those things could happen to you. Or maybe none at all." She smiled narrowly. "Either way, this ain't your daddy's country club. Around here *I* have all the connections, and quiet as it's kept, *I* pull the strings."

Cynthia gulped visibly.

Glancing toward the nearest corrections officer, Fiona added menacingly to Cynthia, "So don't sleep, bitch. 'Cause after I drop this load, your skinny black ass is mine." She winked. "Assuming you're still around."

Chapter 50

Tamia

Seven months later

"Everything was so beautiful, Mama Esther," Tamia reminisced, swaying back and forth on the porch swing. "The flowers, the decorations, the chateau by the lake. It was all so perfect. I wore a strapless mermaid gown that showed off my little baby bump, and everyone said I looked breathtaking. Beyoncé serenaded us with the most romantic love song I've ever heard. But even before that moment, Brandon and I had already been fighting back tears. We were both so emotional, thinking about everything we'd gone through to get to that day. Oh, Mama, you should have *seen* the way he looked at me as I came down the aisle. No man has *ever* looked at me with so much love in his eyes. Words can't even describe it." Tamia sighed blissfully. "It was such an amazing wedding, Mama. Beyond my wildest dreams."

"It sounds wonderful," Mama Esther warmly agreed.

"It was." Tamia held her grandmother's hand against her cheek. "I wish you could have been there, Mama."

The old woman smiled. "I was there with you in spirit."

"I know." Tamia smiled quietly. "I felt your presence the whole time, especially when Brandon and I exchanged our vows. I could feel you standing beside me and whispering in my ear, 'Never underestimate the power of a man's love.' Do you remember telling me that?"

Her grandmother smiled. "I certainly do."

"Well, you were right, Mama."

"Of course. I'm always right."

They shared a warm laugh.

After a few moments, Tamia ventured curiously, "Why did you stay away so long, Mama? My wedding was back in April."

Mama Esther sighed. "I know, baby, and I hope you didn't think I'd abandoned you. But you have a new husband now, and you'll be a mother very soon. Your life will never be the same again, and I want you to experience every moment without thinking about the past . . . or even me."

Tamia's throat tightened. "I hope this doesn't mean you're gonna stop coming to me," she whispered.

"That's not what I'm saying at all," Mama Esther soothed, gently patting her hand. "But last year you were going through very difficult times, and you needed my guidance. Now . . . well, now you and Brandon need to rely on each other. But you know I'll always be with you, Tamia. Do you believe me?"

Tamia nodded slowly. "I believe you."

"Good girl."

When Tamia could trust her voice again, she said, "You know Fiona had her baby."

"Yes." Mama Esther's face glowed. "She's beautiful."

"She is." Tamia smiled tenderly. "Dre didn't want her, but once he held her in his arms, she melted his heart. I think he's going to make a great father, and Brandon and I will be there for him."

Mama Esther smiled. "I know you will."

Sobering after several moments, Tamia sighed heavily. "Fiona was sentenced to nineteen years in prison. The judge was more lenient with her because she was a juvenile when . . ."

Mama Esther nodded understandingly.

They sat in silence for a while, holding hands and gently rocking back and forth on the swing.

"Tamia?"

"Yes, Mama?"

Her grandmother's eyes twinkled. "It's time for you to push—"

Tamia awakened slowly and glanced around the private hospital suite. There were beautiful floral arrangements, stuffed animals, balloons, and chocolates everywhere.

Brandon stood at the window, his newborn son cradled lovingly in his arms.

When Tamia saw them, tears swam into her eyes, blurring their images like a mirage shimmering in the distance.

But these two weren't mirages.

They were very real.

And they belonged to her. Both father and son.

Even if she hadn't already received the paternity test results, Tamia would have known that her son was one hundred percent Brandon's. The baby had beautiful dark skin and the makings of thick black eyebrows, and when he opened his little mouth to yawn, dimples flashed in his chubby cheeks.

Gwen had taken one look at her newborn grandson and burst into tears. "He looks *just* like Brandon did when he was born!"

During yesterday's intense labor and delivery, Brandon had stayed by Tamia's side. He'd stroked her hair, kissed her sweaty brow, whispered words of encouragement, and fervently told her how much he loved and appreciated her. And once she'd pushed out the baby, Brandon had proudly cut the umbilical cord with tears of joy streaming down his face.

Tamia smiled at the memory, watching as her husband gently sifted his fingers through their son's head full of curly black hair. Brandon Everett Junior was a healthy, strapping boy who'd entered the world at eight pounds and three ounces.

Turning from the window, Brandon met Tamia's gaze and smiled softly. "Hey, beautiful."

She smiled. "Hey."

Brandon started toward the bed. "The nurse brought him in for his feeding, but you were sleeping so peacefully I didn't wanna wake you right away. So we've just been chillin' together." As the baby began to fuss softly, Brandon chuckled. "I think chillin' time is over."

Tamia grinned, holding out her arms. "Bring him to mama."

Brandon tenderly kissed the swaddled infant's forehead before handing him to Tamia.

As she gazed down into her son's adorable face, her heart swelled with such love and gratitude she could barely contain it. "Hey, little man," she cooed. "Aren't you mama's precious baby boy? Yes, you are. Oh, *yes*, you—"

"Later for all the sweet talk, woman," Brandon teased. "Whip out that big tittie and feed my son."

Tamia laughed.

Brandon gently brushed her hair off her face, then climbed into the bed and spooned her as the baby latched on to her nipple and vigorously began sucking.

"Dayum," Brandon marveled, watching over her shoulder. "He's definitely gonna be a breast man."

Tamia grinned. "Like his daddy."

He laughed, nipping her bare shoulder. As they quietly watched their nursing child, Brandon murmured, "How're you feeling, sweetheart?"

"Like the luckiest woman in the world." Tamia smiled, tenderly stroking the infant's soft cheek. "Beej is such a sweet miracle—"

"*Beej?*" Brandon echoed.

"Yeah. It's a nickname for Brandon Everett Junior."

Brandon chuckled. "Nah, babe, that ain't gonna work."

"Why not?"

"You gon' have my son getting clowned at school."

Tamia laughed. "Then I guess you'd better teach him how to defend himself, huh?"

"Oh, I'm doing that regardless." Brandon grinned. "But we'll have to talk some more about that nickname."

Tamia sighed. "Okay, Counselor. I'm open to negotiations."

"Smart woman."

She bumped her shoulder against his chest, and he laughed.

After a while they fell silent, watching as their contented son closed his eyes and drifted off to sleep.

Brandon cuddled closer to Tamia and whispered, "Thank you."

She looked back, met his worshipful gaze, and smiled. "Thank *you*."

He leaned down and kissed her so tenderly that tears welled in her eyes. As he gently stroked her hip, Tamia reached for his hand.

Their fingers met . . . tangled . . . settled together.

The story of their romance.

Epilogue

Houston, Texas
April 2013

Brandon stood at the podium addressing a huge crowd of cheering supporters who'd come out to celebrate his primary victory. His family and friends were front and center, their eyes shining with pride and excitement as they waved signs proclaiming BRANDON CHAMBERS FOR SENATE. He was the Democratic nominee, headed into a general election showdown with his rival—Republican nominee Russ Sutcliffe.

"Thank you, my fellow Texans, for not allowing the politics of hate and division to overshadow the important issues of this election. Thank you for turning a blind eye and a deaf ear to the smear campaigns my opponents mounted against me. It was brutal, but together we weathered the storm and came out on top." Brandon smiled at Tamia, the words as much for her as his supporters.

Standing beside him with their handsome son perched on her hip, Tamia gave him a wink.

Turning back to the crowd, Brandon continued earnestly, "If you give me a chance to become your senator, I will fight for you the way I've always fought for what I believe in. I won't be bullied by filibustering senators who have an agenda that doesn't serve the people. If need be, I will go straight *gangsta* on that Senate floor—"

As a wave of laughter and cheers swept through the crowd, Governor Bernard Chambers and First Lady Gwen could be seen shaking their heads and fighting back smiles while Beau, Brooke, Dre, Justin, and Cornel pumped their fists and whooped.

Brandon continued, "I'll do whatever it takes to ensure that your voices are heard and your needs are met. That's my promise to you, and I don't take promises lightly. So thank you all for rolling deep with me. Our work has just begun!"

The crowd clapped enthusiastically as Brandon's speech ended. When he and Tamia gave each other affectionate fist bumps, the applause swelled into a roar of approval.

Brandon stared intently at Tamia. "Still with me?"

She knew he wasn't just talking about his political campaign, but about their future together.

She curved her hand against his cheek, gazed into his eyes, and let her heart speak to his before she avowed, "I'm with you, Brandon Chambers. Today. Tomorrow. *Always*."

He smiled and winked at her. "Then let's do this. . . ."

BETRAYAL

Naomi Chase

ABOUT THIS GUIDE

The suggested questions are included
to enhance your group's reading of
Naomi Chase's
Betrayal.

Discussion Questions

1. When the story opened with a love scene, whom did you think Tamia was having sex with?

2. Did you think Brandon would meet Tamia at the restaurant? Or did you expect him to go to the courthouse to marry Cynthia?

3. Were you surprised when Brandon postponed the wedding?

4. After Brandon chose to be with Cynthia, Tamia decided to cut her losses and move on with her life. Did you agree with her decision to distance herself from Brandon? Did you sympathize with her?

5. Do you think Brandon was selfish for expecting Tamia to wait for him? Could you understand where he was coming from?

6. Do you think Tamia was wrong for getting involved with Dominic again? After everything he'd done to her, was she foolish to trust him?

7. Did you ever suspect that Cynthia was faking her pregnancy? If so, when?

8. Were you surprised to learn that Honey and Lou betrayed Tamia by conspiring with Bishop Yarbrough?

9. Were you surprised that Dominic was blackmailed into extorting sex from Tamia? Did this make his actions forgivable? Understandable?

10. Do you think Brandon and Tamia belong together?

11. Do you think Brandon's parents will ever completely accept Tamia as Brandon's wife?

12. Do you think Brandon and Cynthia could have been happy together if she hadn't lied about her pregnancy? Do you think Brandon would have eventually ended their relationship?

13. Do you believe Dominic genuinely loves Tamia?

14. How would you have felt if Dominic had been the father of Tamia's baby?

15. Were you shocked that Cynthia killed her own mother?

16. Do you think Dre reacted unfairly when he learned that Fiona was pregnant?

17. Do you think Dre and Brooke will end up together?

18. Were you pleased with the ending of *Betrayal*? Why or why not?

19. Would you like to read more about Brandon and Tamia in the future?

Don't miss the first two books in the Exposed series—
turn the page for an excerpt from

Exposed and *Deception*.

On sale now at your local bookstore

An excerpt from *EXPOSED*

Chapter 1

"Tamia! Baby, get up."

Jolted awake by her boyfriend's frantic voice, Tamia Luke opened her eyes and stared at his dark, handsome face. "What time is it?"

"After seven," Brandon replied.

"Shit!" Tamia threw back the covers and sprang out of bed, naked breasts bouncing. "What happened? Why didn't the alarm clock go off?"

"The power must have gone out when it rained last night."

"Shit," Tamia repeated, bending over to retrieve her discarded clothing from the floor. "I can't be late for work. Especially not tod— *Ow!*" she yelped as Brandon slapped her soundly on the ass.

He grinned, dimples flashing in his cheeks. *"That's* for keeping me up late."

Tamia laughed. "I didn't hear you complaining last night, Negro!" she called as Brandon ducked inside the large master bathroom, a blur of mahogany stretched over lean, taut muscles. "And hurry up so you can take me home!"

Brandon's response was muffled by the sound of running water.

If they hadn't been in such a rush, Tamia would have joined him in the shower for round two of what they'd started last night. After attending a cocktail party at a ritzy downtown hotel, Brandon had invited her back to his place to spend the night. They'd doused themselves with a bottle of champagne, then licked, sucked, and fucked each other until they collapsed from sheer exhaustion. They probably would have overslept even if last night's storm *hadn't* knocked out the electricity.

Grinning slyly to herself, Tamia hurriedly tugged on her bra and panties and the black Christian Lacroix dress she'd worn to the cocktail party. Leaving Brandon to his shower, she headed out of the bedroom and made her way to the kitchen. It was a large, ultramodern room with gleaming granite countertops, black-lacquered cabinets, and stainless steel appliances. It was as immaculate as the rest of Brandon's plush condo, thanks to the cleaning lady who came like clockwork twice a week.

Tamia got busy brewing a pot of gourmet coffee, though she knew Brandon usually stopped at Starbucks on his way to the office. It was the thought that counted. If she'd had more time, she would have whipped up some eggs, bacon, and grits, though she knew Brandon often grabbed breakfast with a colleague at the prestigious law firm where he worked. Again, it was all about taking care of her man. Which was why she'd blown off her friends last night to accompany Brandon to some social mixer he'd forgotten all about until the last minute. And she hadn't batted an eye when he'd sheepishly asked her to pick up his tux from the dry cleaner. Tamia would have gone anywhere and done anything he'd asked of her.

Because she was on a mission to become Mrs. Brandon Chambers.

Oh, she knew she had her work cut out for her. Truth be told, Brandon was more interested in making partner at his law firm than getting married. Although Tamia frequently spent the night at his place, she was barely allowed to keep a toothbrush there. And after seven months of dating, she had yet to meet his parents, one of the most powerful political couples in Texas. Whenever she hinted at being introduced to them, Brandon always told her that his folks could be very intimidating, so he didn't want to scare her off.

What he didn't realize was that Tamia didn't scare very easily. So she'd be a good little wifey for as long as it took to convince him to put a ring on her finger.

Smiling at the thought, she poured steaming coffee into two fancy paper cups and snapped on the lids just as Brandon strode purposefully into the kitchen. He was impeccably dressed in a dark pinstriped suit that accentuated his tall, athletic build.

"Ready to go?" he asked.

"Been ready." Tamia straightened his tie, admiring his smooth chocolate skin, midnight eyes, and boyishly sexy smile. Brandon was the total package: fine as hell, rich, smart, and successful. He was going places, and she had no intention of being left behind.

"Here. I made you some coffee."

Accepting the cup from her, he took a long sip and let out an appreciative groan. "Damn, baby, you make the best brew. What would I do without you?"

Tamia smiled privately. *If I play my cards right, you'll never have to find out.*

Twenty minutes later, they turned off the main road and into a lushly landscaped development located in the shadow of Houston's Galleria. Brandon was on his BlackBerry, assuring his secretary that he wouldn't be late for a scheduled deposition that morning. So he didn't notice the way Tamia's hands clenched in her lap as they passed another car on the narrow street, nor did he hear the small sigh of relief that seeped past her lips.

He pulled up to a one-story stucco house situated on a perfectly manicured lawn. Tamia's red Honda Accord was parked in the driveway.

Grabbing her purse, she leaned over to kiss Brandon. "Have a good day."

He smiled. "You, too. Don't be late for work."

"If I am, I'll just *blame it on the rain,*" she said, crooning the old Milli Vanilli song.

Brandon laughed as she climbed out of his Maybach.

Although he was in a hurry, he waited until she'd reached the front door before he pulled off with a wave.

Tamia inserted her key in the lock, stepped inside the cool interior of the house, and closed the door. But she didn't move beyond the foyer. Staring anxiously at her watch, she waited until three minutes had ticked by. Then, opening the door, she poked her head outside and glanced up and down the tree-lined street, watching as cars backed out of driveways and joined the flow of other vehicles headed to various workplaces.

As Tamia locked the house and hurried to her own car, her cell phone rang. She fumbled it out of her purse and answered with a breathless, "Girl, that was close!"

"I know," Shanell Jasper agreed. "I was running late this morning. And so are you! What happened?"

Tamia grimaced, sliding behind the wheel of her car. "The power went out last night, so we overslept."

"Uh-oh. You've got that client meeting at nine. Are you going to be late?"

"I hope not." Tamia glanced at her watch, mentally calculating how long it would take her to get home, shower and change, and make it to the office on time. If only she'd had the foresight to leave a change of clothes at Shanell's place last night. But everything had been so rushed. After picking up Brandon's tux from the dry cleaner, dropping it off at his condo, and hurrying home to get dressed for the cocktail party, she'd reached Shanell's house just minutes before Brandon arrived to pick her up.

"How long do you think you can keep this up?" Shanell asked.

Tamia pulled onto the main road. "What?"

Shanell snorted. "You know damn well what I'm talking about. This crazy charade of yours, lying to Brandon about where you live and using my house as your cover. How long can you keep this shit up?"

"However long it takes."

"And what if it takes that man, like, five years to propose?" Shanell paused. "Or what if he never does?"

"He will," Tamia said resolutely.

Before Shanell attempted to sow more seeds of doubt in her mind, Tamia told her that she'd see her at the office, then ended the call.

She knew her coworker meant well, and God knows Shanell had every right to voice her concerns since she was doing Tamia such a huge favor. But Shanell didn't understand what was truly at stake here. She had no clue what it was like to grow up on the wrong side of the tracks and dare to aspire to greater things. The crumbling shotgun house Tamia still called home was a world away from the lavish River Oaks estate where Brandon had been raised. He wouldn't be caught dead dating someone from Houston's notorious Third Ward— no matter how smart, successful, and educated Tamia now was. So showing him where she *really* lived was out of the question.

Sure, she felt a pang of guilt every time she lied to him or had to inconvenience her coworker. But she was compensating Shanell for her trouble. And once she and Brandon were married, Tamia would spend the rest of her life proving to him that he'd made the right decision.

Chapter 1

Tamia

Houston, Texas
November 4, 2011

Tamia Luke's heart pounded violently as she watched the twelve jurors file into the jury box and reclaim their seats. She was so nervous, she wanted to throw up. These men and women held her fate in their hands. Their verdict would determine whether she spent the rest of her life in prison or walked out of this courtroom a free woman.

She searched their faces, hoping for something—*anything*—that would give her insight into the decision they had reached. But their expressions were unreadable, and none of them would make eye contact with her. Not even Juror Number Eight, an attractive, middle-aged black man who'd hardly been able to keep his eyes off her throughout the trial.

But today he seemed to go out of his way not to look at her.

Like the other jurors.

With mounting anxiety, Tamia leaned over and whispered to her attorney, "They won't look at me. Why won't they look at me?"

"Relax," Brandon murmured soothingly. "It doesn't mean anything."

Tamia hoped to God he was right. She'd spent the past five months behind bars, serving time for a crime she hadn't committed.

She didn't know *what* she would do if the jury found her guilty of Isabel Archer's murder. It was unthinkable.

When the judge emerged from his chambers, Tamia and Brandon rose from the defense table. Her insides were shivering, and her legs were so wobbly, she thought she'd collapse to the floor. Without thinking she grabbed Brandon's hand and held tight, comforted when he squeezed her back.

"Ladies and gentlemen of the jury," said the judge, "have you reached a verdict?"

The jury forewoman stood. "We have, Your Honor."

As the judge read the folded note that contained the jury's verdict, the silence that had permeated the packed courtroom was now deafening. You could literally hear a pin drop.

The judge looked at the forewoman. "What is your verdict?"

Tamia closed her eyes, her heart slamming against her rib cage as she braced herself for the woman's next words.

"We, the jury, find the defendant—"

Tamia held her breath.

"—not guilty."

Pandemonium erupted in the courtroom, loud cheers from Tamia's supporters dueling with shouts of protest from Isabel Archer's outraged relatives. The judge banged his gavel, calling for order. But it was the sight of Brandon's beaming face that gave Tamia permission to believe the verdict she'd just heard.

"WE WON!" she screamed, throwing her arms around Brandon's neck as he laughingly lifted her off the floor. As he spun her around, she caught a glimpse of Dominic Archer, seated behind the plaintiff's table across the aisle. He looked so stunned that Tamia might have felt sorry for him—if she didn't despise his motherfucking ass.

"Thank you, Brandon," she said earnestly as he set her back down on her feet. "Thank you for believing in me. Thank you for saving my life!"

"You're welcome," he told her. "I never doubted your innocence."

"I know. And that meant *everything* to me."

His expression softened. "You know I—"

"Congratulations," a new voice interrupted.

Tamia and Brandon turned to encounter a pretty, brown-skinned woman dressed in a navy Dolce & Gabbana skirt suit that hugged her slender figure. Her dark, lustrous hair flowed past her shoulders in a way that made Tamia more desperate than ever to get into her stylist's chair. Sporting months of nappy new growth and wearing a pantsuit that did nothing for her shape, she felt raggedy next to Cynthia Yarbrough—the scheming hussy who'd stolen Brandon from her.

She forced a smile. "Hey, Cynthia. You're looking well."

"Thank you, Tamia." Cynthia didn't insult her intelligence by returning the compliment. "Congratulations on your acquittal."

"Thanks." Tamia smiled gratefully at Brandon. "I couldn't have done it without this man's amazing legal prowess. I don't know if I can ever repay him, but I'm determined to try."

Brandon chuckled. "You might feel differently after you receive my final bill."

Tamia laughed, then leaned up and kissed his smooth, clean-shaven cheek. She didn't miss the way Cynthia's eyes narrowed with displeasure.

Don't get it twisted, heffa, Tamia mused. *He was* my *man first!*

Soon she was surrounded by a group of supporters who'd been there for her throughout the trial. Lou Saldaña scooped her up and swung her around, while her best friend, Shanell Jasper, took one look at her attire and promised to take her shopping ASAP. Distant cousins Tamia hadn't seen in ages had shown up, along with a few of her neighbors.

Everyone who mattered was there.

Except Fiona.

And she *doesn't matter anymore,* Tamia thought darkly.

"YOU BITCH!"

The enraged outburst came from the other side of the courtroom, where a sobbing woman was being restrained by several members of Isabel Archer's family. As Tamia watched, the woman pointed at her and screamed, "You're gonna burn in hell for what you did to Isabel!"

Before Tamia could open her mouth to defend herself, Brandon silenced her with a warning look. "Don't say anything. The jury has spoken for you, and that's all that matters."

Nodding grimly, she watched as the hysterical woman was led out of the courtroom. Although Tamia knew she was innocent, it bothered her that there were people who would always believe the worst of her, that she'd killed her lover's wife in a jealous rage. The worst part was that she *knew* who the real killer was—and there wasn't a damn thing she could do about it. She'd sworn not to tell anyone, and no matter how horribly she'd been used and betrayed, a promise was a promise.

After accepting more congratulatory hugs and kisses, Tamia followed her small entourage out of the courthouse and into the bright November afternoon. She and Brandon were met by a buzzing swarm of reporters who shouted questions at them.

"Miss Luke, do you feel vindicated by today's verdict?"

"Mr. Chambers, do you stand by your strategy to portray Dominic Archer as the real killer?"

"Do either of you believe he really murdered his wife?"

"Miss Luke, do you regret having an affair with a married man?"

Taken aback by the barrage of questions, Tamia looked askance at Brandon. He gave her a reassuring smile, then stepped to the cluster of microphones. Calmly he surveyed the crowd, waiting for the noise to die down before he spoke.

"Miss Luke and I are pleased that justice was served today. I commend the men and women of the jury for weighing all the evidence and coming back with the only verdict they could have: not guilty."

The reporters fired more questions at him.

"With all due respect, Brandon," one voice rang out above the rest, "how difficult was it for you to defend the woman who cheated on you? Throughout the trial, you were forced to hear the lurid details of Miss Luke's affair with Dominic Archer. How in the world did you remain objective?"

Tamia's face heated with shame, while Brandon didn't so much as flinch. "My prior relationship with Miss Luke wasn't on trial," he answered evenly. "If I didn't think I could handle hearing the 'lurid de-tails' of her affair, as you put it, I wouldn't have taken her case. But I did, because I believed in her innocence. Clearly the jury did, too."

Tamia beamed at him.

"Is there any chance that you and Miss Luke might reconcile?"

Brandon paused, giving Tamia a sidelong glance.

She met his gaze, holding her breath as she waited for his re-sponse.

After several moments he turned back to the reporters, chuckling and shaking his head. "You guys are always looking for a romantic Hollywood ending. All I want to do is celebrate this victory, which reaffirms my belief that the justice system can and *does* work."

"Given your winning track record," someone retorted, "I'd say the system works just fine for you."

Brandon grinned as laughter swept over the crowd.

Tamia was also grinning, but not for the same reason as everyone else. For the first time in several months, she had reason to hope that all was not lost between her and Brandon. Because whether he real-ized it or not, by dodging the reporter's question, he'd left the door open for the possibility of him and Tamia getting back together.

Today's verdict had given her back her life. Now that she was a free woman again, nothing would stop her from trying to reclaim the only man she'd ever loved.

Nothing.

And no one.

Turning her head, she saw Cynthia standing off to the side by herself.

Their gazes met.

Tamia smiled.

Cynthia's eyes narrowed with suspicion.

That's right, bitch, Tamia thought. *I'm taking back what you stole from me. And this time, I'm never letting him go!*